MW00988917

HAPPENSTANCE

PHIL SHEEHAN

WILDBLUE
PRESS

WildBluePress.com

HAPPENSTANCE published by:

WILDBLUE PRESS
P.O. Box 102440
Denver, Colorado 80250

WILDBLUE PRESS is registered at the U.S. Patent and Trademark Offices.

ISBN 978-1-948239-25-7   Trade Paperback
ISBN 978-1-948239-24-0   eBook

Interior Formatting by Elijah Toten
www.totencreative.com

HAPPENSTANCE

IN MEMORY

This book is dedicated to my father, Philip John Sheehan (1933-2012), and my best man, Norman Nissen (1958- 2016).

After graduating from children's books, my father initiated my lifelong journey of reading by starting me off with two SciFi classics: Isaac Asimov's *The Foundation Trilogy* and H.G. Wells' *The War of the Worlds* – and the rest was history. Dad was always supportive of seeing his children attempt new endeavors, with his only request being that whatever we pursued, it be constructive. I only wish I would have started and finished this endeavor sooner so that he could have enjoyed reading *Happenstance* as much as I enjoyed writing it. Semper fi, Dad.

Norman was a longtime friend, a member of the clandestine and fun-seeking "PND" trio in high school (Phil, Norman, Dave), and the most well-read person I've ever met. Better known as Stormin' Norman, or Murky Swampwater. Norman truly treasured books and was a voracious reader of anything he could get his hands on. Norman could frequently be found at the Book House of Stuyvesant Plaza, in Upstate New York, happily assisting customers locate their perfect book. To his wife, Janice, and his two children, Abby and Sam: Norman was a gentle teddy bear of a man, a great father and a true friend. I would have been honored to get his guidance on *Happenstance*. We all miss him.

SPECIAL THANKS

I wish to thank many people for helping me fulfil my dream of publishing this book. It has been fun, and a journey of learning as well. I'd first like to thank my many friends and family members who kept urging me to stay with it, even though my "day job" and seven soccer-crazed kids made that seem like an insurmountable task at times.

Special thanks to my son, Patrick Sheehan, my brother, Sean Sheehan, and my neighbor, Scott Gage, who read and critiqued the story before I ever sent it to a publisher or editor – and then stayed with me and provided support as the editor-recommended mods followed (phew!).

Speaking of editing, Annie Dawid deserves a medal. When the publisher says your first draft has potential, but is "sloppy" … well, you now know the herculean task Annie took on! My only question to her remains: Will you continue to charge me by the hour on my next book, or will you convert to charging by the comma? Yes, reality is a harsh mistress – without a great editor like Annie, my ability to master the comma will continue to drive high odds in Vegas.

To my publishers, Steve, Michael and Ashley at WildBlue Press – thank you for your honesty and direction, and keeping the door open for me.

I hope you enjoy *Happenstance*.

For more on the author, Phil Sheehan, or this book, Happenstance, visit *philsheehanbooks.com*

PROLOGUE

A.D. is the abbreviation for *anno Domini;* Latin for "in the year of our Lord." The term has been used to indicate the number of years that have passed since the birth of Jesus Christ.

A.D. 1484 (2767 C.A.E.$^{(*)}$)
On Board the Stojesst IV

The panoramic view outside the ship appeared empty and devoid of life. Adm. Stjssjen surveyed the endless view before him as he sipped his silver mug of hot, caffeine-laced vystil. Curly wisps of vapor rose from the cup and bathed his nose with their rich aromas. The admiral briefly closed his eyes and drank deeply from the dark liquid, enjoying the serenity of the moment. For the time being, all was well. He had awakened in the middle of the night, and all efforts to fall back asleep had eluded him. There was too much swirling in his head. After an hour of fitful tossing, he showered, grabbed his vystil and surrendered to the sleepless night.

Night was a relative term aboard a ship in interstellar space. There was no rising sun or singing birds to announce the formal commencement of morning. Outside the ship, evening, nighttime, morning and daytime all blended into one continuous flow of anonymity and monotony, indistinguishable from every other moment that came before or was to come. To provide structure and routine, daily cycles were assigned by the ship's computers to adjust lighting in line with the typical Cjarian day back in Phenolsst, the capital of the planet Cjar. Daily routine was not something one deliberately and consciously thought about, but

---

*. **C.A.E.** is the abbreviation for the *Cjarian Age of Enlightenment*, referring back to the year when war on the planet Cjar ended, and a worldwide peace ensued. This peace continued for over two thousand years until the year 2345, when conflict with the Klaxx was first encountered. C.A.E. predates Earth's A.D. by 1283 years.

the brain was programmed such that interruptions of that daily routine subconsciously increased stress levels, the last thing anyone in space needed – especially in wartime.

The admiral reflected over the past few months of battle. The Klaxxstinian Space Navy, frequently referred to as the *Klaxx* or simply "the K," had amassed every available ship it had within the sector, an area of space including at least six neighboring star systems. The planning and logistics behind its operation were impressive, and as best the admiral's recon forces could surmise, its efforts surpassed what the admiral's own fleet was capable of doing by more than a small margin. Yet, as ominous as the assessment appeared, the admiral prayed that it contained a silver lining: the creation of a ship-depleted weakness in the defensive forces around the Klaxxstinian home world – something the admiral desperately hoped to capitalize on.

"Admiral." The commanding officer on deck acknowledged Adm. Stjssjen formally when their eyes met. "Is there anything I can do for you this morning?"

"No, Capt. Fyslyl, I just thought I needed to keep a closer eye on you and your crew," Stjssjen replied with a slight smirk. "Carry on, captain."

Capt. Fyslyl saluted his response with a wordless smile and returned to his console to continue his discussion with the con officer.

As best they could, the Cjarian recon forces estimated that the Klaxx flotilla, forming near Cjar, consisted of one war behemoth, five battle cruisers, 23 destroyers, 75 frigates and an additional assortment of miscellaneous support ships that numbered beyond 200.

The war behemoth was of most concern to the admiral. It was one of only two known vessels of this class; and both belonged to the Klaxx. Cjar had nothing even close. Little was known about the war behemoths, beyond their lethality levels. They were extraordinarily large ships, easily justifying the fear-evoking nickname that had quickly become the standard call sign for these space-faring monsters. Recon estimates had the 1,600 meters in length, 500 meters in width and 200 height, and the exterior hull of the ship was believed to l wall structure that exceeded three meters in thickness estimate was based on a direct hit on a behemoth, recor 10 years earlier, when a Cjarian cruiser, hopelessly outgunned and severely damaged, had committed a final act of gallantry to save other ships in the area by ramming the war behemoth directly on its starboard side. The velocity of the impact, coupled with the mass of the 800-meter-long Cjarian cruiser, destroyed most of the gun ports on the starboard side of the gigantic ship, but never succeeded in stopping it, or even penetrating its hull structure. Nearby ships watched in horror as the Cjarian cruiser simply crumpled around the exterior of the behemoth before ending in a magnificent explosion, incinerating all 1,000 of its crew.

Subsequent simulation and analysis at the Cjarian War College, using its knowledge of Klaxxstinian alloys, the mass and the velocity of the two ships, and estimates of the magnitude of the resultant explosion that included the cruiser's fuel and weaponry, concluded that the ship's shell must have exceeded three meters in thickness in order to survive the collision – a daunting realization. The fact that the Klaxx had not yet deployed the two ships together also said a lot to the admiral: the Klaxx must be afraid of something. Either their home world support was so low that they couldn't afford to allow both ships to leave at the same time, or they were concerned that there was a yet-to-be-identified weakness in the ships that the Klaxx thought the Cjarians could exploit – this was the admiral's only hope.

The Cjarians, not to be outgunned, had engaged their entire second and third fleets. The combined fleets included six battle cruisers, 32 destroyers, 52 frigates, 163 support ships of various sizes and one brand new, highly secret reconnaissance spacecraft called the Jarisst I. The Jarisst I was an odd-shaped ship, approximately 115 meters long and 12 meters wide. The nose of the ship, where the control center was located, was more spherical in shape and slightly larger in diameter than the rest of the ship, with a diameter of 20 meters. A second flat, bulbous area was located two-thirds ᴊ the distance down the axis of the ship. This area housed a secret drive system and was approximately 30 meters in diameter.

"Good morning, admiral."

Adm. Stjssjen turned to see Cmdr. Cel Rylsst.

"Sleep avoiding you as well?" the admiral queried.

"Someone has to keep an eye on you, sir," Rylsst replied dryly.

"Yes, it seems everyone is keeping an eye on someone, right, Capt. Fyslyl?"

"Aye, aye, sir! Trusting bunch we are," Fyslyl returned, and they all chuckled.

Adm. Stjssjen was the senior Cjarian military officer in the two fleets and had been honored by being given the command of the combined fleet. But even as the officer in charge, Adm. Stjssjen knew he had limitations relative to the Cjarian High Command. Adm. Stjssjen was vividly aware that the Jarisst I was rumored to have a raft of capabilities that he was not cleared for. The latter fact did not sit well with him, especially as the Jarisst's commander seemed to think that he didn't have to take orders from the admiral.

Adm. Stjssjen's persona suddenly changed, and he turned to face his first officer, Cmdr. Cel Rylsst, to utter what seemed to be a long, pent-up statement, "What an arrogant bunch the Jarisst's crew is."

"Ahh, that's what you were chewing on; I was wondering, sir. Yes, admiral, they most certainly are," the commander replied. "They seem to think that they can play by their own private set of rules."

It was well recognized throughout the admiral's flagship cruiser, the Stojesst IV, that the Jarisst I would come and go without any warning. It seemed at times that the little ship reported to no one and was created with the sole purpose of pissing the admiral off; and Cmdr. Rylsst knew they had succeeded many times.

Adm. Stjssjen shook his head at his first officer, turned to look out the bridge window, and sighed. "Their cocky tendencies are far too dangerous, especially during a battle of this significance. Glysst[*] knows that everyone's nerves are high and trigger fingers are already set like trip wires throughout the fleet. It's only a matter of time before we have another friendly fire incident."

Months earlier, during a battle with the Klaxx, a Cjarian frigate, the Blysst 24, had been lost to a friendly fire incident. The frigate had suddenly appeared from behind a large asteroid and was closing on the fleet. Numerous attempts to hail the ship had gone unanswered. As the frigate approached a Cjarian battle cruiser, the cruiser opened fire with a salvo of six CJ-876 thermobaric torpedoes, each with a yield of 25 tons of TNT[**]. The frigate never had a chance. The first torpedo separated the ship into two, just aft of amidships, and the successive torpedoes pulverized the ship halves into a sea of debris. Celebration quickly turned to devastation with the realization that the target had been a friendly.

Cmdr. Rylsst responded, choosing to remind the admiral of their orders, "Sir, regardless of their intentions, the last communication we received from Cjar was that it was imperative we protect the Jarisst I at any cost to the fleet. I can only imagine what capabilities that little ship must have to justify this level of security."

Rumors about the ship's capabilities had been rampant among the port loading crew when they left Cjar. As it turned out, Rylsst recalled, many of the rumors actually paralleled research that a good friend of his worked on years ago at the University of Cjar. Rylsst has lost contact with his friend, but he couldn't help think that the stories had to be related to his friend's work. The stories centered on a revolutionary new engine design that combined quantum physics and antimatter technology. Rylsst recalled that

---

[*]. **Glysst:** The common reference for the religious deity of Cjar (God).

[**]. **TNT:** Trinitrotoluene, or more specifically, 2,4,6-trinitrotoluene, is a yellowish chemical compound with the formula $C_6H_2(NO_2)_3CH_3$. TNT is best known as an explosive material with good handling properties.

his friend had claimed that if his invention worked, it would allow a ship to travel over greater distances and speeds than anything the Cjarians, or the Klaxx, had ever fielded or tested – even faster than the speed of light. Rylsst had actually laughed at his good friend when he had made the latter comment, and summarily dismissed the discussion. Now Rylsst was beginning to second-guess his haste, wondering if his friend's hints were more accurate than he had assumed.

"I've also heard the rumors suggesting the Jarisst I can exceed the speed of light," the admiral replied as he continued pacing, seemingly reading the commander's mind. "Yet, we never know where it is, what it is doing, what it is capable of doing, or when it is returning – and we are supposed to protect *IT*?" The admiral muttered a Cjarian curse under his breath. "And if their engine technology is that far ahead of us, what does that mean about their weaponry and defensive capabilities? Perhaps it could be us on the losing side of a friendly fire event." A sobering thought, he mused.

"Perhaps the Jarisst I can help locate and defeat the war behemoths, albeit fighting a behemoth seems to be a bigger task than even that small super ship could possibly accomplish," added the commander.

Adm. Stjssjen nodded his agreement. He was hesitant to believe the other rumors that claimed the ship could literally "skip" through space. That gibberish was a science fiction favorite that traced its roots back to the early days of space flight. Even the brightest scientists simply couldn't grasp the concept of faster-than-light travel, so the academics and book writers created crazy theories that included worm holes, space tunnels and teleport jumps in order to fill their scientific gaps and fuel the fantasies of the common folk. They just couldn't grasp how a ship could arrive before the light, which allowed someone to see it, actually arrived. For most Cjarians, it was analogous to time travel, which was clearly impossible. The Cjarian scientists couldn't get past their own paradigms and see the mental disconnect between believing that faster-than-light travel was impossible, while easily accepting faster-than-sound travel. It was ludicrous that the scientists found it acceptable to acknowledge a ship's arrival before the sound was heard, but not its sight.

There were, however, some exceptions within the Cjarian scientific community. A leading scientist at one of Cjar's oldest universities had long ago proposed a postulate, now known as the Wyrlsst Postulate, named in the scientist's honor after he passed away, that theorized the visual paradigm that would parallel faster-than-light travel. Prof. Wyrlsst proposed that, analogous to the collection and compression of sound waves known as a sonic boom announcing the breaking of the sound barrier, there was a parallel, but even more impressive light show associated with the collection and compression of light waves that would initially blur vision and then conclude in a short flash of light that included all the colors of the rainbow.

"Rumors or not, there seems to be a mounting database that supports that the Jarisst I may indeed present an evolutionary step in technology and space travel for us," added the admiral. "We can only hope that it can also help against the behemoths."

Both the admiral and Cmdr. Rylsst knew that the Jarisst I had been developed at Cjar's top secret military base on a small, desolate moon known as Secretorum[*] that orbited the fifth world in their home planetary system. The moon was selected because the lethality of modern weapons had become so extreme, caution required all development and testing to be removed from the home planet, Cjar. In the event a catastrophic disaster did occur, casualties could thereby be minimized without risking the general populace. The location had the added benefit that secrecy was more easily maintained. Many had commented that the future of a Cjarian victory hinged on the secrets being developed on Secretorum.

If only the admiral knew what those secrets actually were so that he could better attack the Klaxx. The admiral hated the Klaxx, an urge that was typically unnatural for Cjarians. Not so for the Klaxx, who seemed to hate everything and everyone. The two races were so radically different.

---

[*]. **Secretorum:** Secret of secrets

For years, historians and academics had attempted to understand what could motivate one species to be peaceful and explorative, while another species could evolve to be so destructive and combative. Had Glysst designed this difference into the fabric of the universe? If yes, why? If no, what had happened to make the Klaxx this way? It was a safe bet that no one, short of Glysst himself, would ever be able to answer that question.

Cjarians were tall, thin, gentle, almost fragile-looking humanoids that averaged 2.0 meters in height (6.5 feet), but rarely weighed more than 85 kilograms (187 pounds). Cjarians were primarily vegetarians and had an average life span of 130 years, thanks to their diet and a truly rich medical science history that had eliminated most common diseases found on Cjar.

On the other hand, the Klaxx were a relatively short race, typically less than 1.6 meters in height (5.2 feet) and frequently exceeding 100 kilograms in weight (220 pounds). The Klaxx were known to be extremely short-tempered and aggressive, and rarely lived past 75. The Klaxx were true omnivores, but they preferred meat whenever given the opportunity. They were also infamously known to become even more ill-tempered when feeding on raw flesh. The admiral had joked that it was a wonder this insane race hadn't consumed its own young and passed into extinction centuries ago. Instead, it had continued its warring ways with Cjar.

The long-lived war dated back to the year 2012 C.A.E., when a Cjarian science vessel, after over six years of solitary travel at slightly below the speed of light, entered a previously uncharted solar system that was 5.3 light-years from Cjar. The small ship, the Cjar LVII, was unescorted, as were all scientific expeditions at the time. The Cjarians had never been at war, were not aware of other intelligent life forms, and prior to this event, had therefore never considered the need for a military presence. When the Cjar LVII's external sensors picked up signs of a non-natural object approaching them, the crew broke into pandemonium over the excitement of finally discovering signs of intelligent life beyond their planet. The jubilant crew sent video of the approaching vehicle back to Cjar and immediately began hailing the oncoming ship.

Unfortunately for the crew, their excitement was short-lived. The Klaxx ship's response to a flurry of Cjarian transmissions was to simply blow the ship out of existence, instantly killing all 15 crewmembers. Unbeknownst to the Cjarians, the Klaxx immediately began their quest to find and destroy the home world of what they deemed to be an invasive species that had openly challenged their territorial rights.

From the Cjarian perspective, the destruction of the ship went undetected for five years until the initial transmission detailing the alien contact was received back at Cjar, followed shortly by an automatic transmission that the ship sent when its exterior hull was breached. Under normal circumstances, the scientific community would have assumed that the ship might have hit a meteor or experienced a catastrophic system failure. This rare, but unfortunately very real scenario had occurred twice before in the history of Cjarian space travel. In this case, however, no one could argue against the distinct pictures in the initial video transmission and the excitement of the crew's recorded discussion. The object in the center of the video was non-natural and closing quickly. The Cjarian high command now had to face the stark reality that not only was there alien life "nearby," but it was categorically unfriendly and dangerous.

The half millennium following this encounter was populated by a landscape of skirmishes and battles between the two races, without either side ever gaining a significant advantage – a stalemate that consumed time, resources, lives and dreams, without ever changing the outcome. It had begun relatively small and grew to a handful of ships on both sides during the first century, but the following centuries had seen the two races field thousands of space faring vehicles to support the war.

The admiral broke another long silence. "The Jarisst I is due to report back soon. Hopefully, this time, they will have new data that will give us badly needed recon on the Klaxxstinian Navy and perhaps even the behemoths. We will see," he muttered.

*****

"Commence operations to the Klaxxstinian solar system," ordered Zyles Blissiart, captain of the Jarisst I.

"Klaxx …? But, Adm. Stjssjen's orders were for us to oversee sector …"

"Lt. Pfssiast, I know what the admiral ordered, but we don't take orders from him. We are heading to Klaxx, immediately. Only the High Command fully knows what is at stake and they have given us the opportunity and honor to possibly make the biggest impact on this war in over 300 years."

"Is the admiral going to be notified?" Lt. Mentyss Pfssiast asked.

"Not at this time, lieutenant," Capt. Blissiart replied curtly. "The truth is, we must move quickly and engage the enemy as soon as possible. We are going to Klaxx. With this ship's experimental drive, we should be able to cover the five-plus light-years in a little over 10 days. Think of it lieutenant, almost 200 times the speed of light. The Klaxx have no idea that we can cover that amount of space in so little time. Their continued aggressive attacks are based on the assumption that they can fall back as quickly as we can attack, so they falsely believe that they can still cover a retreat.

"But you and I know the real truth. The Klaxx can't. Not even remotely close. We will rush in, target and destroy key planetary defensive targets, recon for the behemoths and quickly escape. They will never see us coming. We will be gone before they realize we were even there. The same holds for Adm. Stjssjen. We will be back in his fleet before he even knows we left.

"Lieutenant, with this ship, we have a unique opportunity to strike a major blow directly to the heart of the Klaxx Empire as well as locate the Behemoths." Capt. Blissiart looked at Lt. Pfssiast with an intensity the lieutenant had never seen before, and continued. "Mentyss, we have another new weapon called the neutron cannon. It has completed development on Secretorum and although we have yet to demonstrate its full capabilities, it was designed specifically to penetrate the outer armor of the behemoths. Therefore, the High Command has determined this is a one-time opportunity that we must exploit, at all costs, before the window closes. If we can locate the behemoths for the new weapon system to target and destroy, then the Jarisst I would be free to lead the First Fleet on a direct attack on Klaxx itself. We need to move quickly."

"Captain, we are still too close to the nearest planetary mass to initiate maximum acceleration. We will require additional time at sub-light travel before we can engage the antimatter warp drive."

"Okay, lieutenant, move us away from the planet at maximum allowable speed, make preparations for the crew and engage the new drive as soon as you determine it is feasible and the ship is prepared. Keep me posted, lieutenant, and let me know as soon as the crew is all buttoned up. You and I will be the last to prep for acceleration."

After decades of top-secret flight tests and the deaths of far too many brave and talented test pilots who had been attempting near light-speed travel, the scientific community finally concluded that its approach to overcoming the impact of the high G acceleration forces was beyond Cjarian science (one G is equal to the gravitational pull on Cjar). The greatest scientists kept trying to solve the problem solely with ultra-complicated G-absorption devices that boggled the imagination. They all knew that to achieve the full benefit of light-speed travel, they had to overcome the extremely high acceleration rates that were required to get to light speed, as well as to slow down from light speed. High acceleration rates were an equation for instant death as each G resulted in a doubling of an individual's weight.

To reduce the impact of high G levels, Cjarian scientists had attempted to design complex systems to absorb the insane gravitational forces, thereby protecting the occupants. Although these systems pushed the Cjarian science frontier forward, they were still woefully inadequate. Then, in 2649 C.A.E., during a freshman science fair, a first-year astrophysics student at the Cjarian Space Academy proposed the simple solution everyone had previously overlooked. The greatest Cjarian scientists had been so focused on creating new science that they had overlooked basic science. The student reminded everyone of what they already knew: the effect of gravitational pull decreased as the distance from the gravitational body increased by a factor that squared the distance between the bodies of interest.

$$F_{Grav} = G(M_1 * M_2)/D^2$$

The simple but brilliant proposal changed the rules of the game from focusing on fixing a problem, to avoiding the problem altogether. The student, Steni Qyissys, proposed that the ship be as far from gravitational fields as possible, preferably in free space where weight was essentially zero, before allowing a ship to exceed 100 Gs of acceleration. In this manner, the Qyissys Rule, as it quickly became known, dictated that a ship must be in a gravitational field of less than 0.01 meters per second squared before it could exceed 100 Gs of acceleration or deceleration.

Previous to this breakthrough, Cjarian scientists had invented other systems that successfully handled Gs below 100, the best of which was known as a G-suit. These inventions allowed a ship's occupants to accelerate at sustained, but lower rates within gravitational fields, while the Qyissys Rule was the breakthrough that finally opened the new frontier to faster-than-light-speed manned flights.

Capt. Blissiart also studied at the prestigious Space Academy on Cjar. Blissiart graduated with a doctorate in antimatter studies. He then completed a second doctorate in quantum physics, afterwards joining the highly secretive Space Force Labs to work on a new interstellar space drive system. Blissiart had been one of the principal researchers who achieved the biggest Cjarian breakthroughs of truly new science in over a millennium: the Quantum Physics Anti-Matter Space drive, better known as the Q-PAMS drive. The Q-PAMS drive was capable of propelling a ship at more than 200 times the speed of light. For the first time in history, star systems seen only through the telescope could now be visited directly and *relatively* easily.

Capt. Blissiart led the research that created a miniature molecular collider that bombarded multiple atoms of a number of specially selected elements together to create rare, high-energy isotopes.

Previous colliders with equivalent capability were measured in diameters of hundreds of meters; the new breakthrough achieved a design within an astounding 4-meter diameter – small enough that it could be packaged within a spaceship.

Capt. Blissiart also led the design and construction of the first and only ship to house the Q-PAMS drive, the Jarisst I, and was now its first captain. The secret to the Q-PAMS drive was twofold. The first breakthrough was the ability to continually generate rare isotope materials and their corresponding antimatter isotopes without allowing them to break down or commingle until the desired moment. The Q-PAMS design included the placement of four of these four-meter diameter colliders immediately next to each other in a double figure-eight fashion. One set of colliders manufactured the targeted isotopes and the other set of colliders manufactured its required antimatter equivalent. The process required timing accuracies on the order of a hundredth of a millionth of a second to ensure that the creation of the highly unstable isotopes occurred simultaneously, and at the exact time and position. The resultant collisions, and energy releases, were then funneled through a specialized exhaust system down the primary axis of the spacecraft, resulting in the creation of thrust for the ship. The amount of thrust created was based on the type of material annihilated and the frequency of the annihilation process.

Research had identified that different materials created different levels of energy. The current energy level record was achieved from two synthetic materials known as Leo-1253 and its antimatter form, known as Leo-3521. Both were highly unstable isotopes that had been created by the famous Cjarian scientist Leo Tjassist 100 years earlier. Tjassist's work focused on creating a material that would attach to cancer cells and reduce blood flow to the targeted cells, thereby allowing other medications to subsequently kill the weakened cell and eradicate the cancerous tumor. One of his most significant challenges was that he was never able to keep the rare isotopes in existence for more than a hundredth of a second – too short a time to successfully attack the targeted cells. Leo died without awareness of the other applications his work led to. Capt. Blissiart's team had identified the new application, but it had still taken years to solve the complex timing issues for the new engine.

To minimize any risks to the crew during Q-PAMS flight, a second breakthrough technology was created on Secretorum by a separate team of scientists. It was known as the gravity cell, or G-Cell – as most troops called them. G-Cells were an innovative life pod that an occupant lay in horizontally. The pod was then oriented axially flat in the direction of the planned acceleration with extreme precision to directional angles. The occupant was placed in semi-hibernation for as long as the trip was planned for, or as long as the ship was accelerating above 100 Gs. Once the ship slowed below a preset acceleration level, the occupant was automatically revived through a series of small steps that required as long as one to two days, dependent on the length of the flight. During emergencies, the crew could be revived much quicker, but the awakening could be very painful and disorienting.

Once in the G-Cell, the occupant was harnessed and immersed in an electrorheological fluid that changed viscosity with changes in an applied electric field. As acceleration levels were increased, the viscosity was increased to better absorb the forces on the body. During extreme periods of acceleration, the liquid became gel-like and a circulation system was activated that allowed the gelatin-like material to be liquefied and extracted from the fore section of the G-Cell and then re-injected into the aft section of the G-Cell at very high rates to resist the force driving the occupant backwards during acceleration. The opposite process occurred during times of rapid deceleration and the pod was swung 180 degrees in the opposite direction to ensure blood flow was not lost from the head.

The combination of zero gravity (no weight) and the G-Cell was adequate to protect the enclosed traveler for sustained acceleration or deceleration levels up to 1,000 Gs when well beyond a gravitational field. During normal travel, occupants would exit the G-Cells after the acceleration phase was completed and the ship was at steady state speeds with minimal to no acceleration. The crew would then re-enter the G-Cells prior to deceleration, and then exit again once sub-light-speed travel was resumed.

To maintain bone and muscular systems during extended G-Cell occupation, a well-known deterioration risk for space travelers, the G-Cell suit was further designed with a membrane around the occupant's body. The membrane consisted of thousands of electrical sensors that induced nerve and muscle activity every 60 minutes by twitching the muscles to avoid muscular atrophy. In addition, the occupant's temperature was maintained at very low levels to minimize aging effects. That, in combination with a series of chemicals introduced into the occupant's blood flow, allowed the body to be maintained in a mode very similar to hibernation. Studies at the Cjar University for Physical Sciences and Biomedical Engineering had demonstrated that the occupant's aging process could be reduced to 1/300 of normal, allowing an individual in a G-Cell to only age 1.2 days for every year inside a G-Cell. The idea for this technological breakthrough had actually been developed in the Medical Research Industry as a technique to preserve terminally ill patients, hoping that a cure could be found while the patient remained "on ice."

A mask that was hermetically sealed around the occupant's face provided oxygen. For extended hibernation periods, food and resultant bodily wastes were collected, reprocessed, salts removed, and the remaining water and nutrients were then fed back into the body's circulatory system through an IV located on the forearm. Due to the reduced bodily function rates, very little nutrition was required and an individual could survive in the G-Cell indefinitely. The longest such test to date had been with a space pilot volunteer who remained for two years and 53 days in a G-Cell. The pilot survived without any detrimental effects, other than the fact that he had missed his favorite sports team, Leicesterstyss, win its first and only championship in team history.

*****

The crew was all loaded into their G-Cells. Lt. Pfssiast and Capt. Blissiart completed their Q-PAMS checklists, donned their membrane suits, inserted their IVs, climbed into their G-Cell harnesses and started the G-Cell initiation process.

The Jarisst I automatically finalized its pre-programmed G-Cell processing steps and subsequently initiated the Q-PAMS to traverse the 5.3 light-years to the Klaxx solar system. If all went to plan, they would arrive in a little under 10 days.

*****

The captain and primary flight crew were awakened first and began the process of emerging from their G-Cells. Non-critical flight crewmembers would remain in their G-Cells until the ship was closer to their destination.

Capt. Blissiart was beginning to regain his senses. The other crewmembers struggled to regain their composure and rid themselves of the dripping electrorheological fluids, the breathing apparatus sealed to their faces and their membrane suits. The captain became painfully aware that alarms were clanging around him, and strobe lights were flashing. Their rotating auras created an eerie light throughout the sleeping ship. Blissiart suddenly panicked as he realized the alarms were actually battle station alarms. He was keenly aware of a throbbing in his head due to what must have been an accelerated revival process, but what he saw on the deck viewscreen quickly made him forget his headache. The captain went pale. "How long has it been since that ship was identified?" Capt. Blissiart demanded, knowing that no one else would know the answer either.

"Based on emergency flight protocol, we must have made the drop from light speed less than six hours ago," Lt. Pfssiast croaked the words out of his still raw throat. "Battle klaxons would only initiate if another ship were close by. Sir, we must have dropped right into their lap." The two men dressed haphazardly and quickly found their way to the control room.

Two Klaxxstinian battle cruisers were bearing down on them from opposite directions. "Weapon systems, are we on line yet?" Capt. Blissiart screamed above the alarms as the ship rocked from the concussion of a nearby explosion.

"Captain, no they aren't; we are the first ones up. We are taking concussion hits from nearby detonations. We can't outgun two battle cruisers, but ... Sir, they don't appear to be attempting to destroy the ship ... I think they are trying to incapacitate us, intentionally detonating missiles near the ship, rather than hitting us directly. Do you think they are trying to suggest we surrender?"

"Lieutenant, the Klaxx have never taken prisoners ..." His face froze with concern, "but in this case, I fear you may be correct. They must be trying to capture the ship. Lieutenant, we cannot let this ship fall into enemy hands under any conditions!"

"What are your orders, sir? The revived crewmembers are moving to their battle stations, but we are not even at 50 percent combat readiness yet. The Klaxx will be on us in seconds."

"By Glysst, Lieutenant, we will not fail Cjar! Ready the Q-PAMS again!"

"The Q-PAMS? We don't have time to re-enter the G-Cells," screamed Lt. Pfssiast with a cracking voice, still impacted by the G-Cell revival process. "The gravity well of the two ships is approaching 0.1 Gs and we aren't even in G-suits, let alone our G-Cells. We can't ..."

"Ready it now, lieutenant. It's our only option – dead or alive. Punch it, NOW! That's an order, lieutenant!"

Without further hesitation, the lieutenant punched the Q-PAMS emergency activation button. Although Capt. Blissiart knew the outcome, he could not allow the highly secret Jarisst I to fall into Klaxxstinian hands. It was the right decision. It was the only decision. It was also the last decision the captain would ever make. In the blink of an eye, the ship accelerated past the battle cruisers, reaching a pre-programmed 500 Gs. Standing crewmembers were violently thrown off their feet – killed instantly from the impact on internal ship structures, and the failing of internal organs under the enormous and sudden acceleration. As this was the first time the emergency system had ever been activated, no one, including the captain, knew what the outcome would be, but it was clear that one of the brightest Cjarian minds in the past 300 years, Capt.

Blissiart, had just ended his brilliant career much earlier than planned.

*****

Three months later
An unknown location in space

The Jarisst I exhausted its antimatter warp drive power cells some three months later. As part of the ship's auto shutdown procedures, the last Q-PAMS reserves were used to decelerate the ship, bring the ship to a stop and send out an emergency distress communications pod, or C-Pod. The C-Pod was pre-programmed to continuously emit SOS signals. The C-Pod was also pre-programmed to scan nearby space for non-natural electromagnetic signals that might identify intelligent life forms. If identified, the C-Pod would head toward it – unless the signals were identified as Klaxxstinian in nature, better known as a K-Sig. In the latter case, the C-Pod would immediately terminate SOS signals and remain in a passive data collection mode until the Klaxxstinian presence passed, or it was hailed by a Cjarian search signal.

As it turned out, neither K-Sig nor other signs of intelligence were identified; the C-Pod defaulted to orbiting the small, yellowish star a few million miles away. The C-Pod autonomously directed its flight path towards the orbits of the innermost planets where, if there were life, it might exist within the habitable zone of the small star.

One part of the automated code, built into the Jarisst I during development 10 years earlier, was a seemingly logical, but little-considered subroutine that directed operating G-Cells to default to full suspended animation during emergency Q-PAMS operation. The intention of this long-forgotten programmer was simply to protect as many of the ship's occupants as possible when an emergency situation arose, especially with the awareness that there was no way to predict the endless array of possibilities that could arise to create the emergency. Unfortunately, the one option that the programmer never considered was the option that the ship could find itself light-years from home, on an unplanned flight path, with no way of disengaging the sleep mode – possibly never to be found again. This scenario would condemn the occupants to a potentially eternal hibernation.

*****

Four years after the emergency C-Pod was released from the Jarisst I, the pod struck a small asteroid in the nondescript solar system, ricocheting the remains of the pod and the asteroid in different directions. Two years later, drawn by the gravitational pull of two different celestial bodies, the C-Pod impacted the fourth planet and buried itself into the alien landscape.

*****

Years streamed by the endless and quiet expanse of time and space.

*****

CURRENT DAY

A.D. Sol 2028

CHAPTER 1

A.D. 2028 (3311 C.A.E.); Aug. 22

Maj. Blake Thompson had seen action in countless conflicts over the past 15 years as the United States pursued what seemed like a never-ending, ever-spreading disease associated with Islamic extremists. The names of the leading factions changed every few years, as did some of the hot spots they created across the globe, but the Middle East maintained its status as the epicenter of all terrorist roots. The worst of the groups included ISIS, Al Qaeda, the Taliban and Boko Haram organizations, but there seemed to be a continuous supply of lunatics looking to make a name for themselves in the harshest manners possible, each one trying to outdo the others' grotesque horrors, all in the name of Allah.

Blake had not originally planned on making a career out of the military; that all changed when his father, one of the many "N.Y. Bravest," was killed during the South Tower collapse on 9/11. Blake was only 13 years old, but he had attended more funerals than he cared to count, honoring his father and the many other fire fighters and police officers he had grown up with – who were all lost on that infamous day.

Like many others impacted by 9/11, that day formed Blake into the man he had become. From that point forward, his singular focus became the protection of the U.S. against future 9/11-like attacks. Blake completed high school, attended West Point and then pursued a career in the Special Forces. Like most Special Forces members, he quickly found himself in the Middle East, but he also visited many other hot spots in countries across Africa and Asia – most of which were intentionally never shared with the media and therefore "never happened."

Soon after learning of his father's death, Blake had vowed to avenge him by hunting down and destroying any and all radical terrorist cells that the government could identify. Deep down, Blake knew that not all Muslims were evil, but his distrust of the Middle East and Muslims was forever fueled by the events of Sept. 11, 2001. Blake promised himself he would never let his guard down, as the U.S. had done that fateful day.

At 2.03 meters (6'6") and 111 kilograms (245 pounds), Blake was considered a "specimen" among his high school friends in the small, upstate New York town of Cobleskill where he and his mother had moved after his father's funeral. Mom's only wish was that her children grow up in a less dangerous and friendlier environment. How she had settled on Cobleskill was never clear to him, but Blake had enjoyed the small, rural town of 10,000 people with its beautiful tree-covered rolling hills, streams and lakes, dotted by cows and family dairy farms; it had been a great town to grow up in. His high school football coach had pushed for Blake to join the football team, trying to convince him he could play quarterback on offense and middle linebacker on defense – the next Jim Kelly. The coach had talked about college scholarships and even crafted dreams about the NFL, but Blake had played and loved the game of soccer ever since he was in grade school.

Blake had the speed and agility to play any position on the pitch, but he gravitated to the goalie position where he enjoyed the pure self-accountability that came with it. With his sheer size, aggressiveness and agility, Blake quickly became the top goalie within the small upstate N.Y. conferences. True to the football coach's expectation for a middle linebacker, Blake feared nothing and brought that attitude to his goalie box. His soccer coach and defenders quickly realized that not only did Blake never back down from contact, but he actually enjoyed mixing it up with incoming attackers. By the start of his junior year, the league's forwards all knew that the 18x44 yard rectangle, known on the pitch as the penalty box, belonged to Blake, and he was truly a general that commanded his battlefield. Blake looked forward to re-enforcing that ownership with anyone who dared enter his domain.

Blake attacked soccer in the same manner he did everything else, with total dedication. Blake studied the game and spent hours working on his skills after everyone else left school to go have fun on the town. He read every book he could find on goalkeeping and studied films from every era of soccer. His unknowing mentor was Lev Yashin, who played for Dynamo Moscow in the 1950s and 1970s. To this day, Yashin is still widely considered to be the best goalie to ever play the game and was known as the "Black Spider" because of his incredible athleticism and reflexes. Yashin coupled those skills with massive strength and power, creating the template for the perfect goalie. With Blake's equally impressive size and agility, and his dedication to the game, he shattered the school record for shutouts and goals, allowing only five goals in his combined junior and senior seasons – two of which were due to penalty kicks. During his senior year, Blake was contacted by multiple colleges offering free rides to come play soccer at their institutions, but none of that was in Blake's plan. Blake remained singularly focused on one, and only one path: to attend the prestigious West Point Military Academy. A congressman from New York City who had known his father prior to 9/11 provided the recommendation letter for Blake, and his acceptance into the prestigious facility was completed so fast that it seemed predetermined.

In addition to his physical attributes, Blake found that he had a natural intuition for logistics and operational planning. During his four years at West Point, he mastered his nuclear engineering studies, aced all of his operations research (OR) and systems management classwork, and also established himself as an expert in statistics. Blake's ability to calmly re-scope plans "on the fly" when things went wrong, as they so often do in the field during a special ops mission, was an innate skill that helped him move quickly through assignments. Every commander wanted someone like Blake in the field with them. One battle-hardened Marine Corps sergeant had been quoted as saying: "The next best thing to having Blake with you was actually not having to go in the first place." The ultimate compliment from an ultimate tough guy.

Three intense years later, after gaining Special Forces status and then applying for SEAL tryouts, Blake graduated and became a

Special Forces Navy SEAL (Sea, Air, Land teams). The Navy SEALs have long been considered among the best and toughest "bad asses" on the planet. Only the best-of-the-best are granted the opportunity to even attempt to become a Navy SEAL; and the fallout among that already select group commonly exceeded 50 percent during the months of grueling training.

During the three-month-long Stage 1 training, better known as BUD/S Prep (Basic Underwater Demolition/SEAL), candidates are challenged to complete multiple objectives including a 1,000-yard swim with fins in fewer than 20 minutes, exceeding 70 push-ups in two minutes, and completing a four-mile run in less than 31 minutes. Stage 2, Intro to BUD/S, is a three-week basic orientation training session. Stage 3, basic conditioning, lasts seven weeks and is typically where candidates start to drop out in larger numbers. History has shown that candidates who scored below 800 on their PST (Physical Screening Test) typically survived Stage 3; Blake scored a 655. In this case, unlike most tests, the lower the PST score, the better.

Stage 4 was another grueling seven-week session that introduced the candidate to underwater skills unique to Navy SEALs. Stage 5 was an additional seven weeks of land warfare training focusing on weapons, demolitions, navigation, patrolling, rappelling, marksmanship and small unit tactics. Stage 6 focused on mastery of a wide array of SEAL skills required to join a SEAL platoon, including HALO (High Altitude-Low Opening), HAHO (High Altitude-High Opening) operations and the notorious *Hell Week,* where candidates are pushed to the edge of mental and physical limits while undergoing extreme sleep deprivation. Once a candidate passed all of the requirements of Stage 6, then, and only then, could a candidate become a true SEAL team member who is rewarded with the pinning of the highly coveted Trident on their uniform.

Blake made it through all of the grueling mental and physical tests. As the challenges intensified, Blake overcame any hesitation, or thought of failure, by recalling his father and friends who had died on Sept. 11. Every time a new barrier arose, Blake focused his thoughts on his memories of those he considered to be his personal heroes, those who had given everything for people they didn't even know. The thought of those firefighters carrying heavy gear up countless flights of stairs into known danger zones, only to meet death halfway up the towers, was fuel enough for him to get through a "simple series of tests," as he was heard to say one time. It was only after training was completed, as Blake and his fellow classmates traded experiences and developed the camaraderie that SEAL training creates, that he found many common threads with his fellow trident winners. Most were driven by something the majority of the free populace would never face or could even begin to understand. There were a few who were simply born with a natural set of gladiator or warrior genes for the SEAL life, but most had come either with a chip on their shoulder, to prove to the world, or like Blake, had experienced something traumatic in their lives that became their personal call to arms.

The SEAL life was their very personal way of dealing with the internal pain they would never disclose, while simultaneously finding a path where they could impact the world and prevent others from going through similar trauma. Contrary to stories that made SEALs out to be cold, heartless killers, most SEALs had a definition of right and wrong that was an order of magnitude above the everyday citizen's back home. SEALs also had an equally strong desire to make things right – or die trying.

Following SEAL graduation, Blake saw action in theaters of war and conflict all around the world, the majority of which were never reported on the nightly news. He and his team were currently deployed in the Tibetan Himalayas on a special assignment before heading back to Afghanistan for what was scheduled to be his final SEAL mission. Over the past decade, tensions had increased between the Chinese and U.S. governments, as the Communist country was challenging the U.S. as the largest economy in the world. China's developing confidence was publicly highlighted in many well-known oceanic areas – especially where the Chinese were creating man-made islands to justify expansion of their territorial waters. But their expansionist efforts were also being pursued on land, frequently in lesser-known areas like the mountains of Tibet. For years, the Chinese had been systematically eliminating the rich Tibetan culture and traditions, ways of life Tibetan monks had practiced for centuries.

Blake had always found the Chinese government's logic to be flawed relative to how it treated its own people, and that, regardless of the country's enormous economic progress, its people were still not free. That was a true power that the Chinese government simply didn't understand, or more likely, was afraid to experiment with. Blake was confident that China would never become a true world leader until it began providing the basic fundamental freedoms to its people that the U.S. had embodied since 1776. At the same time, Blake found it highly ironic these were the same freedoms that were taken for granted by the average American on a daily basis. Unfortunately, as Blake had observed over the years, most people had to experience significant loss, like what occurred on 9/11, before they truly appreciated just how precious American freedom really was. One of Blake's favorite quotes was from Thomas Jefferson, who said, *"The tree of liberty must be refreshed from time to time with the blood of patriots and tyrants."* Blake routinely reminded his teams that there was no 50/50 requirement in Jefferson's quote, and that their goal should be to strive to make that a 0/100 ratio, with the clear "winner" being the tyrants' blood – preferably by the hands of the SEALs.

At 41 years of age, Blake remained in great shape, as good as – if not better than – any professional athletes of the same age. But rather than retirement, Blake was already thinking about the next step in his career. He had recently applied for and was accepted into a position in the new, top-secret U.S. Space Corps program. Even though the announcement of the Space Force goal had been made a decade earlier, and started even sooner than that, the bulk of the activity was classified, and the past five years had seen the biggest jump in U.S. space activity since the space shuttle program became standard fare in the 1980s. Blake treasured his experiences and accomplishments with the Special Forces and SEALs, but he was equally excited to start the next stage in his life. He saw the Space Corps equally important as the SEALs as the Chinese and Russians were both starting to lay claim to greater areas of space – areas that the U.S. firmly believed needed to remain unclaimed and free to all of humanity. Many military strategists believed that tomorrow's wars would be dominated and controlled by winning the space war, just like the wars of the 20th and 21st centuries were dominated and controlled by winning the air war.

Blake was leading his SEAL team deep into the Tibetan wilderness near 6,714-meter-tall Mount Kailash. His team included five elite Special Forces members, including a 26-year-old Chinese-born computer specialist named Li Zheng. Blake had worked with Li for the past four years and considered him both a personal friend as well as the best computer hacker the CIA had ever encountered. The man simply thought in electrons and software, yet surprisingly, had a cutting wit that rivaled the long-stereotyped British, just with a slightly different accent – as Blake chided him whenever he got the chance. Li had also been an accomplished marathoner in college and won the famed 4,393-meter-high Pikes Peak marathon, a true test of altitude running. Taking a "jaunt" in the Tibetan mountains to show up his Chinese counterparts was a "no brainer," he dryly told Blake.

Lt. Sean O'Rourke, 33, was Blake's primary pilot and had been with Blake, on and off, over the past seven years. O'Rourke, originally from Shannon, Ireland, could talk in a heavy brogue when he chose to, but did so only when he wanted to antagonize someone. Sean was a veteran sharpshooter, having won the USAF Distinguished Shooter Badge for both rifles and pistols. During a joint military shooting contest, Sean had so impressed the Marine Corps commander in charge of the event that the commander invited Sean to compete for the Marine Corps Interservice/Marine Corps Rifle Competition Badge – Sean ended up winning the Gold level for both pistols and rifles. Coupled with his sarcastic humor, Sean was the most unlikely oddball of the group, and he reveled in that fact, frequently using his self-deprecating humor to crack jokes and reduce tension levels while in action.

Corp. Diego Velasquez, 27 years old, only 1.72 meters (5'6") tall and 65 kilograms (145 pounds) soaking wet, was one of the best hand-to-hand combatants in the Special Forces for his weight class. Diego had crossed the U.S.-Mexico border as a 5-year-old child with his mother and three siblings. He joined the U.S.M.C. as soon as he graduated from high school and quickly adapted to the Marine Corps theme of "no rules barred, meanest sons of bitches in the world." Marines were Marines on a 365/24/7 basis. They were taught to overcome and win at any cost, pure and simple. That theme sat well with Diego, who had grown up in a tough, gang-filled section of L.A., receiving a third-degree black belt before graduating from Venice High School.

Once in the Marines, Diego quickly picked up boxing, judo and Brazilian Jiu Jitsu, in addition to becoming a master with explosives. Diego had made a name for himself in the Marine Recon group, where it was rumored that his eyesight and hearing were as good as any cat or bird of prey in the jungle. At the end of the day, Diego was as deadly a combatant as the U.S. military could produce.

Spec. Harry Lundrum was both the kid and the brainiac of what was already a way-above-average group of intellects. Blake commonly referred to Harry as "Einstein" due to his ability to conceptualize the physics of a problem and construct mathematical models in his head. Harry graduated from Harvard with a dual Ph.D. in chemistry and mathematics at the age of 24, and then followed up with third Ph.D. in astrophysics from M.I.T. by the time he was 27.

Now at 29, Harry had 36 acknowledged patents, and three times as many government secrets that would have easily become patents had it not been for their classification by the U.S. government. Once Harry tasted the government "black" and "compartmentalized" project world, with its unending supply of high-tech gadgets and problems waiting for his Einsteinian brain, Harry knew he had found his home. Harry maintained an insatiable appetite for the latest and greatest science breakthroughs and had to be on the leading edge of everything. He read and absorbed articles on nano-materials, biotechnology and genetic engineering like others read a *New York Times* best-seller. With his seemingly photographic memory, once read, the material was available for instant replay any time he needed it.

However, the most endearing aspect of Harry was his total humility. Harry never bragged or put anyone down for not being as smart as he was. He was revered for his ability to reduce the most complex issues into simple terms that any layman or soldier could easily grasp – without the recipient realizing what Harry had actually done. To truly understand Harry, all one needed to know was that his favorite movie character was Pavel Chekov on "Star Trek" and his favorite movie scene was the bar scene in "Good Will Hunting" where Matt Damon, playing the character Will, put an arrogant Harvard student in his place. Harry had replayed that role many times in the real world and many a pompous student, or professor, decided they should quickly exit stage left and leave Harry and his friends alone.

Patty Myers was the final member of the elite group. At the age of 31, she was one of the most accomplished linguists in the military, ratcheting up the ranks within the CIA special request rooms. Patty was fluent in English, Arabic, Chinese, Russian, German, French and Latin. It was a thing of beauty and amazement to see how quickly she could flow from one language to the next, without breaking stride or mixing languages. The CIA quickly realized that Patty was also a natural cryptanalyst and moved her into a Ph.D.-equivalent cryptanalysis program that quickly paid off against the Taliban. It was these skills that gained her a rare "female pass" into the Special Forces.

At first glance, neither Harry nor Patty met the standard SEAL "look," relative to the common Hollywood-stereotyped SEAL teams, but both could still fight with the best. Regardless, if the op expected significant military content, it was not unusual to include a second special ops team that was heavily loaded for firepower. This approach was a little more common than what was typically shared with the public, as many Ops were becoming more strategic, not purely for killing hostiles.

Their current black op was a good example of today's strategic Ops. It was focused on taking out the power and computers at a remote communications jamming center the Chinese were using to block Tibetans from accessing the Internet. The Chinese efforts were directed at keeping the Tibetans isolated from the world while they continued to assimilate the country. Furthermore, the objective of the black op was to do it without firing a single shot, as the Americans didn't want the Chinese to know they were ever there.

The op was a success; the team was in and out in fewer than two hours. Li successfully completed the system shutdown and uploaded the virus. They regrouped 200 yards away from the Comm tower under cover of a stand of chir pines.

"Nice job, Hack." Blake frequently referred to Li as "Hack," a term from a bygone era when the term "computer hack" was more in vogue. "How long do you think your little trick will keep them at bay?"

"It'll take those wankers a few days to even know there is a problem, and then a few more days to get around each of the viral shields I set up, so I expect it'll hold them for a couple of weeks before they can start blocking again. That should allow the Free Tibetans adequate time to exchange more than a few messages with the outside world," Li replied confidently.

The Free Tibet movement had started in 1987 in England. The group fought for the rights of Tibetans to determine their own future, campaigned for an end to the Chinese occupation of Tibet, and tried to ensure the respect for the fundamental human rights of Tibetans and their culture. Needless to say, its small, independent efforts were like using a pellet gun against an elephant. As Li claimed, "It made a little noise, but really didn't accomplish much." They all knew that this particular Op, even if successful, wouldn't have a significant impact on the Chinese. It was an op based on principle, a clandestine op that required absolute perfection from the team.

The decision to implement Project Pipeline, as it had been code named, was based on a request from the British MI6 organization, the Queen's secret intelligence service. One of the top MI6 agents, Oliver Wyatt, was married to a Tibetan woman, but her family had remained in Tibet with no means of contact with the outside world. The Brits lacked assets in Tibet, so they contacted the U.S. government and worked out a deal to rescue a U.S. spy being held by the North Koreans, in exchange for assistance in Tibet.

The Brits were good to their word, rescued the spy without incident, and escaped before anyone could stumble across the few Korean soldiers who would never see the sunrise. The British mission was clearly more dangerous, but the Brits also had a little payback incentive that they had been holding onto for a couple of years, waiting for the right opportunity to register the payback. The North Koreans had uncovered a British spy ring a few years earlier, and executed five critical assets the Brits had spent years developing. As typical with the Brits, it wasn't just the investment in the assets; it was the fact that the Brits considered these five individuals part of their family. The Koreans' act had made it personal; it had to be avenged. The Brits escaped quietly, but left an obvious calling card that would be found long after they were out of the country, ensuring the North Koreans would know who had trumped them. The fact that one of the Korean bodies left behind just happened to be the same major who had executed the British assets was considered icing on the cake by Oliver and the Brits.

Oliver was 31 with a background in chemical engineering. Blake worked with him on previous special ops outings, most of which were in Africa and the Middle East against the growing Islamic Fundamentalist movements. The two men respected each other, so it didn't take any arm-twisting when Oliver called him up and requested that he personally lead the Tibetan raid.

Blake reflected over the past few years, wondering when more Islamic Fundamentalist uprisings would spread deeper into Europe, or even breach the Western world. After the 9/11 attack in the U.S. that destroyed the Twin Towers and killed thousands, there had been many more incidents in Europe. Incidents like the 2015 Paris nightclub attack that killed 130 and the 2025 Heathrow International Airport terrorist attack that killed 251 continued to stoke fears of more attacks throughout the world.

If it were up to Blake, he would orchestrate a Western world takeover of the entire Middle East, with the obvious exception of Israel. Although most would argue that it wasn't feasible to govern an area that large, or politically correct to replace their legitimate rights to govern themselves, it was clear to Blake that the past 1,000 years had proven they simply weren't capable of governing themselves; nor were they capable of respecting the various differences in culture and religion elsewhere in the world. It was also abundantly clear that those governments were either incapable of eliminating the violence that forever seemed to emanate from their areas, or they weren't truly interested in stopping it – both options were unacceptable to Blake. A change in strategy, like Blake proposed, would also mean an end to the lucrative weapon sales programs that Russia and the Western world enjoyed. The truth was that Russia and the West had created a great deal of the unrest by removing various strongmen who had previously maintained stability, as well as by continuing their arms sales to these countries.

In Blake's opinion, something different and something significant had to be done, plain and simple. There should be rules established that would allow for legitimate Middle East governments to propose exceptions to the plan based on a track record that proved they were mature enough to join the rest of the world. In that case, they would also be expected to join the Western Alliance and provide troops and financial support at a level equal to the Western countries. The process of determining the readiness for self-governance would be a monumental task when one considered the political implications of countries such as Saudi Arabia, Iran, Iraq, Turkey and Egypt, let alone the multitudes of smaller countries.

An effort of this size would require total commitment and alignment from the West, Russia, and even China. It would require trillions of dollars, and massive semi-permanent military deployments from all the countries, as well as countless checkpoints to control border crossings. The ultimate goal would be to demilitarize the entire Middle East and establish safe zones for each Muslim and Christian sect with borders enforced by the alliance. An effort this large would require a unified worldwide agreement, an alliance the likes of which hadn't been seen since World War II. In essence, it required the worldwide acknowledgement that this series of conflicts was indeed WWIII, although different from WWI and WWII, and therefore needed an equally united world response. Unfortunately, as bad as things currently were, it would have to get a lot worse before the world truly came together to address the issue of Islamic extremists. It was equally clear that the Muslim governments and religious leaders would need to visibly and repeatedly demonstrate support for the end to violence, as well as demand an end to the extremist organizations that freely operated within their countries.

Blake knew his vision of the Middle East was not likely to happen in his lifetime, so he was looking forward to leaving the terrorist ops world and pursuing new challenges in the Space Corps program, where he could have a greater impact; but that was still a few weeks out. Until then, Blake remained a Special Operations combatant and was in one such endeavor right now that required 100 percent of his skills and attention.

Blake surveyed the area the group had stopped in. Although it was nighttime, he could easily see outlines of the surrounding area and its rugged beauty. What a shame it could not easily be shared with the rest of the world, he thought glumly.

"O'Rourke." Blake looked back at his pilot. "What travel accommodations do you have for us tonight?"

"Noottin' boot de best o' course," Sean replied. "How aboot a top o' de line Mercedes and a sporty Mustang?"

"Splendid," panned Li. "Are they at the nearest Avis counter?"

"Ye o' lil' faith me friends," O'Rourke lobbied back with as heavy an Irish brogue as he could muster. "When 'ave I ev'r let ye all down?"

"I don't think we have enough time to detail the evidence to that response," baited Li, "but, please, where should I begin? I know, for starters, how about that boat on the Congo River? You know, that one with a hole in the bottom the size of a silver dollar and we had to bail water just to stay afloat while you slept the entire way?"

"Slept?! Now, now, weren't I nursin' fer bullet 'oles at the time after I 'ad saved yer arse from a 'ole tribe of locals? Is there no shame in ye, man?" He grinned.

Before Li could respond, a light flashed three times in quick succession from the bushes 300 yards ahead. O'Rourke flashed back two times and waited. The light in the bush then flashed four more times. Sean flashed back three times, and the lights went dark.

"See, j'st wait a wee moment more me lads, yer chariots await!" Sean boasted.

"I can 'ardly bear the anticipation," Li mocked back.

The six of them spread themselves out in single file, about three meters apart, one behind the other, and made their way toward the spot that had been the source of the light. Five minutes later, Sean, at the head of the pack, flashed his light two times, and a single man emerged out of the darkness ahead. He motioned to them to follow.

As the group rounded a small hill surrounded by trees and thickets, they made out two horses and a large wagon of loose straw.

"'Air we 'r me laddies, noottin' but d' best!" he proudly whispered. "This 'ere is Mercedes," as he pointed to the horse on the left, "and this 'ere is Mustang. And this 'ere is yer lovely chariot!"

"Absolutely wonderful, Sean. You've outdone yourself once again. You simply never cease to amaze me, but I'm really waiting to see how you pilot this chariot into the air," Patty replied with dripping sarcasm.

It became clear that their newfound guide did not speak English, but as Blake had pointed out ahead of time, that also protected the man from being able to share anything the group discussed if he were ever captured. The man jumped up onto the only seat on the wagon and motioned the group into the straw pile.

"Pile in," Blake directed in a whisper. The group found shelter under the straw; the long, slow and bumpy journey to the border was under way. It would be a good four hours before they reached their planned rendezvous point, just across the Indian border, so most of the team saw this as a good time to get some sleep. The lone exception was Diego, who took the first watch in a forward position of the straw pile to keep an eye and ear out for any unexpected visitors. They planned to stay south of the Chinese G219 National Highway to avoid detection by the Chinese troop transports that frequently traveled that road.

Once on their way, the only sounds the group heard – besides the clip-clop of the horses and the wobbly wagon wheels – were the occasional rich tones of the Chinese nightingales abundant in this area.

CHAPTER 2

A.D. 2028 (3311 C.A.E.); Aug. 23
Houston, Texas

It was nearing midnight and Robert Stern, a third-year aerospace engineering student at the University of Houston, was in the last week of his summer internship at the Lyndon B. Johnson Space Center at Houston. Robert was getting ready to check in on the Mars Rover, but first he had to finish his calculus-laden thermodynamics homework. Robert was 1.82 meters tall (5'10") and 66 kilograms (145 pounds), blue-eyed and had sandy-brown hair. He had grown up in Pueblo West, Colo., where he attended Pueblo West High School and graduated with honors in 2025.

Robert enjoyed playing video games so he jumped at the opportunity to intern in NASA's software and simulation department in Houston. Unfortunately, the Mars Rover software work was nothing like playing the newer video game consoles with 360-degree virtual reality headsets. The technology was so old that Robert wondered if even an old Commodore 64 might provide more advanced technology. So much for *high tech,* he sarcastically told his friends back home. On the other hand, he was getting paid $25 per hour, and he knew this would be one heck of a résumé builder.

Even worse than the outdated technology was the response speed of the overall communication system and its built-in delays. The delays were due to the distance the radio waves had to traverse between Earth and Mars. Radio waves travel at approximately 300,000 kilometers per second in space, the same speed as the speed of light, but Mars was more than 54 million kilometers away. Therefore, every programmed equipment move sent from

Earth took more than six minutes to be received on the Red Planet, and then another six-plus minutes to return to Earth. Each day, Robert would send his orders to Mars and then check the following day to see how many meters, or even centimeters the robot had covered. Sometimes he would stick around for an extra hour or two to make a couple sets of commands, but typically, he would move on and do some of the more "fun" analytical tasks that NASA had him working on. As long as it involved programming, Robert was content. He seemed to have an innate ability to think like a computer, and lines of code flowed from his fingertips.

Robert's desk was located in a sea of small cubicles. Old Dilbert cartoons and NASA calendars covered his cubicle walls. Like many other engineers, Robert's favorite Dilbert cartoons were the series on women who loved engineers. The latest joke was that NASA was hiding them all on a secret moon base. After all, it really couldn't be this bad, could it? It was a well-known fact the engineering profession still lacked what most people considered to be an appropriate level of female candidates. Although the ratios had improved over the past decade, it wasn't by much. The engineering programs across the country still sported less than 20 percent female headcount in the male-dominated industry. In addition, male engineers continued to bear the brunt of the majority of *geek* jokes across the country. It always pissed Robert off that while engineers invented and created new things, they were never seen as "cool."

Robert recalled a saying prevalent at the Colorado School of Mines, where he had attended a campus tour in which a rare female engineering student leading the tour responded to a comment about her dating odds being good at the school by saying, "We have a saying here that the odds are good, but the goods are odd." Everyone had laughed, but that still frustrated Robert every time he thought about it. Why was it that the "cool guys" were always the law school guys? Like lawyers did anything of *real* value? Lawyers were always the wonder boys on the prestigious career track, yet so many of them became the infamous ambulance chasers who advertised day and night on TV about your rights to sue someone – because nothing is ever your fault; it has to be someone else's fault. Engineers, on the other hand, were promoted as geeks, nerds, and just plain weirdos, thanks to Hollywood.

"Damn lawyers," Robert frequently told his friends. "What the heck do they actually create anyway? Nothing, absolutely nothing! All they do is transfer wealth from one person or business to another, while siphoning off huge percentages for themselves. Do they add to the general betterment of humankind? Hell no! But they sure are good at destroying things. How much do those bloodsucking pigs cost businesses and doctors every year? A lot. In this litigation-crazed country, they can sue anyone for anything at any time – without any accountability to anyone. And the shallow women love them for the money that it brings in. What a crock."

Robert actually enjoyed being a nerd, so screw them all, he thought.

Robert refocused his thoughts back to his work at hand. It was a slow and painful process, but at least he was getting paid for doing something. In fairness, the job might have been exciting years ago when the Rover first landed and activated, but after years of nothingness, no one really cared anymore. The fact that the Rover was still working was amazing, a true engineering feat of extraordinary perfection. Unfortunately, other than the handful of "nerdy" engineers who designed it, no one even cared about that anymore, either. The media and general populace had long forgotten the Rover program even existed.

Robert had earlier finished his thermodynamics homework related to determining the maximum efficiency of a gas-cooled, pressurized-water, nuclear reactor that operated between 150 to 160 atmospheres and 300 to 320 degrees C. Good stuff, he thought, but he was ready to play for a while, so he closed down the links on his Dell Latitude VII laptop and opened up the links to the Mars Rover data, slid the file over to his 30-inch monitor and decided he would check the video feeds and take a look at his buddy, Mack. Robert had renamed the Mars Rover robot after the famous turtle called Mack in Doctor Seuss's "Yertle the Turtle." Mack was the everyday turtle at the bottom of the pile that never received any glory, but had to put up with the crap from the guy at the top – kind of like working as an engineer for the government. In the book, the guy at the top was named Yertle. Robert detested people like Yertle and had grown to be a defender of the Macks he met throughout his school years.

"Okay, Mack, what have you got for me tonight?" he asked the screen.

"Let me guess. Red rocks, red sand, red sky, red … huh, what is that?" He knew no one would answer. "That looks hard and polished … almost like metal. Mack, is that really metal?"

Robert started to get excited and sat up straight in his chair, his fingers suddenly motionless while hovering over the keyboard. This was different, *really* different. He wondered if this might be a remnant from the 1999 Mars Polar Lander mission that crashed. He would surely get an A in his astrophysics lab if he were right. Heck, this would make CNN, he thought, getting even more excited. This wasn't just a "find" – this was BIG! But Robert also knew that some Yertle in the organization would quickly take credit over an intern, and Robert would be shielded from the limelight. He decided he would keep it as a secret until he knew more so that no one else could take credit for it. First, and most importantly, he needed that A. He could easily manage the timeline for CNN afterwards.

Robert began programming Mack for the next day's work and directed it to start excavating around the small piece of metal on the robot's right side. The immediate area looked free of rocks and hopefully would be easy to excavate. The shadows from nearby boulders were beginning to creep over the site and nothing else of interest was in the immediate viewing area, so Robert also programmed the robot to conduct a 360-degree panoramic sweep of the surroundings to see if anything else could be detected that was worth checking out. He expected the slow rover would take a couple of days to uncover the object, but it shouldn't be too hard. After all, the exposed object in the red sand looked pretty small, no bigger than the dimensions of the keyboard on his laptop computer.

******

A.D. 2028 (3311 C.A.E.); Aug. 24
Houston

The next afternoon, as soon as his classes were over, Robert headed over to the Space Center quickly. It was after 6 p.m. and he still hadn't shared his secret with anyone, so he scanned the office area to make sure no one else was around. Perfect, it looked like everyone had left for home. The big bullpen area was empty and the lights were all off. Even the coffee pot was cold. As he walked down the hall to his cubicle, movement sensors turned on the lights one bay at a time. Robert knew that the lights would go off in 15 minutes unless someone else came by, so he also knew that he had a built-in warning system that would alert him to anyone else possibly seeing his computer screen and possibly learning about his secret discovery.

Robert typed in his password, clicked down through a number of LAN locations and opened up the video stream for the Mars Rover at the same time he opened up a Ziploc sandwich bag and started eating his PB&J sandwich.

"Oh, my God!" Robert sat back in his chair and dropped his sandwich. "What the heck is that? Mack … what did you find? … That assuredly does not belong to the Polar Lander …" he mumbled with disbelief.

Robert could see that the robot had excavated a small depression around one side of the metal fin – yes, it was definitely a fin, but what was it attached to? There were at least 10 inches of a cylindrical body that had been excavated with strange markings on the exposed surface – clearly not English, nor anything else Robert had ever seen. Robert looked around. No one was present.

"The heck with my Physics lab report, this is ready for CNN primetime right now. Maybe I'll let Professor Lu sit on the stage with me; that'll get me an A!" Robert told the computer screen. Unfortunately, he knew that he couldn't release this information without going through NASA first. He also knew that this information would get classified quicker than he could finish his PB&J sandwich, but he had to call someone. Robert picked up his desk phone and dialed the home number for his supervisor, who was also an adjunct professor at the University of Houston.

"Hello, George here."

"George, Mr. Stratton, Prof. Stratton ... this is Robert Stern." The words fought each other to come out all at once. "I really need to show you something. Can you come in *now*?"

"Whoa, Robert, calm down; I'm sure it can wait until tomorrow. We just finished dinner and I'm getting ready to head to my daughter's soccer game ..."

"No, sir, I apologize for cutting you off, but you absolutely need to see what Mack, I mean the Mars Rover has uncovered."

"Water?" George asked with a smile. "Did you find a drinking fountain?" he asked sarcastically.

"No, not water. It's much, much bigger than that. I'm telling you; you really need to see this. Please come in, sir."

A long pause ensued. Robert could tell the phone was being muffled and George must be talking to someone, maybe his wife. He sounded pretty irritated.

"Prof. Stratton, I'm telling you that I have to show you this tonight! I promise you that you won't be disappointed – I'll quit on the spot if you are," Robert added with a tone that laced together confidence, authority and fear.

"Okay, Robert, you sound pretty keyed up about whatever it is. I'll be there in 30 minutes. It better be good, Robert – this is not the time to try to match Cal Tech for pranks."

"I'll say it again ... I promise you, sir, you will not be disappointed."

Thirty minutes later, George Stratton and Robert were looking at the Dell 30-inch monitor, alternating with screams of joy like little kids, broken by intermittent moments of silence from sheer disbelief as they attempted to absorb what was on the screen.

"What do you think it is?" they both asked simultaneously.

Prof. Stratton took over the replay controls and zoomed in on the markings. "Look, see how linear these markings are? And the swirls are in different directions … no way they could be from entry damage, wind erosion or other natural means. These are definitely intentionally made by someone, or something, likely with a machine, but I don't recognize it from any country … on this world … I hate to jump to conclusions, but Robert, this could … this could …"

"… Be alien?" Robert completed the sentence for him.

"Do you think that means there was life on Mars after all?" Robert asked.

"Could be, but we also can't rule out other sources as well."

"Like what?" Robert demanded. There was no answer.

"What do we do now, Prof. Stratton? Who do we tell?"

"We must keep this absolutely hush, top secret. You can't even tell your father or your class advisor. I'll contact the head of NASA Houston to determine what to do next. This will be bigger than the finding of the Dead Sea Scrolls. Meanwhile, you start working on a program to excavate the object further. You found it, so it's up to you: what would you like to name the object, Robert?"

"The object? Why do sci-fi movies always refer to it as *the object*?"

"Robert?"

"Okay, okay." Robert paused to contemplate Prof. Stratton's question, "Well, I'd like to call it The Big Brag.*"*

"Say what?" echoed Prof. Stratton.

"You know, Dr. Seuss? 'Yertle the Turtle'? Come on, Prof. Stratton, it's a classic from your era, and you don't know it? That was the short story at the end of 'Yertle the Turtle.' "

"Was that the one where the worm ends up winning the battle of the beasts with the biggest brag?" asked Prof. Stratton.

"That's the one! Seemed appropriate as this will be the biggest brag of the century, assuming we are right."

"Robert, I'm not sure how those wheels turn in your head, but they definitely turn. The Big Brag it is."

CHAPTER 3

A.D. 2028 (3311 C.A.E.); Aug. 24
Tibet

The long ride continued without incident until Diego rustled the straw above Blake as he reached to tap Blake's shoulder. Blake passed on the signal to the others. All Blake and the others could know from Diego's signal was that he had spotted or sensed something. Whether that "something" was a threat or not, was impossible to tell at the moment, but years of training and conditioning taught them to always default to "threat." The group prepared for action. Guns were moved to the ready and maximum sensory focus was placed on the auditory systems of each of the team, straining to pick non-natural sounds out of the nightly orchestra of crickets, birdcalls and wagon noises.

Blake spread the straw to his right and peeked out: a crystal clear night with multitudes of stars in the sky, and a continual flow of darkened trees passing by. Blake had intentionally planned their mission around the cycles of the moon to ensure a moonless night, and in so doing, minimize accidental sightings of their team. At the same time, the dark night, aided by the lack of any man-made light sources, allowed his eyes to adjust quickly to the darkness. It was always surprising how much one could actually see once one's eyes adjusted. Blake strained his ears to listen. A minute that felt like eternity passed quietly, until the silence was broken by an owl hooting nearby. Another minute passed and then Blake finally heard it. Just a murmur, but it was clearly human. Blake rustled the straw to his left where Patty had been sleeping and whispered.

"What dialect?"

"It sounds Tibetan," she whispered back. "Likely farmers."

The group relaxed a bit, but still remained focused on looking for any unexpected threats that might be approaching. They had directed their guide that the only time he should stop was if he felt he were in imminent danger, which would be the team's unspoken signal to go into action. Otherwise, he was not to stop for idle chitchat as the group was on a tight schedule to get to its rendezvous point. Every extra minute on the trail increased the chances they might run into a Chinese patrol.

A long minute passed and Blake heard a second rustle from Diego's position. Blake rustled the straw in Diego's direction, but there was no response. Diego had exited the wagon, which meant that he saw or heard something he didn't like. That was Blake's signal to depart the wagon as well. Blake flipped on his night vision goggles and quickly found Diego crouched in the bushes alongside the road, moving forward slowly. Blake followed him quietly, leaving the others in the wagon.

The voice now became two distinct voices and the sounds were clearly getting closer. The wagon slowed, but didn't stop as the driver began conversing with the two voices ahead in the dark.

"Patty?" Li whispered this time.

"I don't know what they are saying, but it's not Mandarin. I feel pretty confident they are likely just local farmers."

Li looked at his watch. The nightglow on his watch showed 3:55. A little early in the morning by any standards in the U.S., but this was Tibet. The driver and the two strangers, who were now walking alongside the wagon, were talking as if they were friends who hadn't seen each other for a few days.

"Be alert," Patty whispered to the others from her headset.

At least five minutes went by, but it seemed like an eternity. The two men were still walking alongside the driver. This really didn't feel good, Patty thought, but she knew that Blake and Diego had left the wagon and she was pretty sure there would not be any surprises as long as they were monitoring the situation.

"Now?" Sean whispered. He was clearly getting tense as there was no hint of his Irish brogue.

"No," Patty whispered back, but she was also ready to pounce at the first sign they were in trouble. She reached forward, felt the rough surface of her silencer and double-checked to make sure the safety was off. Her legs tensed as she prepared to stand and jump out of the wagon. Just when she was sure that the night was going to go badly, the two men stepped aside, said something that sounded like a goodbye, and the wagon lurched forward again at its previous speed. Everyone let their breath out slowly and relaxed, but they were still down two passengers. Patty passed on to the others that Blake and Diego were still off the wagon and that they should stop a couple hundred meters down the rutted road to find out what had happened.

A minute went by and Patty was getting ready to rap on the buckboard behind the driver when she heard straw moving again.

"Blake?" Patty whispered.

"Yes."

Patty had been in the field with Blake long enough to know that the short reply was a statement as well; it meant "later."

Forty-five minutes later, the wagon left the rutted road and headed due west, and the ride got considerably rougher as they moved across open fields. Another 10 minutes passed and they entered a field where the shape of two Sikorsky UH-60 Black Hawk helicopters emerged out of the darkness.

"Let's go, people," Blake stated as he vaulted out of the wagon and headed to the first helicopter. "The sun will be lighting up the eastern sky in less than an hour." The blades had already begun turning. "Diego and Patty, on me." The others headed for the second helicopter.

Two minutes later, they were airborne and heading south, in the direction of the Indian Air Base at Gautam Buddh Nagar, UP, India. The U.S. and Indian governments had quietly become much closer than what was routinely publicized during the past decade of Islamic battles, and it paid dividends in times like these. Not only did they not have to fly into Chinese airspace, but they were able to fly without risk through India, in this case, directly to the USS George Washington currently sailing in the Indian Ocean.

"What happened back there?" Patty asked.

"I detected movement in the bushes a few yards off the road and behind the Tibetans," replied Diego. "I dropped out of the wagon, and waited for Blake; once he joined up, we circled around behind the wagon with our night vision goggles and we could clearly see that there were two Chinese soldiers ahead of the wagon with automatic rifles in hand."

"I suspect it may have been a trap to see if our guide was legit or not," Blake added. "The local farmers were likely used to lure us out, as well as provide the Chinese with what looked like innocent cover."

"Could be," replied Patty. "The Chinese frequently use Tibetan civilians as innocent bait without letting them know anything is going on. By doing so, they also have a better chance of catching unsuspecting farmers that may be conducting illegal trade with the West. Nothing like that happened this time and the farmers, although up suspiciously early in the morning, looked like they were moving on to go about whatever business they were doing."

"Always good to hear we are among innocents, right, Blake?" Patty said, smiling. "What about the two soldiers, why didn't they stop us?"

"Not so for those two," Diego replied before Blake could answer. "We were too close to our pickup point to risk identification or the chance that they would hear the copters take off. Maybe they were looking for an unexpected score, but they just didn't seem right. Almost like they were waiting for something."

"And that meant …?" started Patty.

"They needed to take a nap, real fast," Blake volunteered dryly. "We couldn't risk the chance that they would try something. Diego and I each sang them a lullaby across the back of their heads."

"Okay, that doesn't sound too likely to start an international incident," Patty said, chuckling.

"No risk of that, Patty, and they'll survive. Those two were lazy, clearly not the first-line Chinese army. There were a number of deep ravines and crevices nearby and we stashed both of them where they won't be found until they wake up. I expect the Chinese will write them off as deserters and not look very long for them, if they look at all."

The rest of the ride went quietly. Blake didn't believe in killing just for the sake of killing, but he really had hoped to get out without leaving any signs of their visit. He'd have to trust that the two sleeping soldiers would be more worried about letting their Chinese commanders know they had failed, than of letting them know that something happened.

*****

A.D. 2028 (3311 C.A.E.); Aug. 31
Houston

One week later, NASA had rushed together a team to research "the object" under direction from Washington and the Pentagon. At least two feet of the object, Robert's The Big Brag, had now been uncovered, and what appeared to be an access panel was now clearly visible on the side of the object. One young engineer referred to it as the "Martian Mortar" as it did indeed look like a small missile. As the sole discoverer, Robert had been kept on the team, and given a crash course on the importance of maintaining secrecy on his find.

A number of engineers gathered together in a dedicated conference room, now dubbed the "Mars War Room," while the images on the computer's screen were projected onto a 72-inch flat screen on the east wall of the room. The room comfortably sat eight people, but there were no fewer than 15 in it at the moment.

"Can we open it?" Robert asked from the back of the room.

"There are no apparent screws, knobs or openings that would provide access points," responded one NASA engineer without looking back. "It's highly likely that it's a hermetically sealed panel that isn't meant to be opened. We've tried knocking on it and pushing against the panel to no avail."

"Have you tried acoustics yet?" questioned Robert.

"Acoustics? That's a crazy idea. Furthermore, we don't have any capability to do that with the Rover," the engineer responded, clearly bothered. "Worse yet, the Rover seems to be getting stuck in the soft sand and can't get enough traction to make progress. We need to …"

"Wait!" screamed Robert. "I swear the door just shuddered. Playback the video."

As they all watched the replay; it was hard to tell if it really was a shudder of movement, a video artifact, or interference from the Martian atmosphere. The picture snow came and went fairly frequently, and it was rare to have a crystal clear picture.

"Can you program it to spin its wheels and move its arms at different frequencies, just to see if maybe we are close to an acoustic lock signal?" Robert requested.

"We can, but is this really worth wasting another day of programming with wait-and-see time?" the engineer replied sarcastically.

"That kid is the reason you're here right now, so perhaps you should give him a little more credence," Prof. Stratton answered before Robert could utter a word of defense.

"Okay, okay, point made, professor," the NASA engineer replied. "I'll set something up tonight and we'll see what happens in the morning."

Robert smiled a quiet "thank you" to Prof. Stratton and stepped out of the room to get something to eat. At this point, he'd let the professor deal with the newly minted Yertle at the controls.

*****

A.D. 2028 (3311 C.A.E.); Sept. 1

Both Robert and Prof. Stratton arrived early the next morning to get the first glimpse of yesterday's efforts. Prof. Stratton had picked up three McDonald's bacon and egg biscuit sandwiches, a couple of orange juices and a large coffee for himself. The night operator was there and had a big smile on his face as he accepted the sandwich from the professor.

"Thanks, professor, I …" the night operator was cut off by Robert.

"OMG! It's opened! I'll run the video back and see if …"

"No, Robert," Prof. Stratton said gently, as he placed a hand on Robert's shoulder. "You know this operation is being run by NASA and the Pentagon now. You can watch, make comments and dream all you want, but getting directly involved is now strictly off limits. Your involvement can only be verbal."

"Correct you are, professor, but I can," the operator replied with a smile. "Robert, I like your spunk, and your ability to think outside the box. Too many of these guys are too afraid to be wrong and therefore wait for someone else to voice an opinion just so they can shoot it down. Nice move on your part. By the way, the name is John, John Tatum, but my friends call me JT for short. Nice to meet you."

"Thanks, JT," Robert replied, simultaneously taking a bite of his sandwich.

As they scrolled through the video, they could clearly see when the door literally popped open as if it were spring-loaded. As soon as it did, a series of lights in the interior began blinking on and off with various patterns and frequencies.

"What's that?" Prof. Stratton asked.

"I don't know," the engineer responded, "but if I didn't know better, it sure looks like your Big Brag just turned itself on."

*****

Arak, Iran

The two men were near the city of Arak, Iran, a little less than halfway between Tehran and the Iraqi border to the west. Arak was a major industrial city that supplied Iran with a large percentage of its steel, petrochemical and locomotive needs; the city contained many commonplace warehouses.

"Allah Akbar," the general stated quietly. "We will finally bring the great Satan to his knees and send the world a message that we can no longer be ignored. We will not be treated like second-class citizens anymore."

"Yes, Gen. Shirazi, Islam will rise again. We will create seven stars that will scorch their country, just like their heretical teachings in their Revelations speak about," replied Col. Armeen Khorasani.

With that, seven nondescript trucks left the unmarked facility. Over the next two hours, one at a time, they would split up and head in seven separate directions.

The general recalled with deep hatred the past four decades of misery caused by the hated Americans. Ever since the initial Gulf War in 1990, medical and food supplies had been withheld from the Iranian people in exchange for promises to reduce or stop Iranian efforts to expand their nuclear capabilities. It angered the general to think of how arrogant the Americans were, that they could own the power of nuclear technology, but other countries like his should not? No, that would no longer be the case, and unlike the corrupt Americans, the Iranian people would use the technology to lead the Islamic nations in taking back the world for Allah.

The general was amazed at how easy it had been to delay deadlines with the U.S. and the United Nations, as well as to hide advances from their so-called inspectors. The Americans were clearly weak and had lost their way long ago. Their leaders cared more about appearance than substance. Political correctness was just a feeble country's excuse for capitulation and not taking a stand on principles. They were all disbelievers and sinners – and they needed to be held accountable. The Arak site had been re-commissioned in early 2022 and it had taken more than six years of highly secret development to get to where they were today. Many times over the years, work had been stopped and even destroyed in order to keep the Americans and their arrogant inspectors at bay. When the inspectors brought forth incriminating evidence, the Iranians had to waste valuable time convincing the despicable Americans that their work was only for medical and agricultural purposes. But they had remained vigilant, focused and determined, and therefore successful – as Allah said they would be against the unbelievers.

The general smiled. He reveled in the fact that Allah had shaded America's eyes and clouded its judgment for the past few years, all to ensure that mighty Persia could continue its work and retake its rightful place on the world stage. He, himself, would be Allah's instrument to bring Islam back to its glory days.

"Get the car, colonel. Our work here is done," directed Gen. Shirazi.

"Allah Akbar."

*****

George Bush Center for Intelligence, Langley, Va.
CIA headquarters

The room was dark and lit mainly by the monitors covering every inch of space on the front wall of a limited-access control room.

"Sir, we have been recording movement out of the city of Arak," the analyst relayed to the CIA director over the phone. "Seven trucks left, one at a time, 15 minutes apart, all heading north on Highway 47, but now they appear to be splitting up and heading in separate directions. We have two bogies heading east and west on Highway 5, two heading north and south on Highway 47, one on Highway 56 and two others have gone into warehouse buildings elsewhere in Arak. This looks like the movement we have been waiting for. Perhaps you should come down and see this."

"I'll be there in 30 minutes. Alert the Israelis."

"Yes, sir."

CHAPTER 4

A.D. 2028 (3311 C.A.E.); Sept. 2
Near Pluto orbit

The first to regain consciousness was Lt. Thjars Chjssiast, the ship's communications officer. Lt. Chjssiast felt like he had been in a head-on crash with a space barge. His sight was blurred and his head was banging as if someone were pounding on the hull with an air hammer immediately next to his head. He pulled the breathing apparatus from his throat and gasped his first breaths of unaided air. The fluids from his G-Cell had drained and he was exposed to the dry air of the ship. He was cold. It took every ounce of energy that he had, but Thjars slowly rolled his body across the edge of the G-Cell on the side opposite of the opened canopy, attempting to reach the floor with his left leg – and immediately crashed hard onto the floor.

*****

Thjars regained consciousness and realized he must have passed out. He had no idea how long he'd lain on the floor. He tried to stand, but his balance was unsteady. He felt as weak as a baby, and no matter how hard he tried, Thjars couldn't even get to his hands and knees, each time flopping unceremoniously to the floor until he finally decided to wait it out a little longer. What had happened? He was so weak and his vision was blurred; the lights actually hurt his eyes. Thjars strained to hold back the pain in his head, trying to clear his mental processes, but he couldn't remember a thing. After a few more minutes, he began to collect his composure. He tried to talk, but nothing emanated from his throat. His throat hurt, a raw pain that felt like his throat had literally cracked open.

As his sight cleared a little more, he became aware of a number of distinct shapes on the floor in various areas of the room, but he couldn't quite make out what they were. A few more minutes went by, and Thjars began to regain more of his senses. Finally, he could focus and see clearer. His vision still impaired, but improving, identified what appeared to be at least four crewmembers on the floor. He thought they were crewmembers based on their overall shapes and the insignia on what looked like Cjarian uniforms, but something just didn't look right. Thjars further surveyed the room. Based on the status of the G-Cell control panels, it looked like others might still be in their G-Cell membranes, but from the floor, he couldn't see the actual crewmembers in the units. The four on the floor were clearly dead; their skin had an odd, disheveled, almost gray, leathery appearance. He also noted that they were lying in very non-natural, contorted positions. Thjars strained to understand what he was seeing. He tried again to recall what might have happened. Thjars's last memory was that of entering his G-Cell for the two-week trip to the Klaxx system, but there was a total void of any memories after that. He had never experienced a G-Cell revival like this before.

It had been a good 20 minutes since Thjars woke up on the ship's floor, and he was beginning to regain some of his balance and motor skills. He decided to crawl over to one of the crewmembers, half crawling, half dragging himself across the floor. He stopped twice during his three-meter journey, breathing hard and sweating. He had never experienced anything like this in all of his years of space travel. Thjars began to think that the ship must have run afoul of a deadly virus that had infected the entire crew. But why would some have lived and others died? Was he weakened by it, but on the path to healing, or was he on the path to death? Thjars shuddered. Too many questions and too few answers. He needed to stay focused and not panic, he told himself.

Finally, Thjars reached the first crewmember; the person's back was facing him. Thjars reached out to roll the crewmember over and see who it was, but when he touched the body, it literally crumbled into dust. Thjars recoiled, falling flat on his back, gasping for breath. This wasn't possible. He must still be asleep, in a horrid nightmare, he told himself, trying to find some form of explanation. He closed his eyes, counted to 20, and then recalled each of his family members by name. A sure-fire method to test consciousness. He opened his eyes, but the nightmare remained. Thjars couldn't take his eyes off of the remnants of what had been a crewmember only moments earlier.

"Is anyone there?" his voice finally scratched out. "Is anyone else alive? What happened?" He paused, his breathing still rapid. "Is everyone dead?" It hurt too much too talk; Thjars needed something to drink.

He could see four unopened G-Cells that appeared to be well lit, suggesting the occupants inside each might also be alive, and three more that were clearly empty. During revival, G-Cells were typically opened one at a time so that slowly recovering crewmembers didn't overwhelm the support personnel – none of whom seemed to be around, Thjars noted. He examined the nearby monitors, squinting to focus on the digital displays. The monitors indicated that the individuals inside of the four G-Cells were still alive, but those occupants clearly didn't need his help at the moment. Then he saw it. Behind the last G-Cell was the water cooler. The artificial gravity created by his suit was obviously still on as Thjars was having no trouble remaining attached to the floor, so he assumed that the water would be working as well. Yet, he felt so weak he wasn't sure he could make it to the cooler before passing out again.

Five minutes later, which felt like an eternity, Thjars made it to the cooler like a dehydrated man crawling through a desert on his belly. He reached up and turned the water on. It spat and gurgled for a few seconds and spit out a stream of dark water into the sealed container that collected the dispensed water before finally running full stream and clear. Thjars exerted all he had to pull himself up to the cooler, purge the bottle and then refill it with clean water. He sat against the cooler and drank small, slow gulps of water from the container. After 30 seconds, he lay back down on the floor and abruptly passed out, waking up a full hour later.

Thjars got to his knees and pulled himself to a standing position, firmly gripping the ship's structure near him. For the next 30 minutes, he practiced taking steps, walking and maintaining his balance. He still couldn't understand why he emerged from the G-Cell in such a weakened state. He again wondered if he had caught a viral infection while he was in the cell, but then he recalled the broken, decayed bodies. Nothing made any sense.

Thjars knew he had to make his way to the control room. Maybe once there, he could determine what had happened, or find someone else who could. Thjars made his way to the control room, step by agonizing step – it was almost as if he had to teach himself how to walk again. Thjars had been through many G-Cell flights before, but he couldn't shake the fact that he had never felt this bad before. Had all of the G-Cells malfunctioned or been improperly programmed? Maybe everyone had gotten sick. That reminded him – where was everyone? He knew there would be no immediate answers, but he was still hoping to find someone else alive who might be aware of what had happened. There was dust and long-abandoned spider webs everywhere in the hallways. It had to be a dream. No, he was right the first time: this was a nightmare, a living nightmare. And he seemed to be the lone survivor in this nightmare.

Thjars finally made it to the control deck, where his worst fears were confirmed. More bodies. It looked like both Capt. Blissiart and the First Officer were on the floor, dead and dried up – the same as the crewmembers in the medical bay. It was hard to tell their identity from their faces, but there was no denying the names on the uniforms. There were three others within the room in the same state, broken and dried out. All of the bodies appeared to have been dead for a very, very long time, not just two weeks. "What happened here?" Thjars wondered aloud.

Thjars was exhausted from his trek; he sat down to rest for a few minutes in the nearest chair he could find, near Capt. Blissiart's remains. Every muscle and joint in his body was screaming. It seemed like his body didn't want to respond to his simplest commands. At this point, he had to assume that all of the crewmembers not in G-Cells must also be dead, so his only hope was to find additional, unopened, but operational G-Cells. A thousand questions and scenarios were going through his head, but he had to know who was still alive before he pursued anything else.

Thjars had now been awake for a couple of hours. He headed to the sleeping quarters, where many of the G-Cells were lined up in symmetric rows. Of the 24 remaining G-cells, one was just opening and five more were lit and cycling through the various stages of opening. The other 18 were empty.

"What is your name, private?" Thjars asked the first individual, as he helped him exit his G-Cell. He pulled a chair over and helped him into it. He could see his name on the G-Cell control panel, but he wanted to see how far the crewmember had recovered, and if his mental processes were intact.

The private coughed and looked up, struggling with the side effects of the revival process, "Private ... First ... Class ... Knarls ... Knarls Rjissist," he croaked out.

"Okay, private, you're in charge in this room for the time being. Let me get you some water and once you've recovered, help the others, but don't rush anything," Thjars ordered quietly. "I'll be back after I've surveyed the rest of the ship."

"What ... happened ...?"

"Save your energy, Knarls. I'm not sure yet, but I'll update you when I return."

It took Thjars a couple of hours, but he successfully surveyed the entire ship, stopping many times to rest and recover.

Based on what he had seen from the G-Cells in other areas of the ship, Thjars was confident there were no more than 11 possible survivors, including himself. It had become clear that anyone who wasn't in a G-Cell must have been lost, and Thjars had found most of them as he surveyed the ship. That left 19 assumed dead, including Capt. Blissiart. What went wrong? Where were they? And more importantly, how long had they been in the G-Cells?

His body shook at the thought, and he quickly put it aside to focus on the immediate needs of the crew and ship.

Thjars used the intercom to call all surviving crew to the sleeping quarters and then joined up with them. Four crewmembers were sitting on chairs as Knarls attended to them. Six others sat in a huddle in the middle of the floor with blankets. Clearly, Knarls had been up to the task and was taking care of everyone as directed.

Realizing that he was the ranking officer now, Thjars made a quick role count. The ever-tough, Sergeant-at-Arms Qulys Plyenysst was there, thank Glysst, he thought. If things got tough, it was good to know you had an old timer like Qulys around, Thjars reflected – suddenly realizing it was his first positive thought since waking. Pfc. Knarls Rjissist was next. Although a relative youngster at 35, he would provide good backup for Qulys. The others included medical officer Jenysys Thalysst; military scientist Jarns Blissiart, who was Capt. Blissiart's younger brother; two engineers, Cryells Elysst and Allympht Allsysst; three technical specialists, Zalmyt Wylmysst, Platsys Flysst, Nylsst Volysstmyn; and linguist Juulys Lystnyng – the latter now the only surviving female on the ship.

Thjars handed Juulys a blanket to wrap herself up with. She nodded a silent thank you. He then shared the ship's status, as best he knew it, with the rest of the crewmembers.

In all of the confusion, Thjars had forgotten about Jarns, and he suddenly realized that Jarns had yet to be told that his older brother was not among the survivors. That would be an even tougher blow for the young man, but Thjars would have to tell him soon. For now, most of the remaining crewmembers were content with simply waking up and relearning how to walk and talk.

All of the ship's primary flight crew and command structure must have been up at the time of the incident, and were, therefore, all dead from whatever had happened. A devastating loss, but more critical at the moment was that he wasn't sure that the remaining crew had the required knowledge to operate the ship. Thjars again shuddered from the fear and dread attempting to envelope him. No one wanted to consider dying in space, lost and alone for years.

It would have been better to die suddenly, like the captain, or in their sleep, than to face this. His body shuddered at the thought.

To better concentrate on the here and now, Thjars began recalling as much of the ship's procedure as he could. He knew that an emergency signal and C-Pod would have been sent out if anything had gone wrong. Perhaps it was only a matter of time before help would arrive. On the other hand, it didn't take a brain surgeon to realize that the dead had been dead for a very long time. He knew he had to realize and accept the fact that help was definitely not coming, or it would have been here already. Thjars still had no idea who, how or what had initiated their recovery process and awakened them, but he thought it better to keep that to himself for the time being. Thjars also realized that he needed to re-initiate communications with Cjar as soon as possible.

Thjars also realized that once the ship's emergency mode has been activated, the ship's drive could only be accessed by the captain or the first officer, both of whom were now dead … and he still had no idea where in space they were or even *when* they were. He needed to access the ship's log as soon as possible to determine the "when." For all he knew, they had been asleep for months or, Glysst forbid, even years.

In order to remain in control and focused, Thjars had to remind himself over and over again that he was now the officer in charge. He had to remain in control to make sure that the rest of the crew maintained hope. As he watched the others, knowing that everyone was also struggling to grasp their current situation, he knew he needed to get them into action if they had any hope of survival. Time to start getting things done, he thought, as he started handing out orders.

"Jenysys. You're our only remaining medical officer, so you're it. I need you to be responsible for making sure everyone passes their initial health checks and recovers as soon as possible. I'll expect your report every 30 minutes until everyone has passed your review."

Jenysys nodded agreement.

"Juulys. See if the system has any stored messages from Cjar and start scouring the skies for any electronic signals that you can detect.

"Cryells and Allympht. Get to work on cracking the drive system access codes so that we can re-engage the main drives – you will be our new pilots.

"Jarns. I need you to monitor the skies for celestial bodies that may be in our impact zone. We'll need to reposition accordingly, but only after reviewing with me.

"Zalmyt, Platsys and Nylsst. I need you three to figure out *where* and *when* we are as soon as possible.

"Qulys and Knarls. See if you can bring our weapon systems on line. I'll deal with the task of cleaning up the remains of our lost crewmates.

"Let's go, Cjarians. The sooner we get into action, the sooner we figure out what's going on, construct our options and pursue solutions. We'll meet back on the control deck in two hours unless someone finds new information that requires it be sooner. Now get moving. Jarns, you and I need to talk. Come with me first, please."

Thjars broke the dreadful news to Jarns as soon as the others left the room. He then accompanied Jarns to see his brother's remains, leaving him there alone for a few minutes to pay his last respects. Surprisingly, Jarns requested he be allowed to clean up his brother's remains by himself. Jarns had handled the terrible news about his brother better than Thjars had expected. The kid was a real trooper, just like his brother had been, Thjars noted.

Two hours passed quickly and the group reconvened in the control room.

"Report out, everyone," Thjars directed the crew.

"Lieutenant, close-in defensive weapon systems are on line, sir," Qulys reported to Thjars. "But longer-range offensive weapons remain locked out by the same access codes that have the Q-PAMS drive system offline. Only Capt. Blissiart and Lt. Pfssiast can, I mean could, access those codes, sir." All gave Jarns a quick glance, but he handled it with class. "Sorry, Jarns, that was not very thoughtful on my part," Qulys said with regret clearly in his voice.

"It's okay, Qulys, but thanks just the same. For what it's worth, it actually helps to hear his name spoken," Jarns replied softly, but in control, as he looked at Qulys.

Sergeant-at-Arms Qulys Plyenysst was 125 years old and had seen many conflicts over the years, yet even Qulys was at a loss on how to get out of this situation. However, he knew he had to maintain a presence of confidence and control, lest the group fall into despair. He continued on with his report to Thjars.

"Don't worry, sir, Jarns will have it figured out in no time as I'm sure he knows all of his brother's secrets. Right, Jarns? Simple as walking. Be done before the day is out, right?"

"Thanks for the vote of confidence, Qulys," Jarns replied. "Now that you mention it, I could start trying passwords I know he used in the past. It's not a guarantee that he would use the same ones for something as important as ship safety, but it's a start. I'll write a program that can intermix key words, phrases and numbers and see what we can come up with."

Maybe the kid is more like his big brother than we realized, Thjars thought. Glysst knows, we need everyone to be fully engaged and active, he added to himself.

"Thank you, Qulys. Juulys, what do you have for us?" asked Thjars.

By Cjarian standards, Juulys Lystnyng was a beauty in everyone's eyes, but she could also be pure business when needed. Juulys was a full 1.95 meters in height (6'4"), with long-flowing, reddish-gold hair.

"The quick answer is that there are no general messages in the stored memory. Capt. Blissiart may have messages in his private folders, but we'll have to wait for lil' brother to take care of that. Right, Jarns?" Juulys said, smiling.

Thjars realized that the rest of the crew would draw strength from her. He would need her help to regain their confidence over the next few days. Before he could say anything, Juulys shifted gears back to business and added, "I've started scanning near space with no results anywhere near us. However, I am picking up a tremendous amount of electrical transmission from the third planet of this star system and it's clearly non-natural, but I can't translate any of it yet. It will take at least another day to scan all possibilities and then I'll start working on the signals from the third planet. By the way, whatever it is, it clearly is *not* Klaxxstinian."

"Thanks, Juulys. That's great news about the signals being non-Klaxx, but I have to admit, I'm a little nervous knowing that we have intelligent life here that we don't know anything about," replied Thjars.

"Agreed," replied Juulys. "On the other hand, we may be able to get help from them, assuming we can get to them."

"Okay, fair point, Juulys. Continue to keep me posted on progress. Zalmyt, Platsys and Nylsst, your turn. Any news?"

The group spent the next 45 minutes updating each other, answering questions and brainstorming ideas to establish plans for the next few hours of operation. Considering the situation, Thjars felt the group was handling it quite well, but he also knew that the greatest challenges for the group were yet to come after the immediate challenges were solved and the brute reality of their current situation became clearer. Thjars concluded the meeting by inviting anyone who was interested to join him at the air dock to pay their last respects for their fallen crewmembers. All 10 of his fledgling crew joined in. Without realizing it, Thjars had triggered one of the best-known techniques for building team cohesiveness during trying times, that of simply honoring and maintaining tradition, in this case for their fallen crewmembers.

Thjars talked about each member of the departed crew, taking the time to highlight their greatest accomplishments and personalities.

After he concluded his speech on each crewmember, he invited others to share their memories before starting on the next crewmember. He saved Capt. Blissiart for last and then, with Jarns' help, they transferred all of the remains to the air dock. They stepped back in unison, closed the door, and with one final salute from all 11 crewmembers, saluted their fallen friends as Thjars opened the doors to space and the remains were ejected.

Thjars saluted as he ended the ceremony. "Glysst be with you, my friends, and in your honor, may Glysst guide our decisions going forward." He dropped his salute, turned to the crew and then added, "Friends, let us head to the galley and have our first meal in this new star system."

CHAPTER 5

A.D. 2028 (3311 C.A.E.); Sept. 4
Pluto orbit

Lt. Thjars Chjssiast was at a temporary loss. His two surviving engineers, Cryells and Allympht, were still unable to override the ship's security system. The override was required to enable the faster-than-light Q-PAMS drive, as well as the slower ion drive, the latter of which could still achieve as high as 0.9 light speed. Without these systems, the Jarisst I was limited to the use of maneuvering rockets. The result was that the ship was dead in space, with no chance of getting the crew to the inner planets of this uncharted system – let alone home to Cjar.

On the positive side, Cryells and Allympht were able to access the navigation system. They quickly called Platsys Flysst, one of the technical specialists, who also had background in astrophysics and astronomy. Unfortunately, after hours of trying to reconstruct their flight path, Platsys was still not able to determine where they were. None of the constellations in the sky made sense; nothing looked familiar. He knew that changes in constellation shapes were expected after travelling across space, but in this case, there was nothing that resembled any of the constellations he was familiar with.

However, he did uncover one piece of staggering news relative to the ship's time log. As best he could ascertain, they had been in their G-Cells for more than 500 years! ... Five hundred years. Flysst immediately assumed he made a calculation error, but he re-analyzed the data five times, getting the same answer each time. It was incomprehensible, but that was what the data said.

Five hundred years! It was almost impossible for Platsys to get his head around that fact. What in Glysst's name happened?

Platsys broke the news to the already exhausted crew. Juulys told Platsys it was a horrible joke; he repeated it two more times before she finally realized he was serious. Some cried; others just sat and stared at the floor. It took more than a few minutes to truly sink in. Everyone they knew: their families, friends, commanders, and fellow soldiers … were all long dead. The crew struggled with the realization, but they all knew they needed to come to grips with it quickly; the fact remained that they were all alone, more alone than they had ever thought possible – but they were alive. Platsys realized that the crewmembers in front of him were now his entire world – the only family he now had.

"What do you think happened to Cjar? The war? Admiral …" he stammered out, breaking the long silence.

"Platsys, those are good questions, but none we can answer any time soon, nor answers that will help us right now. We need to put our energy into the things that we can impact, and do it quickly," Thjars responded.

Thjars knew he needed to keep them occupied and laser-focused on *today*. Thjars brought them back to task by asking Platsys to provide the group with a detailed technical summary of the hard facts he'd been able to collect so far in this uncharted star system.

Platsys took his time, laying out all the detail he had gathered. He'd determined they were at the edge of a previously unknown solar system with a G2V star. He continued on, picking up energy and educating the crew like a college professor. A G-type main-sequence star (G V), often called a yellow dwarf, or G dwarf star, was a main-sequence star with a luminosity class V of spectral type G, with a surface temperature between 5,300 and 6,000 degrees Kelvin. Like other main-sequence stars, a G-type main-sequence star converts hydrogen to helium in its core by means of nuclear fusion. Each second, it fuses approximately 600 million tons of hydrogen to helium, converting about 4 million tons of matter to energy. Platsys was convinced that livable conditions might exist on one, or maybe even two of the inner planets – if they could get there.

Platsys also knew that the term yellow dwarf is really a misnomer, so he continued explaining that G stars actually range in color from white, to slightly yellow for less luminous GV stars. Platsys further added that a G-type main-sequence star is capable of fusing hydrogen for approximately 10 billion years, but he had no idea where in that process and timeline this particular star was. When its time came, the star would expand to many times its current size and become a red giant. Eventually, the red giant would shed its outer layers of gas, which would become a planetary nebula while the core cooled and contracted into a compact, dense, white dwarf. It was all theoretical, of course, he went on to explain, as no one had been around long enough to watch the entire process.

"So, Mr. Astronomy," quipped Qulys with a chuckle, "in soldier-ese, what the Hylraxxt[*] does that mean to a layman like me?"

"Oh, sorry, sir, I can get a little carried away at times. I kind of enjoy this stuff," replied Platsys with an apologetic grin.

"You think?" Qulys said, laughing.

"Well, it means that this star really isn't much different than the one we have back on Cjar."

"Come on, Qulys, you didn't follow that? I'm soooo disappointed in you," Juulys replied, dripping with sarcasm. She tilted her head to the side and smiled coyly at Qulys.

"Carry on, you maggots," Qulys threw back at his two antagonists, crossed his arms and leaned back against the ship's wall – with a small, but knowing grin. He had to give it to Thjars; it was a good move getting the group focused on something concrete and *now*, something they could all connect with. And on Platsys went …

"The system appears to have at least six planets, although I have a fair amount of mapping to complete yet, so there may be more that I haven't found yet. Two of the planets are monstrous

---

[*]. **Hylraxxt.** The Cjarian reference for hell.

in size. The first of these monster planets is approximately 1.4 billion kilometers from the G2V star and possesses equally huge, beautiful rings about its orbital plane." Platsys pulled up some pictures for everyone to ooh and ahh over. "My initial assessment suggests that the planet's atmosphere is made up of mostly hydrogen and a small amount of helium."

Platsys expected with its distance from the star and the gas make-up he was analyzing, it was highly doubtful there would be any life on this cold gas giant, so he continued on.

"The second monster planet is closer to the star, at approximately 800 million kilometers, but it's truly a monster in every sense of the word. It's so big that I think it may have been on the verge of becoming a small star itself." Platsys showed additional pictures, including one compared to their own Cjar.

"Good Glysst! It makes Cjar look like a small moon."

"Yes, it does. It may be one of the biggest planets we've ever seen," Platsys replied. "This planet is also composed mostly of hydrogen, but has a fair percentage of helium as well. There are additional traces of carbon, hydrogen sulfide, neon and oxygen, identified by the sensors."

Platsys knew that some of these elements were the basis for life as they knew it, especially carbon. But there was so little of it available, that even if the planet's internal heat could generate enough warmth for life, the environmental conditions on the planet would be highly non-conducive to life, so he elected not to share that set of facts.

Thjars and Qulys caught each other's eyes and nodded. This was therapeutic for all of them, and Platsys looked like he had enough energy to keep it going for hours.

Platsys added that, by analyzing the infrared and spectral footprints of the planets, he had concluded that this giant might also have traces of ethane, phosphine and sulfide, all of which were key elements in the manufacture of Leo-1253 and its antimatter form, Leo-3521, the rare and extremely complex Cjarian-made isotopes that fueled the Q-PAMS system. If they could access the standard ship drive, they could reach this planet and possibly replenish their Q-PAMS fuel system, but they still had to find sources of platinum, gold, uranium, plutonium, thorium, francium and tin to complete the isotope recipes.

Platsys continued his dissertation for a full two hours, answering every question that came up. As good as this session had been for the crew, Thjars reminded himself that the most urgent task was still to determine how to access and initiate the ship's high-speed drive systems. Without that access, it didn't matter what was located on these planets; the planets were visible, but simply not reachable.

*****

A.D. 2028 (3311 C.A.E.); Sept. 6
Washington, D.C.

Blake returned to the U.S. from his "all-expenses-paid Tibetan vacation," as his teammates had jokingly referred to it, and was now in a small, sparsely decorated waiting room at the Pentagon, half a world away from where he had left fewer than 24 hours ago.

Prior to this unplanned trip back to the U.S., Blake had been scheduled to return to Africa with his team for his final op as a SEAL. The op would have been in Borno, Nigeria, where the Islamic Fundamentalists were hell-bent on transforming the country into total anarchy that they could then rebirth as a Fundamentalist State. Blake wasn't convinced there really was any difference between total anarchy and an Islamic Fundamentalist terrorist state, other than the words, but it allowed him to continue his life's passion of eradicating that scourge from the face of the Earth. Regardless, the redirection of his plans had come straight from D.C. and the Pentagon; Blake was to begin his new assignment with the Space Corps sooner than planned. The upside of this redirection was that his team, albeit on a slower and less direct return path home, would also not go to Africa, thereby receiving an earlier-than-expected leave with family and friends. His friends had urged Blake to go with them, or to visit his family in New York and New Hampshire for a couple of days, but they all knew that they were wasting their breath; Blake never took time off. Patty even reminded him that his sister, Cindy, was not getting any younger, but besides the emotionless look she received in return, Blake's only response was that he had spoken to his sister a couple weeks ago on the phone, prior to leaving for Tibet.

Reflecting back over the past 24 hours, Blake had received the coded transmission as soon as they had landed on the USS Washington in the Indian Ocean. He had been "requested" to travel alone to the Pentagon "ASAP," with no further explanation. Blake remembered laughing and thinking it was one of his teammates joking with him, until he was introduced to a Major Pat Sullivan a short five minutes later. The major, flight helmet in hand, informed Blake that his personal F/A-18 E-F Super Hornet flight would leave in exactly 30 minutes, and that he best make haste to be on it.

The trip, albeit long, was relatively uneventful. Major Sullivan had flown the F-18 nonstop to Ramstein Airbase in Germany with one in-air refueling hookup over northern Turkey. Blake had flown on more than a few "backseat hops" during his career, but they were typically for special, "flyover" recon flights and nowhere near as long as this flight; this was his first "special envoy" flight. The two men maintained a long conversation during the flight about their careers, families, frustrations with the U.S. government's endless bureaucracy, and of course, personal experiences with their respective air and ground versions of the war on terrorism. The only tense period had been when they had crossed airspace from Iraq into Turkey and were close to Syrian airspace. The Russians had taken over a large part of Northwestern Syria after coming to Syria's aid to join the fight against ISIS back in 2017. It was still called Syria, but for all intents and purposes it was Southern Russia. The Russians had become touchy after losing a fighter to Turkey's USA-made F-16s in late 2015, when they shot down one Su-24 fighter bomber for invading Turkish airspace. Even though that had been many years earlier, the two majors didn't plan on becoming a retribution case for newspaper headlines, so Major

Sullivan gave the "Syrian" boundaries wide berth, crossing into Turkey just east of Mosul, Iraq, while Blake monitored the threat warning systems for any sign of other aircraft or ground launches. This was the side of the air war that people back home didn't appreciate; just because the enemy didn't have an air force, didn't mean skies were safe. Every time one of these fighter jocks hit the sky, he was marked and tracked by both terrorist and Russian radar systems, waiting for that one opportunity where a lazy pilot might make them famous.

When they finally landed in Germany, Blake thanked the major, shook hands and wished him well for the two days of R&R leave the pilot had earned for volunteering for the flight. Blake had enjoyed the fellow major. He was a personable "get it done" kind of guy. He hoped their paths would cross again in the future.

Four hours later, Blake boarded a C-17 Globemaster III for an 8½-hour, non-stop flight to Washington, D.C., refueling once over the ocean, a few hundred miles east of Newfoundland. Blake was grateful that he was able to catch some sleep on this flight or he would have had to beg off the meeting until the following day, although he knew that wouldn't be an option, based on the cost the government had expended to get him there. Fewer than three hours later, cleanly shaven, dressed and fed, Blake was escorted to an inner room in the Pentagon.

Blake looked around, surveying the small room. It couldn't have been any bigger than 10x10 feet, like a very small bedroom with two doors, one on either side of the room. Blake had entered through the east door. There were two chairs, a small table, one lamp with a dim yellowish bulb, and an unopened Evian water bottle on the table. The walls were a standard, nondescript, beige-gray color with two pictures on the wall. One appeared to be a young John Glenn in a Mercury-era launch photo and the other one was of the space shuttle Challenger crew, the same crew that had been lost in a spectacular and devastating explosion almost a half century ago in 1986.

A young page entered through the west door of the room, handed Blake a big envelope, turned and left through the same door.

Blake pulled out one of the two chairs and sat down as he gazed intently at the envelope, turning it end over end. It was a string-sealed, 9"x12" red envelope that had his name handwritten on it, today's date, a line for him to provide his signature of receipt, and the words "Top Secret, Eyes Only" emblazoned across the front from one corner to the diagonally opposing corner. Blake signed the envelope and carefully opened it while looking back at the door to see if there were a peephole that someone might be watching him through. He saw none, but he was positive that his entire visit was being recorded. He picked up the water bottle, opened it and took a long drink. It hadn't been offered, but he was thirsty and no one else was here, so he took it as fair game and thanked the windowless door with a small nod of his head as he held up the bottle. He returned his focus to the envelope.

"After the past 24 hours, this better be good," he nonchalantly challenged the door without looking up. Within the envelope, he found two reports. He put the bottle down and began reading.

Some 45 minutes later, Blake finished reading both reports and sat there, stunned, staring straight ahead at the second door. Yes, the trip was definitely worth it. Blake knew how well the government could maintain secrecy when it wanted to, but nothing prepared him for what he had just read. This was pure fantasy – turned reality. Unbelievable.

The first report summarized an "object" that had recently been uncovered on Mars. No one really knew what it was, but it clearly did not originate from his current planet of residence, Earth. The object, which graduated to the title of "device" by the time he had reached the middle of the report, had apparently turned itself on, but with no known response or action. As the object had only been recently discovered, the first report was relatively short and contained many hypothetical scenarios of what it might be, where it came from, and what it might be able to do, or not do.

The second and significantly longer report described how more than 20 years earlier, a young engineer at the Space Telescope Science Institute (STScI) in Baltimore had "improperly appropriated" the Hubble space telescope and discovered a different "object." Blake wondered why everything had to be an "object" – most probably written up in a CIA standard operating procedure somewhere, he grunted. The engineer had pointed it in the general direction of Pluto just to get some "guaranteed A" pictures for a master's thesis he was working on. After a couple of days of "playing," the engineer had detected an object near the orbit of Pluto that caught his eye. At first, the intern had simply assumed it was a comet or meteor, or maybe even a small, new moon that he could take credit for, but it was so small, he was having difficulty getting a good picture of it.

After days of monitoring the growing distance between Pluto and the object, he realized that while Pluto was moving, the object wasn't moving with it. He also noticed that the object's position relative to the star field behind it was changing in a very odd manner as well. It was as if the object were holding a non-natural position independent of the general movement of the other "nearby" objects in space. After that final realization, the engineer had contacted his supervisor in the middle of the night and was promptly rewarded by getting his derriere chewed out on the phone for waking him up. That all changed the next morning when the supervisor watched the tapes and nearly passed out at what he witnessed – the young man had been correct. The "object" was definitely not acting "natural" relative to the space about it, nor did it look like a celestial body – rather it had a very odd, but definitively, non-natural shape.

The discovery was immediately labeled a "non-natural celestial event" and classified as "top secret." Unfortunately, the young engineer had gone back to campus that night and talked about it with a number of his buddies before agents could catch up with him. In an attempt to discredit the young man's story and to divert newspapers and the splashy tabloids that frequently promoted "alien" headlines, the CIA was pulled in to deflect attention on the topic. The CIA immediately deployed two very young-looking agents who had overnight, coincidentally, and quietly, become students in the same classes as the young engineer. The CIA, doing what it does best, picked up the young engineer and transported him to a windowless room in a nondescript building where agents "educated" him relative to how he would play the game going forward. They then initiated covert efforts to humorously downplay the engineer's claims while buying beers and alien T-shirts for all of his friends until the topic died away a couple of weeks later. The two new students then quietly transferred back to an unnamed school on the East Coast.

As the news of an alien ship had been picked up by the tabloids, NASA executives launched a parallel mission to aggressively and very publicly back efforts to change the status of Pluto from a planet to a non-planet. This was big news, and every editor in the world wanted to jump on it. Thanks to mainstream media, the message was marketed on every news front, easily deflecting focus from the engineer's findings, which it did even better than Washington had hoped for. On Aug. 24, 2006, the world's scientific communities formally re-classified Pluto as a non-planet and the scientific community's focus was consumed with the highly ignitable debate associated with the reduction of Pluto's importance in the solar system. The only people truly delighted about the news were the textbook authors and publishers who now had a blank check to release multitudes of new science books that schools and students around the country would have to purchase to remain abreast of current science courses. The tabloids quickly forgot about the young engineer and his alleged claim to fame and the story drifted back to "non-status," similar to many of the other hundreds of alien-theory stories. Blake found it odd that the report never once mentioned the engineer's name. He could only imagine where the poor kid was on assignment now ... perhaps the Nome, Alaska, weather station, he laughed.

The report went on to detail how, only three months after the discovery, the 43rd president of the U.S., George W. Bush, secretly initiated the structure to start planning and building the Space Corps, as well as to begin rebuilding the astronaut ranks. The Space Corps became a top secret branch of the government, connecting the NSA with NASA, with a top-secret goal of reaching the object within two decades – highly reminiscent of President John F. Kennedy's decree of reaching the moon by the end of the 1960s. The only difference with this decree was that the public knew nothing about it. Even the leading U.S. aerospace companies including Boeing, Northrop-Grumman and Lockheed, who were jointly developing the technology to support the project, had no idea what the true application was. The only publicly allowed news story was released in *Popular Science* magazine, a well-read platform that would still allow the government ample room to deny the sources and facts, yet still drum up considerable interest. The article talked about the goal to develop a long-theorized light-sail concept that, in combination with a nuclear rocket system, could accelerate a vessel to 0.0025 light speed (750,000 meters per second) or 2.7 million kilometers per hour (1.7 million mph) – a previously unheard of speed. At this rate, a vessel could reach Pluto, or the object for that matter, in fewer than three months, as well as open up the entire solar system to human flight exploration. An exciting new Space Age was dawning for humankind, or at least for a small, micro-segment of the U.S. truly privy to the whole picture, Blake realized.

The report described how light sails, solar sails or photon sails, as they had been conceptualized by science fiction and *Popular Science* writers for the past century, were based on the theory that a large deployable structure could easily be erected in space, where the weight of the sail would not cause it to fail structurally and collapse on itself. The solar sail worked on the premise that solar radiation, or a highly directed, high-energy beam would exert pressure on the sail and propel it through space. Solar radiation pressure is calculated on an irradiance (solar constant) value of 1361 Watts per square meter at one AU[*]. The force on a sail and the actual acceleration of the craft varied by the inverse square of distance from the sun, and by the square of the cosine of the angle between the sail force vector and the radial from the sun.

The final section of the second report detailed the U.S.-based technology that had secretly been developed, demonstrated and thoroughly validated at the unknown cost of billions of dollars to the American taxpayers. Blake was confident that whatever the number was, it was likely greatly understated. The pinnacle of the report was the acknowledgement that a prototype ship, capable of carrying eight astronauts, was ready for its maiden assignment.

---

[*]. One Astronomical Unit, or AU, is equal to the distance between the Earth and sun

And the ship's mission was to investigate the object near Pluto – way before the *Popular Science* article told the world that the technology would be ready.

After sitting in total silence for an additional 20 minutes, staring at the door while digesting the contents of the reports and thinking about the potential impact of their contents, the second door opened without warning. A man dressed in a standard black suit, black tie, white shirt and insanely well-polished black shoes entered. Blake eyed him over. He estimated he was somewhere between 35 and 40, 1.87 meters tall (5'10"), and about 75 kilograms (165 pounds) with an athletic build. He didn't look like one for idle chitchat.

Blake stood up and they shook hands.

"Kay?" Blake asked with a smile, with obvious reference to the famous 1997 Hollywood movie, "Men in Black."

"I get that a lot. You must be Jay, then." He smiled back at Blake.

"Whoever you need me to be, sir. Good to see you have some sense of humor left," Blake answered.

The man went on to explain that Blake was being given two months to prepare a team for the journey and that he needed to know now, on the spot, if Blake were the man. No time was offered to sleep on it. No time was requested. These types of assignments weren't for people who had to sleep on it.

"Where do I sign?" was all Blake had to say, and his grip on their second handshake was met with an equally firm grasp.

"You already did," he replied. Both men liked what they saw. Good stock both ways. No bullshit. The man told Blake to have a seat and he would get back to get him shortly. And with that, the man now known as Kay turned and left.

*****

Two days later, with infinitely more information, after having met and talked with what seemed like an endless progression of people who were all "in the know," it was time for Blake to start proposing team members. He had been given books of résumés on all sorts of candidates, many of whom he had already met, as well as 10 times more he hadn't. He had stayed up late into the night reading and taking notes, as well as risen early to exercise, read and study some more. Yet, with all of the impressive résumés he reviewed, he continued to home in on his own special ops team members. Their training, other than issues associated with weightlessness, could hold up to anything the Space Corps could come up with. Their dedication and commitment to successfully completing any task they were charged with was unparalleled in Blake's mind. Furthermore, with the realization that literally *anything* could happen on this trip, he wanted a group as broad and deep of intellect as he could find, as well as a team that was tough as nails under any conditions – one that wouldn't panic when things went south. That described his team perfectly.

Patty's linguistic and cryptanalyst background was especially applicable in case the object truly was "non-natural." Additionally, there was no way that Blake would entertain going without Harry's brainpower or Li's computer expertise. Okay, it was well known that Sean could pilot anything on the planet, and the U.S. spacecraft was definitely an off-the-planet vehicle that would only be piloted by true astronauts, but it was still Sean. Diego was the toughest dude he had ever met; why wouldn't he fit? Blake had gone over it a hundred times, both in his head and on paper. He was leaning hard toward requesting that his entire team go, regardless of its lack of astronaut training. In Blake's opinion, the other two positions could be handled by well-trained astronauts who were familiar with both space travel and piloting the new space vehicle.

Surprisingly, Blake's proposal was accepted, and quicker than Blake had expected. His crew almost immediately, and humorously, became known as the A-Team around the Pentagon. Blake had been around long enough to know that wasn't meant to be a head-swelling compliment within the military ranks, but rather a way to jab and have fun with him to see what he and his team were really made of. Sure enough, it didn't take long to find out that half of the people "in the know" joked that it was from the movie "Armageddon," in reference to the 1998 Bruce Willis movie where a group of non-traditional, anti-establishment, red-blooded oil drillers had become astronauts overnight. The other half joked it was from the 1980s TV series, "A-Team," led by John Hannibal Smith and anchored by the infamous Mr. T. Although Blake enjoyed both references, he personally thought the "Armageddon" analogy was more appropriate. He secretly coveted the famous line that Ben Affleck said near the end of the movie when he summed up Bruce's ability to complete the mission and set off the nuke on the asteroid: "He doesn't know how to fail." If he had to sum up his team with one sentence, that was it.

The ship was originally planned to be named Terminus after the famous Isaac Asimov book "The Foundation Series," but was later renamed the Armstrong I, after Neil Armstrong, the most famous astronaut in American history, who died in 2012. Neil Armstrong was the long-celebrated first human to set foot on a celestial body, other than Earth, when he had touched down on the Moon in 1969 and uttered the immortal phrase: "That's one small step for man, one giant leap for mankind."

Blake was well aware that he and his team had a lot to do in a relatively short period of time if they were to make this work.

CHAPTER 6

A.D. 2028 (3311 C.A.E.); Sept. 8
CIA Headquarters

"Gentlemen, the attack is a go. This op is code-named *Whiplash*," the CIA director relayed as he hung up the call from the White House. "We have received independent collaboration from our mole inside the Arak facility. This is the real deal, seven nuclear missiles on the way to the U.S. Five of the trucks are being tracked with 100 percent probability of certainty, the other two are p50 as we had no way of verifying what stayed on the truck, or was removed while the two trucks were under roof in the truck depot. An airborne X-ray surveillance system completed a flyover of the two trucks in question 30 minutes ago and verified that they contain similar shapes within the truck bed. Unfortunately, the two remaining trucks at the depot also depict the same missile-shaped footprint. To ensure that all units are taken out, the target field has been expanded to nine trucks. Lieutenant, what is our missile status?"

"Sir, the initial attack waves will utilize BGM-109 Tomahawk cruise missiles from four separate submarines. The follow up, if necessary, will be by Israeli F-16s and our F-35C Lightning II fighters on the USS George H.W. Bush CVN-77. Assuming the trucks are successfully taken out on the initial attacks, the planes will be re-assigned to take out the nuclear facilities at Arak. Probability of success exceeds 90 percent, sir. In case of failure, we have a second wave of missile launches and aircraft ready, but the element of surprise would obviously be lost at that point."

"Load the coordinates and launch the Tomahawks," the CIA director ordered. "I want at least three Tomahawks for each truck, double redundancy to increase the probability of success. Elevate to battle stations for the aircrews. Let me know when the Israelis are airborne as they will need to be ready to launch as soon as we know status from the first wave. There will likely be some collateral damage, so make sure the White House is prepped."

Within 30 minutes, salvos of cruise missiles were launched from four U.S. submarines in the Arabian Sea. The launches were conducted in groups and timed with the intent for all missiles to arrive at their targets simultaneously, thereby negating any subsequent movement by the surviving trucks.

All they could do now was wait and watch the clock.

*****

Iran

The average person doesn't think about, or comprehend, how large cruise missiles really are. The Block VII, Phase II BGM-109 cruise missile is the Navy's premier strike weapon. With booster, the missile weighs approximately 1,600 kilograms (more than 3,500 pounds), is more than six meters long (more than 22 feet) and can travel at speeds of approximately 880 kilometers per hour (approximately 550 mph). The missiles utilize DSMAC, Digital Scene Matching Area Correlation, to locate and identify land targets. A digitized image of an area is mapped and then inserted into the missile's mission profile. During flight, the missile verifies the images stored in its memory and correlates them with the images it "sees" on the ground while flying overhead. Based on comparison results, the missile's inertial navigation system is updated and the missile self-corrects its course continuously. The missiles also carried onboard video with satellite links to the launch station so final guidance could be modified, if needed, by the control room personnel – for example, in the case in which a truck makes a change in direction at the last second.

As planned, the missiles arrived within 30 seconds of each other, and 26 explosions rocked the Iranian countryside. One missile malfunctioned and crashed into the sea, but was easily covered by its surviving twin sisters. Fifteen minutes later, with onboard camera and satellite verification of the targeting and destruction of all nine trucks, the U.S. and Israeli aircraft were re-vectored to Arak.

As the F-35s entered Iranian airspace, three older MiG-29As rose from Bandar Abbas to meet them. All three were quickly wiped from the sky by a salvo of AIM-120 AMRAAM fire-and-forget missiles. It was never meant to be a competition. One could argue that the MiG-29 pilots also knew that and should have stayed on the ground. The F-35s continued northward, unabated, toward Arak as if nothing had occurred.

The Israelis hit first at Mach 1.1, unleashing 14 AGM-142 Popeye air-to-ground missiles and six BLU-109 penetration bombs. Explosions rocked the nearby area. Thirty seconds later, the F-35s flew over at Mach 1.6, dropping 21 British laser-guided Brimstone cluster weapons that were controlled by a room full of guidance operators onboard the George H.W. Bush aircraft carrier, and six 900-kilogram HVPWs – High Velocity Penetrating Weapons. Sixty seconds later, secondary explosions continued to rock the Iranian nuke site.

The mission ended as quickly as it began. All satellite and Reaper assessments verified that the attack had been a total success. The fighter aircraft had all quickly, and safely, exited Iranian airspace at supersonic speeds without incident. It had been almost too easy.

The nuclear reactor was ruptured beyond repair, and all major buildings within the facility were destroyed and on fire. Fatalities would be significant. Nuclear fallout would be worse and become a major issue on world news, but the options had been severely limited, and the Iranians had brought this upon themselves. Tehran, the capital of Iran, would be spared the nuclear fallout as it was far enough northeast of Arak, but the people of Arak would suffer significantly. This would be the biggest nuclear catastrophe since the 1986 Chernobyl disaster – dwarfing that of the 2011 Fukushima Daiichi nuclear disaster after the Tōhoku earthquake and resultant tsunami. Although a nuclear weapon was not utilized, it would become the first intentional nuclear fallout disaster since the 1945 WWII bombing of Hiroshima and Nagasaki.

Sensor-laden drones were already validating that the truck explosions did, indeed, include chemical species and radioactive isotopes consistent with those associated with typical nuclear weapons. On the world stage, this would be an open-and-shut case; the Iranians were guilty of not only manufacturing weapons of mass destruction, WMDs, but also clearly planning on using them – against all international treaties, and more than likely, against U.S. interests.

The president was planning on conducting a live news broadcast in two hours after he first updated key world leaders.

*****

Three hours later
Ardakan, Iran

"General …" Armeen stuttered as he hung up his cell phone.

"Yes, colonel?"

"The news is not good, general. All seven of the bombs have been destroyed and the Arak facility is a total loss. Many brave lives have been lost. We must ensure they did not die in vain – they are martyrs in the name of Allah.

"But that is not all of it. The U.S. president has shared his evidence with the world and even our closest non-Arab friends in Russia are publicly joining the call for more embargos against our country.

"I'm afraid that the Jihad with the infidels is at risk."

"Colonel, was it not Allah's own hand that saved us by having us travel to Ardakan? Had he not, we would be among the dead as well."

The colonel turned to look out the window, hiding the relief on his face.

"You are correct. Allah has saved us for another day."

"Yes, he has," the general paused. "However, it appears that the U.S. spy machine had its tentacles very deep into our organization, Col. Khorasani. Allah warned me of this risk and that is why I elected to have the first bomb trucked out *two weeks earlier from this facility* ..."

The colonel's mouth dropped and he turned to face the general in time to see his grim smile above the barrel of a semi-automatic, nine-millimeter, Beretta M9 pistol that was clenched tightly in his hands.

"I was praying daily that it wasn't you, colonel, but outside of a select few, you and I were the only two people who fully knew the plans. I had to test you, but I also had to have a backup plan in case I was sadly correct – which I was. You are now in Allah's hands, and the Americans you spied for will join you shortly."

The colonel began to protest, just as the 9-mm bullet entered his brain, and exited the back of his skull a brief instant later. The colonel, the U.S.'s best inside connection to the internal mechanisms of the Iranian extremists, died instantly.

The true attack had already begun. The hand of Allah was moving and already on its way to America. The general smiled. After years of planning, all while enduring the pain from the U.S.-led embargoes that were starving and killing his people, the hated Americans were only weeks away from harvesting their payback. Allah would slay the infidels in a nuclear firestorm, but that final destruction would only come after they'd brought great pain to the Americans; city by city.

Gen. Shirazi had also learned about a secret American space project from a powerful contact in Saudi who had spent great sums of money to find out about it. The man had shared that he had proudly sacrificed many infidel lives in order to place a key operative secretly into their program. He planned to blow their ship up at a critical juncture and then expose their lying leaders to the world. The Americans would then be brought to their knees where they could finally be beheaded, once and for all: all in the name of Allah.

"Allah Akbar," the general said softly as he looked to the sky and smiled.

*****

A.D. 2028 (3311 C.A.E.); Oct. 30
Houston

It had been a long, but very productive two months and the crew was ready for the mission to start, their anticipation growing by the day. The training teams had thrown everything they had at Blake's crew, and they had passed every test. The days had been filled with physical conditioning, space ship familiarization, mission training and anthropology studies, the latter to better prepare the group to assess issues associated with a potentially new civilization. Eighteen-hour days had been the standard, starting day one. Various tests were proctored every morning and evening. Failure was not an option.

The NASA training had been initiated at Cape Canaveral in Florida, then at Houston where it included 10 days in space, actually on the Armstrong I. Sean O'Rourke, Blake's master pilot, had demonstrated the capability to pilot the Armstrong I in the simulator, but the plan for this maiden journey would limit him to being the proverbial fly on the wall. The responsibility to pilot the Armstrong I to Pluto was reserved for USAF Cmdr. Jack Pavlik and USMC Maj. James Snyder.

Prior to the "event," as many were calling the discovery of the "object," the Armstrong I had been scheduled to launch in 2031, well after the Reagan I returned from Mars, but the U.S. government had thrown everything it had into accelerating the schedule. Although the ship was now complete, it came with added risks due to the cancellation of three years of development testing that would no longer occur – the actual flight to Pluto would also be the primary development flight.

A good portion of the training had been teaching the rookie spaceship crewmembers about the ship's design and functions, its communications protocols, and the planning of various scenarios that may arise with the object near Pluto. Although NASA lacked data that could verify or deny the existence of life forms in the object, the team still had to be ready for that one-in-a-million chance. Blake had agreed with Patty that there really wasn't a training program that could cover the infinite number of potential issues that could develop on a trip like this, but you couldn't *not* train. If the crew actually did find signs of, or even actual living, intelligent life forms, Blake was most concerned about his options if the aliens were found to be unfriendly. Because of that risk, Blake had demanded that the team be armed for this mission. Assuming that the "experts" were correct, and the object really was "dead," the guns would simply become expensive dead weight, at a cost of approximately $10,000 per pound to get into orbit. But there was no way Blake would agree to leave that risk open. In addition, if the object was found to be a legitimate non-natural object, the team would have to find a way to hook up with it and tow it back to Earth orbit, which was one of the biggest remaining challenges in Blake's mind. The Armstrong I carried a mammoth cable that was intended as a tow cable, assuming they could find some method of attaching it to this yet-to-be seen ship. The truth was that no one knew if it would really work or not – and there was no way they would know until they actually arrived at the ship and attempted it. This was one more reason why Blake wanted Harry on the team; he needed Harry's brainpower to figure it out when they got there.

Blake's team was surprised to learn that they were actually the second launch over the past year. The first launch, including six astronauts led by Cmdr. Dutch Kline, left for Mars a full 10 months earlier on the Reagan I. The Reagan I also was a new spacecraft design, but it would be the last of the pre-light-sail vehicles. The trip had been planned years ago, unrelated to the Pluto mission. The U.S. had been the first to land on the moon, and the U.S wanted to make sure it beat the growing Russian, Chinese and Indian space programs to be the first to explore the outer planets; after all, the Americans had also been the first to set foot on the Moon, and the president wanted to continue that leadership.

As it turned out, the Mars mission was already well under way when the object on Mars had been discovered by the young NASA intern. Sometimes, Lady Luck really did smile on you, Blake had commented. Additionally, as the Mars mission had been shrouded in full secrecy, it was relatively easy to change the mission objective in an attempt to recover the object on Mars. The secret mission would also be able to return the device to the space dock in Earth orbit without needing to explain to the world what was going on.

The 78 million kilometer trip to Mars was expected to take approximately 300 days, based on the pre-light sail technology on the Reagan I, two weeks on the surface and another 300 days for the return trip, for a total mission length of nearly two years. In a crazy turn of events, the new technology on the Armstrong I was so advanced, as compared to the Reagan I, that Blake's team would actually get to Pluto and return to Earth before the Reagan I team could return from Mars. In essence, the glory of being the first men on Mars would quickly pale in comparison to the Armstrong I's journey, creating a devastating realization for the Reagan I crewmembers. To ensure that the Reagan I crew didn't lose focus on their mission, it was determined that what they didn't know couldn't hurt them, so the decision was made to restrict all information about the Armstrong I mission from the Reagan I crew. Cmdr. Dutch Kline, Mars mission, and his five crewmembers would not be happy men when they returned to Earth and were debriefed on the new developments. But that was not Blake's concern at the moment. Blake was focused on his team and his mission.

None of Blake's team members were married, but all of them had family of some sort they were allowed to visit prior to initiating the two months of training. They all left a similar message for family members that they would be embarking on a special operation in a "can't-tell-you-where country." Little did anyone suspect that "out of country" actually meant "out of world."

For the most part, things had gone smoothly. The only exception had almost turned disastrous when Diego had taken his younger brother, Jose, out to a restaurant for drinks one night. The two had been minding their own business talking quietly, when a few local toughs decided that "their kind" weren't welcome in *their* territory. Over the past few decades, the various gangs in L.A. had focused on expanding their territories and frequently went to war with each other over streets and local establishments in the regions of conflict. Diego had always wondered why the U.S. government spent so much time fighting combatants in other parts of the world when there were more than enough targets right here in L.A. that were simply begging to be "taken care of."

Diego and Jose had returned to the area they grew up in and were reminiscing their childhood memories. They sat down to eat at a local eatery that they had both enjoyed as children when five tattoo-covered gang-bangers approached their table and demanded Diego and Jose pay penance for crossing into their territory. Diego had politely responded that they weren't gang members and that they weren't looking for any trouble; they were just there to enjoy a meal and a beer between brothers. Diego had attempted to pursue a diplomatic path, but these thugs were really no different than the many other killers he had encountered around the globe. There was simply no appeasing them. Diego knew they were already long lost from what most would deem "normal" society. In Diego's opinion, they should have been removed from the collective gene pool a long time ago. This type of scum only understood one thing, and that was the need to identify who the alpha male was in any gathering – and then take advantage of that position. Diego was ready to elevate to stage two; the question was, were they? One, possibly the leader, slapped Jose firmly across the back of his head as a second thug pulled his shirt up to expose a big knife under his belt.

So be it, Diego thought. Game on.

Diego tensed and readied himself. Every cell instantly morphed into a different being. A pure killing machine. He knew Jose was out of his league here, but if they wanted a real test, he was more than ready. A smile crossed his lips.

"What the fuck is your problem, skinhead?" asked the gang member who had slapped Jose.

"You, you stupid ass, worthless shit," Diego replied coldly, still smiling.

"Who you talking to, fuckhead?" the now obvious leader yelled back in disbelief.

From years of training, Diego was confident of three things. First, the benefit of the element of surprise. Second, the benefit of a distraction when you were outnumbered. Third, mental toughness was even more important than physical toughness. This idiot was going to be a piece of cake to take down mentally. Diego took a drink, put his beer down and smiled even wider. Total confidence. Come and get it, jackass. Diego looked the man square in the eyes, a look only a killer could know. Diplomacy was over. Full military engagement had the green light. The first step was to throw him on the defense and get him so pissed off that he lost his mental cognitive skills, then take him physically.

"You deaf, Cunga? What's the matter you fucking beaner? You need your boy to hold your dick for you, too?"

The gang leader almost fell over backwards in shock. No one had ever talked to him like that. But then again, he'd never met Diego or anyone else like Diego before. Diego, on the other hand, had seen all kinds of trash just like this piece of work, and most were likely tougher. He noted the man's emotional state. Mental disengagement complete. Diego kept smiling. He knew two more things. One, the idiot had already forgotten Jose was even there. Good. Two, Diego was in total control of the next 60 seconds. Better.

Diego waited until the leader made his first move and leapt into action. As he had learned as a youth, and was re-enforced in the military, always take the leader out first; only then could you gage the true intent of the rest of the group. It was pretty common to see a group of thugs turn tail and bolt when they saw someone effortlessly take out the kingpin of their puny little world. In this case, the leader was about 1.87 meters tall (5'10") and an easy 81 kilograms (180 pounds), with very little fat – a fairly impressive appearance, but clearly a street tough with no formal training. The man had been standing directly behind Jose, facing Diego, and now began to pull a knife out of his boot. The initial motion was all Diego needed in his mind to complete the legal definition of "defending oneself." In one fluid motion, Diego slid his chair back, flipped the table to the left and covered the three feet to the leader in the blink of an eye. The table and flying glasses were a diversionary tactic to buy an extra second or two of free time before anyone else could react, as well as to provide a natural barrier between him and anyone to his left during the initial seconds of the melee. The leader now had his Ka-Bar military style knife up to waist level, but not in proper position to utilize it efficiently. Definitely not trained, Diego noted.

The surprise move caught the lead gang member off guard and he had frozen in place for one brief moment, but one moment was more than adequate for Diego. In a continually flowing motion, Diego provided a quick strike with the edge of his hand to the man's Adam's apple. The leader immediately dropped his knife and began clutching at his damaged throat. Diego spun to his right and somersaulted off the back of Jose's chair, connecting with the second gang member and locked his legs around his neck. The vault carried his full weight past the second gang member, with his legs still wrapped around the man's neck. Diego applied one simple but sharp rotation of his thighs and waist, snapping the man's neck. Diego released his hold and completed the vault. The assailant's body dropped to the floor. The surprise move left the other three members dazed for an additional split second, which in turn provided Diego enough time to roll back toward them. As he rolled, he sideswiped the gang member who had been to the left of the leader, knocking him to the floor while simultaneously grabbing the leader's Ka-Bar knife off the floor and thrusting it up into the groin of the next man to his left. That gang member had been in the process of pulling what looked like a Glock 17 out of his jacket, but immediately howled and released the Glock. Diego caught the gun in midair while spinning up to a kneeling position, quickly shooting the last man on the left in the head with his initial shot. He panned right and snapped off two shots into the bleeding gang member, while continuing his movement to the right where he pumped two shots into the chest of the man trying to get back up from the floor. Only the leader was left, now on his knees, still gasping and holding his throat. He had watched it all in disbelief. Diego waited five long seconds, waiting for him to absorb the end of his wretched reign while looking deep into the man's eyes, hoping to find some hint of humanity. None. Diego shot him, once, directly between the eyes and the ex-leader joined the other four on the floor. Five gang bangers dead. The entire exchange had lasted less than two minutes. Jose was still sitting in his chair and got up only after Diego directed him to do so; he then moved over to the other side of the restaurant where Diego signaled him to move to. Diego simulated making a phone call and nodded to the manager to dial 911 while he maintained guard on the rest of the room. Diego was pretty confident that there were no other gang members present, especially as most of the patrons had quickly fled the restaurant once the fighting began, but he wasn't going to drop his guard and take that chance until the police showed up.

Diego looked back at Jose, who was still white as a ghost.

"You okay, bro?" he asked quietly. Jose simply nodded his head with an affirmative.

"Good to hear, but you may want to sit down before the floor finds its way to you." Jose did as he suggested and sat down, clearly unnerved. Diego surveyed the fallen gang members one last time. He felt no pity or remorse. They had come in here with clear intent to steal and possibly inflict harm on him and his brother. In Diego's codebook, they got what they deserved and society would be better off for it.

Within minutes, sirens could be heard, getting closer to the restaurant. The owner was still behind the bar, saying nothing, shaking visibly.

Ninety minutes later, after multiple police interviews, and one well-placed call to the Pentagon, the lead investigator shook hands with Diego and told him that he and his brother were free to go. As Diego turned to leave, the officer pulled him close and whispered in his ear.

"Retired USMC myself. Hope you can come back again; there's plenty more of this trash that needs to be cleaned up, but our hands are always tied. Sucks for sure. Thanks man. Oorah."

"Thanks bro, take care and watch your back." They shook hands again. "Semper fi." Diego saluted and then turned to leave with his brother.

Once again, Diego reflected that his time in countries far, far away could have been better spent right here in the U.S. Jose might have been aghast over the spillage of blood, but Diego would sleep fine that night. Those thugs were no better than Somalian pirates. Each made his own decisions, without considering the impact they had had on innocent others, so now they had received a final dose of their own medicine. It seemed like a fair deal to Diego. He put his arm around Jose's shoulder and they walked out into the night.

CHAPTER 7

A.D. 2028 (3311 C.A.E.); Nov. 3
Mars orbit

Cmdr. Dutch Kline breathed a sigh of relief. The Reagan I had traveled for more than 10 months to get to the storied Red Planet, and they had finally arrived. Cmdr. Kline reflected on the many science fiction stories and movies that had been written about the Red Planet over the past century, going all the way back to the famous Orson Wells "The War of The Worlds" radio broadcast in 1938. That broadcast caused fear and panic across the East Coast when people believed it was real and that Martians had actually invaded Earth. Dutch chuckled, then took in a big breath, half from the relief of arriving, and half in anticipation of the next phase of the mission, in which his crew would land and walk on the storied planet.

So much had happened since 1938, Dutch reflected, but now … this crew would be the first humans to actually set foot on the planet. But things had changed again, based on a coded transmission received weeks earlier. Now, Cmdr. Kline and his crew were to locate and recover an unidentified object that was reportedly non-human in origin. Based on the communications with NASA over the past few weeks, and contrary to everything science knew, they apparently weren't the first intelligent race to have connections to the Red Planet. The photos were unmistakable and the sheer magnitude of that realization brought Cmdr. Kline shudders of anticipation.

The crew had been alerted to the new information about the object on Mars so that they could come to grips with it prior to the complex and dangerous landing mission that would require 100 percent of their focus. The fact that they had to change landing sites didn't bother the crew at all; landing zone A or zone B was immaterial when compared to landing *on* Mars.

During the final approach to Mars, the crew had theorized countless scenarios relative to how the recently discovered object would alter their lives, as well as those of every person back on Earth. Their excitement was high, and contrary to what NASA physiologists had been afraid of, this was exactly what the crew needed in order to re-energize and refocus their efforts after 10 months of dreary flight from Earth to Mars. It had been a long 10 months, traversing the millions of kilometers of nothingness between Earth and Mars, with no pit stops in between. The latter had become the theme response for the team when anyone complained about anything, and the jokes about "are we there yet" became a standing response to just about anything.

The Mars landing would be accomplished in a similar fashion to the old moon landings made famous by the Apollo astronauts. The driving requirement behind the independent Lunar Module landing back in the Apollo days was no different than with the Red Lander today: fuel constraints. In this case, the Mars mission required such an extensive payload of fuel and resources just to get to Mars, that the possibility of then landing the same ship on the planet, with its massive size and weight, was prohibitive. In addition, the gravity levels on Mars were far greater than the moon – 38 percent of Earth, but still more than twice that of the moon – making landing and taking off even more challenging with limited fuel options.

The Earth orbit launch of the Reagan I had been necessary for the same reasons, but it also provided the additional benefit of secrecy by shielding the construction within the enormous space dock structure. Earthbound telescopes could easily make out the space dock and the magnitude of construction on it, but large solar panels obscured sight of what was actually being built. The space dock had been a five-year, aggressive project by the U.S, started as part of President Trump's public announcement to start the U.S. Space Force. The space dock completed construction in 2026, nowhere near in time to start and finish the Reagan I for a

2027 launch window, so the construction had secretly taken place in parallel with the space dock construction. From Earth, it was too hard to tell where one ended and the other began, thereby creating the appearance that it was all space dock.

The actual Reagan I launch had been further concealed by initiating the trip when the space station was directly between the Earth and the sun, thereby ensuring that the sun would block most amateur attempts, and many less-technologically advanced foreign government attempts to spy on space station activity. It was well known that anyone with a good telescope would have a chance of picking up the flight path once it was under way to Mars, but at that point, no one would know exactly where it had originated from or what it really was. The U.S. planned to continue mock building efforts and flights to the station, well after the Reagan I had departed, to reduce the risk of anyone suspecting anything had changed.

Like the ancient Lunar Lander, the Red Lander was constructed to land and launch vertically to eliminate the need for standard landing strips or perfectly flat Martian surfaces. However, because Mars had an atmosphere, the Red Lander also employed steroid-induced, V-22 like technology to translate back and forth from vertical rocket thrust to horizontal flight. In this manner, the need for landing accuracy was greatly reduced, vast areas of the surface could be explored and the return vector to the Reagan I could be conducted on a much gentler ascent slope, and with a much higher level of flexibility and forgiveness. The 1970 Apollo engineers basically had to thread a needle from a distance of 385,000 kilometers, with only one attempt: a feat still considered beyond astounding even with today's technology. Another historical proof of the Greatest Generation ever, as Blake frequently reminded young recruits who thought they were the best thing to ever walk on the planet.

The biggest difference with the Red Lander, as compared to the Lunar Lander, was computer power. The computing capability of the new Mars Lander exceeded that of the entire Apollo-age space industrial complex by orders of magnitude. The Apollo-class ships had a computer capability of less than half of even the 1980s-era personal computer chips that employed the then-impressive 8086 16-bit registers from Intel, and far less than what a typical wristwatch contains today. The Apollo computer memory storage was a not-so-mind-blowing 32K – hard to even classify as a computer. The Mars mission, by comparison, consisted of multiple computers, each of which was at least five times the Tianhe-2, the world's top computer in 2013, at 33.86 quadrillion flops/s, or 33.86 petaflop/s. Researchers typically measured computing power in "flop/s" or floating point operations per second. The bog-standard 2.5 GHz processor found in a 2015-era office laptop, was theoretically capable of 10 billion flop/s, or 10 gigaflop/s – a babe in the woods compared to the Reagan I's computing capability. The famous Moore's Law from the 1970s stated that "processor speeds, or overall processing power for computers will double every two years." On any given year, the informal rule might or might not have been accurate, but looking back over the years, the thumb-in-the-air rule had actually continued to be fairly reliable until at least midway through the 2010s.

Cmdr. Kline had dreamed of this type of mission his entire life, as had each of his crew. His crew included pilot Maj. John Martinez, co-pilot Maj. Bob Chase, two mission specialists, Lt. Tom O'Dougherty and Lt. Pat Skiles, and one engineer, Jimmy Decker. Dutch was disappointed he wasn't going to the surface as originally planned, but it was his decision to remove himself, rather than one of the crew, to make sure they were not weight-limited on their return with the device. He also told Houston that someone had to have the landing party's backs while they were on the surface – in case something went wrong.

After 10 long months, the crew was finally ready to start their descent to the Martian surface.

"Okay, gentlemen, the free ride is over, time to get your lazy butts in gear. Suit up!" Kline barked with a smile.

O'Dougherty, Skiles, Chase and Decker began suiting up. Both Cmdr. Kline and Maj. Martinez would remain on the Reagan I, so they assisted the other four while they suited up.

"Yo, Marty!" O'Dougherty called out to Maj. Martinez. "What are the oddsmakers in Vegas claiming the object is? Russian? Chinese? It sure as heck can't be Martian, can it? I don't care what those NASA boys say about the unreadable encryptions; there simply aren't any little green Martians running amok."

"Tom, you're all talk, good buddy. It's time to put your money where your mouth is. I've got a hundred bucks that says it's not from Earth. Are we on?" Martinez shot back with a smile.

"You're on!" chuckled O'Dougherty. "My money says it's Chinese. You know how horrible their quality control is; they likely tried to hit Taiwan and missed!"

"I'll be happy to take some of that action, too, O'Dougherty!" added Decker. "Those pictures have me convinced – it's not from Mother Earth."

"Okay, but you guys will be 14 shades of red, and a hundred bucks lighter when you get to listen to me take those NASA boys for a walk in the woods with a made-in-China trinket."

"We'll know soon, gentlemen," added Cmdr. Kline with a serious tone. "Let's get this show on the road. Make sure you don't forget to roll the videos while you're down there debating the foundations of civilization. Time to get serious, gents." Cmdr. Kline was a good leader, willing to join in the humor, but it was clear he was sending a message at the same time: this is a dangerous mission and they were all well aware that there would be no opportunities for "do-overs."

The men continued to suit up in their extravehicular suits. This step of the process, when aided by others, required at least 30 minutes. Equipment checkout would take another 20 minutes. The standard NASA suit weighed approximately 23 kilograms (50 pounds) on Earth and cost in excess of $2 million each. The suits on the Reagan I were made by a spinoff subsidiary from ILC Dover that operated totally in the black and off the books to ensure that no one could connect the new suits to the program. ILC Dover had made the standard space suits for NASA for decades, dating all the way back to the Apollo programs. The standard NASA suit was the starting baseline for this trip, but each had been modified to add additional oxygen that could extend the time on the surface by a full two hours as compared to the typical six- to eight-hour capability that the standard two-tank scuba-like gear provided. The new modifications added an additional 11 kilograms to each suit, but would not have to be put on until the men were actually ready to walk on the surface of Mars.

The men loaded into the Red Lander and completed their checklists to prep for flight. Forty-five minutes later, they were ready.

"Ready to close the door, commander," Maj. Chase spoke into his com.

"Martinez is closing the door. The door is closed. Prep for countdown," Kline replied after a short delay.

"Systems ready for disengagement."

"Roger that."

"Start the countdown."

"10 … 9 … 8 … 7 … 6 … 5 … 4 … 3 … 2 … 1 … initiate disengagement," Maj. Chase robotically stated, followed by a series of metallic "clunks" and a loud hissing sound as the locks on the Red Lander were opened and a nitrogen vent jettisoned the Red Lander from the Reagan I. The vent was designed to push the Lander at least 100 meters past the Reagan I prior to firing the rockets on the Lander.

"Ready to initiate engines." Maj. Chase updated Cmdr. Kline. "3 … 2 … 1 … engines initiated. We are commencing our descent to the surface of Mars."

"Good luck, gentlemen, and you'd better come back bearing gifts, or don't bother coming back." Cmdr. Kline smiled.

"Aye, aye, sir, but we shipped ahead of time from Amazon.com. Last we heard, there were no brown trucks on Mars, so we expect your gift should be waiting on your doorstep when we return to

Earth." Maj. Chase ended with a laugh that both ships joined in on.

The separation was textbook – exactly what everyone trained for in space – a totally uneventful event. The four men were now on their own, heading down to the Martian deck in the Red Lander.

Cmdr. Kline looked over at Maj. Martinez with a contemplative expression. "Our world is about to change, Marty, and nothing is ever going to be the same."

Maj. Martinez nodded, his eyebrows raised as he exhaled loudly. Cmdr. Kline had no idea how prophetic his statement would become.

*****

Ten hours later, after one full revolution about Mars, thousands of pictures and at least as many transmissions to Earth, the crew was approaching their landing target. With the landing site locked in, Maj. Bob Chase rotated the rocket engines and began the descent down through the thin Martian atmosphere. Once within the lower atmosphere, he rotated the engines for a horizontal flight path mode and began sweeping the local terrain around their landing zone, just to make sure they hadn't missed anything of importance from their orbit assessment. Twenty minutes later, Maj. Chase gently touched down on the red Martian surface in a cloud of red dust that was rewarded with a cheer from men who had travelled many millions of kilometers to be the first to set foot on another planet – although they each silently harbored doubt they were no longer 100 percent convinced of that distinction. The flight had been without challenge, and the journey to Mars had continued as "by the book" as anyone dared to hope.

"Gentlemen, welcome to Mars and congratulations for being the first men from the United States to land on Mars," Maj. Chase announced. Everyone noted his reference to the United States, rather than the proverbial "mankind" that Neil Armstrong had used, and the very obvious, but unspoken tie to the object they were being asked to investigate.

"Jimmy, what do you have on atmospheric readings?" Maj. Chase added.

"Yes sir, major, give me one sec ..." Jimmy swiveled in his seat to check the gauges measuring external environmental conditions. "Looks like the atmosphere is at 0.087 psi – wow, it really is less than 1/100 of Earth's sea level atmospheric pressure of 14.7 psi. Hard to believe it's still an atmosphere and hasn't disappeared like the water did," Jimmy added.

"Commander, commencing the shutdown of main engines on your order," Maj. Chase relayed to Cmdr. Kline.

"Roger that, Maj. Chase, shut down the main engines," replied Cmdr. Kline from 150 kilometers above the surface, well above the Martian atmosphere that extended to approximately 50 kilometers.

Minutes later, Maj. Chase relayed that the engines were shut down, and the four crewmen were preparing to exit the vehicle and initiate salvage efforts with their first recon of the object.

"Major, as we really don't know what's out there yet, Houston has recommended we minimize our Day One risks. You and Jimmy are cleared to exit the Red Lander. Tom and Pat will remain in the lander monitoring your progress until we're sure of what we're dealing with. Acknowledge transmission," ordered Cmdr. Kline.

"Acknowledged," Maj. Chase relayed back. "Chase and Decker preparing for initial excursion. Lieutenants O'Dougherty and Skiles to remain on board the Lander." As Maj. Chase spoke, he looked at his two lieutenants and nodded, acknowledging that he knew how disappointed they would be.

"Commander, a private word?" requested the major.

"Okay, what's on your mind, major? I've temporarily stopped both the voice recorder and auto feed to Houston."

"Dutch, to be honest, you know that we had prepared statements to read, based on first the five of us with you, then the four of us standing together, but that won't work now with only two of us on the ground, and there really isn't time to rescript our lines. If it's all the same to you, Decker and I would like to pass." Chase stated calmly, but firmly, and then continued, "Dutch, it's not like we're on national TV anyway. But more importantly, we came as a team and ... and with O'Dougherty and Skiles not joining us for the first steps on Mars ..." Maj. Chase paused, looked down and then back at the camera with a steeled expression. "We understand why, but it still kind of sucks, sir. We think it's better that we keep to the task and skip on the speeches." Maj. Chase was all business.

Cmdr. Kline reflected for a few seconds, respecting the fact that Maj. Chase was actually standing up for his fellow crewmembers. "The fact that we were prepared to talk about expanding the 'one small step for man' speech to the 'first step in humankind's journey to the universe' speech does seem a little contrite now that we know others are already ahead of us. Your call, major; I'm with you either way."

"Thank you, commander." Maj. Chase saluted the commander and then smiled at the other men in the lander.

"Going live again, major. The mic recorder and Houston link are both back up in three, two, one, live." He knew that the tapes would get analyzed back home and someone would wonder why there was a 60-second gap at such a critical point in the landing. The commander smiled as he thought about how many times *sun spots* had been used to explain other oddities.

"Don't sweat it, major," O'Dougherty spoke first. "We are on the planet, aren't we? I really wasn't ready to get these white boots all dirty yet anyway. Go get that flag up." Tom then saluted the camera, fully knowing that Cmdr. Kline would be watching for their reactions, and finished with a big grin.

Maj. Chase looked back at the men. The truth was, they had all become close friends, and situations like this, where they all had each other's backs, was what it was all really about. Lt. Skiles took over the ship's controls and audio feeds as Lt. O'Dougherty helped Jimmy Decker and Maj. Chase into the exit bay. Seals were locked and the atmosphere of Mars was exchanged with the air of Earth with one big swooshing sound.

"Commander, egress is underway. Is the external video feed clear?" Maj. Chase asked in a calm but mechanical voice.

"Good to go, gentlemen, and Godspeed," Dutch responded in deference to Scott Carpenter and the historic Apollo astronauts. Over the decades, the term "Godspeed" had become as commonplace in space operations as the reply "roger" had; the one constant that never changed was that it still carried a great deal of reverence, even after all these years.

Maj. Chase climbed down the ladder and took the first step for humankind onto the Martian surface, with zero fanfare.

"Commander, I'm on the surface," Maj. Chase reported as he looked back over his shoulder toward the lander. "Jimmy! Stop sightseeing and get moving; we don't have all day, son," he said, grinning.

Jimmy had been scanning the planet's surface from the top of the stairs, looking as if he were seeing a gorgeous young lady for the very first time.

"Oh, yeah. Sorry, chief. Guess, no matter how much you plan for it, it's still hard to absorb it all," Jimmy replied with a kid-like grin.

"Sure is, Jimmy. It sure is. Please pass the flag down." Maj. Chase was concerned Jimmy would take a tumble with the flag and decided to coach him down step by step. Jimmy handed the flag down gently.

"Okay, Jimmy, now hand down the two shovels, one at a time, then the rope, and then the tripod and winch."

"Working on it, sir."

Fifteen minutes later, with their supplies on the ground, Maj. Bob Chase and Jimmy Decker planted the flag and stepped back to ensure their headset videos were working correctly. Maj. Chase smartly saluted the flag, and then turned to salute the two men still in the lander – the significance of the latter salute was not lost on anyone.

"Thanks, Bob. Now go get 'em, skipper," O'Dougherty volunteered.

Bob picked up their shovels, motioning to Jimmy to pick up the tripod, rope and the winch. The two men walked over to the object, and the Mars Rover, a mere 100 meters away from the Red Lander.

Walking was easy, as they both weighed less than 32 kilograms in the light Martian gravity, yet the gravity was enough that they didn't create the funny bounce the Apollo astronauts had famously demonstrated on the moon.

"There's Rover!" Jimmy blurted out as if he had found his long lost dog. "Well, old man, what have you found for us?" Jimmy asked.

"Help me out, Jimmy. Let's pull Rover out of the way so we can get a better look at our new friend."

"Ummmm, are we allowed to do that, sir? Shouldn't we have NASA move it?" asked Jimmy innocently.

"Do you really want to sit here and watch the red dust grow older while we just wait for the signal to travel all the way to Earth, get processed, debated, and then sent back here?"

"Sorry, sir, brain fart. Good point. I'll get the front, you get the rear," Jimmy volunteered. "Commander, you want to strike the last 30 seconds of audio, please?"

Cmdr. Kline chuckled. If NASA allowed the crew to sanitize the tapes from the last 10 months, a significant volume of the recorded material would be erased.

The Rover weighed much more than an average man – 185 kilograms on Earth, approximately 70 kilograms on Mars – heavy, but still movable by the two men.

"You have to admit, Bob, the engineers who designed this little guy did one hell of a job. It's hard to believe that it's still working in this environment, over 20 years later. This particular one, Opportunity, was designed to last just a few months – that's really impressive! And on top of that, it actually died during a sandstorm in 2018, but the NASA guys somehow brought it back to life again in 2022. Maybe they should have renamed it the Phoenix," Jimmy chuckled.

"Let's just hope that your fellow engineering buddies who designed our Red Lander and the Reagan I are as good as those guys who designed this Rover – and that they get us all home in one piece," replied Maj. Chase.

"Gee, thanks for the vote of confidence on the general engineering community," Jimmy bounced back sarcastically.

"Any time, Jimmy. Someone has to keep you egomaniacs in line." Maj. Chase said, chuckling.

The two men dragged the Mars Rover out of the way and returned to the object. The lights in the object were no longer on; everything appeared silent. The Mars Rover had excavated at least a full meter of the object.

"I wonder if the batteries ran out." Maj. Chase looked over at Jimmy.

"Hmmm … Good question, Bob. No clue here, yet." Jimmy was on his knees by the object and sat back on his feet with his hands on his hips, looking intently at the object now. "Okay, now it's my turn. Let me see if I can remove some more of this dirt. Major, how about you set up the tripod so we can operate the winch, just in case?"

*****

Minutes passed and Jimmy continued to dig the red sand away from the object. He was making faster progress than they had expected, albeit from his immediate perspective, it still seemed slow and exhausting because of the bulky spacesuit. Jimmy's labored breathing was unmistakable.

"Jimmy, take a breather and switch positions with me."

Maj. Chase took Jimmy's place for the next 15-minute shift. Over the next three hours, Jimmy and Bob exchanged places frequently so they could rest, but also so a different set of eyes could monitor the situation. They could now see the object much more clearly, as well as its inherent complexity. With the new information they were seeing, Jimmy began referring to it as a device.

"Device? Did you say device, Jimmy?" Cmdr. Kline asked from orbit.

"Well, umm, yes I did. The term 'object' just doesn't do it justice. We knew before we landed that it really was a device, but the more I see of it, the more it seems we should call a tree a tree, and a device a device. It is clearly an electromechanical device of some type."

But it was still the first time Cmdr. Kline heard the word "device."

"Okay, I follow you, Jimmy, but I'd still like the two of you to step back for a couple of minutes. Safety is paramount, so let's just spend a couple of minutes looking and thinking, just to make sure our enthusiasm to uncover this … this device … doesn't override our need to make sure we are safe. I don't want to miss something that would end our trip prematurely."

Both men were confident that it was unlikely the device was booby-trapped, but they agreed it wasn't worth taking chances. They reminded themselves that none of them had any idea why it was here, how it got here, when it got here, or who the owners were. Jimmy also reminded Cmdr. Kline that he had received in-depth training from the military on what they had learned in the Middle East; defusing leftover unexploded ordnance and IEDs from the Taliban and ISIS Wars of the 2000s and 2010s – and he wasn't about to forget that training now, millions of kilometers away from the nearest hospital. With that reassurance, Cmdr. Kline gave the go-ahead to continue digging.

"Okay, but make sure you guys do as much looking and thinking as you do digging. Slow and safe, gentlemen."

"Acknowledged, commander." And the two men got back to the task at hand.

By the end of the first day, it was clear that the device, now exceeding two meters in exposed length, was not going to be a willing participant in the removal process. The two men called it a day as their oxygen supplies, even with the additional packs, decreased quicker than expected because of their higher-than-planned exertion levels. When the flight was originally planned, it was focused on the crew walking around the Mars surface and simply collecting rock samples; nowhere in the original plan did it include hard-core labor to excavate a large device.

The two men returned to the Red Lander, re-entered and removed their space suits with assistance from Tom O'Dougherty and Pat Skiles. The men were all ready to eat and get a good night's sleep before hitting it again tomorrow.

"Amazing," Jimmy blurted out.

"What?" the men asked in unison, all looking to Jimmy.

"We've traveled almost 80 million kilometers and we don't have to worry about jet lag, like we get when we travel from New York to Beijing, all because we can set our night and day exactly like Earth's." They all enjoyed a light laugh at that realization. Most people on Earth would not have realized that the length of day and night on Mars was almost identical to that of Earth.

"Jimmy, if that's all it takes to keep you happy, you'll make some woman a very happy wife someday," Maj. Chase added lightheartedly.

"Well, maybe this device can get me a date with someone on its home planet. I sure as heck can't get one on Earth!"

The crew exchanged jibes and reassurances for a few minutes and then recounted the day's activities. They also discussed plans for tomorrow's activities. Before turning in for the night, Maj. Chase radioed the Reagan I and debriefed Cmdr. Kline on the day's progress, and then it was lights out.

CHAPTER 8

A.D. 2028 (3311 C.A.E.); Nov. 3
Orbiting Space Dock

Blake was the only crewmember who hadn't taken time off to go home. He had too much to learn in too short a time to consider leaving the mission right now, so he spent his limited free time calling and using FaceTime with family and friends when he had a chance. He told himself he would have plenty of time to visit people when he returned. His younger sister, Cindy, now lived in New Hampshire, and although they rarely saw each other, they maintained communication whenever Blake was back in the U.S. His mother had passed away after he had graduated from West Point, and Blake had never settled down with anyone, so it was really just him and his sister, and his military family. She was married with three children, who all referred to him as Uncle B, but even though they always begged him to visit, he knew she didn't need some big lug in the way, so FaceTime was more than adequate. He also justified his decision by reminding himself of the many men and women who were there with him supporting their operation. Blake was well aware that the vast majority of them did NOT have the option to go home right now, so he was content staying where he was and supporting them.

Blake started every morning with a 45-minute routine that would punish even a professional athlete, followed by a hard two-mile run that he drove himself to complete in less than 11 minutes. Blake always maintained his physical conditioning regimen as it was an absolute necessity in the SEAL forces, but he fully expected that the rigors of a multi-month trip in space would prove equally challenging, and therefore just as necessary.

Weeks of dedicated studies, as well as the recent on-ship exercises, had honed Blake and the crew for the upcoming mission, and all were well past eager to get started. The one aspect that Blake felt still presented significant risk, was the one-in-a-trillion possibility that the object was indeed a ship, that the ship did possess alien beings – and that those beings were still alive. It was easy to dismiss it as a one-in-a-trillion possibility, but … what if it occurred and they weren't properly prepared? It could be disastrous for either, or both parties. Blake felt strongly about this issue and had enlisted the assistance of one of the top anthropology graduate schools in the nation to help him out: Cornell University in upstate New York.

After discussions with a number of professors, Blake homed in on Prof. Adam G. Rimlinger, whose expertise dealt with complex societies, state formation, politics and archaeological theory. Blake requested clearance for the professor from the Pentagon, and quickly received it. He wasn't sure what the Pentagon had initially shared with the professor, but it was clear the professor didn't want to talk too much about the first contact. The only insight Blake picked up relative to the professor's hesitancy, was regarding a visit the professor had received from three black sedans with men in black suits, a document he was required to sign under their intense eyes, and a commitment to have his university research programs funded for the next 25 years – as long as he kept his mouth totally shut.

Prof. Rimlinger spent numerous sessions on the phone with Blake, as well as sending volumes of information to Blake for him to read during the long flight. Blake wished he could have taken Prof. Rimlinger with him, but he knew this was as good as it would get.

*****

A.D. 2028 (3311 C.A.E.); Nov. 4
Mars

The four men woke at 6 a.m. local time and ate their breakfast-in-a-tube, ready to restart their task in earnest.

"Commander, based on yesterday's progress, what do you think Houston's thoughts would be relative to growing our excavation party by two?" Maj. Chase asked Cmdr. Dutch Kline with hopeful anticipation.

"Sorry, Bob, no can do. We need to keep Tom and Pat in the lander, just in case. As a matter of fact, I received a message last night requesting you move the Red Lander farther away, just in case something goes wrong. The Pentagon and NASA are both pushing for a mile separation."

"Roger that," Maj. Chase replied. They all knew what "just in case" referred to, a possible explosion, but no one dared voice those words.

"Commander," Jimmy piped in.

"Yes, Jimmy?"

"I'll say what no one else wants to say. If it is a *bomb*, or some kind of explosive device, it could be a nuke; we have no way of knowing. In that case, a mile will be no better than 100 meters. Furthermore, we will exhaust our safety fuel if we move the lander, and also shorten our time at the dig because of the time it will take us to get back and forth each day. Can you imagine what it would take to transport this thing a mile when we get it out?" Everyone took note that Jimmy was taking a much stronger stand than he normally did. "We all know the risks. Those guys back home are making calls from the proverbial back seat, with good intent, but not with our firsthand awareness. We need to stay where we are and get to work."

It was the strongest statement Jimmy had made during the entire trip. Bob Chase looked at Tom and Pat, who both quickly acknowledged agreement with a thumbs-up gesture.

"Commander, we are all in agreement. Permission to overrule requested."

"Granted, and for the record, officially justified due to the risk it would create to fuel safety margins. I'll handle the call with Earth. Great point, Jimmy."

"Thank you, sir, on our way."

For the next few hours, Bob and Jimmy took turns at the "Big Dig," as Jimmy had dubbed it, in reference to the monstrous Central Artery/Tunnel Project Boston had undertaken around the turn of the century. It was a slow and tedious process. By noon, Maj. Chase called a break; the men returned to the lander for lunch, and checked in with Cmdr. Dutch Kline.

"Dutch, we haven't made as much progress today, and we planned on having this device loaded by tomorrow morning at the latest. I don't think we can meet that schedule at our current pace."

"If you're thinking about winching, I'm all for it. We haven't seen any signs of booby traps, and to be honest, everything we can see suggests that it crash landed, rather than impacted a target," Dutch agreed.

"My guess is the end we found sticking out of the ground is the front end that contains the brains," Jimmy jumped in, "and the rest of the device is simply fuel containment and engine. Whatever it is, it appears to have survived the crash mostly intact, even if it is banged up a bit. So, either the sand cushioned it or the device is made of some pretty tough materials, or a little of both. Either way, I don't think this is a bomb. Just a hunch, but I'm confident that I'm right."

"I'm leaning towards agreeing with you, but before you become the first humans to walk on Mars, as well as the first humans to die on Mars, I think we'd better get Houston's opinion on this as well."

They all knew Dutch was right this time.

"Roger that," Bob answered, realizing that it would take a half-dozen minutes for the message to get to Earth, and an equal delay to receive their response, let alone the time the NASA engineers would need to debate their answer.

Surprisingly, it only required 30 minutes to receive the green light for the winching operation – even Houston realized there simply wasn't any additional time to waste. If they missed their planned departure window, the distance between Earth and Mars would be increasing, and they would be playing catch-up the entire trip home, possibly extending their trip by months.

The two men had their orders and went back outside to set up the winch. Jimmy decided to move the winch to a large nearby rock, where he could keep it more stationary. He weighted it down now that they realized how big the device was and then ran the cable over a small tripod nearer the device to provide a fixed, directional pull on the device. It would've been easier to provide a vertical extraction, but they didn't come prepared with a tripod tall enough.

"Ready?" Maj. Bob Chase asked Jimmy.

"Yes sir, Bob. Start it slowly and I'll wave you off if I see anything that bothers me. I've moved to the far side of the contact point in case the cable snaps. I suggest you find a safe position as well. If that cable snaps under load, it will become a lethal whip."

Thirty seconds passed and the winch pulled slowly, but seemingly easily as it extracted the device, millimeter by agonizing millimeter, until Jimmy waived crazily and yelled "Stop!" into his headset mic.

"What is it, Jimmy?" Bob yelled as he tied off the rope and ran over to Jimmy and the device.

"The sand started giving way … I wasn't sure what was happening," Jimmy stammered. "Although looking now, I think it means we're close to the device's end, and the soft sand was just filling the void under the device as you were pulling it out. We are damn lucky that the sand was this deep here. Looking around, this thing could have easily smashed itself to pieces on some of these rocky outcrops and we never would have known it was here. Let's pull some more and I'll stand back a little more, just to be safe."

"Okay, Jimmy, on your call."

Five short minutes later, the device was totally exposed.

"It looks like a giant sardine with a rocket stuck up its ass end," Jimmy mocked.

"Sure does, but if that is an engine, it's unlike anything I've ever seen, and I've seen a lot of missile engines in my day," Bob acknowledged.

"Commander, are you seeing this?"

"Quite clearly, Bob, and quite amazing to be honest," Cmdr. Kline responded. The engine was clearly damaged by contact with something, although that might have been due to ground impact. "Do you see any signs of fuel leakage?"

"No, I don't. And our radioactive tags are clean. If whoever 'they' were used nuclear power, then the nuclear containment shell must still be intact," Jimmy answered.

"That's the best news I've heard all week," Bob said, grinning. "Let's get this thing packed. Any guesses on weight?"

"Good question. Let's try pulling the winch cable by hand and see if we can gauge the weight."

They both pulled and found the device could be moved a little easier than expected.

"If I had to guess, which is what you're asking, it's a good 2.2 meters long, 50 centimeters in diameter, and I'd say about 600 kilograms in weight, give or take 10 percent. That would make it about 233 kilograms on Mars. That suggests about 120 kilograms (or 250 pounds) each for us to carry it, and it's pretty ungainly as well."

Bob Chase turned off his transmissions recorder. "Jimmy, there's no way it weighs that much. What are you saying?"

Jimmy turned his recorder off as well. "Maybe, but who's here to disagree with us? Don't you think we *need help*?" Jimmy added with a big grin as he looked back at the Mars Lander.

Maj. Chase paused for a moment and grinned. "You're a genius, Jimmy," finally realizing that Jimmy had found the ticket to allow the others an opportunity to walk on Mars. They both turned their recorders back on.

"I think you're right, Jimmy. We will need Tom's and Pat's help getting the device to the ship. It's too much for just the two of us." Maj. Chase winked at Jimmy.

"Great idea, major," Jimmy smiled back. "How about validating that with the commander?"

"You know I'm listening," Dutch Kline chuckled softly. "And I don't need Houston for this one. Skiles, O'Dougherty! Are you two so lame that you're going to make Chase and Decker do all the work? Get your butts topside now – that's an order!"

"Wahoo!!!!!" O'Dougherty hooted back. "Come on Skiles, it's sandbox time! We're on our way!"

Sixty minutes later, all four men were standing around the device, alternating between taking in the views and examining the device.

"Our biggest issue will be getting it through the lock, then finding a spot to fit it into the lander and tie it down securely so it doesn't kill us all on takeoff."

"What about Rover?" Jimmy asked.

"Great question, Jimmy. Sure seems like he has earned a trip home, doesn't it?"

"Amen! It sure does."

"I'll have the commander check with Houston. There's a possibility they may want this little marvel to keep looking for more surprises."

By the time the four of them had loaded and stowed the device, Cmdr. Kline had received word from Houston that validated Bob's opinion. The Mars Rover was to remain gainfully employed, with no thoughts of retirement. The men spent the rest of the day on the Martian surface, collecting samples and videos from the Martian landscape. It was truly an amazing experience, filled with breakthroughs, but as much as everyone had hoped they would find remnants of water, nothing was found. Cmdr. Kline had also not identified possibilities from above, as he orbited the planet awaiting their return.

"See ya, good buddy," Jimmy called out as he looked out the window at the Mars Rover. "Poor dude, what a lonely life."

"What were you doing over there with Rover before we left, singing it a lullaby?" Pat laughed with one eyebrow raised as he looked over at Jimmy.

"I … ah … I … umm …"

"What did you do, Jimmy?" Now it was Maj. Chase's turn to ask.

"I wrote 'A⁺, Jimmy, 11-4-28' on it." Jimmy replied meekly.

"Great!" Tom O'Dougherty joined the fray. "Jimmy, now you've introduced graffiti to Mars and we'll all be held responsible for the biggest social disgrace in human history!"

The men all shared a hearty laugh until Bob Chase brought them back to the task at hand.

"Okay, time to buckle up, gents. I'm lighting the rockets," Bob ordered.

"How about we change the name to *Red Flyer*? I'd really like to make sure we don't have to land again," Jimmy replied, and was rewarded another round of laughs from the group.

With that, the Red Lander, or newly minted Red Flyer, lifted off, rotated its engines and began the flight back up to the Reagan I with device on board. It would be a long 10 months to get it back home to Earth.

*****

A.D. 2028 (3311 C.A.E.); Nov. 5
Houston

The special, invite-only group was gathered in a large, dimly lit, executive conference room at the Houston Space Center.

"This is wrong," Blake rebuked the room full of NASA and military brass. "This crew has worked hard to prepare for this mission for over two months and you're simply pulling the plug? How do you think you can train others in time, or are you delaying the entire mission?" Blake's face was red with rage, and it was taking every ounce of strength to maintain even a hint of professionalism.

"Maj. Thompson, we understand why you're upset, but you need to understand the playing field we're dealing with. This decision is out of both Houston's and NASA's control, and it's bigger than just the U.S.; there's nothing we can do about it. These orders are directly from President Callahan and the Pentagon – it's not up for debate. Either you are on board, or we'll find a replacement for you as well," Gen. Keith McGraw, head of the Top Secret Space Corps, replied firmly and resolutely. Blake looked around the room with consternation and then rotated back to Gen. McGraw.

"Okay, level with me, fully. What's going on, why, and what's the revised game plan? I agree an order is an order, sir, but frankly, I think I'm also due an explanation I can share with my team," Blake countered.

"Major, like I said earlier, this comes straight from President Callahan himself. Although this project remains top secret, President Callahan has been keeping key world leaders up to date on what we have discovered and what we're planning on doing. He has relayed to each of them that we may be on the edge of one of the most monumental milestones in human history since the birth of Christ – that being the discovery of life elsewhere in the universe. The president thought this was simply too big for just the U.S. to be involved, and based on what he declared were the greater principles of humanity, he invited select other countries to join. As part of the agreements to the seven other countries that signed on, under full secrecy, the Pentagon selected representatives from six of them and they have been training together for this mission – just like you and your team have been doing. The seventh country, Japan, did not offer a crewmember, but has still complied with its financial obligations. The new team is also ready to go now, so there will be no delay to the mission. In actuality, since the very beginning, you were the backup team in case the others were not successful in closing their training gaps.

"The fact is, major, you were also going to be recalled. That changed just last week, when the U.K. member, Sir William Davies, was found to have renal cancer and had to be removed from the roster. Unfortunately, the U.K. did not have a viable alternative. That put the French alternative on the table, but they were not willing or capable of putting the necessary funding on the table. Therefore, major, you have remained on the list, but your team is off and will remain off. Only the two pilots, Cmdr. Jack Pavlik and Maj. James Snyder, had guaranteed seats and would have alone represented the U.S. As it is, the U.S. will now have three of the eight positions."

"That seems fair considering the investment the U.S. has already made in this program. Who makes up the remainder of the team?" Blake asked.

"Before we go there, you should also be aware, as I hinted earlier, that a major part of the agreement to join the mission was a requirement that the invited countries had to pay their fair share of the development and operational costs for this mission. The actual numbers are classified, but they are not insignificant – the total cost of this program was too excessive even for the U.S. to go it alone. I can confirm that each commitment was based on numbers with no less than 11 zeroes to the left of the decimal place – and it was cash up front. No cash, no play. They also agreed to forgive significant percentages of debt the U.S. owed each country. These stipulations greatly limited the countries of interest. In addition, the selected countries had to commit to sharing a classified percentage of any future profits they gain from this endeavor with the U.S. So, Blake, in fairness to those countries, an upfront investment of $100 billion, debt reduction, and an agreement to basically pay royalties in perpetuity gave them a fair position to demand they be physically represented on this mission." Gen. McGraw paused to let that message sink in before continuing.

"Yes, Major, I also see this as more of a political and financial decision, and less of the 'greater principle of humanity' message being advertised to the world leaders, but that is what it is. We all painfully know that the U.S. has been on the brink of financial default for many years now. The U.S. debt is currently over $30 trillion and still growing, and that number, as big as it is, is dwarfed when compared to the trillions of dollars associated with the committed debts of Social Security, Medicare and other long-term entitlement systems that the government has overspent and undersaved on. Granted, the rate of growth has slowed from the out-of-control rates following 9/11 and the subsequent financial crash of 2008, but it has continued to increase every year. Our government sees this mission, and the potential technology on the object near Pluto, as a one-time opportunity to escape financial ruin and become the technology banker for the rest of the world. The fortunate fact is that the U.S. is the only country currently capable of reaching that object, which the Pentagon is convinced *is* an alien ship.

"In this one series of moves and agreements, the U.S. debt will be reduced below $20 trillion and financial future value estimates, assuming that new technology is actually discovered on the object, suggest that the U.S. could break even and eliminate the national debt in less than 20 years. Based on that added information, I expect you will understand why the president felt he really didn't have a choice on this issue. The countries that signed up for the trip obviously also see upside for their countries as well. If even a portion of the expectations of this trip are realized, I believe you are looking at the beginning of the new world order and the countries that will lead it for at least the next 100 years. The U.S. must be and will be a part of that picture. If our wildest dreams are realized, then the U.S. will easily continue to maintain its position as world leader, but in addition, it will have a financial ledger cleanly in the black for the first time in over a hundred years."

Gen. McGraw stopped and let Blake fully digest his last few statements. He then continued, looking directly at Blake.

"Maj. Thompson, the other individuals on your new crew are down the hall in the Kennedy Room, waiting to meet with you. For what it's worth, it's a pretty damn impressive group of individuals. The five include Spec. Rakesh Deshpande from India, Maj. Vladimir Popov from Russia, Maj. Jie Gao of China, Spec. Klaus Schneider from Germany and lastly, Lt. Col. Ataullah El-Hashem from Saudi Arabia, representing the Union of Arabic Countries that was created two years ago." Gen. McGraw turned to face the back of the room.

"Captain, please invite them into the room and we'll get activities started."

"A Muslim?" Blake cracked out like a whip. "On this flight? How could …"

"Stop right where you are, major," Gen. McGraw snapped with the intensity that only a general with his experience could do. "I am well aware of your history, as well as your father's. But it stops this second. While the team members are on the way to meet you, I need to know right now, major, and I mean *right now*," the general stated with steely eyes that cut right through Blake, "are you in or out? And 'in' means 100 percent, now and three months from now, that's 100 percent, with zero-point-zero exceptions, major," Gen. McGraw barked.

Blake paused for a few long, quiet seconds, every muscle and tendon in his body as tense as a drum skin, and then locked his eyes on Gen. McGraw.

"Yes, sir, General, message received and agreed to. I am 100 percent on board." Blake paused for one additional second and saluted as he added, "My apologies for not assuming there was a bigger picture, sir." Regardless of how disappointed or angry he was for his team, Blake now knew there really was no other answer.

"Thank you, major, I was confident you would be. And off the record, I would've responded the same way you did. Matter of fact, I did."

Before Blake could respond to the kind words he had never heard uttered from a general's mouth before, the doors opened and five new participants joined the crowd in the conference room. The newly minted crew spent the next three hours introducing each other and starting the "getting to know" process with their new teammate. Blake left the room to clean up before dinner. He reflected on the day's unexpected, surprising and heart-wrenching events and could only shake his head in wonder. Now he had the unenviable assignment to break the news to his *old* team.

*****

Later that night, after Blake's team had wound down from hearing the disheartening news, they headed off to the on-site pub to unwind a little farther. Blake would have loved to join them, but he had less than 48 hours to prepare for the launch to the orbiting space platform where the Armstrong I was docked and waiting. As the group passed by the dormitories, Blake peeled off toward his room while the others continued on to the pub. He still felt like he had abandoned his loyal and dedicated team. As they disappeared into the night, Sean's voice was the last thing Blake heard before entering his lodgings.

"What a bunch of bollocks! They just put a bunch of corner boys on the ship, instead of us; can you believe it, laddies?" Sean piped up.

"So, now what?" Patty replied.

"I don't know," replied Harry. "At this point, I guess the best thing to do is to hang around Control Central in case anything comes up that Blake needs help with."

"You really do amaze me, Harry," she responded. "We just received the biggest letdown of our careers and your immediate response, without complaint, is to start thinking about how to be there if someone still needs our help. There is no better human being than you, Harry. This news sucks for sure, but you are totally right – thank you for reminding us that we were falling into the victim loop." With that, Patty stood on her toes and kissed Harry's cheek. "Count me in. How about the rest of you?"

"Sure," chimed in Li. "When he is millions or billions of kilometers away, besides telling him Sean's latest crappy Irish jokes to boost his morale, I'm not sure there will be much more we can do, but I'm with you."

"I don't know about you guys, and gal, but I really don't have much to say, other than I'm ready for a beer," Diego added. "I've got the first round. You with me?"

"Like ye even 'ave to ask that, really, ya bloke? I'm ready t' be a bogtrotter, so, let's git a movin', laddies, and lass." Sean smiled directly at Patty and genuflected as low as he could.

Patty was a Special Forces killer when the need arose, but if you met her on the street, you would've bet every nickel you had against it, regardless of the going odds. Patty was 1.77 meters tall (5'6") and an athletic 61 kilograms (135 pounds) with shoulder-length brunette hair that curved in at the neck. It was atypical for her to *not* get the proverbial second look from male gawkers when they entered an establishment, and yet she typically shied away from parties. But this was not a party; this was a gathering of her closest friends. Sean had long had a crush on Patty, but never mentioned it to her as he refused to do anything that would jeopardize the working relationship of their team – the team that was now going to be partially separated by distances they had never dreamed possible.

Three rounds of drinks later, a fair serving of fish and chips, and the conversation had gone serious again.

"I know he's the president and such, but … good grief! China? Russia? India? And even the Middle East? No insult intended to the Chinese, Li," Patty spat out as if it had been bottled up for a long, long time and couldn't be restrained any longer.

"None taken, Patty," replied Li. "Fully understood."

"Pretty strong words for you, Patty. Well, don't stop now girl, keep going!" Sean encouraged.

"Thanks, I think. Harry, what do you make of it? I understand the idealistic dream here to be one happy world, and we all start singing 'Kumbaya' together, especially if it helps to pay the bills, but we deal in reality, and the reality is that we just don't all play very well together, and, damn it, we simply don't trust each other. The world just isn't that friggin' mature yet. People and countries still hate each other and we still have wars that kill simply based on differences in religion. Then there are the Arab nations and their representative. For God's sake, I simply can't get past him … do you even realize what his name stands for?"

"Actually, I do," replied Harry. "You may be the linguist of the group, but I have done a little reading before."

"Really, Harry? Ah neva would 'av' seen that comin'!" Sean replied sarcastically.

"Seriously, you really have to wonder if anyone did their homework on these newbies," added Patty.

"The surname of El-Hashem means 'the crusher' and his first name of Ataullah means 'gift of God,' " Harry replied for her.

"And we are letting him on the Armstrong I with Blake so he can blow them all up in the name of Allah? That way, their entire religious base won't go out the window when it's proven that there really are other sources of intelligent life in the universe." Patty was almost yelling by the time she finished. The group went silent in their own thoughts, all wondering what their government had signed up to.

CHAPTER 9

A.D. 2028 (3311 C.A.E.); Nov. 7
Hawaii-Aleutian time zone, Johnston Atoll

The crew was making their final preparations for takeoff from Earth to the orbiting space platform where the Armstrong I was docked. This was their second stop, the eight-hour flight from Houston being the first, to the farthest journey from Earth any human had ever embarked upon. All told, NASA estimated the round trip for this journey would require more than four months of time, there and back.

To ensure the mental and physical health of the crew during such a long journey, the spacious Armstrong I had a small gym with specialized resistance-based equipment each crewmember was required to spend at least one hour per day utilizing. The crew of the Reagan I would have been beyond envy to see the improvements in living conditions that NASA had built into the Armstrong I. In addition, there was a wealth of electronically stored books, periodicals, music recordings and educational materials on the Armstrong I's mainframe computer – all for the crew to access any time they desired. The onboard library also included an extensive educational section the crew was expected to study and test on to ensure they maintained their mental edge; the results of these were radioed back to NASA on a daily basis so that scores of psychologists and scientists could evaluate the crew to determine if they were still mentally healthy, or to identify psychological risk areas that might develop on the long flight. NASA had to make sure that *if* there really were alien beings in the ship, the crew was 100 percent ready, physically, intellectually and emotionally.

Daily news and sports updates would be streamed continuously from each astronaut's home country. One of the biggest challenges to maintaining updated news stories, as well as operational commands, was that the information transmission lag would grow as the distance from Earth increased – more than five hours by the time they reached the object near Pluto. Most of the average populace was unconsciously programmed by grade-school maps of the solar system to think that distances between planets remained constant as textbooks typically depicted planets in a neat, orderly array on the same side of the sun. However, many orbits, including Earth's, were elliptical, rather than perfect circles. That fact alone altered the minimum and maximum distances between the planets, but those differences paled compared to the fact that the planets are rarely aligned in near radial alignment from the sun, instead being distributed around the sun. It might have been common practice in grade school to simplify the picture by representing the distances between planets based on the assumption they were in line, but flight planners and communication specialists had to consider many more variables, almost all of which were a function of changing distances and time. Blake recalled one example in his training modules where the distance between Earth and Pluto, when they were at the closest to each other on the same side of the sun, was more than 5 billion kilometers, but that distance grew to a staggering 7.5 billion kilometers when they were at their farthest separation on opposite sides of the sun. As it took Pluto almost 250 years to orbit the sun, while the Earth did it every 365 days, it meant that there was only one window per year where the two planets would be linearly aligned with each other, which didn't guarantee a shorter distance due to the specific shape of each orbit and the relative positions of each planet within its own orbit relative to the sun.

One key limitation for the crew, a requirement to maintain mission secrecy, was that no one was allowed electronic contact with anyone outside of the Houston Control teams. The primary reason was to ensure secrecy of the mission. Yet, it was also well documented that a reduction in human contact would add to the rigors of a very long and lonely trip, so psychologists had determined that the best way to offset the risks associated with human separation was to ensure that the daily activity of the crew was strictly regimented. Each day was planned with individual and group activities, with exceptions for individual training or personal requirements, such as the daily prayer schedules for Lt. Col. Ataullah El-Hashem. Sundays were left unscheduled, other than critical flight mission requirements, to respect traditional Christian beliefs, as well as to let the crew enjoy some downtime after six long, work-filled days.

In the case of any pending personnel problems, the three Americans had been provided with a one-word code name that could be sent to NASA: Lebanon. Blake, Cmdr. Jack Pavlik and Maj. James Snyder all knew that the military had a system for creating code names that could spit out words that, at first glance, made no sense at all. However, they also knew that once explained, the madmen in Code Name Central typically always had justification. So Blake had questioned it and asked the Houston specialist for the additional insight on why a Middle Eastern country was their emergency code name.

The Houston specialist had smiled, already expecting their question, and launched into a short thesis. As it turned out, the Armstrong I's launch platform was being maintained in a geosynchronous orbit directly above a small park near Lebanon, Kansas. It was at the intersection of AA Road and K-191, accessible by a turn-off from U.S. Route 281,, approximately one mile north of a small town called Lebanon. The little-known park is the central geographical point of the continental U.S. Although there was no way to stop spying from other countries, this location was selected for the space dock to orbit about in order to minimize unintended spying from ground-based systems elsewhere in the world. As it was also a long way from all of the action in Houston and the Johnston Atoll, it was a safe bet that no one would ever jump to a conclusion relative to the true meaning of it. Blake found it ironic that the small town at the geographical center of the United States, in the middle of nowhere, had absolutely no awareness of its importance or anything that was about to happen. The town's name was well known by everyone in Houston Control as it was depicted as the epicenter of the mission on every Houston control chart due to the location of the space dock invisibly located 35,786 kilometers directly above it.

The men had laughed. Even if someone intercepted the transmission, it was obvious that just as Blake had done, their thoughts would immediately migrate to the country of Lebanon. A great diversionary tactic, Blake thought; score one more for the beloved nerds in Code Name Central.

The crew had next been transferred to the Johnston Atoll in the Pacific Ocean. The Space Corps had taken over the small island and abandoned WWII military airport facilities it contained and set up a secret installation for space launches using a relatively new, upgraded military version of the 1980s space shuttle concept, known as the Night Star. Clearly, anyone with satellite technology could monitor launches, see the Night Star and be aware that space-based flights were taking place on the Johnston Atoll, but the public message was consistently re-enforced that the launches were to support the space dock, and various satellite launches that included both military and commercial applications.

That message seemed adequate for the American public, but NASA and the U.S. government knew that the Chinese and Russians had been doing everything they could do get more insight – and now the U.S. government had invited them in with open arms. Definitely an odd set of bedfellows and contradictory positions.

Blake had not recalled hearing about this island and had to pull out maps of the Pacific Ocean to see exactly where this long-lost, but now all-important destination was. The Johnston Atoll was 1,200 kilometers southwest of Hawaii, thereby giving the citizens of that far-flung state the best seat in the house relative to night launches.

Hawaiians knew little about the island except that the U.S government had spread many stories about using the Johnston Atoll as a nuclear test site back in the '60s and '70s as a means of encouraging curious onlookers to keep their distance. Over the years, the atoll had been enlarged many times by the U.S. government by the dredging of coral beds – a technique now deemed illegal due to the increased concern associated with global warming and dying reefs all around the globe. The island continued in total obscurity until 2003, when the atoll was turned over to the Fish and Wildlife Service. However, by 2014, the military decided that perhaps it had better use for the island and took it back permanently.

In 2021, a major expansion had been undertaken that enlarged and re-enforced the 2,750 meter-long runway on the island. Additional structure was built up out of the sea to support offices and living quarters. A launch pad was constructed 1.5 kilometers to the east of the island. Sea barriers had been constructed around the atoll to protect the runway and structures from flooding and wave damage that came with severe storms. For similar reasons, the offices and launch platforms had been built 15 meters above the water line to maintain safety for the personnel and structures – knowledge from the offshore oil industry had greatly aided the building of the sea structures. Over the past decades, offshore oil industries had poured billions of dollars into developing their technology and construction efforts to protect the bloodline of the world: oil. The fact that Uncle Sam could easily borrow that technology was a fact of life that a number of oil CEOs simply had to deal with.

Although there was no realistic option to eliminate spying activity, there was also no reason to make it easier by allowing free rein to the enemy's prying eyes, so the Navy maintained a patrol perimeter with a 60-nautical-mile radius around the island. This distance was based on the line-of-sight capability that the tallest ship in the world had at slightly over 70 meters above the water, in addition to the height of some of the facilities on the island. At a height of 70 meters, the horizon is a little over 30 kilometers away, as compared to someone standing on a beach who can only see five kilometers from the shore. It didn't eliminate spying from planes or satellites, but again, why make it easier than needed? A ship could stay on location for a long time, but a plane had to refuel sooner or later – or risk becoming a reef at the bottom of the ocean next to the WWII-era ships and planes already scattered throughout the Pacific Ocean.

The Night Star launched vertically on a massive fuel rocket, similar to the space shuttle in concept, but the similarities ended there. The Night Star provided much greater independent flight capability than the shuttle, sported a much sleeker profile to enable atmospheric flight and had electronics and software capabilities decades more advanced than the final space shuttle designs, the bulk of which were highly classified. Most pilots referred to the older shuttle as a flying, or better yet, falling brick with an excuse for wings – they weren't too far from the truth. The Night Star was closer to a true airplane, but it used the rocket launch system to facilitate getting to the edge of space quicker. Afterwards, the airplane-like performance allowed for a much safer, better-controlled return to terra firma.

Due to the size of the Armstrong I crew, and the risks still associated with launch disasters, the plan was to ferry the crew up to space in three separate launches. The transport flights were limited to a maximum of six people, including the flight commander, co-pilot and controls specialist. Blake and the two Armstrong I pilots were on the initial launch scheduled to take off in less than two hours. The remaining five Armstrong I crewmembers would be split over two separate flights during the next few days.

As Blake surveyed the deep blue-green waters around him, he couldn't help think of how beautiful this lonely orb in the middle of space really was. Yet, he and seven other handpicked humans were about to leave its beauty and splendor to spend four months in the empty reaches of cold and lifeless space. But then again, Blake reflected, perhaps it wasn't quite as lifeless as they previously thought.

Blake continued to enjoy the warm air and the sounds of the light waves striking the island. In his short time here, he was already beginning to understand and better appreciate the simple life of the Samoans and other Pacific island people. This was a rare beauty and serenity that only a few people, who had the wherewithal to spend thousands of dollars, might visit once in their lives. The Samoans and Polynesians freely experienced it every day.

"Time to go," Blake spoke to the vast ocean of water in front of him. He turned and walked to the elevator to the launch platform. Blake pondered the scope of potentially new worlds that they might be on the verge of learning about. What wonders and beauties would those worlds open up, he speculated. It was a breathtaking moment of possibilities for both a man and the planet's populace, that both believed themselves alone on the most amazing and beautiful of God's creations: planet Earth. And in a short 90 minutes, he would be leaving it behind for a long, long time, hoping to find that God had created many other things the eight men were about to discover.

*****

Hours later

The director of Flight Control took a deep breath and nodded to his flight control engineer.

"Initiate the final countdown." Simultaneously, Blake felt the rumblings of the launch beneath him. The Flight Control engineer began the final countdown ... muscles tensed.

"Ten ... nine ... eight ... seven ... six ... five ... four ... three ... two ... one ..." The sheer energy of the launch was vibrating every cell in Blake's body. A seemingly long pause from the control tower ensued and then Blake heard the long-awaited words: "Ladies and gentlemen! To those who have helped make this possible, and to the crew on board the Night Star; we have liftoff! Liftoff has commenced at 6:17 a.m. Good luck and God bless, gentlemen. Enjoy the ride and we'll see you in a few months."

The Flight Control officer listened to the sounds of the command center as members of the flight management team communicated status. He knew there would be little response from the astronauts as they were currently being pushed back into their seats by the ravenous thrust of the launch engines, to the tune of slightly over three Gs.

Blake had experienced his first launch weeks earlier as part of his pre-mission space training and came to the conclusion during that flight that the English language clearly lacked adequate words to describe both liftoff and space flight to someone who hadn't experienced it. The sheer magnitude of raw power required to lift humankind to the stars was simply beyond words. It was indescribably frightening, yet exhilarating at the same time. A conflict of emotions that added to the unique experience.

Amazingly, the record for rocket thrust was not held by the rocket Blake was currently in. The most famous record had been established, surprisingly, more than 50 years earlier by the powerful Saturn V rocket during the historic Russian-American race to space. The United States, then under the direction of Wernher von Braun and Arthur Rudolph, had designed the Saturn V rocket in the late '60s and manufactured it with the assistance of Boeing, North American Aviation, Douglas Aircraft and IBM. Multiple launches were undertaken, ending in 1973, when the Saturn V had generated a maximum of 7.7 million pounds of thrust to get a payload of 141,000 kilograms (310,000 pounds) into orbit. The historic effort was an acknowledgement of the sheer brilliance of the engineers in that timeframe who did their work with slide rules, something that today's engineers with a room full of powerful computers still seemed unable to equal. In comparison, both the older space shuttle and the current Night Star generated between 6.5 and 7.5 million pounds of thrust with the solid rockets and main ship engines combined.

The record for thrust was nearly equaled in 2018, when Elon Musk launched the Falcon Heavy with 27 individual Merlin engines that generated more than 5 million pounds of thrust and carried more than 63,000 kilograms (140,000 pounds) of payload into space. The Orion Space Launch System finally broke the Saturn V's hold on the thrust record in 2021, by generating an astonishing 8.8 million pounds of thrust on its maiden flight.

The Night Star thrust was so intense that Blake had recalled thinking during his first launch that the rocket had exploded and they were all within seconds of dying. That feeling lasted for the full 8½ minutes of burn until the primary engines shut off. It was a euphoria only experienced by an infinitesimally small number of human beings.

Fifteen minutes later, after the occupants had caught their breath and their heart rates had slowed, Blake softly said, "What an amazing sight," in pure awe of the picture forming outside his forward window.

The white clouds and blue sky were quickly transitioning to black as the rocket moved through inner space to outer space at an altitude of approximately 100 kilometers, the so-called Karman line. The Karman line was named after Theodore von Kármán, a Hungarian-American engineer and physicist who predicted that normal flight was not possible at this altitude because the air was too thin to support aerodynamic lift.

"It's a sight that you can never tire of," Cmdr. Jack Pavlik replied. It was Jack's 12th flight into space. Jack was sitting in the left passenger seat, just ahead of Blake. Maj. James Snyder was to Jack's right. The two Night Star pilots were in front of them in the first row of seats.

Six hours later, at 28,000 kilometers per hour, the Night Star was closing in on the space station orbiting directly above Lebanon, Kansas. The Space Station was at an altitude of 35,786 kilometers in a geosynchronous orbit and traveling at 27,357 kilometers per hour. As the Night Star got closer to the space station, the pilots used reverse thrusters to slow the Night Star down until they matched velocities with the space dock, just prior to docking.

Blake looked out the forward window and could see for the first time in its full glory, the Armstrong I. It was a massive vehicle by earthly space experience. The ship was a full 55 meters long, 5 meters in height and 10 meters in width. It might have looked like a flattened cigar to the inexperienced eye, but it was a thing of beauty to Blake. The ship was mostly black as its shell was manufactured from carbon fiber re-enforced composite panels. However, the ship had long, flowing white lines on it that made it look sleek and fast. There was a large picture of Earth painted on the top of the ship, and along the sides were large flags that represented each of the six countries funding the flight, with the

United States flag at the front and a little larger than the other flags. Blake laughed when he thought of how important President Callahan had said it was to downplay politics and include all the world in this operation, yet still found it okay to make the U.S. flag just a little bigger than the others. All in all, it was a beauty, Blake thought.

The Armstrong I included a full kitchen; an eating area that doubled as a meeting area for the eight crewmembers; a small exercise room; two bathroom facilities, one of which included an innovative weightless shower system; a small library with video capabilities and an expansive control deck that was also capable of seating all eight crewmembers. The Control Deck also contained the flight control computers, multiple video displays, radar systems and the communications command center. The Armstrong I even contained separate living quarters for each crewmember. They were small by earthly standards, at 2 meters in width by 3 meters in length, but luxurious compared to any previous space-faring ships.

As they got closer, Blake saw what looked like gun turrets at various locations around the ship. Blake recalled that these were installed not for warring purposes, but instead to protect the ship against space-borne debris and rocks. It was well documented that space contained a tremendous amount of debris, and although the ship's skin was a full 5 centimeters thick, an unexpected impact of a rock traveling at 20,000 kilometers per hour could slice through the ship like a knife through butter, killing everyone on board.

To increase protection of the ship, a pair of young engineers at the ARL Weapons and Materials Research Directorate (WMRD) had invented, designed and fabricated a novel, automated firing system that was integrated with the radar systems on the Armstrong I. The automated system allowed the ship to detect and fire upon any debris deemed a risk to the ship. In theory, it could take out anything smaller than a meter in diameter. For items larger than a meter, the experts hoped those would be rare enough not to matter, or big enough to be seen early enough to be avoided. The automated firing system was based on the U.S. Navy's Phalanx anti-missile defensive system that could fire up to 4,500 rounds per minute. The Space Corps scuttlebutt quickly dubbed it "Asteroids," after the famous 1979 Atari video game classic. Disappointingly, there had been no way to trial the system in space before launching the Armstrong I due to the accelerated schedule once the object near Pluto had been discovered. As they would not have the ability to reload prior to the launch, the option of conducting a single test fire was also not approved. Blake was not thrilled about the highly touted system that he saw as more of a research and development trial, but there really weren't any other options, other than not having it.

*****

A.D. 2028 (3311 C.A.E.); Nov. 13
Pluto orbit

Forty days had passed since the "great revival," as Juulys was referring to it. The crew was quickly moving beyond restless, and the battle against despair was becoming a daily checklist item. Nothing had been received from Cjar. No messages, no signals, nothing. No progress had been achieved on breaking the code to initiate the main drive engines or the Q-PAMs drive either. Thjars knew that panic or despair would set in soon without something to rally around. He needed to keep the crew focused, but the only thing he could think of that offered any form of hope, however slim, was the third planet. He gathered the crew together on the control deck after dinner.

"I wish you were all here for me to provide you with better news about the ship, but we have yet to achieve any success with the encrypted codes. Glysst knows that Jarns, Cryells and Allympht have been working day and night to break the code, or find a path around it." Thjars surveyed the tired-looking group in front of him. Half the group had their heads bowed toward the floor and weren't even looking at Thjars.

"Juulys, our biggest hope may reside with you. What have you been able to decipher from the third planet?"

"Actually, Thjars, that's a rather timely question." Juulys knew where the lieutenant was heading and she knew she had to help provide some positive news to keep the crew from sliding into depression, or worse. Everyone looked up at Juulys.

"I still can't translate the signals we are hearing, but they are clearly non-natural. Not only is there life on the third planet, but it is undeniably intelligent, and abundant. There is help there if we can figure out how to interact with them." Juulys' smile on the last comment excited most in the room as she swept from one set of eyes to the next.

"But, there's nothing out *here*, or anywhere near us, Juulys." Knarls jumped in and interrupted Juulys. "I appreciate your effort to provide some hope for the group, but now is not the time to start creating false pretensions. I'd rather know the facts, Juulys."

"Actually, Knarls, I am giving you the facts."

"We're all ears, Juulys; what have you found?" Thjars tried to rein the group back in before Knarls created mass panic. "Have a seat, Knarls; let's hear her out."

"Well, first off, we've known for weeks that there is a tremendous amount of radio activity on the third planet, and as expected, there are extreme concentrations of signals emanating from focal points on the major land masses, likely their major cities. But I can now say with confidence that the inhabitants of the third planet have also mastered atmospheric flight based on signal paths I've traced over what appears to be very large bodies of water separating the land masses. At least half, if not well more than half of the planet's surface appears to be covered by water."

"But, how can you tell they have atmospheric flight?" Thjars added, attempting to set up validation for her. As he looked around, he could clearly see that it was working – everyone was now looking at Juulys, laser-focused, eager to hear what she would say next.

"There are distinct lines of electromagnetic traces across the large expanses of water. Granted, it is possible that these are vehicles that may float on the water's surface, but the change in position of the signals is very fast, more than 800 kilometers per hour, so I think it's fair to assume that they are based on atmospheric flight."

"That is good news." Sergeant-at-Arms Qulys Plyenysst jumped in. "Great work, Juulys. What else can you tell us about *them*?"

Bingo, she thought. We've got the crew for at least a little longer – now for the punch line.

"Yes, actually there is." Juulys paused long enough to ensure she had everyone's undivided attention. "I also have conclusive evidence that they have achieved space flight."

The group broke into loud exchanges of excitement. Juulys waited a few moments to let that sink in as she looked at Thjars.

"Sorry, Thjars, I should have let you know first, but to be honest, I wasn't ready to believe it yet myself. Only today did I finally conclude it is real, and then … well, you asked," she smiled.

"That's fine, Juulys, we're all in this together. Go on," he replied.

"I've been tracking signals near the fourth planet as well. These signals were approaching the planet when we first awakened 30 or 40 days ago. At first, I thought we might have been seeing signs of a second alien life group, but that changed. The signals remained near the fourth planet for a number of days, but as of a few days ago, the signals are now separating from the fourth planet – and heading directly back towards the third planet."

The crew broke into pandemonium.

"Easy, everyone. This is great news, I agree, but it also appears that their travel speeds are way too slow to reach our area of space in a reasonable time. I estimate that the signals are moving between the third and fourth planets at approximately 28,000 kilometers per hour, far less than one tenth of one percent of light speed. At that rate, it would take *years* to reach us, assuming we could contact them and convince them that we're here. I will know more by monitoring them over the next few weeks, but from what I can estimate right now, it will take them at least 300 days to return to the third planet."

It was like dropping a bomb in the room. Sheer joy suddenly changed to total silence, and despair again fought its way back into the group. Juulys was losing them.

"We could be dead by the time they could figure out how to get here. To sit here and know there's life in sight, but not be able to do anything about it, to just sit here and rot in space ..." Knarls was losing it.

Thjars knew he needed to re-enforce Juulys' more positive message and get the crew back together again, but Qulys beat him to it, interrupting Knarls with a very terse directive.

"Soldier, get a grip on yourself, or I'll get a grip on you and sit your ass down promptly." Qulys shot his statement across the room with the authority only a seasoned drill sergeant could muster. "Okay Juulys, what do we need to do?" Nobody dared to screw with the old man; they all knew he was one of the toughest and most dependable sergeant at arms in the Cjarian space fleet, and for good reason. Qulys might have been 125 years old, but he was one tough customer and when he drew a line on the deck, no one dared cross it. Knarls sat down.

"Thanks, Qulys. We are definitely not out of options. Matter of fact, this is actually good news in my opinion. We actually have a lot to hope for and a lot to do. Honestly, for the first time, I'm beginning to think we have a real chance," she added with enthusiasm, but it still wasn't enough to move her fellow crewmembers as she had earlier.

"Look, radio waves are still radio waves – and they should take no more than five hours to reach the third planet, and another five hours for their response to reach us. We just need to figure out who we should be communicating with, how to get their attention and then how to start communicating with them in a manner they understand. It may be that we could help them close their technology gap and build a ship that could come rescue us."

Qulys jumped back into the discussion.

"Thjars, we need to be careful here. I agree with Juulys' optimism, but I think the most important question is determining *who* we want to contact. We know nothing about the entities on the other end of these signals. I think we need to focus more of our efforts on translating their speech and video signals and then, and only then, try to assess who we want to contact - and *IF* we want to contact them. Glysst knows we wouldn't think there could be another race as aggressive and demented as the Klaxx, but we don't know that yet."

Everyone in the room caught the full intent of his words and nodded acknowledgement.

"Well stated, Qulys, and I agree. Okay, everyone, let's get back to work. Cracking and translating these signals is now our number one priority. Cryells, Allympht and Jarns, you three continue working the codes for the drives and control systems. Everyone else, get with Juulys and she will provide you assignments to support her with those translations." Thjars sent the crew back to work. He wasn't totally happy with the meeting, but he wasn't totally disappointed, either. He reflected that he, Qulys and Juulys may have just bought them another week or two of focus.

CHAPTER 10

A.D. 2028 (3311 C.A.E.); Nov. 14
Earth, orbiting space dock

The space dock was a construction marvel. A labyrinth of passages and modules that housed the various living spaces, operational centers and maintenance hubs and were all oriented along a tube-like configuration. The Armstrong I was located directly in the middle of the tube or tunnel area. At any given time, personnel could look down on the Earth, as well as watch the construction activities on the ship. It was a scene straight out of "Star Trek," except for the fact that the Armstrong I looked nothing like the famous Enterprise. Blake spent the few spare hours he had floating through the various sections of the dock and talking to the technicians and engineers who had built the Armstrong I. He was interested in their perspective of the design as a comparison to the engineers back on Earth who would never even touch the ship. But the time to be a tourist and ask questions had come to an end and Blake and the other astronauts were getting ready to board and launch the Armstrong I.

Each crewmember had been authorized to bring personal electronic devices that had various software and personal items preselected and preloaded, including pictures, games, books, and other personal preferences. One month prior to takeoff, the devices had been required to have their wireless systems removed and all content and software checked out extensively to ensure there would be no risk of ship interference or damage. To further ensure the devices remained safe and unaltered, the devices were then stored in a locked cabinet on board the ship that was not opened until 48 hours after departure from the space dock. The latter requirement was to ascertain that the ship was far enough away from the space dock so that nothing could be sent to their personal electronic devices, regardless of the state of the wireless system.

In addition to their personal devices, as the crew prepped to enter the Armstrong I, each crewmember was assigned three iPad-like devices, one primary and two for backup during the long flight. Each unit had a built-in, shipboard-limited, wireless system that enabled them to communicate with each other, access a number of preloaded apps for investigations and other apps required to interface with the ship. Access was granted for all shipboard systems, except for the environmental living, flight control and propulsion systems – those functions were limited to the two pilots and Blake. The devices were hermetically sealed, shockproof and waterproof, fully capable of operation even in the vacuum of space. Although they were not the ultra slim likeness of their Earth-side counterparts, they were still smaller than Blake expected them to be. The device framework included both a Velcro strap that could be used to mount to one's wrist, as well as a mechanical connect/disconnect system that would allow the unit to be worn on a space suit. The spacesuits had specially designed fingertips that could activate the typing functions as simply as their exposed fingers could. The device framework was also lightly magnetized to enable it to be mounted to the ship's wall, thereby allowing it to provide a light source while leaving the crewmembers' hands free to work. They were pretty cool devices, Blake reflected, but then again, at a cool $100,000 each, they ought to be. The devices were officially called Man Portable Communication devices, or MPoCs for short. Regardless of the fancy names and acronyms that the device supplier or NASA had given them, Blake and the crew had all laughed that their governments were not capable of just calling them phones or something simple; instead, there always had to be some cold, mechanical name given to everything. After much discussion, they all preferred to call them their "Little brother" or LB for short. It was a humorous reference to George Orwell's fictional character, Big Brother, in his book "1984." Blake had to explain it to Jie Gao and Ataullah El-Hashem, but once they heard the connection, they were sold. As it turned out, each crewmember had a similar name based on their own country's government and sarcastic humor, but Little Brother stuck, so they all used it.

Ninety minutes later, suited up with their LBs activated, the crew were in their launch seats aboard the Armstrong I. Technicians were going through the final checklist to get ready for the launch that would take the eight-man crew to the orbit of Pluto. Few words were exchanged among the crewmembers as each dealt with the upcoming trip in their own private manner. They all had a common and conflicting set of emotions, simultaneously dealing with the apprehension of the unknown, the long time away from home, or even Earth for that matter, versus the excitement of what they might discover. Like the others, Blake forced himself not to focus on the length of time they would be away from Earth, the excitement of the potential of finding extraterrestrial life, or the potential dangers that lay ahead. Instead, he and the others focused on the "here and now," the details that had to be completed before they could even start the journey. But at this point the training was over, and he was truly tired of waiting: Blake was ready to move.

"Take your places," Joe Dodd commanded everyone in launch central on the orbiting launch platform. Joe had been the director of the Armstrong I Design and Build Teams and was granted the privilege of overseeing the actual launch sequence, an honor he was thoroughly enjoying even though this was his first trip in space and he was still trying to find his space legs. "Cmdr. Pavlik. Any words of wisdom you'd like to share?"

"Actually, yes, there are, but they aren't mine, so I'd like to defer to Maj. Thompson, who was voicing his thoughts to Maj. Snyder just last night." Cmdr. Pavlik turned around, smiled at Blake and extended his hand, signaling Blake that the floor was his.

"Thank you, commander, I am honored, and I surely did not expect to provide the launch speech for this momentous occasion, but I will attempt to do it justice." Blake paused to collect his thoughts. "Ladies and gentlemen. We are on the verge of a new era for the human race that may include multiple, historic, first-of-a-kind leaps for humankind. This may indeed become the single biggest year in human history since the discovery of fire. And it may very well define humankind's future for the next 2,000 years." Blake paused. "We cannot take our responsibilities lightly, nor can we assume that our part of this mission is any greater than that of the thousands of dedicated people who have worked without fanfare for years to make this a reality. I proudly dedicate the Armstrong I and this mission to those people, their labors and their dreams. We, the crew of the Armstrong I, are honored and humbled to be given the opportunity to carry your work and dreams into the future. God bless you and God bless this journey. We will see you in four short months."

The next voice that was heard, unexpectedly, surprised everyone. It was President Callahan himself. Due to technical difficulties with communication equipment over the past two days, no one had expected the president to be able to provide the historic launch speech – something NASA had taken significant heat for. Somewhere, a worn-out IT team would surely sleep better tonight.

"Maj. Thompson, I am thoroughly impressed. I had a speech written and ready to go, but winging it from your hip, you just out-wrote my own speech team, and out-speeched me. Congratulations for a job well done – hear, hear! But based on that speech, I must question if you are gearing up for a run at the White House upon your return!" The president and everyone else on line shared a hearty laugh. The president then continued. Obviously, as Blake and everyone else on board already knew, no president ever born, or yet to be born, would ever miss the chance to add their own words to an historic occasion.

"The first new step for humankind that Maj. Thompson spoke of is the launch of this mission on the Armstrong I, a manned flight to the edge of the known solar system, where only the unmanned Voyager probes have gone before. The second new step is the maiden flight of a technology that will open a new age for humankind's exploration of space, something that was previously only dreamed about in science fiction. The third new step may be one long flight in human terms, but one short historical milestone in humankind terms, the interaction with extraterrestrial life. An event that carries the weight and opportunity to alter the path of humankind's awareness, knowledge, and actions forever." The president allowed for a long pregnant pause for that last message to sink in. "As Maj. Thompson so eloquently hinted, the eight brave men of Armstrong I carry the dreams and hopes of the 8 billion people of Earth with them, most of whom are currently unaware of this historic trip, but someday soon will be. Furthermore, their future existence may, indeed, depend on the actions and interactions that each of these eight men will be responsible for. Finally, in the famous words of Scott Carpenter: Godspeed, gentlemen. We will be with you in mind, heart and spirit, and pray that God oversees every day of your historic journey."

"Thank you, sir. Well stated." Cmdr. Jack Pavlik broke in. "Not to chat and run, sir, but in the famous words of Scott's crewmate Alan Shepard, it's time to *light this candle!*" Laughter erupted as everyone connected his order to the infamous 1961 line from Alan Shepard when he had been waiting, uncomfortably, for hours on the Freedom 7 launch pad – a line made even more famous in the 1983 movie "The Right Stuff."

With that, the astronauts buckled up and the flight engineers and technicians left the Armstrong I and returned to the Orbital Control Center, or OCC for short.

"OCC, we are ready for separation and initiation of thrust," Cmdr. Pavlik stated as calmly as if he were leaving to get a cup of coffee.

"On your order," the OCC voice replied.

"Disconnecting in three ... two ... one ... we have disconnection," Pavlik verified.

"Engage thrusters and move to two kilometers."

"Thrusters engaged," replied Maj. Snyder.

The Armstrong I began to separate from the orbiting docking station, slowly at first, but picking up speed. What seemed like an eternity of seconds passed, and Maj. Snyder finally broke the intense silence.

"Separation distance of two kilometers achieved."

"Blake, would you like to do the honors again?" Jack Pavlik turned around and asked Blake. The two of them had become close over the past two months, creating a bond based on mutual respect of what they had accomplished in the military and what the two men stood for.

"Thank you, Jack, but you already did that, remember? It's all yours. Besides, I don't want to be responsible if we scrape the paint on President Callahan's new ship before we even get out of Earth's orbit."

Even the president chuckled at Blake's parting comment.

"I really do feel like I'm in an old 'Star Trek' series … Ready, captain." Maj. Vladimir Popov chuckled as he attempted a near perfect imitation of Pavel Chekov to Capt. Kirk.

"Okay, Chekov, take us … out there," Pavlik boldly stated as he waggled his hand toward the forward window.

The crew all shared in another light chuckle.

After pushing a series of buttons, Maj. Snyder initiated the solar sail as everyone watched in anticipation. The technology had been tested many times in smaller scale, and even on smaller unmanned craft like the NASA Sunjammer in 2014, but this was the first full-scale deployment on a manned craft, as well as the first time any of the crew had ever seen the equipment deployed in real life.

Blake watched out the windows, and simultaneously on the monitors, as the cosmic wonder unfolded in front of them. It was like a gigantic kid's erector set on steroids, Blake thought. First, the outer shell of the ship seemed to split on the top side of the ship and a mechanical arm that was at least 20 meters long and a half-meter in diameter slowly emerged from the gap. The arm slid forward along the flight line of the ship until it was directly in front of the ship's nose. A manmade umbilical cord approximately 15 centimeters in diameter was attached to the end of the mechanical arm and to the nose of the Armstrong I in a tripod format.

Next, a small reflective set of panels, similar to a drogue parachute that extracts the primary parachute in atmospheric applications, began to unfurl from the far end of the arm, the farthest position from the ship. Once locked in place, the solar panels extended a full five meters and the light force on the drogue sail began to deploy the rest of the structure as the musical sounds of "Also Sprach Zarathustra," the song made famous by the 1968 movie "2001: A Space Odyssey," streamed out of the control deck speakers.

Blake laughed. "Wow, you guys thought of everything for this roll out. Thanks, guys, well done and greatly appreciated," he relayed to the OCC.

"No problem, gentlemen, we're enjoying it on this end as well," replied the OCC director. "It's pretty impressive from this angle. We flipped coins between this and the 1986 classic song, 'The Final Countdown' by the band Europe, but we got a little hung up on the word 'final'."

"Good decision," replied Pavlik with a chuckle.

As the crew and OCC watched, the structure continued to unfold itself and move farther away from and ahead of the ship. It was an amazing sight to behold. Approximately 15 minutes later, the structure was fully deployed and looked like a mammoth umbrella structure without the protective canvas on it.

The diamond-shaped structure was a full 500 meters to a side and was positioned 400 meters in front of the ship.

"The grid is locked in place," Maj. Snyder relayed to Cmdr. Pavlik. "Approval requested to deploy the first phase of light sail panels."

"Approval granted," replied the commander.

The deployment was dependent on the selected speed and auto-controlled by the onboard ship computers. If the entire sail were deployed at one time, the sudden force would risk failing the carbon-fiber based umbilical cord and could separate the sail from the ship. As complicated as the grid was, the umbilical cord was even more complex. It was fabricated from millions of strands of continuous carbon fiber and rumored to have cost more than $200 million.

The grid was separated into thousands of individual panels. As an increase in speed was requested, the computer slowly deployed additional panels to manage the acceleration forces. As the distance from the sun increased, the amount of sail required to increase velocity would also have to be increased because the energy from the sun, per square meter, decreased as a ship traveled away from the sun. In the case of the Armstrong I and its nuclear reactor, however, the ship also had the ability to apply a laser beam to the sail to make up for lost energy from the sun.

As the crew watched, hundreds of panels in various, but symmetric areas of the grid were deployed and the ship began to accelerate.

"This is both mesmerizing and absolutely amazing," Maj. Jie Gao spoke out to no one in particular.

Blake recalled that the Sunjammer had a maximum solar sail area of 1,200 square meters. The Armstrong I, which had taken five years to construct once the design had been completed, had a maximum solar sail area of 250,000 square meters, a staggering increase. He wondered if the NASA engineers really knew the max speed of this technological wonder, or if they were simply estimating.

The Sunjammer, named after a solar-sailing spaceship in an Arthur C. Clarke short story, and the Armstrong I sail both used Kapton for the sail material to minimize system weight. The structural elements were made from carbon-fiber re-enforced composites. In contrast, the Sunjammer sail system had weighed only 32 kilograms, while the monster attached to the Armstrong I tipped the scales at slightly less than 8,000 kilograms. As significant as the added weight of the sail was, it was still much less than what would have had to be carried in the form of fuel to make the roundtrip journey. Even considering the fuel-saving sail, the Armstrong I still had to carry a significant amount of fuel to be used for near-station maneuvering, slowing down, emergency power assuming the sail malfunctioned and finally for the return flight home when the sail would be too inefficient by itself. In comparison, the space shuttle launch weight was actually more than 90 percent fuel. By constructing the Armstrong I in space and utilizing the space sail technology, the fuel to total weight ratio had been greatly reduced, to approximately 65 percent of the Armstrong I's massive bulk.

This ratio was still larger than designers had hoped for, as their initial target design had been 50 percent, but that changed with the realization that the return trip would require the utilization of a nuclear reactor that was in turn coupled with a new laser system developed at the National Ignition Facility (NIF), a laser test facility at Lawrence Livermore National Laboratory in Livermore, Calif. Scientists had spent the last decade developing a "laser octopus," as it had become known within Lab confines. The laser was actually an array of lasers that could be turned on singularly, in clusters, or all at once. The lasers were combined with an ingenuous invention that consisted of a second array made of prisms that looked like giant cut diamonds. Each prism was approximately 25 centimeters in diameter and individually controllable within a small three-dimensional v--vspace, as well as possessing a plus/minus five degrees of rotation about any of its axes. Independently, the lasers could create a combined burst of more than two mega joules. That level of energy, if focused, was so intense that it could obliterate a given section of the solar sail, so scientists were able to decouple and defocus the lasers, while achieving less than 5 percent energy loss. This also allowed a more effective spreading of the energy across the entire solar sail, or selected portions of the sail, thereby enabling the sail to be set to a desired speed even in the absence of light from the sun. The control system and software behind the system, known as the Dual Phased Array Laser Distribution System, or D-PALDS for short, was a technological breakthrough in itself.

Blake and the crew had thought long and hard about the light sail and the options they would or would not have if something went wrong. Historically, NASA was famous for using quadruple redundant safety systems in case something failed in space, as nearby repair stations were not exactly an option. In this case, however, with the fact that the laser system had not yet been proven capable of returning the ship home totally on its own accord, there was no guarantee of return if the sail suffered a major failure, and it was definitely not feasible to store a replacement sail on the ship. Instead, all of the crew had been taught how to repair the sail so that a return trip to Earth could be assured. Blake and the others were not too confident about the "assured" probabilities, but that wasn't why someone did or did not sign up for an opportunity like this. Blake firmly believed that if someone were uncomfortable with the level of risk in a given mission, they shouldn't have signed up in the first place.

"*Do svidaniya*," Maj. Vladimir Popov spoke softly while looking back at the OCC.

"Excuse me?" Blake asked.

"That was 'goodbye' in Russian," Popov added, looking over at Blake. "It seems to me that we were thrust together in such a way that we really don't know each other as well as most cosmonauts would. And yet, we have no choice but to work together for the next few months or more, *da*?"

"You are correct, major. So, how do you propose we break the ice, Vladimir, with some Russian vodka?" Blake said, chuckling.

"Actually, yes, my Special Forces friend, I know your history well. I myself am a 10-year Spetsnaz veteran." Popov got up from his chair and left.

"Okay, Blake, what did you say to upset our new Russian ally?" Pavlik lobbied over to Blake.

"Um, no clue, Jack. I sure hope I didn't start a new international incident less than an hour out of dock."

A minute later, Popov returned with a shiny, decorative metal container. "Let me share some of Mother Russia's treasures with you so that we may start this trip the right way. Speeches are speeches, but Russian vodka? That is a celebration!"

Blake let out an intentionally large breath of relief, and everyone laughed heartily. With that, Popov opened the container to expose a small, specially designed bottle of Stolichnaya vodka and eight small, equally specially designed shot glasses.

"We toast, to the flight and to a future that could make many positive changes for all of our countries."

Popov poured the precious vodka into the glasses, designed to encapsulate the vodka during the pouring process, and then handed them out, one at a time. Each had a port for drinking. He then looked over at Lt. Col. Ataullah El-Hashem thoughtfully.

"Lt. Col. El-Hashem, is this within bounds for you? I do not wish to insult you or any religion of the world. I am sure that I can find a substitute in the galley if need be."

"Maj. Popov, your thoughtfulness is most appreciated, and respected. I do believe that given the circumstances, Allah would be understanding, especially as I do not intend to overindulge. At the same time, I do not want to insult you or the customs of anyone else aboard this ship. I am truly honored by both your offer and your understanding. Thank you, sir," and Ataullah took the glass with a nod. "Please feel free to call me Ataullah."

"An honor that is mine as well, Ataullah. *Zdorov'ye*, comrades, salute." Popov smiled, held his glass aloft, put the port to his mouth and then drank it empty. Blake and the others followed suit.

"This trip is looking better all the time," Maj. James Snyder offered as he emptied his glass. "Excellent choice, Vladimir."

"I'm not going to ask how you ever managed to get that on board, Vladimir, nor would I even think of reporting it, but I do hope that you managed to store away a little more of your Russian contraband for this long trip." Blake challenged the Russian with a not-so-innocent chuckle.

"Ahh, but only time will tell, major." Popov smiled and leaned back in his seat.

"So tell me, major, you seem to know a lot more about me, than I of you," Blake tempted the Russian.

"For that matter, I guess that's the same for all of us. I'm pretty confident that the dossiers we received on each other only scratched the surface of our backgrounds," added Ataullah. "In addition, ever since the first day, you've all been looking at me like I belong to the Taliban, especially you, Maj. Thompson. And, by the way, the Taliban has never resided within Saudi Arabia. So, how about we get that on the table first?"

"Well, I can't fault your openness Ataullah; I'd be lying if I hadn't thought that myself," Spec. Rakesh Deshpande blurted out as if he had been waiting to say it for a long time.

Rather than speak and say something he would later regret, Blake simply nodded to acknowledge the moment. Neither of Ataullah's comments about Blake, nor Blake's non-verbal response, was lost on anyone. There was definitely a hint of tension in the air, but everyone decided to let it remain unspoken.

For the next eight hours, the group talked, discussed, proposed, debated, shared and challenged each other on topics ranging from family and work experience to politics and religion, all while Cmdr. Pavlik maintained one ear on their conversations, but focused the rest of his senses on his flight duties. When all was said and done, the crew had a newfound respect for each other and had gotten closer than all of the preflight training and gatherings had been able to accomplish. Blake looked over the group and thought it really was an impressive slate of astronauts.

Rakesh Deshpande was 29 years old and an expert computer specialist. He hailed from the state of Maharashtra on the western side of India, not too far from Mumbai, one of the wealthiest states in India. Rakesh was a devout Hindu, and the middle child of three siblings. Both his mother and father were medical doctors. Rakesh had been married, but lost his wife in a car accident before they were able to have children. He joined military operations shortly after her death and never looked back. Prior to that, Rakesh attended Mumbai University, within the biggest city in Maharashtra, to attend its prestigious computer science program and graduated top of his class in the master's program. He then received his Ph.D. at Oxford University in the U.K. before meeting his future wife. They relocated back to India and were both employed by TATA Consultancy Services until his wife's death. When the chance opened up for him to join India's fledgling space program, Rakesh jumped on it immediately. Rakesh also loved sports, especially cricket, but had recently begun following American football, with a special liking for the Miami Dolphins.

Lt. Col. Ataullah El-Hashem, 43, was a veteran F-16 pilot in the Saudi Arabian Air Force. An only child, at the age of 13, he and his family moved from Sana'a, Yemen, the capital of Yemen, to the border town of Sharorah, Saudi Arabia, and then to Riyadh, the capital of Saudi Arabia, when he had turned 17 to attend the Imam Muhammad bin Saud Islamic University, where he received a B.S. in mechanical engineering. Ataullah had also studied Quran studies extensively at the Imam University from 2005-2010.

Major Jie Gao, 27, was a missions specialist in the China National Space Administration (CNSA). He had been scheduled to be on the initial crew to open the Chinese Space Station this year, but had been requested to join the Armstrong I mission instead. At first, he had been concerned that he was being demoted, until the general secretary of the Communist Party had spoken to him in person, explaining the importance of this trip and how China could not be left behind by the United States. Jie was an only child and a devout Chinese dominoes player, which he thought would come in handy on this long flight.

Klaus Schneider, 38, was an astronomer at the Max-Planck-Institut für Astronomie, (MPIA), a research institute of the Max Planck Society in Heidelberg, Baden-Württemberg, Germany. Klaus was married and the father of two children, both in high school. It had been a tough decision for him to miss almost six months of his children's high school years, especially without being able to explain the secret mission to his family. He'd left behind a less-than-happy family, and that remained the case until two weeks later, when the chancellor of Germany personally stopped by their house and explained that Klaus was on a crucial assignment for Germany, at the chancellor's request. That was the best get-out-of-jail-free card anyone could receive. In his younger days, Klaus had been a semi-pro football player, trying out for the FC Bayern Munich team in the Bundesliga league some 18 years ago. He had made it through the initial cuts, but was heartbroken to be eliminated on the final day of roster cuts. He played in the minor leagues for a few years before starting a family and working at MPIA.

Major Vladimir Popov, 39, was a major in the Russian Spetsnaz GRU and had conducted many secret Ops in Chechen. Vladimir had grown up in St. Petersburg and was a lifelong hockey enthusiast. His hockey dreams were realized when he played three years as a defender with the SKS Saint Petersburg hockey team in the Russian Super League. Vladimir had subsequently studied chemical engineering at Lomonosov Moscow State University. Vladimir, a master chess player, had also won the annual chess championship three years in a row while he was in the 2nd Independent Spetsnaz Brigade. Vladimir was also married, to a fellow Spetsnaz Special Forces member.

USAF Cmdr. Jack Pavlik, 32, had majored in mathematics at the USAF Academy in Colorado, flown F-117 stealth fighters, and been on two tours in the Middle East with the 9th F-117 Fighter squadron. Jack had grown up in Traverse City, Mich., where he always looked and acted like an All-American kid. He'd been the class president and captain of his high school hockey team. Now in his early thirties, he still sported the boyish smile that had endeared him to so many through the years.

USMC Maj. James Snyder, 42, looked exactly as you would expect a 20-year Marine veteran to look: serious, leathered skin, tough as nails, dependable, and one calm and cool customer under any conditions. James came from a long line of Marine Corps members including his older brother, father, grandfather and great-grandfather; all had seen action at one time or another around the world. His grandfather had been in both Guadalcanal and Iwo Jima during WWII and was awarded a Silver Star. James, himself, had endured five tours in Afghanistan and Iraq, as well as a number of other locations on the planet that remained classified to this day.

It truly was an impressive team.

CHAPTER 11

A.D. 2028 (3311 C.A.E.); Dec. 1
Aboard Armstrong I

After two weeks on board, one thing was certain: all had given up trying to beat Vladimir Popov at chess, even Blake. The man was a machine, or perhaps a computer, Blake had joked. No one had even come close to besting the Russian. It was then that Maj. Jie Gao suggested that perhaps everyone try a *simpler,* more friendlier game of Chinese dominoes.

"I smell a setup," Vladimir said as he eyed his Chinese companion with a twinkle in his eye.

"Dominoes are as simple or complex as you care to make them, and there are many, many game forms so that one will never tire," replied Jie.

Jie explained that Chinese dominoes are used in several tile-based games, namely, Tien Gow, Pai Gow, Tiu U and Kap Tai Shap. In Cantonese, they are called "Gwat Pai," which literally means "bone tiles"; it is also the name of a northern Chinese game, but the rules are quite different from the southern Chinese game Tien Gow. He added that references to Chinese domino tiles could be traced all the way back to writings from the Song Dynasty in A.D. 1120.

Jie went on for the next 10 minutes to further explain that the tile set contained two each of 11 civilian suit tiles (6-6, 1-1, 4-4, 1-3, 5-5, 3-3, 2-2, 5-6, 4-6, 1-6, 1-5) and one each of 10 military suit tiles (3-6, 4-5; 2-6, 3-5; 2-5, 3-4; 2-4; 1-4, 2-3; 1-2). Each civilian tile also had a Chinese name (and common rough translation to

English): The 6-6 is tin (heaven), 1-1 is dei (Earth), 4-4 is yan (man) …

"Whoa! Hold on Jie, how about a rulebook; it will take me some reading to keep up with you!" Rakesh held up his hands.

On the other hand, Vladimir was truly looking excited.

"I never dreamed dominoes could be so challenging. You and I need to talk my good friend, Jie." Vladimir and Jie headed off to develop training material, but of course, Vladimir's primary interest was to make sure he learned first, and the most.

Blake looked around; each of the crew was becoming more comfortable with his daily routines.

Rakesh was reading an Indian novel in his iLibrary called "The White Tiger" by Aravind Adiga. The state-of-the art on the iPad and other competitive tablets had become so extensive that Apple had finally retired the iPad moniker and launched the new iLibrary. Rakesh was an avid reader, and his new 10 TB iLibrary could hold millions of books and songs, so it was doubtful he would be left wanting for any reading material on even this long journey.

Klaus Schneider was on the flight deck with Cmdr. Jack Pavlik monitoring star clusters as well as keeping a log of the object they were flying out to rendezvous with. Although many were watching it, nothing had changed relative to the object in the weeks since they had departed from Earth.

Maj. James Snyder was sleeping in preparation for his turn at the controls, so that Cmdr. Pavlik could then rest.

Ataullah looked over at Blake. "Well, it's just you and me, Blake. How about a game of backgammon?"

"Sure, my friends and I played it for years. I didn't know you had games like backgammon in Saudi."

"Ah, but you do not know your history very well, Maj. Thompson. Backgammon was actually invented in Arabia over 5,000 years ago."

"Well, I'll be … I never knew that," Blake replied. "Do you actually have a set with you, or are we confined to playing on the computer?"

"I am confident that we are each guilty of requesting special contraband from our countries of origin; and mine is this." Ataullah pulled a small 25-centimeter-long, 15-centimeter-wide, 2- centimeter thick box out of his pocket and opened it, unfolding it into a miniature backgammon playing board, outfitted with two miniature dice. The game was beautifully adorned, yet had a distinct look of age and antiquity.

"Is it safe to assume this is a family heirloom, Ataullah?"

"Your history of games may be poor, but your powers of observation are excellent, major." Ataullah broke into a wide smile. "This game has been handed down through many generations of my family. It is, indeed, a priceless heirloom to me. You can only imagine how hard it was for me to agree to modify it with magnets to ensure the pieces would not float off into the ship. The dice are to be shaken in this flexible tube and once you pull on the two ends of the tube, it will constrict the dice and then you read the numbers that are under the blue stripe."

"Ingenious. Whoever would have thought of space dice, let alone make and sell them?" Blake queried Ataullah.

"Well, Blake, that would be me. Perhaps I should patent them, yes? Although I doubt there would be a very big demand for sales." They both laughed, and Blake proposed that Ataullah, as the master inventor, should be the first to "roll" the dice in the actual first game of space backgammon.

And with that, the friendly competition began. Blake and Ataullah spent the next two hours playing backgammon, but more importantly, getting to know each other. Blake found Ataullah to be a proud and very religious man. The two men talked in length and detail about the continued struggles within the Middle East and the territories that were shared by Christians, Jews and Muslims. Both men found it unacceptable that indiscriminate killings continued.

"Don't get me wrong, Maj. Thompson, I love my country and I believe in my Quran, but I do not support the fanatical killings that seem to spawn so easily from my culture. I find it to be both a curse and an embarrassment to an otherwise proud and tradition-based society. At the same time, I also feel that the lack of understanding the West has demonstrated of our culture has led to decisions that fanned the fires of hatred and extremism. Furthermore, the random killings that go on within your major cities every day are no less senseless. One has a religious claim and the other is clearly a lack of religion, decency or respect of any authority other than their own, the latter of which is truly anarchy, is it not, Blake?" Ataullah asked with a mixture of sadness, firmness, frustration and respect, the latter primarily for Blake, not the West as a whole. Ataullah continued.

"The bombings that have killed Arab men, women and children have been conducted either directly by the West, or indirectly by the many facets of Muslim sects that the West thought they could arm and control, only to find out time, and time again, that they could not. Instead, they created new tenets of terrorism, armed to the teeth with Western weapons. It has been a failed policy since it began, and blossomed into a reality that has created a lose-lose reality for all. If the West pulls out, the chaos will engulf new areas, and everyone will blame the Western pullout for allowing the disease to grow and spread its death and destruction to a wider audience across the globe, just like ISIS blossomed after the Obama administration withdrew from the area. Yet, if the West stays, it will continue to be declared to be the Great Satan that needs to be attacked and driven from our lands, similar to what occurred under the prior Bush administration. I'm sorry Blake, but I believe the West helped create this monster – and I have no idea how to fix it."

Ataullah's face spoke volumes of sincerity and Blake felt both empathy and guilt over the current situation. Blake also felt the beginning of compassion for this man, Ataullah, but it was still hard to overcome decades of hatred for that area of the world and its people. Blake knew he had to keep the discussion from becoming personal, but he also knew that Ataullah's world of experience was not one-sided either. If honesty was the theme of the day, then so be it. They would talk openly – something their two cultures had not done very well throughout history, and something even Blake had refrained from doing.

"Ataullah, you have made some very valid points about the West's involvement and the murder rates that continue to plague our inner cities; we should discuss those more at a later time, but I need to share something else with you now." Blake paused. "My father, a New York City fireman, was killed during the 9/11 attack on the Twin Towers."

Ataullah looked up, surprise and dread on his face.

"I did not know. I'm sorry to hear that, Blake. I really am."

"Thank you, Ataullah, I appreciate that and I believe you. He was a great man, Ataullah. He lived his entire life to help others – and died proudly proving that fact. Yet, that singular act of violence, from people he had never met, that demonstrated total callousness to life in any form, steeled me to join the U.S. military and take that fight to the people who killed him. During the two decades I was in the military, I fought many battles against people in many lands that call themselves Muslims. People, who in my estimation were not religious. They operated freely outside any form of true government – creating indiscriminate havoc and death everywhere they went. In my opinion, they do not deserve the right to live. They gave up those rights when they began their acts of violence and terrorism, and they alienated themselves from whatever religion or country they falsely claimed allegiance to. Ataullah, you need to know that I have personally caused the deaths of a great many of them."

There was an even longer pause, as both men listened to their inner consciousness, fought their inner demons that sowed thoughts of revenge and weighted the words and sincerity of the other man. Ataullah spoke first.

"Blake, it hurts me deeply to hear that. Yet, I also find myself deeper in trust of you with those statements. I will admit that I already expected you to have done what you stated. But hearing about your father's death creates understanding of the why. Hearing your statements prior to any accusation, creates trust that you are a man of your word. Hearing the fact that you differentiate between ordinary Muslims and extremists by your statement of who you targeted proves you have wisdom."

Blake struggled with how to respond. Ataullah spoke sincerely, but ... he was also a devout Muslim. Blake was still not convinced of the right answer, but he chose to take the higher road until he knew more about the man in front of him.

"Thank you, Ataullah, I believe we are developing similar opinions of each other, and I trust and pray that perhaps others, in higher positions of authority, can one day spread that message better than we can, and that the voices of understanding will drown the voices of extremism in all of the free countries of the world. Until then, perhaps we can continue to pursue and identify common ground by these discussions ... and perhaps settle our remaining differences non-violently by backgammon."

The two men smiled, shook hands and the game was on, but Blake was seriously questioning himself. His long-held convictions and distrust for anyone from the Middle East told him not to trust the man across the table from him. Yet, his instincts also told him that Ataullah's responses were sincere and fair. The Armstrong I team was in for a long journey with plenty of time to figure it all out, Blake reflected, but he would still keep an extra eye on Ataullah.

*****

A.D. 2028 (3311 C.A.E.); Dec. 3
Aboard the Reagan I

The three men had been working on the device steadily since they'd left Mars's orbit. They had collected dimensional data on anything that they could see to measure, and taken hundreds of photographs within the first couple of days, but the effort to collect additional data seemed to become more tedious the longer they worked on the device.

"Pat … Jimmy … What was that kid's name? You know, the intern that recommended the frequency changes to open the first door while it was still back on Mars?" Tom asked.

"Robert? … Yes, Robert Stern," Jimmy replied without ever taking his eyes off the device.

"How did he open the panel? Wasn't it an audible signal?" Tom asked.

"Yes, it was. That's a great reminder. Thanks, Tom. I'll send him a series of questions that he can staircase down through depending on each answer; that way we can save time from sending one question at a time and waiting for the answers to go back and forth across space."

"Good idea, so what do you need to know?"

"So, let's see, what do we need to ask … hmmm." Jimmy paused and looked up at the ship's ceiling for a long minute. "The main things I need to know are: what was the frequency that worked, was it a single frequency or was it a series of frequencies, and how long the audible signal was applied before the door opened. Now that I think about it, I don't think I need anything else if other doors will open with the same approach. Can you think of anything, Tom?"

"Not really … except …"

"Except what?"

"Maybe only one door opened because the others were buried in the sand, but … but what if each door has a different audible sequence that is required to open it?" Tom asked innocently.

"Holy cow, Tom. Talk about raining on the parade. But still, that is a great point. Once we know what Robert did, we can program a computer to go through various sequences and frequencies to see if other doors open. It may take a lot of time, but it sure beats sitting here and just looking at it."

Thirty minutes later, the message went out to Robert Stern. Tom left to get something to eat and then lay down and shut his eyes for a bit.

"I sure hope the kid is there. What time is it back there?" Jimmy asked.

"Well, let's see ...." Pat looked down at his iLibrary, typed in the current shipboard time into the clock function, followed by "Houston" and a click for "track my location," and the computer shot back:

8:30 p.m. Houston local time.

"Gotta love these little devices; they track us all the way to Mars? There's no escaping Big Brother anymore," Pat replied with a chuckle. "It's 8:30 p.m. Houston time – and it's a Friday night. Where else would a good engineering geek be on a Friday night? The study lounge! You'll have your answers in less than an hour."

"Sure, Pat, rub it in. You just can't imagine what it's like to be a young, dedicated future engineer, can you? He might become your boss someday."

"Okay, I say the boy has no social life whatsoever, and I've got a 20 spot that says you have an answer within 60 minutes, starting now. Put your money where your mouth is, Mr. Engineer." Pat continued to toy with his good friend.

"Okay, you're on. He'll answer in no sooner than four hours after he comes back from the pub, and then proves his dedication by working late into the night. You will be bowing to the two of us before this trip is over, Sir Patrick." Jimmy gave the most confident, in-your-face look that he could muster, but he couldn't help think that if it had been him, he *would have* been sitting by the computer day and night, just hoping to get a response, any kind of response, just so he could feel like he was still part of the mission.

Thirty minutes went by. The message would have easily reached Houston by then.

"Want to double the bet, Jimmy? You're down to less than 30 minutes." Pat was clearly enjoying the anticipation.

"Wings, beer and a brunette accounting major. He's enjoying himself. Why don't you go take a nap and come back in, say … five hours, Pat."

"And miss seeing you at the exact moment you need to hand over a crisp $20 bill to me? Not only no, but hell no! This isn't a bet; it's like stealing money from a baby … or should I say, an engineer?!" Pat was beside himself with laughter.

"Pat, if I didn't know better, I'd think you were getting a case of space sickness … I think I need to call Cmdr. Kline and let him know that you need to be strapped onto a medbay table to keep from hurting yourself!"

"Twenty minutes, Jimmy, then I'll go to the medbay by myself!"

The two of them laughed at each other and instead decided to go get a cup of coffee together in the kitchen.

Fifteen minutes later, the two men returned to the device, just in time to hear the computer *ping*.

"Pay up, Capt. Geek, 52 minutes on the button. You owe me 20 big ones!"

They both rushed to the console.

"Ha! A little cocky, aren't we, my friend? It's Cmdr. Kline. He says it's too damn quiet down here and he wants to know why the U.S. government is paying our lazy asses for doing nothing."

"I'm making a schematic of the wiring. Pat is sleeping." Jimmy typed back.

"What, you little weasel!" they were both laughing now as they fought for the keyboard.

Cmdr. Kline was listening *and* watching. His only thought was how amazing the impact of a lengthy space stay could be on two grown men. He also knew that this was probably the best medicine either of them could get right now.

"Ping-ping-ping."

Both men stopped dead in their tracks. A triple ping clearly meant a message from Houston.

"That's my boy!" Jimmy stated in glee.

"What? That means you lost. What are you gloating over?" Pat shot back.

"Engineering superiority." Jimmy had been ready to spring that baby ever since Pat made the bet, hoping that Robert really would be there. "Best 20 dollars I ever spent!"

The two quickly started reading Robert's message.

> *Wow! Thanks man. I'd begun to give up hope that anyone would ever talk to me again. It was like I found the Big Brag and once the Feds took over, no one needed me anymore. I've got a thousand questions! So many things I want to ask .... But, I guess I better answer yours first, right? Okay, here goes. The truth is, I don't really know because it happened accidentally and we weren't recording anything, but it sounded like a frequency I remembered from playing with my Capsela toy as a kid, so I went home, dug the toys out of my parents' spare room closet, replaced the batteries ...*

"Capsela? What the heck is a Capsela?"

"It's a cool toy. I actually thought everyone had one until I went to college. Then I just learned to not talk about it, unless I ran into another kid with electro-mechanical aptitude. It has a series of encapsulated gears and motors and battery packs that could be hooked up together with wires and then integrated into a structure. I made boats, cars, elevators, all kinds of stuff as a kid, all of which could slowly drive across the floor. It was really cool to build stuff that was functional, but it wasn't the fanciest looking toy around. Then Battle Bots and toy-based robotic technology came out and the rest was history; everyone left Capsela toys behind. But it was a trendsetter and way ahead of its time. Well, enough of Memory Lane. We're forgetting about Robert."

> *... and, oh yeah, I brought an oscilloscope home with me. Sure hope I don't get in trouble for that, but I didn't have one at home, and I really wanted to know what the frequency was. It wasn't like anyone was talking to me anyway ... I set it up in my bedroom and played around for a while until I thought I heard the sound again. Based on the oscilloscope, my best guess was that it was around seven kHz, almost like a high frequency squeal from your car brakes. Based on memory, I think the sound was on for maybe five seconds when the door opened.*

"Dang, this kid really is lonely, isn't he? I'm actually starting to feel bad for him," Pat interjected softly.

"Welcome to engineering school, Pat. While all the business majors were out playing around, we *geeks* were studying. Sorry, I appreciate your empathy, but those are the facts, my man. Let's see where he goes with it."

> *But, and I think this is important because it relates to one of your questions, I think multiple tones opened the door. There was a low 10 Hz sound in the background. I know it was 10Hz because I hear it all the time, obnoxious as heck; it's from some of the equipment in the lab below me, and it's loud, so I'm sure it could have carried through the microphone. I measured that too and it was exactly 10Hz. Is it possible that it had to hear both sounds at the same time, rather than in series? Let me know what you think. Thanks for asking. I'd love to hear any updates you can share with me. You won't rat me out on the oscilloscope, will you?"*

"The kid is a budding genius, Pat. I don't think I would've thought to overlay the different frequencies because I was too focused on creating a frequency series, one after the other. Get the gear out. Let's replicate what he thought opened the door for starters and see if we can get the door to close again."

"What about Robert? Are you going to answer him?"

"Ahh, good point. Thanks, Pat. You're not starting to like the kid, are you? That would be a horrible rumor to start, suggesting that you actually liked an engineer." Jimmy laughed with an evil grin. "Let me send him a quick thank you, and promise to send him something in detail tomorrow so that he can go to bed. Thanks again, Pat."

Jimmy sent Robert a note, as he had promised Pat, and then, in turn, promised Robert that he would give him a detailed report tomorrow, but that he would likely have to send it through Houston for approval first. He thanked him again and told him that if anyone gave him grief about the oscilloscope that he should tell them that Jimmy Decker requested it. He then typed goodnight and ended the message with a salutation that said: "Great work, Robert – from your biggest fan, Jimmy Decker."

"That should hold him for a little while." They both chuckled and immediately started to test out Robert's theory.

Pat looked over at Jimmy, perplexed, "So how is it that this thing is still operable after sitting in the red Martian landscape for as long as we expect it has been here? Batteries surely don't last that long."

"Great question, Pat. I wish I knew the answer. I agree that the batteries that *we* are familiar with can't survive this long, but it wouldn't surprise me to find out that there is some type of miniaturized nuclear heart in this thing that maintains a certain level of energy based on the decay rate of whatever isotope they are using. Now *that* could last forever," Jim continued. "Typical nuclear power plants work on the concept of nuclear fission where molecules in fuel rods from a specific material, like uranium 235 or uranium 238, are split and thereby release heat energy. The thermal energy is then used to create steam, which turns a turbine to create electricity. It's a highly efficient process. Now, granted, that takes a fairly massive and complex system to maintain for a long time, a system that wouldn't fit in this itty bitty little device, but that's why I think they must have come up with a very novel technique to harvest the energy from the actual radioactive decay process, and that *can* last a very long time, as well as with very little infrastructural requirements."

"I think I'm following you, but how could the decay last forever, Jimmy?"

"Radioactive life is measured in half-lives ..."

"Ahhh, I think I remember some of this from my high school physics class. Keep going, Jimmy."

"A half-life is the amount of time it takes for half of the material to decay, which is why we use carbon dating to estimate how old an artifact is, as long as that artifact has some form of organic material in it. The process uses radiocarbon (14, C), which is why it is commonly known as Carbon-14 dating. In this case, the creators of this device may have used something more like Uranium 238. U238 decays via a process known as alpha decay and has a half-life of 4.5 billion years. Plutonium is another common material. Pu-244 is a very stable material with a half-life that is still 80 million years long. So it wouldn't take a lot of material to last a very long time if all you were powering was a very small electrical circuit. In this case, a device known as a radioisotope thermoelectric generator could be used. This device harvests the thermal energy of the material as it decays and releases heat. The energy is collected by an array of thermocouples that then convert it to electricity. Now don't get me wrong, in theory this could work, but we don't possess the technology that could do what I am proposing ... even though this device *might*. I really can't wait until we can get into the heart of this thing."

With that, the two men went back to audible trial and error on the device.

Two hours later, they found it. "*Slllickkk,*" and the door closed.

"Voila, we did it! I mean, Robert did it!" Jimmy squealed, "The panel has closed! 10 Hz overlaid by an 8.5 KHz signal for 10 seconds. Damn, Robert was really close. Now let's hope it reverses, or all of NASA will want to tar and feather me for closing the door and locking them out again."

"Well, Jimmy, look at the bright side; you have a long time to figure it out again." Pat laughed.

"Thanks, but somehow I'll feel a heck of a lot better when it reopens. Let's try it again. God, that 10Hz sound really is as obnoxious as hell … S*llllickkk*," and the door opened again. "Whoooeeee! Now we're making some real progress! We just need to find the magic whistle calls for each door."

"Whoa! Just don't go setting anything off, Jimmy," Cmdr. Kline responded over the intercom. "How about I come down and we all look at it a bit slower before you go any further?"

"What?? Ummm … Of course, sure thing, commander. I just didn't realize you were listening in."

"Leave you alone with the device? I don't think so, Jimmy." Cmdr. Kline chuckled. "That's like putting a 10-pound jar of candy in the middle of the living room floor and telling a 5-year-old not to touch it. T'ain't happening!" Cmdr. Kline laughed again.

"Waiting starts now, honest Abe." Jimmy looked up at Pat and Tom and quickly added in a very low whisper, "He said don't set anything off. That doesn't mean I can't look, right?"

Jimmy immediately bent over and started counting what looked like other openings. Without rolling the device over, he could make out what looked like three more panels. This was really going to be fun, he thought.

CHAPTER 12

A.D. 2028 (3311 C.A.E.); Dec. 5
NSA Headquarters, Fort Meade, Md.

"Colonel, I think you need to see this."

"What is it, lieutenant?" Col. Bill Stevens replied dryly.

"This just came in from our Bluffdale, Utah, office. A search string caught 'Night Star,' 'Armstrong,' 'Space Corps' and 'El-Hashem' in a phone conversation between someone in Yemen and an unknown person in Kailua-Kona, Hawaii."

The highly classified Bluffdale Center had been established back in 2014 as a means to protect the agency's data center from electromagnetic pulse (EMP) damage that could occur from coastal-based nuclear explosions. During the Cold War with the Russians, the U.S. government had become keenly aware of what an offshore nuclear detonation could do to electronics and equipment on the East and West coasts, including Washington, D.C. The Soviets had established detailed plans to detonate a series of explosions off the East Coast, well within international waters, that estimates predicted would have shut down 80 percent to 90 percent of the operating capability of Washington, D.C., without ever killing anyone or starting a war, although the latter was not a commonly held opinion in Washington circles. Regardless, the U.S. government had spent more than $1.5 billion to build this secret installation and to ensure select systems and data would be protected from anything other than a direct nuclear hit. The facility was also rumored to be a backup to the highly publicized NORAD facility that was buried in the heart of Cheyenne Mountain in Colorado Springs, Colo. What other capabilities the center had when it was constructed, or had been added in the past 15 years, were not known.

"Okay, pardon my ignorance, lieutenant, but how does Hawaii tie in to this?"

"Sir, the classified Space Corps's Armstrong I launch to Pluto was initiated from the Johnston Atoll, southwest of Hawaii, just a couple of weeks ago. The flight to the orbiting space dock was achieved through a number of Night Star launches."

"The Armstrong has already launched, correct? If so, the threat must not have materialized."

"I'm not sure about that, sir."

"Continue ...."

"Well, sir, first, this call took place *two days* ago, well *after* the launch. Secondly, the Saudi crewmember on this flight is a Lt. Col. Ataullah El-Hashem. Thirdly, a quick dossier on the colonel shows that he is originally from Yemen and attended Imam University night school for Quran studies. It's possible that his Saudi Air Force background is a cover."

"That doesn't make him guilty, or verify this as a terrorist action, lieutenant, but I agree, it's enough to make it suspect. We need to escalate this immediately to the Joint Chiefs of Staff. Good catch, lieutenant. Have the report on my desk in two hours."

"Yes, sir."

Col. Stevens looked up at the lieutenant with a look of mixed disbelief and frustration.

"If you are correct, how the bloody hell could someone have slipped through the intensive Saudi vetting nets, let alone ours, and be put on that ship? This will make the damage Rosenberg did back in the 1940s pale in comparison. The president will have someone's head on a platter if this connection is found to be legit."

*****

Dec. 6
Pentagon, Washington, D.C.

The Joint Chiefs of Staff had assembled a day later to review a number of recent intel alerts and debriefs. The "El-Hashem" debrief was the third on the list and prepped for presentation. The various screens in the room showed a collage of pictures including Yemen, the Armstrong I, the Johnston Atoll, a Night Star photo, the solar system, the orbiting space dock and Lt. Col. Ataullah El-Hashem.

"Gentlemen. We have reason to believe that the Armstrong I crew and the mission to explore the object near Pluto may have been compromised and is now at risk," opened Col. Bill Stevens.

"Come on, colonel, aren't we letting our imaginations run a little wild? No one on the planet has a system that can reach that ship. How could it be at risk?" the chief of staff of the U.S. Air Force chided Col. Stevens.

"You are correct, sir, no one on this planet. However, the picture of the individual on the lower right is of the Saudi colonel, who is actually on board the Armstrong I right now."

There was a good deal of background noise as almost everyone in the room shifted in their chairs, opened the report copies and immediately became more engaged.

"All right, colonel, please continue, but make sure you clearly differentiate between facts, theories and opinions," replied Army Gen. Landon McMullen, the chairman of the Joint Chiefs of Staff. "If you are right, we'll need to debrief the president immediately."

The presentation had been prepared for a 15-minute duration and presentations to the Joint Chiefs were expected to be timely based upon the limited availability of the attendees and the multitude of agenda items typically on the docket. Thirty-five minutes later, Gen. McMullen had heard enough.

"We have a situation, gentlemen, and it appears to be the result of our own decisions. Be prepared to prep President Callahan and his staff by 0700 tomorrow. By 2100 tonight, I want dossiers on each of the crew of the Armstrong I, and I'd like some next step options from your perspectives as well. Any questions?"

"No, sir," replied Col. Stevens.

*****

A.D. 2028 (3311 C.A.E.); Dec. 6, 2028
Armstrong I, past Mars

Maj. James Snyder opened the door to Blake's small room.

"Blake?"

"Yes?"

"I need you upfront right away, and quietly."

Maj. Snyder maintained the night watch while Cmdr. Jack Pavlik had the day watch. They were already three weeks into the mission and, until now, it had been tediously boring. As Blake made his way to the flight deck he saw that Jack was already there, waiting for the two of them.

"What's the matter, Jack, can't sleep?" Blake said, chuckling, trying to break what he could feel looked like a pretty tense air on the deck based on Jack's expression.

"Blake, over here. I need you to read this message, but before you do, it goes no further than the three of us. This may be an international crew, but this is a decidedly United States op as of right now – and I am even happier to have you with us, knowing what I know now." There was no questioning Jack's eyes. Blake nodded.

> *Mission possibly compromised. Intel identified terrorist possibility. Ataullah El-Hashem and the country of Yemen identified as possible connections. Criticality, red. Maintain absolute secrecy from crew. Do not*

restrain or confront El-Hashem at this time. Confirm receipt of this message.

"Damn it, I knew I shouldn't trust him, yet he seemed ..." Blake was struggling for his words as the anger began to swell. "Jack, I've spent hours with him playing backgammon and we talked about everything from his childhood through his military assignments. The man hit me as a straight arrow ... yet, this is pretty damning." Blake pounded the table with his fist, trying to control his emotions. "Damn it, Jack! He came across so sincere ... yet, could he really be that diabolical? Maybe they're wrong," Blake added trying to be fair to Ataullah.

"Are you ready to bet your life, and the success of this mission on that, Blake?" James asked.

"No, of course not, James, and I would have asked you the same exact question if our places were reversed. It's just ..." Blake paused. "It's just hard to believe. I don't misread people very often. Granted, we haven't proven anything yet, but that message would look pretty incriminating in a court of law."

"Yeah, and the nearest court is how far away?" commented James.

"Blake, you also need to know they weren't going to let us bring you into this at first ..." Jack added.

"Yeah, I'm kind of getting used to that, ever since I joined the Space Corps. Things were much more direct and upfront in the military."

"Amen, Blake. To be honest, James and I had already decided that we were bringing you into this regardless of what the top brass said back home." Jack was dead serious.

"They're a million miles away and they think they can tell us how to fix things, when we are right here? Right," James added confidently.

"Thanks guys." Blake looked over at James, "Semper fi." Blake paused again, "Any thoughts on what's next?"

"Actually, we were kind of hoping to see what ideas you might have, Blake." Jack was all business now.

The three of them spent the next hour discussing options on how they might secretly search Ataullah's room, how to covertly question him without making him suspicious that they were onto him, how to search for clues, and how to avoid alerting the other crewmembers. From this point on, it was a three-person clandestine Op. Then Blake had an idea.

"Jack, my home team is currently sitting in Houston with their thumbs up their derrieres."

"Yeah, sorry about that, Blake. That was not our call and I'm sure that was a pretty big disappointment."

"Absolutely, with a capital B-I-G, but ... it may have been our first break."

Both men turned back to Blake, curiosity in their eyes.

"How so, Blake?"

"That team, the same one that is sitting in their dorm rooms on the atoll right now, is the best I know in the U.S. special ops inventory. They have the highest average IQ level of any team in the U.S. Forces, bar none, and they can fight. We need to convince the Pentagon boys that they need to open this op up to my *old* team."

"I don't know them, Blake, but your word is good enough for me. I'm just not sure we can convince Washington. And they aren't here, either," Jack cautioned.

"Relative to the team, they can chase down leads to see how real this threat is. If they can validate something earthside, as real or a misdirection, that will make a huge difference to us. Relative to Washington, I hear you, but remember, we have the ace of trump right here. We are the ones in danger. No one else is here, which by definition puts us in control. We give Washington the option; if they don't take it, I'll do it myself. What are they going to do, fire me?"

The three of them shared a quiet chuckle.

"Okay, Blake. I'll set the next call up for tomorrow night when everyone is asleep again. Jack, speaking of sleep, you'd better go get some sleep now. It's going to be in short supply for a while."

Jack pounced on James' comment. "To be honest, it was starting to get a little boring around here, anyway." They all chuckled again.

"James, remind me to introduce you to Diego when we get back. He took over command of my group until I return. Somehow, I think you two jarheads might just hit it off." Blake smiled at James as he headed to his quarters.

This was a whole new ballgame, Blake reflected. The possible options Ataullah might have at his disposal were almost unlimited, and the resources and time for Blake to resolve it were clearly critically limited. Boredom was no longer on the mission risk board.

*****

Turkmenbashi, Turkmenistan

A small truck quietly, but expeditiously, unloaded its stores at an inconspicuous, temporary, seaside dock. A group of men in long white robes loaded a single large crate into the hold of an old barge that was set to sail across the Caspian Sea to Baku, Azerbaijan.

After unloading in Baku, the shipment was scheduled to start its land trek through Azerbaijan on the Baku-Shamakhi-Yeviakh Highway, following one of the many major drug trade routes established over the past four decades, and then transfer ownership at the Armenian border city of Lachin Rayon. From there, the package was scheduled to travel to a small town on the western side of Armenia called Margara. Selected Turkish border guards had already been paid off to allow the shipment to be picked up and transported across the wide expanse of Turkey, to a small city on the Mediterranean Sea called Dortyol. From there, the shipment would be placed in the hold of a luxury yacht, called the Manchester United, to start its cross-Atlantic journey to its final destination, the United States of America.

The trip had been agonizing slow so far, hiding and evading searching American and Israeli eyes, but it was almost in the clear. Soon, nothing would stop it.

*****

A.D. 2028 (3311 C.A.E.); Dec. 7
Johnston Atoll

Houston and the Pentagon had agreed to bring Blake's team in, with surprisingly little debate, signaling how desperate the situation must really be. Diego, Patty, Li, Harry and Sean were all crowded in a small conference room in the Johnston Atoll control center reading Blake's message to update them on recent events. The growing distance between the Armstrong I and Earth was now making verbal communication nearly impossible.

"Wow, that's quite a load Blake just gave us. And today is Dec. 7, Pearl Harbor Day. Somewhat appropriate, eh?" Diego stated.

"You could say that, but at least the bombs haven't detonated yet, Diego."

"Good point, Patty. Read on, what's Blake's play for us?"

"He wants us to get the team on a military red eye to D.C. tonight so that we can meet with Gen. Landon McMullen tomorrow afternoon. Harry can start planning options, but Blake wants us all in Yemen and possibly Saudi Arabia ASAP. He doesn't know how much time we have, so he needs us to assume we *don't* have any time. Once there, we'll need to track down everything we can find on Lt. Col. Ataullah El-Hashem and the connections he may have over there. There's a brief dossier in the folder he prepared for us, and the Pentagon boys are putting a more extensive package together that we'll receive tonight when we get there." Blake's message continued:

"While you're at it, twist Gen. McMullen's arm to see if we can pull Oliver Wyatt into this as well. Some of the UK's Mid-East connections may help out. I know I don't need to tell you how much is riding on this. I expect you will have questions, but you will need to figure those out among yourselves."

"I've got one," Sean piped up. "What's his comment about the possible contact in Hawaii?"

"You'll love this; check out a little lower. I think he can read our minds." Patty chuckled.

"Relative to Hawaii, we already have the NCIS (Naval Criminal Investigative Services) and the Secret Service involved. They have started interviewing every individual who has been associated with this project, as well as all previously identified Al Qaeda suspects in Hawaii. We'll let them handle that side of the investigation while you guys take the Middle East."

Good luck people.

Diego, I have a separate message for you that should be lined up after you close this one."

Diego typed quickly and hit reply, knowing that it would be quite some time before Blake would read his response.

"Got it. Thank you, sir. We're moving."

Diego clicked off the projector and read the next message by himself.

"I heard through the back channels in the Pentagon about your unexpected op at a restaurant back home. From what I understand, it sounds like that place might be significantly safer than it used to be. Glad to hear you are both ok. Good work Diego. Over and out."

Diego began typing again,

"Yes, thanks, Blake. Jose was pretty shook up. Doubt he will ever return to that restaurant again, or even that area of town."

Diego clicked off the message and smiled to himself.

"Diego, what was that all about?" queried Patty.

Diego hadn't told anyone about that night at the restaurant with his brother and the five gang bangers.

"Here he is, millions of kilometers away in space, preparing for a potential interface with an alien race for the first time in recorded human history, traveling with a possible terrorist that might want to blow up the ship, and the man still takes the time to stay abreast of how my family and I are doing. I swear to God and the Corps, Patty, that man ever needs anything, I'm there, no matter what it takes." Diego shook his head and got up to leave.

"Everything okay with your family, Diego?"

"Yes, I'll catch you up while we're on the plane. Let's get moving."

Patty watched Diego leave and couldn't help think how they all shared the same thoughts about Blake. They definitely broke the mold after that man came out.

*****

A.D. 2028 (3311 C.A.E.); Dec. 8
Over the Atlantic Ocean

It had been a long trip so far, and Diego and the team still had over a day's worth of travel remaining. They had planned on catnapping whenever they could grab a couple of hours of sleep on the various legs of the journey to make sure they weren't totally wiped out when they arrived. They'd left Johnston Atoll on a dedicated C-17 Globemaster III flight fewer than three hours after the communication from Blake, refueled at Pendleton Marine Corps Base in California, and were airborne fewer than 60 minutes later on a non-stop flight to Washington, D.C., on the same C-17. The C-17 had three sets of pilot crews to ensure no time was lost between flights. The five-member team met with the Joint Chiefs of Staff, Army Gen. Landon McMullen, for two hours at the Quantico base in Virginia, ironed out plans, verified connections, communication contacts and extraction points, and received documents and money that would get them into both Yemen and Saudi Arabia. Whatever was going on, it was clear that the Pentagon had bought into Blake's plan hook, line, and sinker, resulting in the total elimination of red tape for the five of them. Anything they wanted, anything they needed, and it was faster than ASAP-squared.

Their next stop after leaving the U.S. on their now personal C-17, tail number 77179, was Ramstein Air Base in Germany, where a limo would be waiting to take them to Frankfurt International Airport. From there, they would fly to Dhamar, Yemen, by commercial airline to maintain cover, travel northeast by car to Marib and then head farther north into the desert to meet up with Oliver Wyatt and his British team. After meeting with the Brits, the teams would split up again, but both heading west to Sana'a.

Harry was pensive. He had played all of the options out in his head numerous times and was convinced that D.C. was wrong for not taking immediate action on the Armstrong I. He thought Blake needed to confront Ataullah, and the sooner the better. Blake would know instantly if there were a potential connection and they could in turn subdue Ataullah for the rest of the flight if needed. There was no way in Harry's mind that Ataullah could withstand a physical confrontation with Blake, let alone the fact that Maj. Snyder and Cmdr. Pavlik were also available to assist. This was a no-brainer in Harry's mind. If Ataullah were truly part of a terrorist cell trying to blow up the Armstrong I, he would have done it already. More likely, he would have done it where it could easily be seen by backyard Earth telescopes and only then after a national broadcast was made to ensure maximum witnesses. It made no sense to wait until they were millions or billions of kilometers away to blow up a secret flight that no one knew about.

"What the heck would that accomplish?" Harry bolted straight up in his chair and spoke aloud.

"What would what do?" Patty squinted her eyes and looked over at Harry.

"Sorry, didn't mean to speak out loud. I was thinking."

"Okay, but you did, so catch us up. We're all in this together, Harry."

"It just doesn't make sense. Why would they blow up the Armstrong I where no one can see it, and when no one knows about it in the first place?" Harry stammered out.

Everyone was now looking at Harry.

"Well, they sure aren't waiting to do an interview with the alien ship," Li threw back sarcastically.

"Oh, my God!" Patty blurted out. "They know!"

"Know what?" replied Sean with a confused frown.

Everyone else looked puzzled, until Harry spoke up.

"To be honest," Harry sat back in his seat, "I hadn't considered that option."

"They know what?" Sean was getting frustrated. It was as if Patty and Harry were talking in riddles and he was the only one not in the loop.

"They know about the alien ship," Patty stated flatly.

"If that's correct, then we need to determine how they found out," added Diego. "This may be bigger than just Lt. Col. Ataullah El-Hashem. He ..." Diego hesitated, "They had to have someone on the inside who knew the details of this mission, and knew the details way in advance."

"Whatever it is you guys are talking about, that statement is a pretty scary scenario," Sean added.

"Yes, but it makes sense. Patty, nice job, you one-upped me on this one. It's the only thing that makes real sense based on what we know right now. We still need to look for connections in Yemen and Saudi, but D.C. needs to start backtracking their trails to every person connected with this mission that Lt. Col. El-Hashem might know."

"I'm still lost," Sean said dejectedly. "What the 'ell did these aliens do, if they really exist, to cause a terrorist cell to want to blow them up?"

"That's a great question Sean, and we need to keep working theories on that," replied Harry. "Assuming they know the reason for the mission, one option is that they must think they can gain something by blowing it up billions of kilometers from Earth."

"There's a second option I can think of right now," added Patty.

"And what's that?" Sean still looked confused.

"They see the alien potential as an even bigger threat to their Islamic ways. A potential joining of demons, the aliens and the Great Satan, i.e. the U.S. The Islamic fundamentalists would never allow that to occur."

"But why not blow the Armstrong I up here near Earth where they could be sure that they achieved their mission," Sean asked.

"They could've blown the ship up at any time, and hurt the Great Satan, but the demons near Pluto would still be there and the U.S. would just build another ship. They need to eliminate the alien demons if they really do exist."

"If this wasn't so damn serious, I'd say you've been watching too many sci-fi movies, Patty, but … wow, it does all line up, in theory, anyway," added Diego.

"If you're right, then we have time on our side," Harry added and continued, "And it makes even more sense to have Blake confront Ataullah in order to close this down before they reach Pluto."

"See, you were right after all, Harry." Patty smiled at him.

"Okay, I think I'm finally catching up," Sean piped in. "But this all assumes there are aliens out there, and live ones at that. There will be a lot of disappointment if this mission ends up being a wild goose chase and there's nothing out there. Then what?"

They looked at each other, wondering what the next surprise was going to be that was already queuing up for them. Their small world was getting very complicated, quickly, and whether or not there were aliens near Pluto was becoming a smaller piece of the puzzle by the day. Too many unknowns, too few knowns and way too many variables that seemed to be changing by the day. SNAFU: systems normal, all *fouled* up.

CHAPTER 13

A.D. 2028 (3311 C.A.E.); Dec. 9
Pluto orbit

"Juulys, any luck yet?" Thjars had walked in and unexpectedly surprised Juulys as she was listening intently to a series of radio transmission from the third planet of this solar system.

"Actually, yes, Thjars, but I lost a lot of time until I finally realized that there are multiple languages spoken on the planet and multiple frequencies and spectrums that they communicate across. I wasn't expecting it to be so complicated; it is so unlike Cjar. I'm guessing that their world is not a single united group of people, more similar to what Cjar might have been like millenniums ago. Once I was able to determine their key frequencies, I started seeing and hearing a lot more. But to be honest, Thjars, it's still confusing, and actually a little scary."

"So they don't have a planet-wide, common language. That's not insurmountable. How many do you think they have?"

"I gave up counting when I passed 200 different languages. It honestly wouldn't surprise me if there were over a thousand languages. Worse yet, even within areas that appear to have the same language, there are multiple dialects present. It's crazy! The same words or phrases appear to mean different things in different areas."

"I've learned a lot from three video broadcasts that they refer to as CNN, FOX and BBC. I think they share the same basic language known as English, but sometimes you would think they were seeing the same picture from different sides of the universe. One will call something black, the next will say it's white and the third will say it's gray. I don't think they agree on anything. It's like the entire race has a form of innate insanity. I don't know how they function as a global unit," Juulys continued, showing a mix of frustration and concern. "Thjars, I simply can't figure them out."

"What about making contact? Are you ready to recommend an approach?" Thjars tried to push past her uneasiness.

"Thjars, I'm not sure where to even start. I see videos of war and death all over the planet. Yet, I see videos of passion and care – and both come from the same land masses. There is a lot of violence on this planet. So much, that at first, I thought we were seeing another race similar to the Klaxx! But, unlike the Klaxx, I see them coming to the aid of each other during times of crisis with what appear to be acts of true compassion.

"Frankly, it scares me because I don't know who to trust, and who not to, and I still can't say that I fully understand what they are saying. For example, this little country in the northern hemisphere calls itself the United Kingdom, yet within that *United* Kingdom they clearly don't get along with each other, especially two groups that refer to themselves as the Irish and the Brits, and there are at least five different sub-countries just within that small collection of islands. The series of islands that make up this country is less than 250,000 square kilometers; tiny by Cjarian standards. Thjars, this planet seems so partitioned that I don't know how they could have evolved into space flight."

"Juulys, you're starting to sound like you aren't comfortable contacting *anyone* there," Thjars replied thoughtfully.

"That is a fair assessment, Thjars, but I haven't given up yet. That BBC group sounds trustworthy because they appear to be one of the less emotional and more direct sources I've seen so far. The other sources seem like they try to make emergencies out of everything. Every new story starts with 'breaking news alert,' like they are *trying* to work their people up into a frenzy. It's really hard to decide, but I think I would start with the BBC group.

"One more example just so you can see how hard it is to understand their languages. Look here." Juulys fast-forwarded through some video to a pre-marked section. "In the United Kingdom, this little thing is called a 'rubber' and appears to be used to remove markings that they make on paper with a writing utensil called a lead pencil. Yet, in this other area on the other side of a large body of water, called the *United* States, 'rubber' refers to a *thing* that is used for, umm, this is a little embarrassing, Thjars." Juulys blushed a little. "For very private interaction between two people, and no, I'm not going to show you how I found that out!" Juulys shuddered. "These people have no modesty. And you almost have to have video present in order to know what's really going on, so I've reduced my focus on radio discussion and have increased my focus on what they refer to as television, or TV, to ensure that I can actually see what they are referring to. Unfortunately, as in the case with the rubber, you can be caught off guard at times. As I mentioned, they are not a shy people."

Thjars laughed to relieve her tension a bit and shook his head before Juulys continued.

"There is another problem that I'm up against. The same exact audible for a word can have different spelling and meaning from what I have discovered so far. It's really confusing. I actually found a video source on some system called 'Google' of a yellow and black book they call 'English for Dummies.' That book helped a lot. The book showed an example with three words like this, the words 't-h-e-i-r,' 't-h-e-r-e,' and 't-h-e-y-'r-e' all sound exactly the same in that area called the United States, but each has a different meaning – and there's a lot more examples like that. It's really confusing.

"But back to who to contact. If we do talk to the BBC, I like this guy they have on in the mornings. He seems genuine."

"How can you tell?"

"Because he's on TV every morning calmly telling the people of the United Kingdom what has happened the previous day and what may be taking place during the day."

"I see," Thjars replied; he wasn't sure he really did, but it seemed like the respectful thing to say at the moment. "What are you thinking about relative to actually making contact with this individual?"

"I'm really not comfortable about that yet, Thjars, but it may not matter."

"Why's that?"

"I've been hesitant to share this, as Jarns didn't want to yet, but …"

"Whoa, you two have been holding out …?" Thjars was getting a little agitated.

"No, no, Thjars, it's not like that, but I do need to update you. Let me get Jarns."

Fifteen minutes later, Jarns had updated Thjars about an object that appeared to be heading in their direction, very slowly, but directly toward them, and it came from the third planet.

"It could be a satellite, or a planetary exploration probe, right?" Thjars asked.

"I really doubt it," Juulys answered. "The probability that a random launch would be heading directly for us, and *not* be intended for us, is next to impossible considering the volume of space we are talking about. We have to assume that somehow they spotted us and they are coming to check us out."

"Juulys, have you picked up anything in the transmissions relative to this flight?"

"No, at least nothing that I can decipher. There are definitely signals emanating from the object, but they are clearly encrypted and I don't have the tools to decipher them. That suggests that whatever the object is up to, they don't want anyone else to know about it, either," she replied.

Thjars was silent for a minute.

"I'm not sure if I should be excited, or nervous," Thjars said quietly.

"Neither are we," Juulys replied. "But I think we need to be both. How about we get Qulys involved, as we may want to prepare defensively, just in case."

"Agreed, but before you do, I thought we agreed that they were nowhere near having the ability to reach us out here, at least within our lifetime, correct? So … what changed?" Thjars challenged the duo.

"Great point, Thjars, I think we forgot that in all of the confusion, but that is a question we definitely need to answer, and answer fast," replied Jarns. "We'll get on it immediately."

"Thanks Jarns, and please keep me updated a little quicker than what just happened."

"Yes, sir, it won't happen again."

*****

A.D. 2028 (3311 C.A.E.); Dec. 10
Dhamar, Yemen

The Lufthansa flight landed at 2:25 in the afternoon. Passengers disembarked, followed the river of people in front of them, gathered around the dingy luggage conveyor to collect their luggage, and exited through customs as the daily routine repeated itself in the same manner as it had every day of the week, week after week, month after month. The ever-knowing cameras recorded three nondescript, Western-looking passengers among those who hailed cabs, and the cameras also showed that the three took separate cabs. Two hours later, after stopping to eat a late lunch, two additional non-Caucasian passengers rented a car together, and then left the airport.

Li had a Chinese passport, Diego a Mexican passport, Patty a dual Canadian-Saudi passport, Harry had the only U.S. passport and Sean had a very natural-looking Irish passport. The five had entered Yemen with little scrutiny and although they knew there were cameras everywhere, they were confident that they had not been identified or followed. By late evening, each had reserved a room at the luxurious Bilquis Hotel in Marib at various times through the afternoon and evening. The hotel was frequented by customers from all over the world, so five more, apparently independent reservations and arrivals, was nothing that would raise anyone's alarms.

The next morning, the group woke up, ate breakfast – again at intentionally different times – and then individually headed into town, all under the guise of exploring the rich history of this ancient city. The continual flow of tourists and historians made it easy to blend in.

Marib, founded in 1200 B.C., once known as the Sabaean Empire, had been the home of the legendary Queen of Sheba. The Queen of Sheba was both a biblical and Quranic figure. According to the Bible, the queen actually met with King Solomon in Jerusalem, exchanging many gifts during what was recorded to be a mutually positive meeting. Jewish and Islamic history have similar accounts of the meeting between King Solomon and the Queen of Sheba, but over the years, different religious groups had taken a great deal of liberty describing a multitude of versions of that historic meeting. Some also proposed that the queen was the person whom the scriptures referred to as the queen of the South.

While the group had been aboard the trans-Atlantic C-17 flight, they all agreed that Patty's proposed theory for Ataullah's goal was their most likely scenario. Although time was of essence, Patty's theory suggested they might have more time than they initially thought. This, of course, assumed that her theory was correct and that Lt. Col. Ataullah El-Hashem would wait until the Armstrong I arrived at the object prior to initiating his own private version of Jihad. This meant they could take the extra time to make sure they weren't being followed and to look like the tourists they were trying to be.

Patty started her day by heading to the Temple of Bilqis (Sheba), while Sean visited the Great Dam of Mrib. Harry started his day at the hotel, waiting for two hours, and then headed out to the Temple of Bilqis as well. They all wanted to keep an extra set of eyes on Patty, even though it angered her to no end. Li went to The Sabaean Wall and Diego volunteered to remain at the hotel as an emergency backup if any issues were to occur.

The city was indeed as rich in history as the brochures had advertised. The Temple of Bilqis, also known as the Mahram Bilqis or the Awwam temple, was built around the 6th century B.C. by Mukarrib Yada'il Dharih I. The temple was a stone ruin that boasted megalithic stone pillars, each of which was approximately 10 meters tall with a 1-square-meter cross-section. Patty spent hours walking through the ruins, taking extensive pictures and videos; it was a marvel like none she'd ever seen. When Harry finally showed up two hours later, he made sure to follow distinctly separate paths and directions than Patty did. Whenever they did accidentally cross paths, Harry made sure he was taking a picture of something so that Patty could walk by without suggesting a connection to anyone that might be watching him.

Sean was at the ruins of the Great Dam of Marib, very near the current Marib Dam. The Great Dam of Marib was built in the 8th century B.C. and considered to be one of the great wonders of the ancient world, as well as the oldest known dam. The dam was a central part of both the Sabaean and Himyarite kingdoms. The more Sean read, the more he continued to realize that this area of the world, one that at times he actually loathed, truly had been the center of the world and the foremost in trade and technology back in its time. It was no wonder that the Islamic religion frequently referred to "regaining" its leadership position within the world power structure.

Li found the Sabaean wall to be equally astonishing. Large rectangular blocks had been cut and mounted to build the series of walls, an impressive feat in itself based on the size of the blocks and walls. But the most impressive aspect was the sheer volume of writings and symbols covering the walls. Although no one had yet been able to fully translate the symbols, there was an extensive trove of data scholars could work with.

After lunch, at 1 p.m. local time, the five began heading toward their planned rendezvous point in Old Marib City. Once there, they used Sean's Land Rover rental to head north into the desert. Three hours later, the group met up with Oliver Wyatt and his group of four Brits.

"Blimey mates, who eva' thought we 'ould run into a bloody Brit out 'ere in d'middle of nowhere?" Sean spoke up first.

"Well, well, if it isn't my old friend Lt. Sean O'Rourke. I see that you've still not mastered the Queen's English, such a waste." Oliver smirked and continued. "Must be quite a letdown to have to use your land legs to travel around. What's the matter, Uncle Sam couldn't afford to send you in on Apache helicopters this time?" Oliver returned with his stereotypical dry and minimal British smile.

"Unfortunately, not this time, 'boot I'm sure we could call in a drone strike or two to send you Tommies back to kingdom come, eh laddies?"

"Okay, could you two kiss and make up now?" Patty jumped in. "Sorry gents, but we really have pressing issues to attend to. We can catch up on pleasantries later. So, Oliver, what's the game plan?"

"Happy to oblige, Miss Patty. As I understand it, the five of you will attempt to assemble as much as possible of our good colonel's past life in Sana'a, but most importantly, see if you can determine if there are any current connections that light up your radar screens.

"Patty, with your dual Canadian-Saudi papers, and your physical appearance, you should be able to fit in better than anyone, so I recommend that you be point on this operation. Your teammates will be nearby at all times for support and backup if anything should arise. If the situation becomes dire, you are to contact my cell immediately and we'll bring the firepower. I've got my immediate team that will remain here for quick support, but there is a second team in the desert north of Sana'a under Lieutenant

Bobby Smith, and trust me, he's packing. He has some pretty heavy stuff out there that can be brought to bear fast."

Oliver didn't specify any further, but Patty knew him long enough to know that Oliver was not one to exaggerate, so she was comfortable that the Brits had their back, and then some. She was also sure that Blake must have upped the ante on this one as well.

"If, for some unpredictable reason, we need additional backup," Oliver continued, "the USS Avenger Carrier Battle Group is stationed just offshore in the Gulf of Aiden, and the USS Wasp and its battle group are moving into position in the Red Sea. At that distance, they can have six heavily armed Blackhawks loaded with Marines and a couple of Pave Low CSAR helicopters, screaming across the bay at 159 knots that can be here in less than 60 minutes. And beyond that, the HMS Prince of Wales Battle group is heading to the Arabian Sea for a post just west of Oman. And just to top it off, every airbase in the Middle East is now on high alert, i.e.: if D.C. decides a full military action is required, and I mean a *full* military action, we're ready.

"Lady Pat, I don't know all of the details yet, but whatever you and your Yanks are into, it must be big. For what it's worth, it looks like the entire U.S. and British militaries have been lined up to make sure you get it done."

CHAPTER 14

A.D. 2028 (3311 C.A.E.); Dec. 10
Armstrong I

Blake was sitting at the desk in his room, reviewing one of the reports that Prof. Rimlinger had given him called "Potential Issues Associated with Contact with Alien Civilizations." His first reaction to the title had been one of skepticism, thinking that it was just another paper from one more UFO-chasing extremist, but once he attempted to open the electronic document, he was immediately stopped with a "SECRET" notification and a request to use his thumbprint to gain access. Okay, he thought, that brought a little different level of expectation to it. He dove into the report and had been reading intently for the last two hours. The document had been written within the last six months by a professor at MIT whose name he couldn't even pronounce or spell – the last part of the four-part name had been 13 letters by itself, "Narayanaswamy," but the prior portions weren't much shorter. The name was so unusual to him that Blake actually wondered if it was a real person, but his best guess was that it was Indian. He knew from talking with Rakesh that southern Indian names were typically quite long. Although modern-day names were frequently shortened, the historical approach had been to include your caste, the town you came from, your father's name and then your own name. Blake laughed when he told Rakesh, "No wonder Indians are all so smart; you have to be so you can spell your own name before you start Kindergarten!" Blake wondered if this report had been requested under short notice once the mission to Pluto was approved.

The chapter he was reading was educating the reader on how common gestures with positive intentions may not mean the same for other cultures. The example he was using was the common thumbs-up signal the United States had developed as a sign of "all good" or "count me in." Some parts of Europe, including France and Germany, used it primarily to signal a quantity of one, and in Finland, it's predominantly used as a signal of good luck. Even though the U.S. meaning was now generally accepted across the globe, the Greeks still rarely used it. For the most part, Greeks understood that the Western intent was good, but in their culture the thumbs-up signal had a negative meaning of contempt or disapproval. The main point the author was making was relative to how much thought, preparation and awareness had to be put into a first interaction with another culture … or other intelligent life forms, as Blake was actually hoping would be the case. This was really good, well thought-out material, Blake thought.

Just then, his LB vibrated. He touched the speaker button and said, "Blake here."

"Blake, I need you in the Control Room. We have another issue."

"What now, Jack?"

"I'll tell you when you get here." And he clicked off.

Blake sat back in his chair. Now what, he wondered. That was definitely not a "when you have a chance" request; it was more a military command. Blake put on his shoes, strapped his LB to his wrist and made haste to the Control Room. Less than two minutes later, he was with Jack.

"Blake, apparently, we may be in a race to the object."

"What?"

"Houston has been so engrossed with tracking our progress, as well as that of the Reagan I, that they didn't detect a new launch that appears to be heading our way – until just recently."

"Damn. Where did the launch come from?"

"They aren't sure yet, Blake, but as crazy as this will sound, they think it came from the moon."

"The moon? Are they thinking that this might be another alien ship?"

"They aren't sure about that, but the ship does appear to be faster than ours. Best estimates suggest it launched 10 days after we did, but it has already cut our lead in the race for Pluto. Houston expects that at the current velocities of the two ships, the new ship will definitely catch us before we reach the object."

Blake looked quietly out the control room window at the stars ahead. Jupiter was actually looking big enough to easily separate itself from the star field. The stars were beautiful, but the night sky ahead of them was quiet and lonely. What had he gotten into, and on an unproven, unknown potential battlefield without any of his normal weapons, tools or teammates. First an alien ship. Then a device on Mars. Followed by a potential Al Qaeda threat. Now an unknown second ship. It was nearly impossible that they were related, but that consideration couldn't be eliminated yet. The Arab League had launched satellites to orbit the moon in 2023, but the Chinese and the Russians had been there earlier. It seemed unlikely that either could have established a base on the moon without the U.S. knowing about it, but then again, the U.S. had not returned to the moon in almost 50 years. The Russians had visited the moon more than anyone over the past few years, and on multiple flights during some years. Many in the inner circles of the Pentagon believed that the Russians maintained a secret goal to build a manned station on the moon, and they had been working on it over the past decade. In the case of the United States, with so much money being spent on the Reagan I and Armstrong I journeys, there was little appetite to spend even more money on a rumor associated with Russians on the moon.

"Jack, when was that Russian moon rocket lost? Wasn't it about five years ago? As I recall, the Russians had talked about it being the greatest spaceship ever constructed, but after it was lost, we couldn't get anything out of them, and the case has gone silent even since."

"I think it was in late 2022. Are you thinking this ship might be Russian, Blake?"

"I don't know, but maybe their vessel wasn't lost after all. If it's the Russians, or the Chinese, or any other Earth-based country, then the lack of radio contact suggests we need to assume their intentions are hostile until proven otherwise, regardless of who they are. If it's an alien vessel, then maybe they are just looking to protect their property, assuming the object really is a ship. Maybe it's their mother ship and the craft from the moon is a returning scout ship. Either way, if the roles were reversed and I saw someone heading to my ship, and I was billions of kilometers from home, I would assume it was a threat and I would prepare to act accordingly – at least until the evidence at hand proved otherwise, with a very high level of probability. So, net-net, we need to be safe and prepare for conflict."

"Agreed."

"Has anyone tried hailing the ship yet?" Blake asked.

"Good question, Blake; regardless of what Houston is doing, we can at least do that. I'll get James on it as soon as he's up for his night shift. We can send messages in English, Russian, Chinese and Morse code. Do we let the others know?" Jack queried.

"I was pondering the same thought, Jack, and I think the answer is *yes*. If Ataullah really has plans to do something, this may throw a wrench into them, so we may be able to gain some advantage because of our new visitor. If Ataullah panics, it may increase the risk of him making a mistake, or showing his cards earlier. Let's schedule a crew meeting tomorrow and watch Ataullah closely as we make the announcement. Let's also keep an eye on Vladimir while we're at it, just in case there is a tie to Mother Russia."

"I like it, Blake. I'll let James know tonight and I'll set it up for 0800 tomorrow. Speaking of Ataullah, have you noticed anything different about him so far?"

"I've been watching him as close as I can without setting off his radar and he seems just as calm as can be. He continues his daily prayers in private, so it's possible that he could be making private calls during his prayer time, assuming he managed to steal communication gear onboard. That possibility seems slim, especially as I'm confident that we would be able to pick up some type of outgoing transmission, even if we couldn't decipher it, and James is convinced nothing has gotten out that wasn't planned. I've seen him down near the nuclear reactor a couple of times, which raised the hair on the back of my neck at first, but each time, nothing happened that I could detect. I've also managed to scope out his room a couple of times when he was in the gym, and although I didn't dig deeply anywhere, nothing looked suspicious, either. He's either the coolest customer I've run into, or this is all a bad read, and I'm definitely hoping for the latter," Blake added optimistically.

*****

Mediterranean Sea

The power catamaran yacht, model 70 Sunreef Power Bounty, was registered to Great Britain under the name Manchester United and was now flying both the Union Jack and the red and gold Manchester United football team flag on its main mast. The yacht was designed for around-the-world travel, held 20,000 liters of fuel, sported two 500 horsepower John Deere engines, could cruise at an average speed of 11.5 knots, and had a range of 4,000 nautical miles. The yacht was a full 22.3 meters long, with a maximum beam of 9.3 meters. It displaced 48 tons and had a 1.6-meter draft. It was the top of the line for non-custom luxury yachts.

Members of the yacht were visible on both the main deck and the smaller upper deck. They waved lazily to people on smaller crafts as the ship departed the Mediterranean Sea through the Strait of Gibraltar. It was a long 3,350 nautical miles to the East Coast of the United States, but it would only take the Manchester United a little less than three weeks to cover it – as long as the weather held. Its cargo bay held more than adequate food, drink and supplies for its long journey.

The specially modified hold also included one large, 4-meter-long crate; it was well-anchored to avoid movement during rough seas.

Alongside the large crate were two moderate-sized crates and six slightly smaller ones, the latter each about 2 meters long; all had been on board the yacht prior to picking up the crate in Dortyol. One of the smaller boxes had been pried open, exposing a French-manufactured Mistral infrared homing surface-to-air missile. The moderate-sized boxes contained two Lockheed Martin-built Nemesis man-portable missiles for ship attacks. The Nemesis used proven technologies from the Hellfire II, direct attack guided rocket (DAGR) and Scorpion missiles. How these relatively new, highly protected missiles had been obtained was not known to anyone on board, but they were considered as big a heist as any in the history of the black weapons market. The Nemesis is a surface-launched missile designed to help troops engage targets from as close as 100 meters, to well beyond the line-of-sight during operations. Fired vertically from its launch tube, the missile featured a 360-degree engagement capability, and also enabled users to select the height of burst or point-detonation fusing options to help enhance engagement options with enemy personnel, lightly armored vehicles, structures – and small ships.

On top of the smaller boxes were a number of small arms and automatic machine guns. To anyone flying overhead, or passing by on another ship, this was clearly a personal ship for someone with money and prestige – and time to burn while enjoying it. But the ship's hold beneath the deck painted a very different picture. This was a ship of war.

The only risks that the crew had been warned of were the North Africa-based pirates, which they had no fear of thanks to their cargo hold, and the weather. There was, however, some concern about the risk of an enterprising young U.S. Coast Guard captain identifying the boat as a potential drug runner. To reduce that risk, the captain of this ship, with a heavy British accent, had fully clarified his intention with the U.S. government to sail from the Mediterranean Sea to Atlantic City, N.J. The captain had gone even further, in the name of safety, and requested the names of Coast Guard boats and their captains so that he could maintain continual contact with them and reduce the risk of a surprise visit. As a further insurance policy, he had plenty of Manchester United paraphernalia and French Alfred Gratien Cuvee Paradis Brut NV Champagne to celebrate with them – if needed.

The financiers of this jihad had clearly planned for all possibilities.

*****

A.D. 2028 (3311 C.A.E.); Dec. 11
On Board the Armstrong I

The crew all met in the galley where Jack, James and Blake provided a quick update of the news of the unidentified ship. Klaus, who had kitchen duties for the day, prepared breakfast for everyone. It was nothing fancy and required little effort as everything was pre-packaged and only needed to be extracted from the storage containers, warmed and passed out.

"We really don't have any idea who they are or where they came from?" Rakesh asked in clear disbelief.

Klaus Schneider looked at Vladimir and in typical, blunt German practice, simply asked, "Is it Russian, Vladimir?"

Vladimir responded quickly, "It is not Russian. Absolutely and categorically not Russian."

"How can you be so sure, Vladimir?" Blake asked slightly suspiciously.

"I'm sorry, I should have clarified, but I have been a sitting member of the Russian Space Board for the past five years. That is not public knowledge, but seems appropriate to share at this moment. I know and approve of every Russian launch. I am just stating the fact that this ship is definitely not Russian."

"Okay, Vladimir. Thank you for clarifying." It was a fair answer, Blake reflected, just delivered somewhat defensively. "I want to look at all the options to make sure we don't get blindsided, or so that we can learn something we can leverage to our advantage."

Vladimir grunted his approval.

Blake then looked at the rest of the crew and added, "We haven't received any responses to our hailing calls yet, and it will be weeks before we can see enough of the ship to know more. The guys back home have also tried, but the ship is dark, without markings, and they can only see the aft end of the ship. One thing that they could validate was that the craft does not possess a light sail, so NASA is convinced that their drive technology is not only different than ours, but clearly better. And based on current ship velocities, they will beat us to the object. We also know they will have to pass very close by us to do so," Jack added.

Blake watched both Ataullah and Vladimir closely, but nothing beyond sincere surprise was evident in their faces. Over the next 30-plus minutes, the crew discussed options and risks, as well as all kinds of theories relative to who the new entrant might be. Jack and Blake caught each other's eyes a couple of times and acknowledged "no hits."

"Perhaps," Vladimir volunteered, "You can have them send what pictures they were able to obtain with their satellite telescopes. After all, the ass end, as you Americans would say, is better than nothing, da?" Vladimir smiled broadly and added, "Good thing this flight has no women on it."

"Good idea, we will request photos. As to your parting comment, recall Patty would have been on this flight. She would have been happy to oblige you by kicking your ass, major," Blake added with a slight smile, but his point was made.

"Da, I know this Patty Myers. Pretty lady, but very smart as well, and talks Russian. I would apologize to her my good friend Blake if she was here, and I would enjoy her being here; we would have good talk, in Russian." Vladimir nodded to Blake.

"You know Patty Myers? How might this be, Vladimir?"

"It pays to know one's friends …"

"And adversaries," Blake added.

"Exactly, but right now, I prefer to use friend, da? She is good linguist and also quite good at, what you call it, code breaking? Da, that's it, code breaking."

"Yes she is, Vladimir, top shelf in all aspects. No disrespect to anyone on this crew, but I also wish she was here. I think she would be our best emissary to interface with the owners of the ship we are visiting, assuming there is anyone there. Who else do you know from my team, Vladimir?"

"With all respect, Maj. Thompson, I know all of them … Lt. Sean O'Rourke, Li Zheng, Corp. Diego Velasquez, and Spec. Harry Lundrum. I would like to meet this Harry Lundrum. He is, should we say, a cut above the rest in intelligence, da? By the way, that special op in Tibet, nice work, major."

"How could you possibly know these things, Vladimir?" Blake looked over at Vladimir with a mix of surprise, concern and admiration.

"We have our ways, major, but I will call you Blake as we are friends, da? You don't share all your secrets with friends and family, correct? At the right time, I will share more, but only when it brings value to both of us. As you know …"

"Yes, we know, it is good to know one's friends … and adversaries." Blake cut in.

"Ahh, we are in agreement, then." Vladimir folded his arms and sat back in his seat.

Blake chuckled lightly. He knew the Russian spy and intelligence agencies were good, but sometimes it was downright embarrassing. There was nothing Blake could do at the moment, so he filed the thought away for future discussion when they returned to Earth … which right now seemed like might happen in another lifetime.

CHAPTER 15

A.D. 2028 (3311 C.A.E.); Dec. 14
Sana'a, Yemen

Patty was dressed in the common Yemen attire for women, known as a Sana'ani curtain-style dress. The Sana'ani includes a wrap of brightly colored cloth, called an Al-Masoon, wrapped around the wearer. Patty was also wearing an Al-Momq, a black face cover made of silk.

It had been three days since they had arrived and had nothing to show for it. They were getting ready to write off Sana'a and head to Saudi, but finally something, the first hit with potential significance, had been uncovered. Patty was walking down 26th September Street, returning from Tahrir Square, where she had just met with a contact Oliver Wyatt had identified for her. The individual, who would only respond to the code name Sana'a 42, had known Ataullah since they had been young men in the military. Sana'a 42 was not aware of any formal Al Qaeda connections that Ataullah had, but Sana'a 42 had numerous information bytes that suggested Ataullah's brother Ahmed did. At the least, that ensured Ataullah remained on the primary suspect page. After a series of short messages, the group decided to head back to the hotel so Patty could provide a more detailed update to the team. With the new information, the team hoped they would be better armed to search and identify additional people associated with Ahmed to add to their investigation.

Patty was still a little uneasy about the secret meet. Sana'a 42 had not been even a little bit nervous. That was unusual, Patty reflected. Typically, informants like this were always looking over their shoulder, in a hurry to exchange their information, take their payment and depart. That was especially true in countries where people could be beheaded for actions that could easily deem one a traitor to the State or religion. But Sana'a 42 had been quite calm, almost comfortable, Patty recalled. She would have to bring that up with Oliver to see what he thought the next time they met. Had the individual not been recommended by Oliver Wyatt, she would definitely have called in reinforcements.

The day was hot, dry and sunny. Dust was everywhere. At least there wasn't any wind today, Patty reflected. Everything was brown in this city and the ground was barren without signs of plant life growing anywhere. Even the buildings were brown and looked like they were made of hardened dirt that had been cut from the ground nearby. It was hard to believe that people could live here, or for that matter, *wanted* to live here, she thought.

Patty was on her way back to the 10-story Movenpick Hotel on Berlin Street where she and the rest of the team agreed to meet. It was a long, hot five-kilometer walk from Tahrir Square to the hotel, which was less than a kilometer south of the U.K. Embassy and fewer than two kilometers south of the U.S. Embassy, a relatively safe zone to be in.

"God, what a desolate place this is," Patty spoke quietly into her headset. "I know beauty is in the eye of the beholder, but I think I can safely pass on this place."

"Amen, sister," Sean chirped back. "Keep your eyes open. Ugly is one thing, but dangerous and ugly is even worse."

It had been about 15 minutes since Patty left Tahrir Square and she'd walked about a kilometer. She crossed Zubayri Street and decided to take a short cut down Sailah Road South. About 100 meters down Sailah, directly in front of the Defense Military Complex, Patty caught movement behind her out of her right eye as she had glanced at the houses to her right. A car had just pulled off the road and three men had gotten out. The men, all wearing nondescript white robes, were walking in her direction.

Patty walked quicker. Under the cover of her dress, she clicked her radio three times, waited five seconds and clicked it another three times, waited another five seconds and clicked it another three times in quick succession. That was their emergency signal. Patty knew that Sean and Diego would be close by as they had agreed to stay within 400 meters of her throughout the day. Harry and Li were back at the hotel exchanging updates with the Pentagon and maintaining home base.

As it turned out, Sean and Diego had also noticed the car stop behind Patty and the three occupants unload, seemingly without a care in the world, as they didn't even look back to see if anyone else was on the street.

"Cocky or stupid bastards, this is a busy road and they didn't even care to look around." Sean quickly followed with a string of expletives once the three men began following Patty, with the car following close behind. Then the three men started jogging toward Patty.

"They're after her, Sean – Patty is their target!" Diego yelled as their radios began clicking. The two men started sprinting toward Patty before the second set of clicks announced their arrival on their radios.

"Take 'em out, Diego!"

Sailah Road turned hard to the left. The right side of the road was a continuous run of small houses with precious little space in between. Patty was now running.

"We're going to lose sight of her for a brief time when she rounds that bend ahead. Sean, when we catch them, you take the driver, I'll stay with Patty."

"Get to her quick, Diego." The gap was closing, but there were still at least 200 meters between them.

As they approached the bend, they both cut across the road and traffic in order to shorten the distance. As they cleared the edge of the bend, Patty was gone. So were the three men and the car.

"Damn! Diego, they got her!" Sean yelled in desperation.

"I'll try calling her. You call Harry and Li, and also let Oliver know what's going on. Oliver's contact was either followed, or he's been compromised and notified someone as soon as they were done talking."

"It was a white Toyota Corolla, plates 18898. Find it, Diego."

Both continued running back across Sailah Road to where Patty should have been, continuing to look in all directions. The car was nowhere to be seen. Harry answered the phone on the first ring and Sean updated him quickly. Harry agreed to call the embassy while Li called the Pentagon and demanded satellite tapes be pulled up immediately to help track what happened.

"No answer from Patty," Diego stated, emotionless, as he moved into battle mode.

"There's no way they caught her that quickly; she still had at least 50 meters on them."

"There may have been a second car ahead of her, and the three men simply chased her straight into their hands. We've done that ourselves before; remember Kabul?" Diego replied, looking intently at the houses off the right side of the road.

"We messed up, Diego. We left her wide open. We have to find her. Try her radio again," Sean responded.

"You call her, Sean; let me check between these buildings to make sure she didn't attempt a side run."

Five minutes later, Diego returned.

"Nothing, absolutely nothing."

"Same here," Sean said, looking down at the radio.

A few seconds later, Sean's radio beeped.

"Hello? Patty?"

"No, it's Li. Harry's on the way to pick you both up."

Jarisst I

Thjars was enjoying a quiet snack in the kitchen when the intercom crackled to life. It was Juulys. "Thjars, can you join me in the Comm Center for a few minutes?"

"I'll be there in five minutes."

"Okay, thanks."

Thjars looked down at his half-eaten rajhstallyst, took one last bite, wrapped the remainder up and stuffed it into his pocket to finish later. He squeezed the last remaining drops of water from the sealed pouch he had selected, dropped it into the disposal and headed out to find Juulys, which he did three minutes later.

Juulys was so engrossed in what she was typing that she didn't realize Thjars had arrived.

"Juulys?" Thjars quietly said, but the result still caught her off guard, and she jumped back against her seat with her hand over her chest.

"Sorry Juulys, I didn't mean to startle you. Is everything okay?" Thjars offered while placing his hand on her shoulder.

"Yes … yes, it is, well … I hope it is. I guess I was too deep into my report and just didn't hear you come in. Thjars, I'm not sure how to say it, but … I have identified two more ships and it appears that one of them is now heading on what looks to be an identical, but opposite trajectory to the initial ship between the third and fourth planets – based on their current trajectories, they will meet up. The other one appears to be heading towards us on as close to the same path as the first ship we identified." Juulys looked up at Thjars.

"From the third planet?"

"No … yes … I think so, but I'm not positive."

"That seemed like a straightforward question, Juulys," Thjars responded.

"Sorry, Thjars. The one heading this way actually appears to have come from the small moon that orbits the third planet. The other ship, a very small, possibly one-man vehicle, appears to be traveling between the fourth and third planets, might have also started on the small moon and is heading towards the fourth planet, in the direction where the ship we detected earlier is coming from."

"Can you determine if they are communicating with each other?"

"I don't believe so. I'm now picking up signals from the first ship heading towards us and have detected attempts to communicate with the other ship in at least three different languages, the most common of which appears to be what they refer to as English. It seems they have stopped using encryption and are sending messages openly. The second ship traveling between the third and fourth planets is clearly communicating in English. I've not picked up any transmissions from the two newest ships. The messages are not encrypted, so I'm pretty confident that the first ship is requesting the third ship to identify itself, but as I mentioned earlier, there have been no responses. Matter of fact, I have not picked up any signals from the third ship, and the third ship is clearly gaining on the first one. I expect they will overtake them before the first ship can reach us."

"Is there any chance this second ship is Klaxxstinian?" Thjars asked, clearly concerned.

"I don't think so, but as our *recent* misfortune has shown, it's actually been hundreds of years since we have seen the Klaxx. We have no way of knowing what types of scout craft they now have around the galaxy, but we may know better by the time they get closer to the first ship. If it's a Klaxx ship, they'll likely start firing as soon as they're within range, but I highly doubt it is as its current speed is much slower than what we knew the Klaxx had ..." Juulys hesitated ... "and that was hundreds of years ago. If anything, I would think they would have made improvements by now."

"So, we now have four space-faring vehicles identified so far, possibly more. I'm having a hard time remembering which is which. We need to identify and name each of these ships in the ship's log and keep track of them with their names."

"Agreed and already done, Thjars. The very first ship that is on a track to intercept us is logged as contact 1, or C1. The ship now following it is C3. The ship currently traveling from the fourth planet to the third planet is C2 and the last, smallest and newest ship heading towards the fourth planet is C4. I am looking for more ships, but so far, this appears to be it."

"Thank you Juulys. Let me know immediately if additional ships, or changes in any of the four flight plans is observed."

"I will, Thjars."

Thjars left the room, reflecting on the irony that only a few weeks ago they thought they were all alone. Now it was getting more complicated by the day and they clearly were not going to be alone much longer.

*****

Sana'a

Li was on his phone and looked over at Sean.

"Sean, we've got the NSA on line; apparently they were already requested to provide surveillance as soon as we were on the ground. According to the call I received, the guy told me '… ah … sir, you may not believe this, but I was told, quote, unquote, that it was from a billion kilometers away.' Yep, gotta be Blake. As usual, he has our back and is letting us know, so, it turns out the NSA was already monitoring the situation prior to her intercept. Harry should be there shortly as well."

A Lacrosse class, Onyx II Reconnaissance spy satellite, manufactured by Lockheed Martin Space Systems, had been re-deployed by the NSA, at Blake's request, to monitor the city of Sana'a while the team was on site. This newer version of the 1980s Lacrosse upgrade included radar imaging, infrared, Hubble-telescope-level video capabilities and a new narrow-beam, long-distance, variable-magnitude, variable-frequency X-Ray (RIVVVX) known as "RIV-X." The price tag for this surveillance platform was rumored on the Hill to exceed $2.5 billion. The level of detail that was recorded was highly classified, but anonymous sources at *Jane's Defense Weekly* claimed it could cover an area of five square miles continuously, with image fidelity accurate to the centimeter level, thereby also providing face-recognition analysis.

"They're analyzing the stored recordings, but it looks like your hunch was correct," Li continued. "There was a second Toyota and Patty ran directly into a second set of guys who pulled her into the second car. The hounds chased her straight to the hunters; she never saw it coming – nor did we. The first car picked up the three runners and they both took off south on Sailah. NSA says they took a number of turns on side roads, apparently to see if they were followed, and then returned to Sailah. They followed Sailah to the intersection of Al Cuds Street, also known as Ring Road, and then headed up Algiers Street to a small warehouse on Mahrogat. Oliver has been notified and he has already checked in and is waiting for orders."

"Have you requested that they pass on word to Blake?" Sean replied.

"Yes, I did, but whether they decide to share it, or *when* they decide to share it I can't guarantee. As we talked earlier, it's not like he doesn't have enough on his plate right now."

"Fair point, Li, but thanks for trying," Sean replied. "Call Oliver and tell him to get a team ready – no heavies yet, just vehicles, men and firearms."

"Got it."

Sean was agitated as he looked over at Diego. "They've taken her into what looks like a small warehouse off of Mahrogat, just north of the 60 Meters Highway. We have to move quickly."

"Get a grip on it, Sean; you can't help her if you go E-state. We'll get to her in time. If they wanted her dead, they would have shot her right there on the street. They want info, or collateral for an exchange; either way, they need her alive. That gives us time, and with the NSA tracking their every move, Oliver and his gang, and ourselves, we have most of the trump cards. Let's go." The two men started jogging down the street as Diego talked with Harry on the phone to set up a rendezvous point.

E-state was what Blake's crew referred to as "going emotional." Their team had coached hard against this in every training session, ever since they had started working together. It was well studied and thoroughly documented that a person's cognitive powers were compromised once someone went E-state because of anger or fear. The quick surge of adrenaline and noradrenaline from the amygdala that accompanied extreme anger or fright was instinctually important for the so called "fight-or-flight" needs of a body in danger, but not beneficial for the deep thinking, cognitive, planning processes needed in Special Forces Ops. Ops like these almost always encountered surprises or unexpected twists that required team members to think on the fly – without going E-state. Many scientific and psychological studies had shown that cognitive thinking processes of a typical person were compromised for a full 15 to 20 minutes after the amygdala kicked in. Every minute counted during a special op, so it was imperative that team members maintained absolute control over their emotions. That was typically "easy" in the field, but this time, it was different. This was personal for Sean. This was Patty.

"Don't worry about me. Just get us to that building," Sean sniped through gritted teeth.

Five excruciating minutes later, Harry pulled up in an unmarked van with no side or rear windows.

"Get in. Take this radio; it's a direct connection to the NSA. A second van with six fully armed Marines from the U.S. Embassy is already on the way, but will stay at a distance until we call them in. Oliver has three men with him, also heading to the warehouse. Diego, it's your lead and your call from here."

Sean and Diego piled in and Harry hit the gas, heading toward the warehouse.

"NSA has given us a different vector and road sequence to get to the warehouse to minimize the risk of a posted lookout seeing us, but we will still be there in less than 15 minutes," Harry relayed to Diego, nodding toward Sean. Even if it was never openly voiced among team members, everyone knew Patty was more to Sean than just another team member.

"Diego. In case there are any possible communication windows, tell them to send a quick update to Blake. Make sure he knows what our current status is. It sure feels like this is a real connection that may further implicate Ataullah."

"Good idea, Harry. I'm on it."

CHAPTER 16

A.D. 2028 (3311 C.A.E.); Dec. 14
On Board the Reagan I

"Reagan I, this is Houston. Come in, please."

Minutes later, after the inevitable communication delays, Cmdr. Kline responded.

"This is Cmdr. Kline, Reagan I. What's up this fine morning, gentlemen?" He sat back in his chair, drinking coffee and waiting for their response, which came a few long minutes later.

"We're not sure yet, but we are tracking an unknown vehicle heading towards you. We are sending you encoded information. Please read and respond."

"What?! From where? … Hello?" Kline stammered while sitting up abruptly and spilling his coffee. He knew there would be no immediate response, but the sheer surprise of the call's content had thrown him off balance. He again reminded himself of the obligatory radio signal time delay as his response travelled back to Earth, and they in turn responded and sent it back, so he added, "Sorry, Houston, will do." It was an uncomfortable and sometimes frustrating manner in which to communicate, but it was the only option available. A few minutes later, he received Houston's response.

"You're not going to believe this, commander, but as best we can tell, it launched from the moon. We have attempted to contact it, but there has been no response yet. We are in the process of re-deploying satellite imaging assets to get a better look at it, but it is small enough that, at this point in time, we feel it appropriate to warn you that we have not yet ruled out a missile."

"A missile, what the f ..." Kline blurted out and then trailed off in order to hear the rest of the message.

"It is still many days, or even weeks away from you, commander. We are looking at a number of options right now and will get back to you as soon as we know more. It's up to you if you want to share it with the crew immediately, or wait until it gets closer." Then the speaker had paused, clearly waiting for a response.

"Roger that, Houston. I will alert them immediately so that we can start looking at options. If your worst case scenario is real, it's not like we have many options."

A few more minutes later, he received the final verbal communication. "Understood, commander. Hang tough. We will get back to you as soon as we know more. If you have ideas or questions for us, send them and we'll get engineers on it ASAP. By the way, everyone is getting called in on this, and I mean everyone."

Cmdr. Kline looked out the cockpit window at the blackness of space. How could this possibly be happening, he wondered. It was unbelievable. Kline knew there would be plenty of time for hundreds of questions, but first he needed to get Jimmy and the others up to speed.

*****

"O'Dougherty, come check this out!"

"What's up, Jimmy?"

"Pat and I have been attempting to remove what we think is the nose cone for what, a week now? Well, we finally got the nose cone off it, whatever *it* is. This looks like a programming panel with keys on it," Jimmy stated incredulously while pointing at a panel. "I have no idea what the markings are on the keys, but it's not a far stretch of the imagination to connect their style with the markings we found on the outside of the device."

"What happens if you type on it?"

"Are you crazy, O'Dougherty? No way am I going to try that! Well, at least not *yet*." Jimmy leaned back with his hands in the air, smiling, "Knowing your damn Irish relatives, the Murphys, it would likely trigger a spontaneous detonation and turn us all into space dust." Jimmy grinned like a high school kid.

"Okay, genius, what next then?" O'Dougherty challenged.

"That's the million dollar question. I don't know, Tom … this is waaaay beyond my pay grade. We need some real brainpower on this. Let's get some photographs and send them over to the geeks at NSA; maybe they can figure it out."

"Sounds like a plan, Jimmy."

Jimmy went to work taking as many pictures as he could, from different angles and magnifications. In the cramped quarters, and especially with the unexpected guest that took up most of the room's free floor space, it was not a simple task to get good pictures that showed what he wanted to emphasize and yet still keep overall perspective. The lighting had to be right, the position had to be right, and even then, it was clear that a picture did *not* always paint one thousand words. In many cases, Pat had to literally lie over the top of the device to hold disassembled pieces at the right angle, while staying out of Jimmy's way.

The photo session took a good two hours and they were sweating profusely by the time they were done.

"Okay, let's load these onto the computer and start transmitting. We'll see what brainy ideas the NSA boys can come up with." Jimmy looked up as Cmdr. Kline entered the bay.

"Gentlemen," Kline said as he entered the makeshift lab area. "We may have company soon."

"What? Like a twin brother to this tyke?" Jimmy said pointing to the device.

"Sorry, Jimmy, but no joke." Cmdr. Kline spent the next five minutes updating his crew before asking for ideas. As usual, Jimmy was the first to speak.

"Commander, are you sure you don't have any more surprises for us? I'd just as soon get it all on the table at one time if that's okay with you. An alien device ... a UFO or missile heading our way ... it's quite an earful, Commander. I don't know. It'd be one thing if it came from Earth, but the moon? That seems to rule out a lot." Jimmy paused and then looked up, quickly changing his expression from sarcasm to consternation, "Oh my God, Commander ... is it possible .... is it possible that whatever is coming towards us is the owner of this thing ...?" Jimmy asked softly as he pointed to the device.

They all looked at Jimmy with what would have been a look of insanity just a few short months ago, but was now fully replaced by equal parts of astonishment and consternation.

"Jimmy, get that off to Houston ASAP. I'm not sure if that is good or bad news, but you may have something there."

*****

Armstrong I

Blake received the double encoded message, processed it through the decryption software, entered two passwords and read the message. He shook his head in disbelief. It didn't seem possible, but the latest update on Patty continued to support a tie to Ataullah. How else could this have blown up so quickly? But right now, his main concern was for Patty and his earthbound team. Valuable time had already been lost due to the transmission time between Earth and the Armstrong I; Blake knew he needed to respond quickly.

Code Red: Transmit to Corp. Diego Velasquez immediately upon receipt. Maj. Blake Thompson.

"Diego, Blake here. Time is critical. Hope you have already acted. If not, do not wait for approval or backup. Hit quick. Hit hard. If you can capture any of them to interrogate, that's a go. Any risk or doubt, eliminate ALL resistance. Kick ass. Blake out."

Blake hit the transmit button and then updated Jack and James on the most recent news.

"Sorry, Blake, but it sure feels like your instinct may have missed on Ataullah this time."

"Disappointing, but I agree, James."

"Should we take him down now?" James asked the question they were both considering.

"It's a fair question, but I'd rather wait a little longer. We have plenty of time before we reach the ship. Agreed?"

"To be honest," James jumped in, "I'm not sure; I could argue either way, but I'm willing to go with your recommendation for now – unless of course, new information requires faster response."

"Agreed, James. Jack, your thoughts?"

"Count me in, but I think I'll sleep with one eye open the rest of the way."

"Okay gents, eyes and ears open 24/7. Share even the smallest new information, or any tiny thing you find that seems out of place or abnormal. If anything changes with Ataullah that increases our perception of risk, I'll take him down pronto."

*****

Sana'a

Diego had been talking quietly on the radio with Oliver, and was now ready to update the team.

"Oliver will be on site shortly. He will locate in the parking lot of the Expo Apollo Hall with his team, just west of the target in a gray Range Rover. We'll park in the Sana'a Trade Center parking lot, on the east side of the target, until we can finalize plans. The view of the warehouse matches what the NSA analysts had relayed, so we're pretty confident of the data. There are fences around 90 percent of the complex, with only the entrance to the actual building open to access. Unfortunately, the road leading to that entrance appears to have a guard shack out front. The park behind the Expo Apollo Hall has a natural barrier of trees, ditches and shrubs in addition to the fence behind the warehouse."

"Great. Do you have any good news for us?" Sean asked sarcastically.

"Actually, I do, two things. First, Blake already responded." Diego relayed Blake's message. It wasn't like any of the group needed permission, reassurance or specific directions from Blake, but just knowing he was tracking with them was a real morale booster.

"Oorah," Sean spoke for the group with his *this is business*, deadly mode. Diego continued on.

"Secondly, only one car remains at the warehouse, so we are pretty confident that only four of the eight men involved are still at the warehouse. NSA verifies that Patty is still inside. On the other hand, we don't know how many were already inside the building."

Sean had a militarized iPad-like device that was receiving downloaded images directly from the NSA and shared the view with the team.

"This must be a standing safe house for these guys. There's even a fenced alleyway that leads from the back of the building directly to the 60 Meter Highway in case a quick escape is needed. We'll have to post someone near the highway in case a getaway car shows up."

"Sean, there's no way we can do this right now as long as there is still light in the sky. It'll be dark in 30 minutes, but I think we need to wait until the town quiets down or we'll risk getting more company. Once a few hours have gone by, they'll think they got away scot-free and might start to let their guard down. We'll hit them around two in the morning. Until then, we watch and make sure they don't go anywhere. All agree?"

Everyone in the van nodded. Ironically, everyone in the ops world knew that the best time to hit a target was between 2 and 4 in the morning. Everyone knew, including the bad guys. Yet, data was data. op after op, it continued to be the most successful attack window. There was just no fighting Mother Nature, and a man's internal body clock.

"Okay, that will also give us time to plan the details. We know that Patty is at risk, but I don't see any other choices. She's going to have to tough it out a little longer. I expect they will take a few hours of interrogation before they do anything risky with her as they don't know what's going on, either. I'll tell Oliver to hustle over and join us so we can develop plans for taking the warehouse. I'll also have Li call the NSA and see if they can use thermal or X-ray sensors from the satellite to tell us how many people are in the building," Diego finished and picked up the radio.

*****

Jarisst I

Qulys, Juulys and Thjars agreed to meet in the control room.

"Qulys, we still don't know what the intentions of these two ships are, but every bone in my body is telling me that neither ship, especially the second ship, has positive intentions. What defenses do we have back online so far?" Thjars looked over at Qulys, hoping he had good news.

"Unfortunately, nothing has changed, lieutenant. Close-in defensive weapon systems are online, but long-range offensive weapons remain locked out by the same access rights that have the drive systems offline. That means no nukes or beam weapons, but the cannon and directed cluster weapons are online. Based on their current speeds, I am confident that, if needed, we could destroy them both once they get close enough, but we don't know what kind of long-range weapons they might have. We could slowly move the ship right now, but once we start to move, they will know for sure that the ship is manned and active. By remaining motionless, with exterior lights off, they may think they are on a salvage operation and focus more attention on each other. Once they bring their ship or ships in close, then we would have the advantage of surprise."

"Qulys, thank Glysst you made it through with us as I'm not sure what I would do without you. I agree with your plan. Make sure the weapons are manned and trained in their direction so that no movement is required until the last split second – if and only if needed. I'd also like to make sure the crew is armed and ready in case we are boarded. Once the two craft are within a day of reaching us, break out the handguns and distribute accordingly. What about training, as I expect we are all rather rusty right now?"

"You are correct, sir. I've been working with Zalmyt, Platsys and Nylsst on the simulator. They are coming along fine and I expect they will be adequate when the time comes. I will start the rest of the crew's training once the ships are within five days of us."

"Thank you, Qulys."

"Juulys, how about you. Anything new on the translation efforts?"

"Actually, yes. Jarns and I have made a couple of minor breakthroughs. We haven't cracked their encryption codes yet, and to be honest, I'm not confident we will without help from Cjar – we simply don't have the computer capability or time to do so before they get here. However, we are feeling much more confident about translating the language they call English. We picked up enough from their unencrypted transmission efforts to the second ship that we could begin to decipher other segments we have obtained from their home planet, the third planet in this system. We are now fairly confident that they call it Earth."

"Have you figured out what their plans are?"

"No, I expect that tactical transmissions have all been encrypted. It is also clearer now that there are definitely many different groups or governments on their planet. Unfortunately, or fortunately, I believe this verifies what we hypothesized earlier – we are dealing with a race in this planetary system whose evolutionary maturity is hundreds of years behind ours, if not more."

"That may be true, but we are currently rather limited in our ability to demonstrate our superiority."

"Point taken, lieutenant. On the positive side, if they are receptive to discussion, I believe I know enough now that I could send or respond with some basic help or introductory messages, mainly in what they call English, if and when you decide to."

"That is good news, Juulys," Thjars replied. "Right now, though, we will stay with Qulys' recommendation and play dead until we better know what they are up to. You may also want to start thinking about some threatening messages that you can use if we want to attempt to bluff our way out of this."

"Good point, I'll start working on that, but keep in mind, *if* English transmissions work, then a message may only work on the first ship. We have no way of knowing what the second ship will respond to as they have yet to communicate with anyone – and based on our calculations, they will be the first ship to arrive here."

"Keep reminding yourself that we have made tremendous progress from where we were just a month ago and we have over a month to go. I expect we will be quite ready for their arrival, especially as they have no idea that we are here, or any way to review our transmissions, like we are doing with them."

"Great point, Thjars. We will be ready."

*****

A.D. 2028 (3311 C.A.E.); Dec. 15

Sana'a

"Okay, mark time. We commence in three-zero minutes," Diego spoke quietly into his radio.

The night was cloudless and the half-moon had risen two hours earlier: great to see by, but also great to be seen by. Unfortunately, there were no other options as Patty had to be extracted tonight. Traffic was almost nonexistent, even on the 60 Meter Highway behind the warehouse. The NSA satellite had identified six human shapes inside of the warehouse. One was stationed by the main entrance, likely an entrance guard, two appeared to be sleeping in beds in a side room on the northwest corner, and the other two were with what appeared to be Patty on the far southwest corner of the building. Knowing that one had to be Patty left five enemy combatants to dispose of.

As soon as the sun set, Diego and Oliver slipped through the bushes and grass, and worked their way up to the fence. Diego cut a small hole in the fence and then maintained guard while Oliver set up a 12-inch-tall black box on adjustable legs just inside of the fence, pointed at the building's wall and pushed the "on" button. He gave Diego a thumbs-up sign and the two men quickly and quietly returned to Harry and the others.

"Okay, Harry, it's all yours," Diego whispered as he patted Harry on the back.

Harry placed a large headset over his ears and began picking up voices within the building. Harry had developed this unit a couple of years back, starting with an off-the-shelf $400 listening device from KJB Security products – plus of course, some of Harry's own personal modifications he subsequently added. The device, as purchased, could pick up discrete sounds from up to 300 feet away due to a specially designed parabolic dish and a 3-band equalizer. Harry had increased the signal-processing capabilities of the unit and tripled the amp as well. As a final improvement, Harry mounted the unit in an open-faced composite shell. The box was mounted on top of a motorized tripod that could be remotely controlled from a distance of 100 meters. Harry could manipulate the controls to get amazingly clear audio from inside the building within an audio cone of 10 degrees, sweeping the focal point through the building to investigate every room in the building, one at a time. The unit was so sensitive that Harry could easily hear the sleeping sounds of two of the men. But that also meant he had been able to maintain clear awareness of what the men were doing to Patty. It had been a rough night so far and he decided it was best not to share that with the rest of the group, especially Sean.

As it turned out, the terrorists had immediately gagged and tied Patty up in the car when they captured her. Once inside the warehouse, they tied her up in a chair and initiated interrogations. The first two hours had been fairly straightforward with no more than yelling and a few slaps. The terrorists had taken an hour off to eat dinner, conduct their ritualistic prayer sessions and then resumed the interrogations, but it quickly became clear that the level of physicality had been upped. Another three hours went by and Patty actually passed out twice during the beatings. Harry almost gave Li the attack signal around 10:30 p.m. when Patty passed out the second time, but there was still too much activity in the neighborhood and Harry was convinced that the terrorists' conversations and actions didn't appear to be hitting the "final" stages yet.

Embassy Marines were lying in the ditch, guarding the alley escape near the road, as well as making sure that no last-minute re-enforcements could surprise them from the 60 Meter Highway. In a pinch, they could also join the upcoming firefight. The Marines were well armed and experienced; anyone coming or going down that alley was not going to have a good day. Oorah and Semper fi, none better. Diego knew that confidently.

The alley was also going to be their own primary escape route. Oliver's second squad had commandeered a van in addition to their second Range Rover, and the embassy was providing a third van. The combination of all three vehicles would be adequate for a quick escape out of town for all team members, even if they left their original vehicles behind. All vehicles had been swept for prints, and traceability of the vehicles to any ownership had been eliminated prior to starting the mission.

Oliver's men joined them on the east side of the warehouse. Just past midnight, they cut down a few key shrubs on the east side of the park, placed a few planks that they had been able to muster from the various garbage piles that spotted the area across the ditch to allow access by their Range Rover. They then quietly cut the fence in multiple locations, in a manner that the fence remained standing, but was weakened enough that a strong impact from the Range Rover would easily break through. The satellite had detected very little metal in the building structure, making it a fair bet that the walls were wooden framework and drywall. Based on that structural information, and the location of the sleeping quarters, the plan was for Oliver and his men to crash the Range Rover through the east wall of the building directly on top of the two sleeping occupants, cutting the bad guys down to three with the commencement of the attack.

Expecting the guard to instantly move toward the unexpected chaos, Diego, Li and Sean would follow through the hole in the fence, move around to the front of the building and blow the front door immediately after. The guard would be frozen between two separate events, each of which required his attention. That short delay would be more than enough for them to take both the guard and the electrical power out, as the electrical wires to the warehouse entered by the guard station. Those actions would shift the odds heavily in their favor at seven versus two, and the seven still had the element of surprise and darkness at their advantage. Diego, Sean and Li would then rush the backroom where Patty was being held, and where Oliver would likely already be after crashing through the wall. If all went according to plan, they would be in and out in less than five minutes. Harry would remain on guard at the outside door until he was hailed by Diego to exit via the alley.

Five minutes to go. Each of the men had NIVISYS AN/PVS-7B/D night-vision goggles and Dupont Kevlar body armor on. Each man carried stun grenades and hand weapons of choice. At Diego's command, they automatically checked their guns, ammo belts and unclicked the safeties. No one spoke. They all knew their next moves and had mentally rehearsed the various issues and surprises that could arise and how they would counter them. The single best approach to success was clear to teams like this – go in hard and assume that the primary plan never went as planned. The single biggest risk was friendly fire and they had planned and rehearsed fire lanes to minimize that risk. Crashes and loud noises might wake neighbors up, but they typically didn't panic people at night. Gunfire on the other hand, was an unmistakable sound that had a high probability of call-in to local police. For that reason, priority was given to silencers and knives for the initial entry. Expectation for gunfire was high in the final room, but at that point, they would be very close to extraction and arriving police forces would find nothing but bodies.

"Five – four – three – two – one … Go!"

An engine roar was followed shortly by a large crash on the east side of the building. Seconds later, the front door disappeared in a cloud of smoke and dust and a small pop was heard near the entry door three seconds later. Within seconds, the lights in and around the building went out.

They all flipped their night vision goggles in position and Diego crashed through the broken doorframe before the dust could clear, with Sean and Li close on his heels. Harry turned his back and crouched against the wall, facing outward to maintain a clear view of any uninvited guests.

As expected, the guard was disoriented. Diego popped him twice in the head with his Sig Sauer 9mm XM17 pistol, outfitted with a GEMTECH G-CORE suppressor. The guard was done. The heavy Range Rover had crashed through the wall with little resistance and landed on top of the two beds. The two individuals in those beds were crushed instantly. Even if they were still alive, the pressure on their chests would eliminate any ability to speak, move or breathe. It was only a matter of time until suffocation claimed them. Three down, two to go. Oliver and his three men were already heading to the back room as the door opened.

"Screw the knives," someone yelled, "just take 'em out!"

Oliver fired one round from his silenced Glock 17 service pistol, striking the first man in the center of the forehead, as his team landed four more shots to his chest. The lieutenant next to Oliver simultaneously lobbed a stun grenade through the now open door. Red lasers danced past the dead man from two modified Colt Canada C8 carbines, looking for a target. Before any did, the stun grenade detonated, followed in perfect succession by Sean bursting through the door with his Sig pistol in his right hand and a Ka-Bar knife in his left hand. The final target was stunned and rolling across the floor in an awkward attempt to stay low and retrieve his AK-47 that was on a table against the far wall – a too distant three meters away. Sean was on him in a flash and tackled him, stomach first, to the ground. Sean dropped his Sig Sauer pistol, switched the knife into his right hand, cupped the man's mouth with his left, pulled his head back and sunk the knife slightly into the man's back just between the shoulder blades.

"One yell, one move, and you're a dead man. It only takes another inch with this knife, but I'll put it clean through you just for grins. Are we clear, mophead?" The man struggled in pain for a few seconds and Sean tightened his grip. "Are we clear?" Sean repeated in the man's ear, this time with a deadly coldness that surprised even Diego next to him.

"Yes," the man croaked back.

"Ahh, so you do know English. How fortunate," Sean replied with distinct coldness still in his voice. These guys might be good at snatch-and-grab operations, but they were clearly novices when it came to a planned op with professional killers.

Oliver whistled for Harry and double-clicked the Marines twice on the radio for the extraction notification while Diego untied Patty. They were going to need to carry her out.

"Tie him up; he's coming with us," Sean ordered.

Li tied the abductor-turned-prisoner up with plastic straps, duct-taped his mouth and blindfolded him. Oliver pulled a syringe from his side pack and injected the man with a heavy dose of Ketamine and Versed. Unlike the movies, tranquilizers like Ketamine never worked immediately, typically requiring five to 15 minutes before the full effects were realized. In reality, they worked more like a scene from "National Geographic" where one had to track the targeted animal through the jungle brush until it finally collapsed. Versed worked quicker and ensured the individual didn't remember much, but either way, this guy would be no problem in a very short period of time.

Diego opened the backdoor and let two of the Marines in who had come down the alleyway from the road position.

"Thanks, guys. Take this trash to the van; we'll get Patty – we need to get her to the embassy ASAP. Call ahead for medics to be ready. We'll take the second vehicle."

Sixty seconds later, the group exited the building through the back door to the alleyway, carrying their wounded teammate and the captured terrorist. They reached the 60 Meter Highway just as the three vehicles pulled up. Thirty seconds later, the first two vehicles with Harry, Patty, Sean, and Oliver's crew were heading northwest toward the predetermined escape route. Total time, four minutes and 28 seconds. The remaining vehicle with two Marines already in it waited for Diego and Li, as well as their two Marine comrades.

"Get those hard drives," Diego ordered as he pointed to a bank of at least a dozen computers against the wall. I'll check the rest of the building."

Eight minutes and 30 seconds later, the three men were sprinting down the alley with knapsacks containing what they hoped would be a horde of information. As the vehicle took off, Diego called Harry's radio, "On the move."

Sean replied with a simple, "Roger that."

*****

Sixty minutes after arriving at the U.S. Embassy and getting debriefed, Blake's earthbound team was on the embassy's helipad for a flight to the USS Avenger. They were accompanied by Oliver Wyatt and the prisoner, as well as one medic for Patty. As unbelievable as it seemed, the remaining terrorist was none other than the same contact Oliver had provided them with: Sana'a 42. Oliver wanted a little "alone time" with this guy. He was pretty confident that he could get info out of him and he knew that no one here was going to bring up the Geneva Conventions. That was for damn sure.

Patty was banged up pretty good, but the medic cleared her of any serious damage and said she would be as good as new in a couple of weeks.

"That was quick, even by our standards," Li quipped to the group. "We'll be long gone before the locals wake up. It'll be even longer before someone reports the incident."

Sean looked over at Patty. "Patty, you've been pretty quiet. You doing okay, considering?"

"Yes, still a little shook up. That was the closest I've been to being …" Patty shuddered and paused. "I know, I'm not supposed to ever say that, but … damn it! I didn't know where I was and I didn't know if you guys knew where I was. I'm pretty sure they were going to finish me before the sun came up. I hurt everywhere." She shook a bit more and was quiet for a minute, pulling herself together.

"Did they … do anything else, Patty?" Sean asked quietly; not confident on how he should ask Patty if she had been raped.

"No, thank God, Sean, they hadn't yet, but I was afraid they would before the night was out." Patty shuddered again, then looked at Harry.

"Harry, they wanted to know why I was asking about Ataullah, so that verifies we're onto something. Hopefully, either Sana'a 42 or the hard drives Diego recovered will tell us more."

"Get some rest and we'll talk again later," Sean replied for the entire group.

"You're right, Sean, I do need some time to regroup and rest, but … I'll be fine. Thanks for coming after me, guys," she added as her eyes welled up with tears.

*****

USS Avenger

On board the USS Avenger, Diego called Houston Space Center and was connected directly with a line that would record and encode verbal discussions prior to sending the message to Blake onboard the Armstrong I. The growing distance between Earth and the Armstrong I made live discussions more awkward due to the time delay, but Diego knew that Blake would be waiting. During the brief message, Diego provided Blake with a quick update on Patty and the Op, and verified all were safe and back in U.S. protection. The team would be staying on the USS Avenger until the prisoner and the hard drives they recovered could be analyzed; only then would they know if they would be heading back to the U.S. with answers, or returning to Yemen to gather more information. Diego added that he would send a message later in the day with additional details.

Hours later, Blake received the message alert, put on his headset and listened to Diego's message.

"What was that all about?" Jack asked Blake as he hung up the headset.

"That was Corp. Diego Velasquez. He assumed command of my special ops team while I'm gone – that's the group I thought would be on the Armstrong I with me right now." Blake smiled at Cmdr. Pavlik. "Apparently, they did touch a trip wire in Yemen. Patty Myers was actually abducted after talking to a supposedly safe Brit contact and they questioned her specifically about her knowledge of Ataullah. Fortunately, the team, with help from the Brits and the USMC, were able to recover her 10 hours later. They also captured one terrorist, the actual contact from the Brits, and they recovered a number of computer hard drives that may shed light on any possible connections with Ataullah."

"That's good news," Jack replied. "Speaking of that, I've been thinking. This is a big ship, and there are many areas that are unreachable or unsearchable, such as the nuclear reactor bay, but there are a lot of easily accessible areas as well. I think it's worth you, James and me taking turns to covertly search the ship for anything that might be deemed suspicious."

"I agree, Jack; I've been thinking the same thing. My biggest concern is Ataullah's sleeping quarters. How do we search his room and not risk his finding out?"

"We could tell him we took a straw vote and the bad news was that he lost, and we voted him off the island. Just hand him a spacesuit."

They both laughed, and Blake added, "Jack, make sure you let me know if I ever piss you off so I have time to make amends or at least start watching my back, okay?"

"Absolutely Blake, you'll be the first to know." Jack grinned back.

"You know Jack, you said that as a joke, but it may actually be a good idea."

"Really, how so?"

"Think about it. I could ask him to help me conduct a spacewalk to check out one of the exterior radars we are having trouble with …"

"What? I didn't realize we were having trouble with … oh, sorry, brain fart. I follow you; keep going."

"Correct, we have to make him think we have a problem. It would take us at least three or four hours to suit up, check the sensor out and then re-enter and remove the suits. You could keep everyone in the control room to help monitor the space walk, while James sweeps his sleeping quarters, as well as some of the other more public areas that are hard to search without alerting someone who has something to hide."

"Interesting idea, Blake, and I think it has a great chance of working. Either we find something, or at least we feel a little bit better if we don't find anything. I'll let James know when we make the shift change tonight. When do we want to give this a shot?"

"Everything we know suggests we have time, so let's give it a few days. I'd like you to report the intermittent problems with the radar system for a couple of days so that it doesn't come across as a surprise. I'd also like to spend time with you and James reviewing the ship, developing a plan of attack and prioritizing locations so that James can get the most out of our spacewalk."

"Sounds like the basis for a good plan. When I talk with James tonight, I'll see what else he comes up with."

"Okay, thanks, Jack. I'll also give Harry a call. He might be able to drum up an explosives sniffer concept for us, kind of like a homemade unit from the what-you-have-in-your-house type thing. I'm sure Klaus could help build it; Germans can build anything, right?"

"Yes, but it sounds more like that scene out of the Apollo 13 movie, remember? We need to build that, out of this." Jack laughed back.

"Great movie! Works for me."

CHAPTER 17

A.D. 2028 (3311 C.A.E.); Dec. 19
Aboard the Jarisst I

"Thjars, our latest calculations project that the second ship will catch the first ship in approximately 21 days if nothing else changes, about nine days before reaching our location. They are both still heading directly towards us, so there is no doubt in my mind that we are the intended target. These two ships are both significantly faster than the ship traveling between the two inner planets of this star system."

"Thanks, Qulys, any change in your game plan recommendations?"

"No, with our limited capabilities and their unknown capabilities, I still believe that the element of surprise is our biggest insurance policy, at least until we know otherwise. If the two ships are indeed competing ships, then they may expose their firing capabilities within the next few days. Based on what we learn, we'll still have plenty of time to change our minds."

"Is Jarns getting any closer to cracking the access codes? It sure would improve our odds to be able to access the long-range weapons and the Q-PAMS drive."

"I wish I could report otherwise, Thjars, but we're no closer than where we were three weeks ago. It appears the designers of that self-protect system accomplished their goal, and then some."

Thjars was deep in thought. He wondered what Capt. Blissiart would be doing right now, that is, assuming he didn't have the codes, either.

"Wait, where are Cryells and Allympht right now?"

"I believe they're with Jarns, why? An idea?

"I don't know, Qulys, but something they had said earlier just hit me."

"What's that?"

"We don't know where we are."

"Okay …? I kind of thought we knew that already, Thjars …."

"Well, yes, I didn't mean it that way. We don't know where we are, so we could be close to Cjar, to Klaxx or in some new part of the galaxy. We haven't picked up any Cjarian or Klaxxstinian signals yet, only the signals from the third planet, right?"

"Yes …"

"We've been monitoring signals passively, not actively, so as to not accidentally alert the Klaxx. However, I think it's safe to assume that if we were within a light-year of either Cjar or Klaxx, we would know it by now, so I'm thinking of sending out a local, encrypted distress signal … thoughts?"

"Still risky, but I follow your logic, sir. I think it's worth a shot. Cryells and Allympht can verify, but I think we can degrade the signal to make sure it dies out before it can exceed a light-year in distance. If there are any Cjarian scouts within a light-year of us, they could pick it up."

"Okay, Qulys, get with the two of them and let me know. If they can pull it off, go ahead and have them send the distress call out."

"Will do, sir." Qulys turned and started to leave the room.

"Wait Qulys, I don't want to get everyone's hopes up, just to dash them against the rocks again. On second thought, get with Jarns and have him do it. Just the three of us will know – no one else."

"Yes, sir." Qulys smiled.

"Sorry Qulys, one more thing. I got excited. Maybe we should be a little more cautious before we jump too quickly. Let's think about this from another perspective. What could possibly go wrong if we try this? That's what Capt. Blissiart would be asking if he was still with us. The biggest negative that I can think of is that it gives us away to the oncoming ships – then we would lose the element of surprise. Thoughts?"

"That would be a problem, sir. I'll double-check with Cryells and Allympht, but I'm pretty sure that our distress signal goes out on a frequency that we have not seen the Earth people use yet. In addition, it's encrypted, so they wouldn't be able to read it even if they did intercept it. So the biggest concern is if they can detect noise coming from this area of space and make the assumption that it is us and that we therefore must be alive. I think we can transmit in a highly condensed packet mode and in a very short period of time so that it's highly unlikely that someone would even detect it unless they were programmed for that frequency and packet encryption. If by some crazy chance it was intercepted, then without multiple reception points, there is no way someone could triangulate it and identify our location. It feels very safe, but as I mentioned, I'll verify with Cryells and Allympht."

"That makes sense; let me know what our two engineers decide. By the way, for what it's worth," Qulys turned to salute, "you're growing into the captain's shoes rather nicely."

"Thank you, Qulys, I appreciate it, but I still don't know what I would do without you and Juulys."

*****

USS Avenger

Patty walked slowly along the flight deck with Flight Cmdr. Doug "Hammer" Jones.

"It's hard to believe something this big can actually float," she said, surveying the broad expanse of the flight deck.

"It is impressive, isn't it? I've been involved with aircraft carrier operations for almost 20 years now and it still never gets old."

The fresh sea air actually felt good. Patty had spent the past few days healing and clearing her head from the events in Sana'a.

"So, give me the lowdown on this ship; just how big is it?"

"This little baby cost over $6 billion to build and entered service back in 2009. It was the 10th and last of the Nimitz-class aircraft carriers and she is closing in on her 20th birthday. Her name is the Avenger. And even though she is an old lady by military standards, she was overhauled in the earlier part of this decade at an additional cost of $5 billion. She now packs as much technology and punch as the newer Gerald R. Ford-class carriers do."

"Let's hope that name holds up; where did the name come from?" Patty questioned him further.

"Amen, she will. That nickname happened to be President George H.W. Bush's call sign when he was a Naval Aviator, in reference to the TBM Avenger Aircraft he flew as a lieutenant in WWII. She'll do 56 knots per hour at top speed – well, at least that's what I can publicly acknowledge," he added with a smile. "There are over 6,000 men and women on this ship, so it literally is a floating city – every function that a city has, so does this baby – plus more. The ship is 333 meters long and displaces 100,000 tons. Her flight deck covers over six acres and she carries over 90 aircraft, each of which carries their own devastating punch, so we can provide a fast, deadly force when and wherever it is needed."

"Amazing. The majority of my career has been focused on small teams of six to 10 soldiers. Although I've made hops on carriers before, it's usually been at night, and I've never been given a tour before. This was truly amazing. Why is every ship referred to as *she*?" Patty added.

"That has been debated, but it is tradition, and you know how the military is on tradition. The best reason I've ever heard, and the one that I favor, is because ships are vessels, analogous to a woman's womb. On the humorous and somewhat off-color side, many sailors say that it's because they are very expensive, need a lot of paint and always have a lot of men around them!" Doug said, laughing.

Patty joined in on the laugh. "Okay, both work, but I'll side with you and stick with the first analogy."

Just then her radio buzzed and she answered it.

"Patty here. … Okay, I'll be right there, Diego."

After four days of working around the clock, the computer spooks on board the USS Avenger had identified at least 10 references to Ataullah, and no fewer than 300 references to his brother, Ahmed. Ahmed was guilty of many sins against the West, there was no doubt about that, but they had yet to find the hard connection to Ataullah – other than the fact that they were brothers. They had also identified what they believed were ties to a contact somewhere in Saudi, but further insight on that tie would require extensive encryption analysis back at the NSA or CIA.

"Apparently, they've found some new, key information. We need to get back to the CIC ASAP, but I really appreciate the tour, commander. Thank you."

With that, they hustled, as best Patty could muster, over to the command tower and headed to the Combat Information Center. The rest of the team was already seated in the briefing area.

Commander Jones ushered her to an open seat. Commander or not, the CIC logged this meeting as a "Limited Access, Invite Only" meeting, so he left as soon as Patty was seated.

"Houston, this is Diego. We are all here and the room is cleared."

"Houston is on and the room is cleared."

"Honolulu, are you also on and is the room cleared?"

"Yes, Honolulu is on as well, and the room is cleared."

"Mr. Phalen, the meeting is yours." The young lieutenant moved back from the podium.

"Hello. My name is Mike Phalen. I am a senior operative with the NSA. This briefing is classified top secret, eyes only. There will be no sharing of information on any level with anyone not on this call, without explicit permission from me, the directors of the FBI, CIA or the NSA. There will be no written notes allowed. Are we clear on the ground rules?"

All heads nodded in all three conference rooms scattered across the globe.

"Please sign the attendance roster being passed around."

He waited a minute until all had signed and received acknowledgement from those on the phone.

"We cannot incriminate or declare Ataullah uninvolved. However, we can verify his brother Ahmed's guilt in a number of Al-Qaeda incidents. He has also been connected with a number of calls to Honolulu and Saudi, in each case, to the same untraceable numbers. We expect the number is to a paid cell phone card, and all of these calls took place within the last twelve months. We have identified one name in Honolulu, 'Aikane,' which we believe may be a code name as it means 'friend' in English. The terms 'Armstrong' and 'NightStar' have both been identified, so we believe with 95 percent confidence level that we have a probable connection. The NSA has begun reviewing phone records to see if they can get a better hit. In parallel with that, the FBI and CIA have flooded the Hawaiian Islands with operatives to locate leads on Aikane. How someone in the Middle East came to know anything about the Armstrong I mission is beyond us at the moment, but we have reason to suspect someone high in the Saudi royalty."

Harry raised his hand first.

"Yes, Harry."

"Does this mean you want us back in Yemen, or will we be able to join the effort in Hawaii?"

"You're ahead of me, but *yes*, you and the rest of the team will be heading to Hawaii to join the search. The computer drives have provided adequate justification to connect Lt. Col. Ataullah El-Hashem to the investigation, as well as a wealth of information that our in-country assets can follow up on. As needed, we can also now pull in President Callahan himself, who can deal directly with the Saudis at their highest government levels."

"Good, Sean was looking forward to seeing Patty in a bikini." Li laughed, and received a well-placed elbow to the ribs from Patty.

"Gentlemen, may I remind you of how serious the situation is?"

"No disrespect intended, sir," Harry asserted himself calmly, "but I think they are due some slack in this case, and believe me, we know the criticality. Sometimes a little humor goes a long way to relieving stress, something that allows the mind to focus better. You should read up on it when you have time. I recommend a book called 'Resiliency: Who goes the distance and why?' by Dr. Edward T. Creagan. He's connected with the Mayo Clinic and it's a pretty good read."

The NSA operative looked at Harry like he was speaking in a foreign language until Li volunteered assistance with his warped English accent.

"Don't sweat it, my good man, he's not pulling your leg. If you haven't met him yet, Harry is the next coming of Einstein, but on steroids and with a photographic memory. He most probably read that book while he was still in grade school – assuming he actually went to grade school." He looked over at Harry with a smile and then continued, "Many of us think he skipped grade school and just went straight to MIT at the age of 5. To save time, we just take whatever he says as fact and move on."

"So you're telling me that my meeting rule of 'no notes' was somewhat of a waste of time relative to Harry."

"That would be an affirmative, sir."

"Well stated," Oliver added in as heavy an English accent as he could muster, "but you really need to work on your Queen's English dialect – that accent is bloody horrifying."

With the exception of a very stoic Mike Phalen, the whole room laughed. They spent another 30 minutes reviewing details, asking questions and building theories and plans for when they got back to Honolulu – the latter almost without involvement from Mike as he stepped back and let Harry take over the "next steps" aspect of the meeting. By the end of the briefing, Mike had a totally different view of Harry and the others in the room. This team was not just a bunch of muscle-bound, Oorah jarheads. This team was one hell of a mix of brain and brawn – not one to take lightly.

"Mr. Phalen."

"Yes, Harry?"

"We need to tie Maj. Blake Thompson in on this effort as well," Harry replied factually, rather than asking for permission.

"Already approved, Harry. Straight from President Callahan himself."

"Damn!" Diego replied, "It's good to see that bureaucracy can still be overcome when needed."

"You have no idea, Corp. Velasquez," Mike replied with the first small smile anyone had witnessed. With that, he turned and left the room, leaving a group of ultra-high energy people looking at each other with questions and curiosity on their faces.

*****

Reagan I

"Jimmy, what's that little town you hail from?" Pat was bored and trying to break the silence as Jimmy continued to toy with the device. Jimmy hadn't spoken in at least 20 minutes.

"Saratoga Springs, New York. One of the prettiest places you will ever see, Pat, especially in the fall. The tree colors are literally insane – beyond words or description. Reds, yellows, oranges, purples. You just have to see it for yourself, in person. Trust me. Should be one of the great wonders of nature, and with less than 30,000 people, you can actually enjoy the quietness as well. It's a well-guarded secret my good friend, yet voted in the top 10 places to live in New York State. Sure beats that God-forsaken swamp you came from. What the heck was it … Oldsmar, Florida?" Jimmy winked at his good friend.

"Swamp? Sunny Florida, home of oranges, palm trees and beaches of pure white sand." Pat was up to the challenge. "Come on, a young man like you? Single? … You ever see what covers those beaches? Ladies, Jimmy, and beautiful ladies at that, as far as the eye can see – everywhere you look, dude. Ten degrees below zero, wind blowing, and three feet of snow in your upstate New York? Never happen, my good man. Come see the sunshine state; you'll change your tune."

"Yep, and more kinds of bugs then you could count in a lifetime, right? Palmetto bugs as big as the palm of your hand, fire ants by the trillions, nasty little bastards they are, and alligators … like really, Pat? Jurassic Park in your own back yard. Screw that noise man, I like to *go* fishin', but not *be* the bait! Wrap 90 degrees, 90 percent humidity and sea-level air density and there ain't nothin' you can do but stay indoors during the summer just to keep from sweating to death. Sorry dude, I'll take the north any day of the week. Winter makes you appreciate summer, summer makes you appreciate winter, and then you get spring and fall in between – God's gift to us mere mortals."

Jimmy had his head almost inside the object and was intent on getting to the center of whatever the device was.

"Pat, please pass me that screwdriver. I want to see if I can disconnect the keyboard."

"Keyboard? Now you're calling the panel a keyboard. Are you sure it's a keyboard?"

"What else could it be? It's got a bunch of separate keys with what looks like an alien letter form on each one. It's not rectangular and it has a different number of rows and columns, but in concept, it looks like a keyboard."

"Okay, Jimmy." Pat was looking a little questionable about Jimmy's efforts. "How about it's a control panel, and one of those keys turns it on, one turns it off, and maybe another one, like that red one, actually initiates detonation?"

"Look, Pat, we have months ahead of us before we can get home. I can't just sit here any longer, doing nothing except looking at this damn thing. I'll go nuts!"

"Go? Aren't you already there?" Pat was trying to make him rethink his plans before he did something he regretted. "You know what the NSA guys said – *don't do anything without our permission*. It didn't sound like an option – sounded pretty much like a court order to me."

"Yeah? Well what the heck have they accomplished? Absolutely nothing! And they're how far away? What are they going to do; come lock me up?"

"Maybe."

"Look Pat, I think if I can get to the back side, we might be able to put some jumpers on the bottom of each key and at least start tracing what these keys do."

"It's a great idea, but let's review it with Cmdr. Kline and if he agrees, we can send the request in to our NSA contact."

"Pat, this isn't a bomb. Yes, it's alien, and I know we don't understand their technology, but look at it. There are no liquids, no solids, no components that look anything like a weapon. It's not a weapon, plain and simple. It has to be a communications device, or some type of miniature satellite that collects information. This is the nose section that contains the brains, followed by the mid-section of the device that must have contained fuel, and the back end that looks like an engine – there's nothing else that would suggest a bomb." Jimmy stopped tinkering and looked up at Pat confidently. "I'm sure of it, Pat."

Pat just nodded and Jimmy continued.

"So, if I'm wrong, the worst that can happen, is I piss off a bunch of NSA geeks who are months away from seeing us – they'll forget everything before we even get home."

"Cmdr. Kline won't," Pat replied dryly.

"Okay, fair point, but watch … one key, pick one, nothing will happen. You liked the red one, watch."

"Wait a sec; weren't you the one that didn't want to type on it the last time we had a discussion on this thing?"

"Yes, but I'm getting sick of waiting, and it's not like we don't have a crap ton of time to whittle away, right?"

Jimmy pushed the red key before Pat could stop him.

"Jesus, Jimmy! Don't do that again!" Pat nearly jumped out of his chair.

"See? Nothing happened, Pat. There's nothing to worry about. Watch, I'll push it again." This time Jimmy pushed the red key and held it down.

"Look, I'm holding it down and nothing is happening." No sooner did Jimmy end the sentence, when the unit started beeping and whirling and lights began flashing in the interior of the unit. Jimmy's hand recoiled as if he had been shocked.

"Holy shit, Jimmy, what the hell did you just do?" Pat stepped back as if the device was alive.

"I don't know …" Jimmy trailed off.

"Jimmy, put the screwdriver down and step away from the device, right now! We need to get Cmdr. Kline down here; he's going to need to let Houston and the NSA know what you just did. Good God, Jimmy, we have no idea what you just activated."

The two men had no way of knowing that the unit was actually responding to an externally received signal.

CHAPTER 18

A.D. 2028 (3311 C.A.E.); Dec. 21
Honolulu, Hawaii

It had been another long flight, or series of flights as it turned out, but the team was back in Honolulu, via Germany; Washington, D.C.; and San Francisco. The warm sunny weather wasn't much cooler than Yemen, but the blue waters and extensive vegetation made it clear that they were far from the barren landscape of Sana'a. A light breeze carried the scent of the ocean that was not far away from where the team had assembled. The sounds of evening birds and a far off Christmas melody floated through the awakening sky. Christmas lights adorned a number of nearby palm trees.

"Somehow, I could never get used to Christmas lights on palm trees," Patty said quietly.

"I agree, Ms. Patty; Christmas lights definitely need to be on a snow-covered spruce tree. But, it is what it is, so we have to make do like the locals, right? So, now what about that bikini, Patty …" Sean aped with a big grin.

"Stow it, O'Rourke, or I'll have Blake send you back to Yemen where you can only see a small section of a woman's face; then we'll see if you can finally develop some appropriate respect." She laughed and flipped her hair to the side with her hand, tossed her head back, turned and started walking away, still laughing.

"Man, I get no respect." Sean wagged his head in comical dismay.

"You're a bloody Irishman, mate. What the 'ell did you expect, O'Rourke?" chided Oliver.

"Well, there goes the neighborhood," Li added dryly.

"Oh God, here we go again, the orange and green versus the red and white, squaring off against each other. I thought you guys finally stopped the warring and decided to get along with each other. Belfast, bloody heck, that was decades ago," Harry chimed in from over his laptop.

Diego jumped in to cut them all off.

"Okay, people, get some rest, clean up and have a good meal on Uncle Sam. If I know Harry, and I'm pretty sure I do, we'll each have a dossier to read by tomorrow morning. We'll plan on meeting at 2:00 p.m. at Hickam's Air Force Base Officer's Club and determine what our next steps are. Get moving. Oliver, thanks for coming with us. We really appreciate it – even Sean."

"Cheers, mate, thanks for making sure I could drink some real suds instead of that watered-down stuff you Americans call beer." Oliver laughed, saluted and gulped the last mouthful of the Allendale Pennine Pale pint he was drinking, and they all headed off in different directions to their rooms.

Diego could still hear Oliver talking as he departed, to no one in particular, "Yes, mate, you Yanks may outnumber us in people, dollars and armies, but where it really counts? Football and beer, yer all a bunch of land-lumbering, rookie wankers …" And Oliver's British laughter faded into the darkness.

*****

Jarisst I

"Qulys! Come here, quick!" Jarns was yelling for him to get to the Comm Center.

"I'm coming; what's up, Jarns?"

"Look, remember that distress signal you asked me to send out a couple of days back?"

"Yeah, I remember; don't tell me you just got a response." Qulys laughed as he said it, hoping to calm Jarns down.

"Not 'just,' look at the log. Try two days ago!" Jarns yelled at him. Qulys was speechless. A response had not been expected by anyone.

"Two days ago? That means we received a response in …" Qulys stammered.

"We received a response almost immediately, Qulys. Considering that the signal had to travel there and back, that means it is less than four hours away. It's in the same system we are!" Jarns was nearly jumping out of his seat.

"Sit tight, Jarns; let me get Thjars down here before we do anything. See if you can determine exactly where it is."

"I already know," Jarns whispered. "It's between the third and fourth planet. I'm pretty sure it's actually from the second ship we identified earlier – the one traveling between the two planets."

"You think that ship is one of ours?" Even the toughened Qulys was beginning to show uncharacteristic cracks in his normally steady demeanor.

"No, Qulys. I'm positive it's *not* one of ours."

"Then … what does this mean?"

"I have no idea, Qulys. No idea at all. Get Thjars down here immediately. That signal may be our only hope."

*****

Honolulu

The team had regrouped at the Officer's Club, ready to get down to business. Even Patty seemed relaxed and back to normal, barring the bruises that were still evident on her face and arms, and the obvious blackened eyes and fat lip, but definitely refocused. It was amazing what a hot shower and a good night's sleep could do for all of them. Harry apparently hadn't taken the time to sleep, as he had spent the night laying out plans for each of them, just as Diego had expected. Harry's plans had been drawn up under the premise that backup wouldn't be needed in the U.S., at least not like it had in Yemen.

"Is there any new information from the hard drives or the captured terrorist?" Li asked Harry, once they were all seated.

"Still trying to break the encryption codes to Saudi, but the NSA call analysis has been able to verify that the majority of the calls with Hawaii originated from the 808 area code, which is the Kailua-Kona area on the island of Hawai'i. Most of those calls were in the morning from the Coffee Bean & Tea Leaf Kona shop at 75-5595 Palani Road. Patty, I want you to become a daily regular there until we find this guy. We were able to get you a job behind the counter serving coffee. You start at 0600 each morning and work until 1400."

"Sean and Diego, you'll stay in town with Patty in case we identify our target."

"Oliver and Li, I've got a list of construction sites and contract construction employee services companies that are on each of the Hawaiian Islands, so you two will be doing most of the traveling. The main focus is on men who have been working on federal government contracts."

Li chuckled. "Piece of cake, Harry. Knowing Hawaii, I'm assuming that must include at least 20 percent of the population."

"Correct you are; it's a big number, Li. There are currently no less than 34,000 people employed by the federal government in Hawaii, and at least 18,500 of them are working for the Department of Defense. That obviously does not include people who previously worked for the government."

"And we have how long to find this needle in the haystack?" Li raised his eyebrows.

Harry actually looked a little disappointed. "And how many of those do you think actually travelled to the Johnston Atoll over the past 12 months? That should be your first data sort, yes?"

"Okay, good point, Harry. Maybe I'm still suffering from jet lag."

"Any updates from Blake?" Patty interjected to save Li.

Harry wasn't quite ready to let it go, though.

"If you look further in the package I've given each of you, the FBI has already provided a sub-list of names for us. The list includes 350 names that fit all of our highest criteria, including that they worked on the Johnston Atoll during the past 12 months. As you might guess, there are no visitors allowed on the island, so by simply signing up to work there, one has already been provided key information. However, I think it's safe to assume that if Al Qaeda is involved, they would've used false names and aliases, so it won't be as simple as just visiting 350 people."

"By the way, Patty. The owner's name is George. He knows you are undercover, but he has no idea why. He suspects that you are in a federal witness protection program, and your lingering bruises will help support that theory. I suggest you avoid any discussion on the topic."

"Got it. Now, what about Blake, any updates?"

"As I understand it, Ataullah still remains our number one suspect. And no, Blake still hasn't been allowed to confront him about it." Everyone knew that was a sore spot with Blake.

"There is one major new event that I was saving for last." Harry updated the group on the new ship that launched from the moon. The discussion lasted for a good 20 minutes as the stunned audience asked questions and tested various ideas and theories. When they were done, Sean asked the only question that remained on everyone's mind.

"And what will you be doing, Harry?"

"Ahh, good reminder, Sean, thank you. I guess there was one more, small item I forgot to share with you. Apparently, while we were away in Yemen, the Reagan I, recall that is the ship that actually travelled to Mars. Well, they recovered something that the Mars Rover discovered – a large, missile-shaped alien artifact they are bringing back to Earth."

"Alien?" Oliver asked incredulously. The entire group was equally stunned. Earth had only just begun its manned journey beyond the moon, yet all sorts of activity seemed to be popping up. Li wondered out loud just how busy the galaxy really was. When the flurry of discussion was over, Harry resumed his update.

"One more thing. Although the unit no longer appears functional from a flight perspective, it appears to still be at least semi-operational electronically. While investigating the unit on board the Reagan I yesterday, the crew accidentally turned it on. The device began making sounds and lights on the interior began flashing, but nothing more has happened since then – at least nothing that we know of."

"I'll bet someone on that ship needed a new set of clothes when that happened," Li joked.

"Likely so," Harry smiled as he continued, "I'm scheduled to have a call with the crewmembers at 6:00 tonight to see if we can figure out more about the unit. The NSA has been working with them, but I think most of those guys are more about electronic spying than they are about pure science or electro-mechanical apparatus."

"Do you think it may be tied to the object Blake and the Armstrong I are pursuing?"

"That is the million dollar question many people are asking."

*****

Iran

"Gen. Shirazi?"

"Yes. Who is this?" replied the general.

"It is I. You do not need to know more. All you need to know is that we have learned something new that will require a small change to your plans."

"Why would I …"

"Listen! I have very little time. The American ship you are planning to destroy is actually on a mission to meet with what they believe is an alien ship near Pluto – Satan himself. We cannot allow them to do so!"

"Yes, we will have blown the Americans up before they ever get close to it, but not until all of our assets are in place."

"No, general, and that is why I previously told you that you needed to await my final orders. Exploding their ship now would then leave the alien devil ship free to join their cause on Earth. We must destroy both. You will inform your people that they will delay the explosion until the ships are together. Is that understood?"

"Yes, but that will also delay the other plans we have in store for them."

"That is correct, general, but it will work out even better than we originally planned. Have faith in Allah. I must go now."

"How can I be sure that you are who you claim to be?"

"That is a fair question, general." The unknown caller then recited every major step of the general's plan, including names of all personnel involved. "How would I know these details if I was not who I claim I am, general? Furthermore, do you not recall the voice that first exposed Col. Armeen Khorasani's traitorous lies to you? Yes, that was me, and that should eliminate any questions you have."

With that, the unknown voice disconnected the call.

Gen. Shirazi was astonished. Where was this person getting his information from? It was almost too much to believe that the Americans were forming an allegiance with aliens – like a child's storybook! But hadn't the unknown person been right on everything else so far? Had he not invoked Allah's name and desires in the same way that the general would himself? Yes, he thought. This man must be guided by Allah, and I must follow his requests accordingly, he thought. Gen. Shirazi immediately began to revise his long-developed plans. There were only a few people he would need to bring into confidence, and he knew without any doubt that all of these men were true soldiers of Allah.

*****

Armstrong I

Blake had, once again, nonchalantly followed Ataullah as he worked his way back toward the nuclear reactor. As Ataullah stood near the bulkhead door to the reactor, he was checking something under his coat. Blake flipped a mental coin in his head a few times and decided that 3-out-of-5 was a winner. It was time to push the edge a little further and see how Ataullah responded to a surprise interruption. Blake was ready to elevate to action mode at the slightest hint of concern.

"Ataullah, what brings you to this corner of the world?"

Ataullah was startled, but recovered quickly.

"Blake, hello, you caught me by surprise. Looking for another game of backgammon?" He smiled back at him.

"No, I've taken enough beatings at your hand." Blake smiled back, trying to gage Ataullah's true intent. "Is something amiss back here? It looked like you were concerned and checking up on the reactor."

"Actually, I *am* checking this unit out. Fortunately, everything seems fine." Ataullah flipped his coat back and displayed a standard radiation medical badge.

"A radiation badge?" Blake queried.

"Yes, sorry to say, but I am not a trusting man when it comes to humankind's ability to truly control the atom. An individual that I befriended at the hospital, one of the doctors that conducted our medical reviews before leaving the Johnston Atoll, told me that as long as there were no leaks, I would be safe. So, I'm checking with my badge."

"Did it help?"

"Not really." They both laughed.

"We're getting closer to our final destination," Blake offered.

"Yes, we certainly are. Only, what, four more weeks to go, give or take a day?"

"That sounds about right. Just out of curiosity, from your religious background, what are your thoughts if we actually find signs of life? It could become a definitive day in human history that would challenge many things that we've held as unquestionable," Blake stated calmly as he watched Ataullah closely for a response.

"Yes, indeed it will be, Blake, more than you or I will ever know and a day the world will remember for centuries to come. I thank Allah for allowing me to be part of that historic day when it comes. But excuse me Blake, it is my prayer time and I must return to my room to prepare." With that, he bid Blake adieu and headed back to his quarters.

Blake wasn't sure if he should push his questioning further or not, but decided to wait until another time. Ataullah looked fully poised and confident in his statements, but at the same time, his comments could be taken two different ways. The next few weeks were going to be very long and challenging indeed.

*****

A.D. 2028 (3311 C.A.E.); Dec. 24
Kailua-Kona

"It's been three days and we have nothing, nothing at all." Patty was frustrated and not bashful about letting everyone on the team know it. "Maybe the individual identified on the hard drive is simply a local contact and others are doing the work. If that's the case, then the list of names we have is totally useless."

"You may be correct, Patty, but we don't have anything else to go on right now. Keep in mind that the military, NASA, the NSA, CIA, and FBI are all working on this. We are just one small arm of the investigation and we have little awareness of how the others are progressing. This is tedious work and it takes time," Harry replied.

"I know, Harry, but an investigation like this could take years, and we only have three or four weeks left. Maybe even less if the second ship is involved."

"What did you just say?" Harry asked with excitement in his voice.

"Maybe less time if the second ship is involved," she replied.

"No, before that … you said it might take years."

"Yes, this is a big, complex case that includes multiple countries and continents that could take years to figure out."

"Bingo. God, I can't believe I missed it." Harry was looking at the floor.

"Missed what?" Sean questioned.

"Years. The investigation could take years."

"Yea, that's what Patty already said," Sean replied, getting a little bothered by the exchange as he didn't see it going anywhere.

"Exactly," Harry added. "How long do you think it took to build the Reagan I? It surely wasn't 12 months. I screwed up."

"Oh, my God! I follow you." Patty's face lit up, but Sean remained confused.

"What the hell am I missing now?" he stammered.

"This list of names *could* be totally useless. We should be looking at names that could have been involved two, three, maybe even four years ago!" Patty answered.

"Precisely. I'm sorry, guys. I screwed up and possibly sorted our suspect out of the database." Harry looked totally dejected.

"Okay, don't sweat it, Harry – welcome to the human race after all. It just took you 25 years longer than most people to make your first mistake." Patty patted Harry on the back. She knew she needed to get Harry re-engaged quickly. "How long will it take you to get a new set of names for us?"

Harry looked up, still frustrated, but acknowledged Patty's effort.

"Thanks, Patty, I'll get on the phone right now. We should have a new list of names by tomorrow morning."

"But it's Christmas tomorrow; will anyone even be in the store tomorrow?" Oliver asked.

"No, but the more I think about it, I'd be willing to make a wager based on Patty's idea, that whoever our suspect is, they intentionally stopped working quite a while ago in order to distance themselves from the project. I'll add that filter to the search as well."

*****

Armstrong 1

"Not sure I would've predicted this one. Nice work, James. Blake, I think you'll want to take a look at this." Jack waved Blake over to the computer screen. "The ship chasing us is still weeks from catching up, but it has gotten close enough that James has been able to get some higher quality pictures of it."

"Well, at least we know who we are dealing with now. In some way, I'm relieved to know it is from Earth." Blake looked up with a wry smile. "Perhaps we should open up our secret to include Major Popov. I'm curious to see what his reaction will be – he sure denied it pretty strongly. First, an alien vehicle, then Al Qaeda came on the scene, now it's the Russians. Who's next to the party, the Chinese? Can it really be the Russians?"

"I can't imagine anyone would purposely hide behind the hammer and sickle, but the only way to verify it is to get Popov in the loop. So, yes, I agree – let's see what he has to say."

Blake picked up the phone and called Major Popov's quarters.

"Vladimir here."

"Good morning. Sorry to wake you, but we have some pictures that you need to see. Can you come up to the control room?"

"Sure, major, may I take a shower first?"

"That depends, Vladimir. The second ship does appear to have taken off from the moon. It is gaining on us and will catch up before we get to the object. By the way, just in case you have any interest, it appears to have a definitive Russian red hammer and sickle on it, but with what also appears to be a picture of planet Earth behind it."

"I'll be right there."

"Thank you, Vladimir, I expected you might be."

Less than a minute later, Vladimir was standing next to Blake and James, looking over Jack's shoulder at the computer screen.

"Please tell me that your Russian president is not playing chess with us, Vladimir." Jack looked back over his shoulder at Vladimir.

"It's not Russian," Vladimir repeated his earlier statement again.

"Vladimir, these pictures are rather telling, you think not?" Blake was not in the mood for debate.

"You said that it launched from the moon, yes?"

"I'm not sure I understand why that matters, but our experts are convinced it came from the moon, even though we're not sure how that could have occurred. NASA verified that there weren't any recent landings, or Earth-orbit launches, so we are thoroughly confused at the moment and hoping that you can shed some light on our new friends."

"Unfortunately, gentlemen, it may matter."

"Pardon my lapse here, Vladimir, but I'm not following you." Jack stepped in for Blake. The three men were now focused on Vladimir and what he would say next.

"The moon *is* a very distinct possibility." Vladimir paused to let his message sink in.

"Please continue, major," Blake interjected.

"I may need to talk to my government before ..."

"No, Vladimir, right now we are billions of kilometers from Earth. *We* are the government for all intents and purposes. They cannot help us more than we can help ourselves. Your ship will be upon us in a couple of weeks." There was no mistaking the commanding tone of Blake's voice. Vladimir paused and exhaled a long breath.

"It's not exactly *our* ship."

"Not *exactly*? What the hell does *not exactly* mean, Vladimir?" demanded Blake without raising his voice, but it was clear his patience was done.

"Do you recall the space vehicle we lost a few years ago?"

"I believe so. Go on."

"This is not easy for me, or for my country, gentlemen. Please forgive me for my hesitation, and some background first."

He looked at the three men, and Blake nodded for him to continue.

"A little over three years ago, my country launched a special rocket that was to land on the dark side of the moon at a location we code named Pink Floyd. You know, in honor of one of those bands from the 1960s and 1970s you Americans loved so much. More on Pink Floyd in a moment, but first, looking back four to five decades ago, our space program had finally caught back up with your U.S. program in the '70s, and we were positioned to regain our leadership in space. This was a very important goal for our country. After all, we were first in space. We did beat you and would have stayed ahead if not for your President Kennedy. He was a good president, better than you Americans realize because you couldn't see past his Camelot image. But enough of that; we can discuss Camelot another time. In 1973, a year after your last manned flight to the moon on Apollo 17, the redesigned Soyuz 13 carried the Orion 2 Space Observatory into space. That was our first big step to catching up with you and then passing you. That was the same year that Pink Floyd released their famous album, "The Dark Side of the Moon" – it seemed like a natural connection for our future base. Over the years, we had many failures that your government and press became very aware of, but we also had many successes you were not aware of. The failures successfully hid our progress from your prying satellites. Not because you couldn't see it, but because you let your guard down and didn't see us as a competitive threat anymore. That was a major mistake for America. You went to sleep and we were operating on overdrive.

"Anyway, pardon my regression into history as I doubt that is what you called me here to discuss, but this is all important background so that you understand what you, I'm sorry, what *we* are up against. By the late 1980s, we had already landed a number of unmanned payloads on the moon – at the Pink Floyd location to be exact. By the late 1990s, we actually had a base established there. As I said, this has been a long-standing strategic goal for Russia. Not knowing for sure if you or anyone else would send satellites or other manned vehicles to circle the moon, we set the base up to be dark, externally, at all times – only internal building lights were allowed. We also went through great lengths to insulate the modules and exhaust any heat footprint we had deep underground into the moon to minimize any possible thermal profile. It was a massive undertaking, far dwarfing your '60s race to the moon. As it turned out, it wasn't until the Chinese began sending lunar orbiters in 2007 that our facility was ever at risk of being detected. By 2013, we had living quarters and self-sustained garden areas, complete with rabbits for meat and vegetables. We were finally in a position that could maintain sustained, permanent life on the moon; including labs and moderate manufacturing capabilities for equipment repair.

"Then in 2020, we sent the final sections to complete a revolutionary new rocket design, one that would allow us to exceed 3 million kilometers per hour – nothing the U.S. or Chinese have made, including this ship we are on now, would touch it. Ironically, we expected to celebrate our maiden launch in 2025, before this flight we are on would ever take place."

"Okay, Vladimir, I believe I can speak for all three of us when I say I am truly floored, intrigued and near speechless, except for the obvious question … What happened?" Blake asked.

"Maj. Anatoly Domashev happened. Today, he goes by the title of general, General Anatoly Domashev."

"Who is this? The name actually sounds a little familiar," Jack asked.

"It may; he was the commander of a 2020 space flight, but you would not know of that flight. You would, however, know of him from the secret file you've read about the shooting down of Malaysia Flight 17 in Eastern Ukraine in 2014, killing 283 innocent people. The plane was shot down because of him; he dictated its termination because of one person on the plane that had broken trust with him. You did not know his reasoning from those files, but you would have seen his name if you read them. He is a truly ruthless man. He would make Stalin pale if he had equal power at his disposal. No, you do not have all of the file information – as we know. We know all of your files you keep on us. WikiLeaks. You do not have the stomach to deal with people like the Wiki group, so they see that as a weakness to exploit. Those Wiki people would not have survived if that had happened to Russia – no matter where they traveled to for safekeeping. No courtroom required."

"Okay, let's not take on the American justice system and due process yet. I guess it wasn't lost then. Am I correct?" Jack added.

"Yes, and no."

"Your answers can be somewhat confusing and misleading at times, Vladimir."

"Let me explain. Yes, it was lost relative to Russian control and ownership, but no, it still exists, so it wasn't totally lost."

"Are you suggesting that this major, I mean Gen. Domashev, is acting on his own, independent of the Russian government?" Blake was leaning forward in his chair.

"That is a correct statement, Maj. Thompson. Let me remind you that I did not lie to you about the ship not being Russian, and you did not ask if I did know what it was." Vladimir paused to allow that to sink in.

"I concur, Vladimir, but you sure didn't go out of your way to be forthright with us."

"That is true. My apologies, Blake, but at the time, I didn't think it was necessary. Now, I can see otherwise. But we digress. Back to Gen. Domashev. The general handpicked his seven-member crew and when he reached the lunar base, they gave the occupants two choices: join or die. We know that two cosmonauts were killed trying to defend the base. We are assuming that the eight other cosmonauts and dozens of engineers and technicians that remained decided to join Gen. Domashev, or also perished. We have not heard anything from the base since they landed in 2025 – three years ago. We secretly hoped that they had all perished, as my government was very concerned that Gen. Domashev would complete the rocket. Apparently he has done just that, and he now sees this as an opportunity to acquire technology that would allow him to pursue greater domination over Russia, and perhaps even more than just Russia."

"Why have you not investigated the site?" James jumped in.

"We have not launched another ship to investigate the site as no other vehicle is currently flight ready, but our current plans would allow for a flyby by 2030."

"You could have talked to us," James volunteered.

"Really? I think not. You are sounding way too idealistic, my good friend James. How do you think that would have gone over, da? Mr. President, sir, we have lost a rocket on the moon where we were building a secret base that we would use to dominate space activities. We would like your help in recovering it." Vladimir paused. "I think not, Sir James."

"How could he ever hope to accomplish this goal?" Blake steered the discussion back to the now.

"Think about what you yourself have seen over the past 40 years. You have witnessed the end of the Cold War, and the escalation of China and India from third world countries to economic, technological and military world powers. They were able to achieve in two or three decades what took our countries a century or more to do, yes?" Vladimir continued without waiting for an answer. "You are well aware of the so-called Technology S-Curves. It takes years of heavy investment on a new technology with little return, then at a certain point in maturity, the rate of return in benefits begins a steep upward climb with relatively little investment and time. As the technology reaches full maturity, the rate of return of benefits begins to level off, regardless of the amount of time and investment. At that point, one needs to retire that technology and find a new technology to invest in, one that begins its s-curve at an already higher level of benefit. If a company or a country can skip one of those s-curves, they can accelerate their technology growth and skip an entire generation of investment. Like the Chinese cell-phone paradigm."

"Whoa." James turned away from the console he was at. "How the hell did we get to Chinese cell phones?" he asked, looking perplexed.

"I can answer that one, Vladimir," Blake volunteered. "There have been many economic studies written relative to the benefit of so-called technology leapfrogging where developing countries can accelerate their development and gain significant economic benefit that eludes already developed nations, like the U.S. Look at the investment that the U.S. made in landline telephone infrastructure during the 20th century, and the maintenance of that system – it was astronomical. Decades and decades of time, worth billions and billions of dollars. The Chinese literally skipped over that technology and era, as if it never existed, and moved directly to cell phones – without ever spending a penny or a day on older technology. In so doing, they became the largest cell phone user in the world and saved hundreds of billions if not trillions of dollars in investment that could then be used on newer technologies for newer, more powerful capabilities. Yet, those same U.S. companies have a harder time investing in the new technologies because of the investments they already made in landline technologies. That is part of the reason the U.S. marketplace has such a long list of *has beens* in the telecommunications industry – those companies were held captive by the success of their previous investments."

"Very good, major," Vladimir responded, "and that is exactly what we think Domashev is hoping to do. Imagine what power a single person could have had back in the revolutionary war if they had a squad of your M1a Abrams tanks or one wing of F-35 fighter aircraft? They would have been unstoppable. Now magnify that by a thousand times and imagine what Domashev, as ruthless as he is, could do with it. Absolutely frightening. Yes, it sounds crazy, but what if what we all hope for *is* actually found in the object? That is a potential reality that we need to understand and acknowledge. Domashev would see himself the equal of an Egyptian god, but with even more power." Vladimir paused for a few seconds and scanned the faces of the three men in the room before continuing. "We on board the Armstrong I, as big as our roles already were relative to steering the future, we will now possibly need to play an even greater role in human history – more than we ever could have foreseen."

That hit home. The four men sat in silence for a couple of minutes, contemplating the many angles of Vladimir's final statement. Finally, Blake broke the silence.

"How did he get into such a high position undetected?"

"His parents were from Chechnya and they were killed in the first Chechen war, back in 1994. As you may recall, things got a little dicey after the USSR was dissolved in 1991. Major Domashev was already in the Russian Army at that time and he openly stated that his parents deserved death for breaking from the Motherland. He was so strong in his statements and his actions, leading many efforts to attack terrorists from the Chechen State that no one ever saw it coming. He was considered a hero of the homeland to many Russian people, but we believe that is when he actually began his plans against Russia, and possibly beyond. It is the biggest embarrassment for the Russian government since Chernobyl. The only difference was that until now, it had been kept secret from others. Now it will make Chernobyl look like a simple car accident."

"For the people of Russia, I am sorry to hear that, Vladimir, I truly am, but your government? This redefines the phrase 'international incident' beyond anything I could have ever imagined."

"Thank you, Blake, your sincerity means a lot to me and to the Russian people, and yes, I agree with the distrust this will create. It truly could beget a World War that would shame the previous two World Wars put together. Alien technology may allow him great power without the need of massive armies.

"Our countries are both proud people, but it will require both of our countries to address this – Gen. Domashev must be stopped before he reaches the alien ship. If the ship does contain superior weaponry and technology, this madman will attempt to overtake the planet."

"How many people do you think his ship can hold?"

"I expect there are 10 crewmembers on board, including Gen. Domashev."

"That is a formidable force; especially assuming they are all armed."

"Yes, Blake, they will be. Of more concern is what weaponry he may have been able to build into this ship over the past few years. We have no idea of his ship's capability. We built it for speed and distance into space. There honestly was no consideration for a war machine when this specific ship was built."

"Okay, I can accept that, Vladimir, thank you. But there is still another piece of this puzzle missing, Vladimir, and one that does not allow me to totally free Russia from ownership."

"What is that, major?" Vladimir looked stunned.

"How could he have possibly known about the ship near Pluto without help from someone on Earth?"

"Ah, yes. I did not see that question coming. You do not miss much, do you, Mr. Blake?"

"That is why I am still alive today, Vladimir. I make it my top priority on every mission to see as much as possible. Please continue."

"I wish I could Blake, but I, too, would like to know that answer. I am gravely concerned that there must be someone high in the Politburo that still favors this Gen. Domashev."

"I need to share this with my government, Vladimir. Would you like to notify Moscow as well?" Blake suggested.

"I think that is a wise decision. Let us make those calls, but ..." Vladimir looked down as he trailed off.

"But what, Vladimir?" Blake asked.

"If what you say is correct, and everything I know says you are likely correct, Blake, then I no longer know whom I can trust within my own government. Da?"

The room was speechless.

Vladimir continued. "I think you need to make your call first, Blake, and I think it needs to be at the highest level of your government, and I do mean the highest level. Perhaps he will know something that will help me determine whom to call."

"That's a tall order, Vladimir – President Callahan himself?"

"Do you have a better suggestion?"

"I'd prefer that your Mother Russia find the traitor within and provide him with a brain hemorrhage as you so frequently referred to your 20th century executions by pistol, but I expect that would take longer. President Callahan it is, although I doubt I will be able to be as eloquent as I was when we first left the space station. I will set up the call, but you, James and Jack will join me. No word to anyone else on the ship. Agreed?"

All agreed and Blake headed for the Comm Center.

CHAPTER 19

A.D. 2028 (3311 C.A.E.); Dec. 24
Manchester United

The Manchester United was nearing its target location 25 miles off the East Coast. The winter weather had stayed uncharacteristically calm and warm, providing further confidence that Allah was indeed guiding their mission. They had communicated with a number of U.S. Coast Guard ships as they got closer to the coastline, even sharing one crate of wine with a particularly friendly captain who overstayed his welcome. They were within days of making their announcement that would finally bring the Great Satan to his knees. The ship had intentionally remained just outside U.S. coastal waters to reduce chances that someone would stop to investigate them, yet close enough that if they needed to get to shore for safety, they could do so.

A man on the bow of the yacht was holding a laptop, enjoying the day. He sent a short email out to a number of memorized addresses and then closed the laptop, lay back on the deck to enjoy the sun, closed his eyes, and smiled. The moment was close at hand. The message was simple:

> *"Our travel across the Atlantic is almost complete. It was a breathtaking journey and I can now check one more item off my personal bucket list! The U.S. Coast Guard has been very helpful, ensuring our safety as we neared the East Coast – greatly appreciated. I look forward to seeing you all soon."*

There were multiple parties on the email distribution that had been waiting for verification of the last statement. Stateside efforts could now commence.

*****

Many hours later, the reply to Blake's message from President Callahan was finally received by the Armstrong I. Blake was pleased to see it was in video format, not typed text. Blake turned on the speakers so that the four men could hear Callahan's response.

> *"This is President Callahan. Thank you, Maj. Thompson, excellent summary. And Maj. Popov, no apology needed. I will trust you. It also helped that, and you should know this, Vladimir, Maj. Thompson also included a short dossier on you, based totally on his own private opinion. For what it is worth, it is quite complimentary."*

The president paused before continuing, almost as if he expected the men to talk before he continued. The video content showed true sincerity in his face. Vladimir looked directly at Blake.

"I do not deserve your president's comments based on the decisions and actions that my government has made or not made. These decisions eventually led to this situation. However, having said that, it appears we are in the midst of a mutual admiration gathering." Vladimir grinned broadly. "I am most impressed with you American cowboys, but I am equally impressed with how your president has dealt with this, and for that I am humbled. I look forward to our return and the sharing of good Russian vodka with him. This vodka will be like none else on the planet as it will have aged more kilometers than any other heavenly fluid man has ever known!" All four men laughed – just in time for the president to continue – almost on cue.

> *"I would be honored to share some of your famous Russian vodka with you when you return home,*

Vladimir, as I expect you are already proposing, and I will provide some rich American bourbon in exchange. I look forward to that day, especially as we will be able to talk and laugh without this damnable time delay."

President Callahan grinned slightly, and confidently, as only a president can do. The men all looked around the room in pure surprise, until Blake broke the silence.

"I agree, Vladimir, it sure feels like they had the room bugged, and by the way, I'm sure they do," he added with a chuckle, "but there is no way that he could have responded that quickly. I believe you are seeing an example of how observant and deep thinking the man is."

"Okay, I'll buy that," James volunteered, "but ya have to admit, that was more than just a little freaky."

"It sure was … wait, he's continuing …"

"Vladimir, as you might expect, or already know, we do have a red phone between our countries. It dates back to the calamitous days of 1962 when President Kennedy elevated the Russian threat to our Defense Readiness Condition to DEFCON 2. That was during the historic Cuban Missile Crisis that we both know all too well – even if we only read about it in history books. That phone line between President Kennedy and your Soviet premier, Nikita Khrushchev, saved the world from nuclear war. Trust me, it was closer than the world knows, or cares to know. I will leave it at that. However, having shared that, I, too, am not sure who, beyond you, that I can trust in the highest levels of your government, but I do have a friend within the Kremlin that I can trust. I cannot share his name, or how we have come to know each other. All I can share is that I trust this man as much as I trust Maj. Thompson, perhaps even more because of how long I have known him, as well as the pure fidelity of everything he has ever shared with me. Yet, you must understand, Vladimir, this man is not a spy against his, or your, country. He is a deep

patriot of Mother Russia and would die to protect her without hesitation. Confusing? Contradictory? Hard to believe? Yes, but all true.

The reason I requested a delay between Maj. Thompson's digital response and this call is because this was my second call this morning. Correct, my first call was to my long-time friend. The short version of a very long story is that there is indeed a Domashev ally high in the Kremlin structure. My friend does not know who this person is, but he is convinced the connection is there. As it also turns out, he has been secretly and independently trying to identify the individual ever since your ship disappeared on the moon. He has not shared this with anyone until now because, like you, he did not know where the lines of safety and danger lay. He has full intention of ending this traitor's life if and when he can identify the traitor, regardless of what happens to himself. As we all know, two minds are better than one, so we agreed to cooperate. We were able to discuss some ideas on how we may be able to use the current situation to lure the traitor into the open, but it will take time. As I am sure you will understand, that is the extent of which I can share with you at this time. The awareness of my Russian friend is not to be shared with anyone, period. We will talk more, gentlemen. Godspeed and good night."

With that, the president clicked off, leaving a stunned, but thoroughly captivated room of men.

"Well, gents, I do believe that is a cap. With everything that keeps popping up, I can only imagine what tomorrow will bring, so let's get some sleep and be ready for it. Except for you Jack. Sorry about that, but I guess this is your shift, correct?"

"Correct it is, Blake. Hit the sack, you poor excuses for wing nuts!"

*****

A.D. 2028 (3311 C.A.E.); Dec. 25
Kailua-Kona

The group was sitting in a windowless room, scanning hundreds of names. They were so engrossed with their effort that no one even seemed to realize it was Christmas Day.

"Hey, I know this name," Patty blurted out and pointed down to a name on the sheets that were spread out on the table in front of her.

The names had been collected from the previous five years and were provided in three formats: one with all the names, a second that was a subset that included only people who were no longer working for the U.S. government, and an even smaller subset that included people who had left their government job at least six months ago; the latter list had 425 names on it. They had started with the smallest list. There were 50 names on each sheet. It was on the fifth sheet that Patty saw someone she recognized.

"Harold Bessimer."

"That doesn't exactly sound Arabic. I was expecting an Arabic name," Sean stated, scratching the top of his head.

"Unfortunately, we have many lost individuals in our own country who have become Islamic fundamentalists because they can't fit into normal society. They take on Arabic names, but still retain their original American name as well, like Harold Bessimer for example."

"Do you recall what he looks like, Patty?" Diego asked.

"I think so, but I'm not positive. If it's who I think it is, he uses a debit card every time he visits. I'd guess he was about five-foot, nine-inches and maybe 165 pounds with dark brown eyes."

"The shop reopens tomorrow morning. How often does he come?"

"I'm not sure, but he was there each day I was – if I am thinking of the right guy. Harry, can the NSA guys tap his bank and find out, or would it be better to get the owner to look into her transactions?"

Diego answered before Harry could.

"I think we are better off keeping the owner at distance, even if it would be quicker. Let's get the NSA to tap his bank. Do you remember what bank it was?"

"Definitely, each time I saw it, I wished I was there. It was a Bank of Hawaii Visa debit card with a picture of a beach on it."

"Actually, I already convinced the NSA to give me direct acccss. I'll have the info for you in less than 20 minutes," Harry stated without emotion.

"Harry, I'm almost afraid to ask, but … how on earth did you convince the NSA to give you direct access?" Patty queried.

"He was an arrogant man. The easy part was reminding their head analyst that this was a national emergency. I stretched the truth a little when I said I had to update the president tonight and would be more than happy to let President Callahan know that he wouldn't help me."

"Harry, I am surprised. I hope you don't make a habit of lying." Patty feigned a broken heart, while trying to hide her shock at Harry's surprising announcement of guilt.

"I could easily convince a jury that I'm not lying. Just look at our current reporting structure; within three levels we connect indirectly to the White House. It doesn't take too far of a stretch of imagination to assume that something this important would be on the president's short list."

"Okay, you win, Harry, not like we would ever have a chance anyway." Diego chuckled.

"Thanks, Diego." Harry continued typing on his computer.

"You're welcome. You suggested that there was more reasoning for the access you were granted …?"

"Oh, yeah, the final hit was that I beat him in his own challenge, a bet relative to who could recite the most consecutive values of Pi."

"Pi? A challenge on Pi … the mathematical term? What was this, a geek's anonymous conference you attended, Harry? And you won, of course. How many did you get?"

Harry ignored the joke. "That's not the important question. The important question is how many did he get? He managed to get 233 places."

"Good Lord, that's impressive. But that still leaves the question open as to how many you did."

"234."

"You only beat him by one?" Patty was truly surprised.

Harry never even looked up. "That was all that was needed. What was the purpose of going further? The contest was over. Additional places would have wasted time for both of us without changing the outcome."

"Good grief, Harry. Okay, but how far could you have gone?"

"I've never bothered to try, as I see no value to it – although others obviously do. The Guinness World Records site claims that a man from China actually recited 67,890 places back in 2005. Good for him, but I have better things to spend my time on."

"But you memorized at least 234 places, didn't you?" Patty seemed perplexed.

"Incorrect. I simply calculated the values, one place at a time, until he exceeded his memory limit," Harry replied, getting bored with the discussion.

"So with that, he simply gave you access?"

"Well, not exactly. He reneged on his agreement and wasn't going to follow through, so I wrote a quick subroutine and hacked his bank account. Found a few things that he wasn't too happy about."

"Good God, Harry, you blackmailed an NSA director?" Patty was flabbergasted.

"No, I just showed him factual data. He chose to use a poor access code."

"Harry, have I ever told you that you are a true enigma?" Patty laughed.

"Yes, at least 1,000 times. Ahh, here it is. All of Harold's transactions from the past four years."

"Thank you Harry. By the way, I know it may not seem appropriate this year, but Merry Christmas," Patty said with a smile that warmed everyone up.

Ten minutes later, they came to three separate conclusions. First, Harold was as close to a daily customer as any business could hope for, and secondly, he was punctual: 7:15 every morning. Thirdly, there were no coffee shop transactions for a six-month period during the second half of 2027, but there were a lot of transactions in Houston, Texas, during that same timeframe.

*****

Armstrong 1

The lines between Moscow and Washington, D.C., hadn't been this active since the Cuban Missile Crisis in 1962, but this time, it was the closest to full détente that the U.S. and the old U.S.S.R. had ever achieved. Many barriers had been removed in a joint effort to share information and develop plans, but nothing about President Callahan's friend or intention was ever mentioned, nor did Mother Russia acknowledge more than it had to about the ship or its general. The growing risk, however, was that the sheer magnitude of discussions would increase the probability of alerting the mole soon, if not already accomplished.

Blake decided that the others needed to be brought into at least some of the information loop relative to the second ship, regardless of what Ataullah's plan was. The Russian ship now required top priority. It had taken more than an hour of discussion to get Ataullah, Rakesh, Jie and Klaus up to speed on the latest events and answer their myriad of questions.

"Vladimir. We need to understand what type of weaponry they might have on board, and especially how close they will have to get before they can begin firing on us. What estimates have your people in Russia made?"

"They are working on it, Blake, but as I mentioned to you earlier, they have precious little information and can only hypothesize. At least our ship has some means to defend itself with," Vladimir replied without emotion.

"How the hell did you know that?" Blake was clearly caught off guard by what had been considered to be a secret relative to the non-American crewmembers of the Armstrong I.

"Da, da, da. We know everything that you do in your American government. Your security systems are like a slice of well-aged Swiss cheese." Vladimir smiled broadly and looked over at Blake.

"When this is over, if you really want to know what happened to your President Kennedy, we will talk. And the 2016 presidential election … ahhh, that was such great entertainment. Your media and the Democratic left … they are most eager people. Blame Trump for everything because it is so easy to believe. Da, you should have locked his cell phone away; it makes him such an attractive target. His tweets, although entertaining, were so distracting to finding the real truth, yet it was right there in front of you all. Russian collusion? Ha! That was classic misdirection, something we Russians would have been proud to say we did!"

"Yes, Vladimir, we do need to talk. We will discuss that, but later, Vladimir. I must admit that when we boarded this craft, I never imagined how eager you would be to support a rebirth of glasnost." Blake smiled back. He also made a mental note that he would need to relay Vladimir's claims to both the Pentagon and the White House at a later time.

"Maj. Thompson, come here. I just received an update from Moscow."

"That is rather timely," Blake stated dryly as he walked over to see Vladimir's screen.

"We now believe that they may have been able to steal and stow aboard two or three of our newest air-to-air missiles, the K-77M. It is a highly accurate and especially deadly missile that utilizes active phased array antennae for improved targeting."

"Those missiles would only be viable in an atmosphere, correct?" asked Jie.

"Yes, Jie, you are correct, but you asked for my estimate, did you not? He stole the missiles, so it's a fair assumption that he had plans on how to modify the weapon for space flight, as he surely knew he lacked an atmosphere on the moon. His primary challenge would be to replace the fins that no longer carry air load, with small booster rockets that could steer the rocket in the void of space. That technology already exists; it just has to be applied to this platform."

"Do you know what the range of the missile is?" Blake followed.

"The Russian K-77M has a range of 100 kilometers. I remind you that all of what I am sharing with you is highly classified."

"I think the recent current events have eliminated the need for classification, or perhaps greatly increased the list of people that qualify for a *need to know,*" James replied flatly.

"Amen, I'll second that," added Blake.

"Da, da, I agree. Now keep in mind that the 100-kilometer range was back on Earth where gravity and aerodynamic drag have a very real impact on the performance of a missile. We are now in space where there is no drag and no gravity to slow the missile down. Theoretically, one could shoot a missile and it would go forever – until it hit something. Do you not remember your own Voyager I space probe? It left our solar system back in 2013 and is still going based on the momentum it had prior to running out of fuel."

"So they could shoot at us now?" Rakesh asked with consternation.

"Yes, they could, but …" Blake interrupted Vladimir's response.

"You are correct, Vladimir. They could shoot, but the chance of hitting us after the fuel ran out would be pretty slim, as we could simply move the Armstrong I to a slightly new location and the missile would go by harmlessly."

"Correct again, Maj. Thompson, but as I said earlier, that assumes nothing else has changed. Gen. Domashev is an intelligent man. He has had three years to work these issues out, although I expect his early plans were for destroying less mobile satellites, not spaceships."

"How so, Vladimir?" James turned and asked.

"It all comes down to design criteria. In atmospheric battles, one designs for full burn as fast as possible in order to close with the target before drag and gravity can overcome the missile and allow the prey to escape, like an aircraft that has significantly more fuel reserves; time is key. Designing in space requires a new set of requirements. Time is no longer the primary driver of design. Yes, speed is still important, but stealth and the ability to redirect multiple times over a very long flight path are more critical. Therefore, a design that can turn rocket ignition on and off, while conserving fuel during long coast phases, would be very deadly indeed. This technology is also available today."

Everyone suddenly looked grave.

Blake tuned to Maj. James Snyder and said, "You'd better start scanning our rear – starting now. Infrared and radar. Let us know immediately if you see anything and keep in mind that this missile would create a very small signature, and it may not have an infrared signature when the motor is temporarily turned off."

"I agree with you," Vladimir acknowledged. "But, at the same time, unless the general created missile manufacturing capabilities on the moon, which is highly improbable after such a relative short period and the lack of additional resources, he only has a maximum of three shots. He will want to make sure of those shots. He may also want to reserve something for the object, just in case there is a potential threat from that direction. If what you shared about the Reagan I is correct, he may have already committed one."

"If I were him ..." Blake had been thinking, it was now time to engage the group's collective thoughts, "I would wait until I got closer and then launch one for a potential lucky hit. If you think about it, between his ship and ours, he is likely assuming that he has all of the trump cards, so he will think that time *is* on his side. In addition, it would be a shame to come all this way to blow up his ticket to fame and then have no safe harbor back on the Earth, or the moon now that he has exposed himself. I expect he would rather die out here in a ship-to-ship battle and impress upon his crew that there is no other way. In that scenario, he has a maximum of two shots for us, so a lucky long shot still leaves him one final roll of the dice when he gets closer."

Rakesh looked concerned. "If he has all the trump cards, then what are we to do? Just wait until he closes and picks us off?"

"That is what I want him to think," Blake responded coldly.

"I'm not following you, Maj. Thompson," Rakesh responded quietly.

"Neither am I," added Klaus.

"Keep going, Blake." Jack prodded with a small smile and a knowing twinkle in his eye. He could tell that they were about to experience what he had heard about Blake.

"Okay, gentlemen. Based on what I know about this crew, as well as people we all know that we have at our disposal back on Earth, there is no doubt that we possess more collective brain power than they could possibly have, no matter how smart they are. So it's up to us to be the brain, while the brawn pursues us. We need to keep Domashev thinking we are helpless prey, all the while as we create a new trump card. For starters, I am going to pull Harry into this. I have an idea, but I want to pass it by him first. In parallel, we need to start sending some misinformation back to Earth."

"Misinformation? How so?" Rakesh was perking up. Good, Blake thought.

"Yes, we need to increase the volume of encoded messages with Earth, and we need to create the perception of concern. Not panic. They know we are too good for that and would smell a trap."

"I'm still not seeing how that helps by simply sending encoded messages out," Rakesh volunteered, looking for more.

"Correct, Rakesh, they know that we know they are there, so it should be expected that our volume of communication will increase, like it already has. They don't need to know what it's about, just that we must be concerned, and then at the right opportunity we let slip an unencrypted message that tells them what they want to hear. Something that will make them totally over-confident of their kill."

Jie finally began to understand. "I see, finally. You want them to think they only need one shot and that they can wait until they are closer to guarantee a kill. Is that correct?

"Exactly, Jie. When you are outgunned with missiles, you need to force the fight to a close-in hand-to-hand battle in order to change the odds. As I said earlier, if I was him I would chance the long shot, so we need to set this bait soon to avoid that risk. This is where Klaus can help."

"You name it, but … how?"

"You are the only one with children, so by definition you have the most to lose of anyone on this ship. Start thinking about a way you can slip up and attempt to send a father's goodbye to your children, but it has to be a message that can be intercepted, translated and believed to be sincere. Can you handle that?"

"Absolutely, and to be honest, it has already been on my mind." Klaus paused and then continued, "Unless you have another assignment for Rakesh, I think I could use his computer skills to make sure we pull this off to look real."

"Done," Blake answered and smiled. Now we are moving, he thought.

"Jack, I need you to work with Vladimir and Jie. This is the most critical issue and it needs to be done soon. We need to come up with an anti-missile system. It doesn't have to be smart, it just needs to work once – just in case he takes that long shot. If he does, and we can stop it, he'll definitely hold onto the other missile. That will force him into the close-in brawl I want. Let's get to work, gentlemen. I'll contact Harry from my room and join you shortly."

Jack looked over at James and quietly said, "Not only do I think he actually likes a good brawl, but I'm willing to bet that he is pretty damn lethal when cornered."

"That's a claim that I wouldn't bet against, nor would I want to have to validate. Regardless of all of our own training, at 6-foot-6 and 245 pounds, I think I'd rather get in a ring with a grizzly bear!"

******

Jarisst I

"Jarns. You have been working this for days, and the ships continue to get closer to us. Any progress yet?" Thjars did not seem to be in his typically patient or jovial mood today; he wanted answers.

"Some. We have verified that the signal we received was from a C-Pod. How it got here, I can't guarantee, but the ship's log does show that a C-Pod was launched when flight operations were shut down after our long journey. It is an automated feature. So there is a high probability that it is actually our own C-Pod."

"Let's assume for a moment that it is; does that provide a benefit to us?"

"Absolutely, sir. If we could reach the probe, we could remove the nose cone and program the cone to send a message to our ship, cancelling the emergency condition. That would immediately release full ship control to us."

"That is good news, Jarns, however, and don't take me wrong, but I don't see many options to getting the C-Pod delivered to us at the moment. So unless you figure out how to get that thing here, I need you to keep working on developing command routines that might bypass the controls so that you can program it from here."

"I will, sir, but the fact that it hasn't responded to anything except our initial distress signal suggests that something in the receiver circuitry may have been broken or malfunctioned. The distress code receiver and the programming receiver are separate subsystems, so that scenario is very possible."

CHAPTER 20

A.D. 2028 (3311 C.A.E.); Dec. 26
Kailua-Kona

It was a typical beautiful Hawaiian morning, another day and setting most people dreamed to be on vacation in. Diego, Li, Sean and Oliver were outside the coffee shop at their planned locations, north, south, east and west of the business, each was within 100 meters of the business. If the suspect showed up, they could quickly shut down every possible escape path – once the trap was sprung. Diego made it clear that they might have only one shot at this guy, and they had to make certain they nailed him.

Patty was behind the coffee bar making espressos. She had a radio below the countertop that she would trigger the button four times in quick succession as soon as the suspect showed up, which was the call sign for the four men to converge on the shop. Sean and Diego would enter the shop and stand in line behind the individual, while Oliver and Li guarded the back door.

The line was currently six people deep and had been like that since the shop opened. This place was definitely operating in the black based on what Patty could see; it was the day after Christmas and people had been waiting in line at 6:00 a.m. when they arrived.

Patty wondered if this were the only open coffee shop in town. As customers came and went, Patty reflected on a comment that Blake had always preached during training: *nothing ever goes as planned*. That idiom had already been proved correct a few times over the past couple of weeks, and in this case, the suspect hadn't even arrived yet. Customer after customer, at least seven out of every ten, had shown up with a Christmas present – a brand new gift card they were using to buy coffee. Each was adorned with Christmas decorations and contained a chip with embedded funds, but no names. Patty would have to go on her memory and somehow get the suspect to trip up and inadvertently identify himself. They couldn't risk a bad call on the wrong person and jeopardize losing the suspect.

The clock ticked to 7:15 and Patty looked toward the door as she heard the bell jingle. It was him; there was no doubt in her mind. Harold was right on time. Patty clicked her radio four times as she handed an espresso to the lady in front of her, smiled and said, "Thank you."

*****

Armstrong I

It was 0600 and the crew was meeting; all hands were in attendance for the daily briefing. Cmdr. Jack Pavlik started like every other day had started and reviewed the current status of the Armstrong I, as well as the object, and that, once again, nothing had changed relative to the position of it. They were now only three weeks away from reaching the object. Then Jack smiled and added:

"But we do have some good information, finally. For the first time, we are close enough to independently verify what the Hubble space telescope had already identified – we will no longer refer to it as an object. From today forward, it is indeed a ship."

Multiple discussions broke out among the crew and Jack held up his hands for silence before continuing.

"I think I can answer the most common question I heard first; it clearly does not resemble anything from Earth."

Cmdr. Pavlik handed out some grainy computer printouts.

"The ship's appearance is long and thin, almost cigar-shaped, with the exception of what we believe is a larger, spherical nose section. Our best estimates place it at over 100 meters in length, and possibly 10 meters in diameter. There is a second, wider bulge in the ship located towards what we believe is the rear end of the ship, but we have no idea what that is."

"Has it moved at all?" Klaus asked.

"No, not that we can tell. NASA has not been able to identify any signs of activity, either. We could ask a lot more questions, but the truth is that other than knowing it's a ship, we simply don't know anything else yet. Blake, how about the ship that is closing on us?" Jack wanted to keep the morning meeting short and looked over to Blake to move on to the next agenda item.

Blake picked up the hint and immediately continued with the latest status of the rogue Russian ship.

"No missiles have been detected yet, but they have closed the distance and are continuing to gain on us. We are approximately 4 billion kilometers from Earth and we have approximately 1.4 billion kilometers still to go before we reach the object. At our current speed of 2.7 million kilometers per hour, we should reach the object in a little over 21 days. The Russian ship appears to be traveling at a little over 3 million kilometers per hour, so they are gaining on us at a rate of 7.2 million kilometers per day. They are currently a little more than 86 million kilometers behind us. At our current rates, they will be alongside our ship in just 12 days, nine days before reaching the object.

"We are working ideas with both the U.S. and Russian governments," Blake continued, "but, clearly, the situation is unacceptable. We have limited options available to us, assuming the Russian ship truly does have negative intentions, which at this time we are assuming they do."

"Maj. Thompson, I have one request." Vladimir's head had been down through most of the discussion so far, but now he was looking directly at Blake. "Could we please not refer to this as the *Russian* ship? It would not sit well with Russia and makes our people look as if they are behind this heinous general."

"That's a fair point, Vladimir. I apologize. What then, or how then, would your government propose we should refer to this ship?" Blake offered.

"I have talked with my government; we are in agreement to refer to it as the Domashev."

"That makes sense to some degree, but doesn't that give him the credibility he craves?" Blake countered.

"Yes, but it is the lesser of two evils. The fact is, he is an individual and he is on a ship that he controls, so naming it after him as a singular enemy makes sense to the Russian government. What we want to avoid is the option that creates even a hint of him as a legal entity, a sovereign country or a representative of Russia."

"Understood and agreed, Vladimir; that actually makes a lot of sense. We will communicate your desires to our various governments, and I will assure you that from this point forward, on this ship, we will refer to that *other* ship as the Domashev."

"Thank you, Blake, both my government and I appreciate your understanding and cooperation."

"While we're on the topic," Blake continued, "as you know, the Domashev has refused to answer all attempts to communicate, but all transmissions have been in English. It may be worth having you, Vladimir, attempt a contact in Russian. Perhaps you can connect more personally or invite him to break radio silence. What do you think?"

"I can't see how it would hurt. Let me give it a try. If my mental math is correct, it should take four to five minutes for him to receive our message. Assuming he takes a little time to consider it and formulate a response, say 10 minutes, then we should expect a response in no less than, what, 20 minutes?"

Blake laughed. "If I can't beat you in chess, why should I question your math?"

"I'll take that as a compliment, thank you." Vladimir smiled back at Blake.

"Let us start looking at some options."

"One more thing," Cmdr. Pavlik added, "We are continuing to have problems with the sensor on the radar unit that I've been mentioning for the past few days. As the Rus— I mean, Domashev …" Jack bowed toward Vladimir, who nodded his approval "… approaches us, this will become even more critical. We need to investigate and fix this sensor. Which means we need volunteers to conduct a spacewalk." Jack scanned the room and stopped at Blake.

"I think I just got volunteered." Blake laughed and then added more seriously, "I think we all realize that you and James need to stay on board as we can't risk the pilots of this ship. That means we need another volunteer."

It was now Blake's turn to scan the room, and he stopped on Ataullah, as planned.

"Ataullah, as you demonstrated yourself the better man in backgammon, how about you joining me."

"I'd be honored. When do we start?"

Blake looked over at Jack. "The sooner the better."

"Can you support us doing the walk tomorrow?"

"Blake, it will take a little more prep with Houston first. I'll need James's assistance during your walk, so we will need to work his schedule out as well. It's not mission-critical at the moment, so let's target later this week." Jack replied, attempting to make this look as realistic as possible.

"Sold," Blake responded. "Ataullah and I will check out the space suits in the meantime."

Blake felt his confidence rising. Once they were outside the ship, the men inside would search Ataullah's room. At the first sign of sabotage, Blake would cut Ataullah's lifeline and hold him at bay until he talked. If he balked or lied, Blake would launch him on a one-way flight to oblivion and register one more 9/11 payback.

*****

Hawaii

Harold Bessimer was next in line and asked for a double espresso as he stepped up to the counter. Sean was two people behind Harold. Diego was leaning against the doorframe, holding it open for the previous customer. Patty made the espresso and handed it to him. Harold handed her what she hoped was his debit card, but it was another Christmas gift card. She tried her best not to show her disappointment. She was afraid she would lose him and simply did not want to wait another day. It was a big risk, but she had to do it. Patty swiped the card, took a breath and handed his card back to him with a sweet smile, saying in as personal a tone as she could muster,

"Thank you, Aikane."

Harold was clearly caught off guard and dropped his coffee. His mouth opened in total surprise as he attempted to say something, but no words came out. Patty's smile disappeared and was replaced with the look of a cat who knew she had cornered her prey. Harold spun and started to run out of the building, but Sean was ready for him. Sean hit him mid-center as if he was playing linebacker for the NFL. An ESPN highlight tackle. The two went down in a heap as Diego stormed into the store, holding an FBI badge in the air with one hand and pulling cuffs out with his other hand. The tackle had knocked the air out of Harold's lungs and he offered little resistance. Diego cuffed him, and the two of them hoisted Harold to his feet. Diego made a fair attempt at reading Harold his rights, not that they were worried about legal issues at this point, and the threesome worked their way outside to the front of the coffee shop as quickly as they could.

As soon as they knew that Sean and Diego had Harold, Oliver had immediately driven the van the short distance around the building. Li caught up with him and jumped in.

A few seconds later, they pulled up to the coffee shop entrance. Li opened the sliding door from the inside and welcomed Harold.

"Merry Christmas, Harold; we've been looking forward to meeting you."

The radio beeped and Oliver answered. It was Harry, and he had information about Harold's time in Houston.

"I've got a better idea. I'm looking at Harold right now." Oliver smiled, "and you'll be able to ask him directly when we get him to you. See you shortly."

*****

Reagan I

Jimmy was feeling a little better about accidentally turning on the device, as nothing bad had occurred that any of them were aware of, but he was growing more frustrated with each passing day that he didn't know what to do with it. Neither Jimmy, the NSA, nor even the prodigious Harry Lundrum had been able to make any progress. On the positive side, Jimmy had really enjoyed talking with Harry; the guy was a bona fide genius, yet he seemed to treat Jimmy as an equal and didn't exhibit even an ounce of arrogance. It was hard *not* to like the guy.

The device was still active based on the constant whirling noise emanating from the interior, as well as the lights that remained on, with an occasional flicker of one specific set of lights. Jimmy had timed the flicker and it occurred every 72 minutes, like clockwork. Harry had liked Jimmy's idea of jumping each of the keys on the back of the board, but so far, they had not been able to take advantage of the connection. It was almost as if the unit were waiting for a specific command before it would act. Harry theorized that the 72-minute cycle was likely a refresh operation to reset timers while the device awaited orders.

During their last call, Harry recommended that Jimmy complete the jumpers, number the wires and then disconnect the keyboard from the device. By so doing, they could analyze the signals from the keys and determine to which numbered wires the signals would have gone. In that manner, they could maintain safety while they hopefully learned something. There were 149 wires and Jimmy was on wire number 71. It was going to be a long night.

*****

Armstrong I

Vladimir sent his message 30 minutes ago. It simply stated, "Gen. Domashev, we need to talk – Major Vladimir Popov, Russian GRU and Space Committee."

Vladimir had hoped for a response five minutes ago, but like many chess experts, he also knew that part of the *play* was to control your competitor's response. Most people thought of chess strategy relative to the actual movement of player pieces, but the real experts knew it was also critical to control the emotion and pace of the match, sizing up your opponent and leveraging anything that could get under your opponent's skin. The only differences in this game were that they couldn't see each other and they didn't have a chess clock that limited their response to seconds and minutes. At 45 minutes, Vladimir finally received his response.

"What is there to talk about, comrade?" Vladimir translated for Blake.

Blake looked over at Vladimir with a questioning look.

"What value is that response? He knows it will be at least another 10 to 15 minutes before he gets your response."

"Patience, my new American friend. That is something your country has never been good at. Your TV shows solve the toughest problems in the world in 30 minutes, including commercial breaks. If your team doesn't score by half time, you get upset. You detest the beauty of a 0-0 soccer score because there are too few thrills. Your country can't see the magic in the strategic aspect of the game. You expect immediate resolution on things that should take time. Perhaps that is why your country does not succeed in chess and soccer, but loves football and basketball, eh? You need patience and intelligence to excel in games of strategy."

"What about Bobby Fischer; was he not a world champion and a Grandmaster? Did he not beat your Boris Spassky?" Blake triumphed.

Vladimir was more than up to the challenge – he lived for this type of banter.

"Oh, please. That was back in, what, 1972? Over 50 years ago – da? You were not even born yet. One winner in half a century does not make for a case, more like a statistical anomaly, da?"

They both laughed. "You win another round, Vladimir. Perhaps I need to wait until I have Harry to help me out. I am not sure Harry plays chess, but I think he might be able to take you to task." Blake chuckled. "So what will be your response to our newly minted general?"

"We need to figure out what he is really up to, how he plans to do it and perhaps get under his skin a little, in an attempt to get him to show his cards a little earlier."

"Won't he expect that?"

"Of course, but doing nothing gets nothing. How do you say in America … nothing ventured, nothing gained?"

"Okay, Vladimir, but it doesn't look like Domashev wants to let us in on his plans," Blake volunteered. "Keep me posted. I need to check our spacesuits with Ataullah."

"Be careful on your walk, Blake. I'd hate to miss out on more opportunities to tell you about the inadequacies of your country." Vladimir chuckled, waved to Blake and then turned back to the screen to compose his response.

*****

Jarisst I

Juulys had been monitoring the radio signals of the approaching ships and modifying her deciphering analysis for many days now, spending a minimum of 16 hours per day doing so. The goal of cracking the three or four primary languages she had identified was consuming her; not much else mattered anymore. She had identified English first, and then Russian. There were three others that she had concluded from parallel English transmissions that were referred to as Chinese or Mandarin, Spanish and Indian, but there seemed to be so many variants of these three languages that she had not been able to pin down a reliable translation yet. Juulys believed her task to be one of the most critical on the ship, second only to restarting the engines. If they could not escape, and were still to survive, they needed to communicate with this new race before they arrived, and that window of opportunity was quickly shrinking.

Juulys also maintained her vigilance over signals that were external to this solar system, hoping to find something that might connect them with Cjar again, but remained mostly unsuccessful so far. For one short period, during the previous week, Juulys thought she'd found something. As far as she could estimate, it was a message that must be from billions of kilometers outside the solar system, and heading outward. It was very faint, on a frequency of eight GHz, and she was only able to pick it up that one time. Unfortunately, after a day and a half of analysis, her excitement was short-lived when she realized that the radio signals appeared to be communicating with Earth. In addition, the second communication validated that the source was moving *away* from the solar system, and at a ridiculously slow speed of 61,000 kilometers per hour. All signs supported that this must be some type of primitive, unmanned satellite that had been launched from Earth years earlier.

Juulys looked around the Comm Center; the room was a mess. Documents and food trays littered the floor and counters. She had always taken pride in maintaining a clean office, but that had all gone to the wayside as the insidious addiction of resolving their current situation consumed more of her strength and passion each day. For a brief instant, Juulys wondered what she must look like. The thought passed quickly as the Comm Center panel came to life again, like it did every few minutes. Juulys resigned herself to the panel again, put her headset on, and dove back into her mental abyss.

But this time there was something different. The latest messages, spaced less than an hour apart, were both well out into the system – closer to the Jarisst I than they were to the third planet called Earth. Over the past few weeks, Juulys had been able to finalize that this system had nine planets in it. The two ships they were monitoring were currently past the orbit of the seventh planet, more than 4 billion kilometers from the star at the center of the system, and fewer than 2 billion kilometers from the Jarisst I. It had to be from the two ships.

"Thjars! I just picked up new transmissions from the two ships," Juulys screamed into the Comm Center radio.

A minute later, both Thjars and Qulys ran into the Comm Room.

"They are not in English this time, and they weren't encrypted. I may be wrong, but I think it's in what they call the *Russian* language. The second ship appears to have answered about 45 minutes after the first ship started the communication. Both transmissions were short, but both unmistakably came from the location where the two ships currently are."

"Could you determine what they were saying? Are they working together?" Thjars asked.

"Not fully, but it sounded like something you would say when you simply pass someone you don't know. I know that sounds odd, but there wasn't anything of substance stated. I can't guarantee it, but I don't think they're working together."

"Juulys, this is interesting new data, but you look exhausted. We are going to need you even more as the ships get closer, especially if or when we actually initiate communications with them. But they are many days away, and until then, you need to go get rest. We can record anything else that comes up and you can review it when you get back."

"Thjars, I can't …"

"Don't even start with me Juulys; that was an order, not a request. Do I need to have our medical officer, Jenysys, come up here?"

"No. No, please don't do that," Juulys responded dejectedly, but then perked up a little. "I'll go, but only if you get Jarns to take over for me. If anything new comes up, you'll allow him to come get me. Yes?"

"Okay, Juulys, yes. Now go get some rest. I'll call Jarns." He ordered softly.

With that, Juulys plodded out of the Comm Center, looking back at the panel one last time as Thjars was picking up the radio mic.

"Jarns."

"Yes, sir?"

"Come up to the Comm Center. I'd like you to spell Juulys for a couple of hours while she gets some sleep. She picked up our first communication between C1 and C3. It wasn't much, but it was communication."

"Okay, I'll be right there, Thjars, but keep in mind I will have no idea what they are saying. Only Juulys seems to understand some of it."

"Agreed, I just want to make sure we are aware if and when the communication continues. Thank you, Jarns."

*****

FBI Office, Hawaii

After hearing from Harry the day before, the FBI had quickly established a temporary interrogation room at the Hawaii County Police Department in order to quickly get everything they could from Patty's coffee shop suspect once he was captured. The police station was a little more than two miles north, following the

Queen Kaahumanu Highway, so Oliver pulled the van into the police station six minutes after they had rolled Harold into the back of the van.

As they pulled in, Oliver saw three black Cadillac Escalade SUVs with darkened windows, two SWAT vehicles and one urban assault vehicle. There were barricades and police cars everywhere, some clearly unmarked government vehicles, and no fewer than 15 heavily armed guards already standing outside waiting for them, each carrying a German-made Heckler & Koch MP5 nine millimeter submachine gun. It was obvious that not only was the facility on lockdown, but they were ready for all-out war if needed.

Oliver looked up into the rearview mirror at Harold and said: "Looks like the guest of honor has arrived and the party is ready to start."

"FBI, CIA, NSA, NASA, Secret Police … Hey, Harold, lookee that, you have the entire alphabet soup of U.S. security waiting for you," Sean sneered. Harold had yet to say a single word during the short drive, but his eyes looked like a deer in the headlights. "If you have any brains at all, you'll make this quick, or I'll finish up what all of us would like to do to you," Sean added with a sharp edge to his voice.

Harry was already inside the police station waiting for them, and Patty was expected in just a few minutes as she had been driven separately by two heavily armed state police officers. Although they all wanted to conduct the interrogation, it had been made clear that the FBI was running this portion of the show. Blake's team would have to sit in a separate room and wait for the FBI to determine what tidbits of information they would be entitled to hear. It didn't sit well with any of them.

"Bloody crock of cow dung," Sean muttered, loud enough for all to hear.

"It is what it is, Sean, leave it be. I'm sure the feds will get what they need, but they have to play by the rules to ensure that he doesn't get freed by some liberal, rights-loving, no-clue-in-the-world judge," Diego replied.

*****

It had been six hours since they had delivered Harold into the FBI's waiting hands and they were still in the same room. No one had come to see them, with the exception of the local Big Island Pizza delivery boy, and that was more than an hour ago.

"This is bullshit, Diego." Sean was agitated and pacing the floor. "*We're* the ones that found the guy and *we* are the ones that are part of Blake's team, not them." He stopped and looked at Diego. "And this is connected with the same sons of bitches that took Patty!"

"Settle down, Sean. We already paid those guys back, and then some, remember?" Diego replied. "We're not in Yemen or Africa anymore, we're back in the U.S., which means we have to follow the law, *capisce?*"

Sean grumbled something unintelligible and sat down, just as the door opened. Sean was the first to bolt back up.

"What have you got?" he asked before the door could even close.

"I'm agent Pete Sullivan."

"Well, at least your name isn't Lynch," Harry smirked as he said it. Everyone in the room just looked at him blankly, except Sullivan.

"Yeah, we get that all the time, ever since that A-Team movie."

"So, what have we, I mean, *you* learned so far?" Harry asked.

"First, I want to say nice work figuring this all out, and finding the guy. First-class work you guys did, and faster than I would've expected any team to do."

"Thanks, Pete, let's just say we were personally incentivized," Diego replied before Sean could say anything that might be taken wrong.

"Secondly, I don't have much to share with you yet. This guy is scared to death, but he isn't talking. We've got every agency working every angle right now. From what we have found so far, this guy is at the bottom of the food chain. Don't get me wrong, he knows something about what went down, and the chances are he even helped do it, but he doesn't appear to know the organization behind this."

"How can you tell that?" Harry asked.

"He's been out here for years, moving from one job to another. We had a separate group raid his house and there's nothing there that would suggest he's heading up a terrorist organization or even a cell. He acts like a loner that may be acting independently. We have his computer and the guys at the lab are going through it now, but as all of you well know, that will take some time. My recommendation is that you guys take off and we'll call you if and when we find anything new."

"It's not like we have anywhere to go right now, so we don't mind waiting this out," Patty said.

"I understand, but we also have a transfer truck coming in 30 minutes. We're moving him to another location that is better suited for this."

"Better suited?" Patti asked the question on everyone's minds.

"I can't share that, but I can tell you that in a police station, a person can feel somewhat protected by their rights. However, where we are taking Mr. Harold is to a place where he will quite quickly fear that those rights are no longer available. Let's just say that the new location will provide a little mood environment change that might incentivize him a little more. Trust me, we do have our ways; it's just that some of those ways are better off not getting publicized."

With that, Pete smiled a confident and knowing smile, turned and left.

CHAPTER 21

A.D. 2029 (3312 C.A.E.); Jan. 2
Chicago

Jim Morrati had finally received the email. The initial meeting had been at least two months ago, so long ago he had actually forgotten about it until the email arrived. Jim had to open the box stored in his closet to find the directions that verified the email. Then the package had arrived just two days ago, in the form of a large backpack that must have weighed close to 23 kilograms. Less than a minute after the backpack had been delivered, he received a call from the loan shark clarifying that if he opened the backpack, told anyone about it, or didn't deliver it as agreed, then he would regret ever being born and that the impact to his family would be even worse. He hadn't slept all night; he was so scared. His palms were sweaty and his head was still spinning. It was the beginning of a new year, and he just wanted to get this over with and move on, hopefully with a new lease on life.

All he had to do was deliver this single backpack to a predetermined location, then leave. When he returned the email with the preplanned message, his bank account would automatically be credited $25,000. He felt guilty as he knew it had to be something bad, drugs of some kind maybe, but he needed the money badly. How the loan shark knew so much about him was still a mystery, but the man with the odd accent and the confident smile had been very reassuring and persistent.

He had been told to deliver the backpack within the next three days. The envelope that accompanied the package had the address, the drop location, a key and a $27 one-day museum pass in it. As the location he was to deliver the backpack to was only a couple of blocks down the road and he wanted to be done with this as soon as possible, he put the backpack on his back, climbed on his bike and headed down East 57th Street to the Chicago Museum of Science and Industry. It was a little more awkward than usual to ride his bike, as a 50-pound load on your back definitely changed one's center of gravity and balance. Thirty-five minutes later, he was in the museum, surprisingly without anyone checking his backpack. The guard at the front whisked him through the line with no waiting; it was as if he knew he was coming. He then found the designated janitor closet next to the boiler room. He looked around and didn't see anyone, so he pulled the key out of his pocket, opened the door and ducked inside the closet. He placed the backpack on the top shelf in the back of the room and built up a wall of tissue boxes in front of it to hide it, just as he had been instructed to do. Someone had really done their homework, or more than likely, this wasn't the first time they had used this drop point, he reflected. As quickly as he had entered, he left, not looking back a single time. He pedaled back up East 57th Street and turned right on South Blackstone Drive back to his apartment. As soon as he was in his apartment, he sent the required email text.

> *"Glad to hear your ship has arrived. Congrats on the Bucket list. Call me when you get to Chicago."*

Jim Morrati exhaled a heavy breath of air. "Almost done," he whispered.

*****

The next day, Jim headed out early on his bike to a part-time job he had recently started. He was feeling upbeat after seeing that the $25,000 had been posted in his account during the night; he need only wait three days for the deposit to clear and he could use it freely. It was an average day in Chicago, which meant cold in January. Jim was riding down South University Avenue. There was an old couple walking hand-in-hand down the sidewalk in the opposite direction, and a young lady was waiting for her dog to finish watering a tree the city had planted the previous summer. Jim had just passed the Henry Crown Fieldhouse on his right and was about to cross East 56th Street when a car pulled out in front of him so abruptly that he almost face-planted on the passenger side of the car. Jim started to yell at the driver when the other man, in the passenger seat, rolled down the window. The last thing he saw was the barrel of a gun pointing at him, followed by a small flash of light.

Jim Morrati was dead before he hit the ground and the car was quickly on its way.

No one realized it yet, but Jim Morrati's death would be the first in a sequence of unusual events to take place in a number of other major cities across the U.S.

*****

A.D. 2029 (3312 C.A.E.); Jan. 4
On the Armstrong I

To save movie time, Hollywood typically showed the suiting up process, prior to a spacewalk, to be fairly quick and easy, almost like changing into one's nightclothes: slip it on, zip it up, snap the helmet on, twist it and presto, ready to go. Not so. It typically required more than an hour to suit up and check out all of the systems in the suit. After completing the process, Blake and Ataullah entered the air dock and connected their fixed safety lifelines to the inner wall as Jack closed and sealed the door. Through the intercom, Jack wished the spacewalkers well, had them recheck their safety lines and successfully restate safety requirements before he purged the air from the air dock and opened the outer door. One could never be too safe when dealing with space.

Blake looked over at Ataullah and nodded. "What a grand way to welcome in the New Year, Ataullah, don't you think?" His voice was muffled by the suit.

"Yes, four days into the year, Blake, and we are taking a stroll in space, billions of kilometers from home, looking at sights no one on Earth has ever been able to behold, and might never see again. None of us could have predicted this a year ago!"

Although Ataullah's comment, *might never see again*, bothered Blake, he played along and they both chuckled, gave each other a thumbs-up and propelled themselves up and out of the dock using the hand rails, Ataullah first and Blake a few seconds behind him. When they had both reached the surface of the ship, Blake called Jack on the radio.

"Jack, ready to open the retrieval line door." Blake watched as Jack activated the retrieval system outer door and it slowly rotated open as two separate lines played out to a length of two meters. Blake and Ataullah attached the primary retrieval line to their suits at the waistline connection point. Only after double-checking the attachment of the new lines on each other and themselves, did they detach the temporary lines from the air dock. The disconnected lines were then attached to the retrieval door for reuse upon their return.

"Ready?" Blake asked.

"Too late to say no now. Lead away," Ataullah replied with a smile.

The two men began their journey to the rear of the ship as Jack released additional line. In the event of an emergency, Jack could initiate the retrieval system and pull either or both of the space walkers back to the dock.

Back on the ship, Jack and the recently enlisted Klaus were turning on Harry's homemade bomb sniffer. They called it Fido-Mutt, in reference to the military's device developed back in the late 1990s known as FIDO. That device was used in the Middle East to detect IEDs, but Harry's version clearly wasn't a direct purebred offspring, henceforth the mutt moniker. The original FIDO was developed from a team including DARPA, MIT, the Pacific Northwest National Laboratory and Flir Systems, with the intent to imitate and replace the proven expertise of a dog's nose with a machine. The machine worked by vapor-detecting compounds of RDX or PETN, both of which were known, common explosives. RDX is an organic compound, known chemically as a nitramide or $(O_2 NNCH_2)_3$. It is a white solid, more energetic than TNT, and first used in WWII. PETN, or pentaerythritol tetranitrate, was also known as PENT, and pretty similar in structure to nitroglycerin. PENT's chemical formula is $C_5H_8N_4O_{12}$.

Harry had gone on to explain in detail about FIDO's ionization sources, charged particles, mass spectrometers and other aspects of the equipment, most of which was beyond Blake, or anyone else on the Armstrong I. Blake just wanted one; he didn't much care for how it worked, but it was Harry after all, so he paid him the respect he was due and read it all the way through, then thanked him. It had taken quite a while to find the necessary pieces, solder some printed circuit boards together and scavenge ship equipment without letting others know, but it was finalized and loaded on a wheeled cart for easy transfer. The final touch had been to use one of the spacesuit air-lines as the intake hose, or wand as Blake had referred to it, so that it was long enough to reach areas without having to lift Fido-Mutt up. It was a pretty odd-looking contraption, but Harry seemed confident it would work. The fact that Harry mentioned he had first read about it in *Popular Science* bothered him a bit, but Blake well knew that Harry would have researched it much further. He also knew, knowing Harry and the mods he would make, that the mutt would likely be better than the purebred version.

Ten long minutes later, with their labored breathing coming through on the ship's intercom, Blake and Ataullah reached the suspect radar unit.

"Jack, we are at the unit … and have connected our temporary lines to the ship. There is no apparent damage to the exterior of the dish … and there are no signs of exterior contact from debris on this area of the ship. Connecting to run diagnostics."

"Roger that, Blake. Nothing is showing from this side, either."

Blake knew that meant that James had not been able to find anything in Ataullah's quarters either. Was he guilty, or not? Yet, he had to be, Blake thought.

It would take five minutes to run diagnostics. Blake looked around the sky. It was a breathtaking sight. The black sky was alive with stars, everywhere. Clusters of stars and constellations that couldn't be seen through the thick Earth atmosphere had sprung to life as soon as they had arrived in space at the Armstrong's docking station, but this … this was even more. Without the bright light of the sun, Earth and moon, the stars were even more astonishing. The brilliance and clarity of his favorite childhood constellation, the Big Dipper, was incredible. But the biggest difference was the lack of twinkling that the Earth's atmosphere created, replaced in space by unwavering dots of bright light. Blake and Ataullah soaked it in for a full minute or two, until Ataullah broke the silence.

"Allah, or God, no matter what you call Him, has created more than the human mind can comprehend, yes?"

"Yes, Ataullah, it is truly stunning. You can look at a thousand photographs from the Hubble Space telescope, all of which are individually magnificent, but nothing can compare to standing here and actually seeing this endless panorama across the heavens. It's like trying to show someone a photo of the Grand Canyon and knowing that it comes up woefully short of the spectacle that your eyes beheld, only this is a thousand times more than even that."

"We are blessed to see this, are we not? Something this magnificent would make even the most arduous doubter realize that there must be a God."

"You would think so, Ataullah. Let's hope that the good Lord helps us complete this mission safely."

"This mission, like all else, is in Allah's hands."

"You really believe that, Ataullah, that everything is in God's hands? That we don't play a role in the overall chaos?"

Blake was a religious man himself, raised in a Baptist church, but he struggled with the statement that *everything is God's plan*. He believed that he had God-given talents that he should utilize to the fullest. Yes, he believed that God's ability to impact anything and everything was limitless, but he simply didn't believe that God worked that way. Blake believed that part of his test and responsibility was to determine how and when to use his God-given abilities to his best. It was a debate that would likely never be resolved and there were very ardent supporters on both sides, as well as many iterations of opinions in between.

"Of course we do, but we are all instruments of Allah, and it is up to us to do what Allah commands us to do."

"If Allah commanded you to detach yourself from the ship and float into space, you would do it?"

"Absolutely."

"How would you be positive that's what Allah wanted you to do?"

"I cannot describe or theorize the process, Blake, but I would know, and if that was His wish for me, then I am bound to obey. It is that simple."

Blake was struggling with the discussion from two perspectives: first from a purely religious perspective, and secondly, but more importantly, from the risk that Ataullah really was the threat to their mission. "How could there be any possible benefit from you floating off into space and dying?"

"That is not mine to question, Blake. There is no way I or any man can understand the perfect and infinite knowledge of Allah. It is the will of Allah."

"Your faith is as strong as anyone I have ever met, Ataullah. I would love to discuss this further when we are back inside, but perhaps God will be okay with us if we get back to the immediate task at hand, that is assuming he hasn't told you to detach yet."

They both laughed, but inside the suit, Blake was sweating not only from the exertion of the spacewalk, but from the last few comments from Ataullah that made the hair on the back of his neck stand up. Was Ataullah truly intent on destroying this mission, in Allah's name? Blake was going to bring this to a head when they were back inside, of that he had convinced himself – regardless of what his orders were.

The light on the diagnostics unit began flashing before Blake could respond. Perhaps that was God's plan as well, Blake thought, as the discussion was heading in a direction that was not conducive to maintaining their focus on the dangerous tasks associated with a spacewalk. This discussion would be better pursued inside the ship.

"Jack, I see a number of hits that show the system went offline, and the diagnostics reference the same set of registers as having a *fatal error* in each case."

"Blake, this is Rakesh, perhaps we should do what every IT expert starts with: reboot the system and see if the problem goes away."

"Good grief, IT 101, reboot the system and see if the problem goes away before you call for assistance. Why does that not make me feel good when we are over a billion kilometers from home?" Jack added. "Blake, give me two minutes and we'll reboot it."

"Wait," Rakesh interjected again, "Blake, disconnect the power to ensure that all registers reset. Keep it disconnected for 10 seconds and then reconnect. Then we will reboot."

In the bulky space suits, it took much longer to disconnect and reconnect the connector then the 10-second delay required. Ten minutes later, the system was rebooted and they were rescanning the diagnostics.

"Blake, you are down to the 20-minute window where your oxygen will hit the yellow line. You need to start thinking about heading back," Jack alerted the duo.

"We're just about done, Jack, but thanks for the reminder. The diagnostics check looks clean. Tell Rakesh to send Uncle Sam the bill. We're heading back."

Fifteen minutes later, the outer hatch door closed and the air dock began re-pressurizing. Blake was looking forward to getting out of the suit, but he was even more anxious to talk to James about *his* investigation.

*****

A.D. 2029 (3312 C.A.E.); Jan. 7
On Board the Reagan I

"Houston, not to state the obvious, but we are closer to that rocket reaching us, just days away now, and we are starting to get a little nervous up here. Do you have any more insight for us?" The frustration in Cmdr. Kline's voice was clearly evident, but the time delay between transmissions added even more angst to the discussion.

"No, not much, Dutch," Houston's response came back an agonizing 186 seconds later, "but we are convinced that we need to assume that the intentions of the people who launched it are categorically unfriendly."

"Great," Dutch replied dryly.

"But here's the catch we're most concerned about, Dutch," the transmission continued. "Images from our long-range telescopes are fairly conclusive that this rocket must be unmanned. It's too small and has no windows. That would suggest it is a very likely scenario that we are dealing with a missile."

Dutch sat back from the console. Neither man spoke right away.

"A missile? Why? How do we defend against it?" Dutch asked quietly. "Are you guys sure about this? If they know what we have, why would they want to destroy it?"

One hundred and 86 seconds passed.

"Dutch, there's a lot more going on than we have shared with you. Unfortunately, you are not cleared for us to share the information."

"What?" Dutch yelled into the radio, breaking his normally calm demeanor. "I don't give a rat's ass what level I'm cleared for or not. You go find whoever it is that you need to and you get that clearance, today!" Kline paused, knowing there would be no immediate response, and then continued, "Look, Houston, this may be life-or-death up here, let alone trying to get this device back to Earth. You need to level with us, and now," Dutch replied tersely.

This time, five agonizing minutes passed …

"Dutch. I understand your frustration. Look, I'll do everything I can, but there is concern that someone is listening in on our transmissions. If that's the case, then they would learn everything we share with you, as well as be prepared to counter anything we discuss that might protect the ship. That means they may also know what you have on board. It's pretty complicated, Dutch, but I'll run it up the ladder as soon as we disconnect."

"Thank you, Houston." And he disconnected the call.

Dutch sat in his seat, still in dismay. Houston was clearly empty-handed relative to helping the Reagan I and its crew, and there was obviously much more information out there that wasn't being shared with them. That meant there was only one option left for him: his crew.

*****

Jarisst 1

"Oh, my Glysst!" Juulys uttered out loud. "Thjars! Come quick," she yelled into her headset.

Sixty seconds later, Thjars was back in the Comm Center.

"What happened, Juulys, you sounded pretty upset …"

"I don't know if I should cry in frustration, or joy."

"You're losing me, Juulys. Slow down. Now tell me, what did you just find out?"

"I'm sorry, Thjars; it's all my fault. I just never thought about it."

Thjars was starting to get a little frustrated, but was trying as best he could to be supportive.

"Thought about what?"

"Thjars, it's right there, right in front of us. The C-Pod," she continued, "it sent out transmissions trying to communicate. With someone. With anyone. With us." She looked up at Thjars. "It's waiting for an answer. We, I, was so consumed about not giving away our position that we never thought to communicate with our own C-Pod – it's our C-Pod!" Tears freely flowed down her cheek.

"Sorry, Juulys, but I'm still not sure what you're saying. We were pretty confident that it was our C-Pod … what could we possibly tell it?"

"We can send it our ship's confirmation code simply by replying to it. That will allow the C-Pod to begin communicating with our ship's computer – and turn on the drives. It's part of the basic emergency recovery system built into all of our ships. Under normal operations, the ship drives require access from the bridge officers. Under emergency situations, the access simply requires computer-to-computer communication from another Cjarian ship … or system, like the C-Pod. In that manner, rescue operations are greatly enhanced once it has determined that the contact source is Cjarian and not an enemy ship. This definitely fits a rescue scenario." She smiled through her tears.

Juulys turned back to the console and typed in a string of characters that represented the call sign for the Jarisst I, as well as a help request.

For the first time since this nightmare began, Thjars was beginning to think that they might be onto something. Hope renewed.

*****

Reagan I

Cmdr. Kline walked into the makeshift lab area just as Jimmy fell back from the device. Noises were emanating from the unit and lights were flashing rapidly in various sequences.

"Damn it, Jimmy, now what did you do?" Kline bellowed.

"Nothing, commander … I swear to God; I honestly didn't do anything this time."

"That's correct, Dutch, I'll back him on that. He was getting ready to complete the jumpers to the keyboard, but he wasn't touching anything when it came to life again," Pat added.

For the next hour, as the men watched, the unit blinked and whirled for various lengths of time, went silent, and then restarted. This pattern continued throughout the hour, but with different sequences in each pattern set.

"Any ideas, Jimmy?" O'Dougherty asked.

"If I didn't know better, Tom, I'd say it's attempting to communicate with someone or something."

"That's more than my head can digest right now, so let's get back to a more immediate and pressing problem that only we can resolve, and we need to resolve it in the next 36 hours," Cmdr. Kline stated. "I think I finally understand what we didn't understand from Houston before."

Everyone turned to the commander.

"Houston just told me that we were not cleared for a lot of other things that are going on right now. Based on what Jimmy just said, I'm beginning to think that they know that someone or something is out there, and they haven't told us yet. But that's not all of it."

Cmdr. Kline spent the next few minutes updating the crew on what he had just learned about the oncoming vehicle and why it was believed to be a missile. Jimmy looked distraught.

"So you're telling me that we'll all be dead in less than two days, and we'll never get to see and meet whoever these people are?" Jimmy stated, dismayed.

"Jimmy, no, not if we can help it. At this point, I don't expect any help from anyone in Houston, so it's going to be up to the six of us if we're going to survive. We need to start thinking about ways to protect the ship."

"We have no weapons, Dutch," Pat stated succinctly.

"Yes, we do." Jimmy stood up.

Everyone looked at him.

"Continue, Jimmy. What are you thinking?" Dutch asked.

"Speed is a weapon. We and the missile are already at speed, so we are both weapons."

"Agreed, Jimmy, but I'd personally not like to be a weapon," Maj. Martinez stated bluntly.

"We need to make the space equivalent of countermeasures on a fighter aircraft and get it out in front of us," Jimmy stated confidently.

"Okay, that sounds great for a movie line, but we don't have any countermeasures and we have no way of launching anything. We also don't know if this thing is homing in on us with radar, thermal or electronic-seeking sensors," Martinez added.

"Those are great points, major, but actually, we don't have to launch anything per se. We simply need to locate appropriate items in front of us and then slow the ship down. It's the opposite of the old bear joke." Jimmy smiled.

"Bear joke?" the major questioned, "Have I ever told you how hard it is to follow your thinking?"

"Yeah, you have … you know the old joke, the one where they describe two people in the woods who surprise a bear and then ask how fast do you have to run to escape the bear? The answer was 'just fast enough to outrun the other guy.' Well this is the reverse. We want to run just slow enough that the ejected items win the race – i.e.: we will slow the ship down after we eject everything and build up enough separation to minimize damage due to the explosion. With the missile on direct line of sight with us, it won't be able to see the separation between the countermeasures and the ship."

Cmdr. Kline's face lit up. "Jimmy, that's brilliant. It's not surefire, but it's the best idea I've heard in a long time. We need to consider all of the sensor options the missile may have and get them out in front of us in the next few hours – time is critical."

Cmdr. Kline and Jimmy then led the group through an hour-long discussion, brainstorming ad hoc countermeasures.

"This actually sounds feasible, gentlemen; I am thoroughly impressed." Dutch smiled with pride. "Let's get moving and launch this idea of yours. Jimmy, at the least, you'll go down in history as the first person to use a space-bound countermeasure in a space-bound war."

"Thanks, commander, but if this device is what we really think it is, I expect we are way behind in that competition."

*****

A.D. 2029 (3312 C.A.E.); Jan. 8
Museum of Science and Industry, Chicago

It was a Monday morning, five days since Jimmy Morrati visited the Museum of Science and Industry. The building was filled with people. Many were enjoying the final day of a three-day weekend, others were there with school groups and many were just tourists enjoying the museum. There were no fewer than 2,400 people in the building, including staff.

The bomb, consisting of 20 kilograms of C4 explosive, detonated in the janitor's closet in the back of the building. The location had been purposely selected due to its proximity to the boiler room. The explosion obliterated the storage room and ruptured the nearby boiler, causing a secondary, and significantly larger explosion.

The simulated coal mine and the Numbers in Nature exhibits were the nearest to the explosion and at least 150 people were instantly incinerated in the blast and subsequent fire. Another 300 were injured, many critically. The destroyed and burning coal mine exhibit collapsed into the Coleen Moore Fairy Tale exhibit on the floor below, trapping scores more inside that exhibit. Pandemonium broke loose. CNN carried broadcasts live, interrupting the world much as 9/11 did, captivating the entire country. Scores of fire trucks, police cars and ambulances descended upon the carnage.

*****

Thirty minutes later, a man with a distinctively Middle Eastern accent called the main offices of the *Chicago Tribune*.

> *"The attack on the Chicago Museum of Science and Industry is the first of many attacks that we have planned for your country. You will pay for the lives of innocent women and children that your airstrikes have killed in Iraq, Iran, Syria and Afghanistan. Unless you revoke your allegiance to Israel and announce the withdrawal of all troops from the Middle East, we will continue to detonate other bombs at major public settings until you renege on your ties to Israel. If these continued bombings are not adequate, then we will escalate the severity of our attacks. We are prepared to go beyond anything you can imagine. There is no way you can stop us."*

The caller paused for a moment.

> *"Allah Akbar. The jihad on America has begun."*

CHAPTER 22

A.D. 2029 (3312 C.A.E.); Jan. 6
On Board the Jarisst I

The lights on the drive control board lit up.

"Thjars, the drives are on!" She jumped up and hugged Thjars. "Can we accelerate away from these ships now? I don't trust any of them."

"I'm not sure, Juulys. Keep in mind that all we have are the sublight speed drives; we still lack fuel to replenish the Q-PAMS drive. There's a part of me that wants to run away as fast as we can as well, but to where? There's another piece of me that wants to head to the third planet, but that may be very dangerous. So, I'm thinking that the best option is to wait it out a couple more days and not show our hand yet until we know more. We can always escape at a later time if the situation worsens. Let's update the rest of the crew and see what ideas they have." Thjars picked up the ship's radio mic and ordered everyone to meet on the Control Deck, immediately.

The group was assembled five minutes later and Thjars provided a brief update. Once the initial Q&A died down, Qulys spoke up.

"Thjars, I believe your option to wait and see is correct, but I recommend that we hit the go button at the first sign of aggression from either ship."

"Agreed, then wait it is. Qulys, you and Knarls are to rotate keeping watch and alert me immediately if anything changes."

*****

White House Situation Room, Washington, D.C.

It had only been two hours since the explosion at the Chicago Museum of Science and Industry. An emergency meeting had already been convened with the president in the White House Situation Room to review the status of the burgeoning crisis.

The Situation Room was a 5,000 square foot complex of rooms on the ground floor of the West Wing. Contrary to popular belief, the White House Situation Room was not a bunker located deep underground. It was also frequently referred to as "the woodshed." The nickname "woodshed" was rumored to have arisen during the Richard Nixon administration when Henry Kissinger was so frustrated with the CIA that he "took them to the woodshed." The Situation Room was originally born out of frustration during President Kennedy's presidency after the failed Bay of Pigs invasion. Kennedy had become so irate when he could no longer trust the information coming to him from the various sectors of the nation's defense departments that he knew he needed to do something different. As a result, McGeorge Bundy, President Kennedy's National Security Advisor, created the Situation Room in May 1961.

The main table in the Situation Room had chairs for 13 people: six chairs down each side, and one for the president at the head of the table. Additional chairs lined the walls. The staff of the Situation Room, including the National Security Council (NSC) Secretary, helps the president connect with intelligence agencies and key contacts overseas. The Situation Room, or "Sit Room" staff is comprised of approximately 30 personnel, organized around five "watch teams" that provide 24/7 monitoring of international events and brief the president every day. A typical watch team includes three duty officers, a communications assistant, and an intelligence analyst.

Muted live video and pictures of the museum carnage played on multiple screens while the meeting continued. Gen. Landon McMullen, Chairman of the Joint Chiefs of Staff, was listening intently as Tom Garrett, Director of the FBI, and Brad Watters, director of the NSA, reviewed what they knew so far about the terror attack in Chicago, as well as a projected top 20 line-up of other key U.S. cities that might now be at risk.

"Okay, ladies and gentlemen, settle down. If I follow what I've heard so far," interjected President Callahan, "you believe we are dealing with a Mideast terrorist cell, that this is a highly planned attack and that it is likely not a singular event; is that correct?"

All heads in the room nodded.

"Have the Brits and Israelis been contacted yet?" Callahan continued.

"Yes, Mr. President. They are looking at all of their intel as well," replied Ben Tellinino, the National Security Council (NSC) Secretary.

"Ben, please pull up the script from the post-explosion phone call again."

"Yes, sir, Mr. President. One minute, please," Ben responded to President Callahan. "Okay, here it is now." He punched the return key on the keyboard and the wall screen came to life.

"All right, everyone, I need opinions. This last statement has me very concerned."

All looked up to see the message from the terrorist displayed across the main screen;

> *"If these continued bombings are not adequate, then we will escalate the severity of our attacks. We are prepared to go beyond anything you can imagine."*

"I was told that the missiles from Ardakan, Iran were all destroyed. Can someone validate that statement so I can sleep without concern of a nuclear threat to the American people?"

Gen. McMullen was the first to respond. "Mr. President, we have verified all sites where the missiles were destroyed with plutonium sensors. Unless they had more, we got them all, sir."

"Bingo, general. What if there were more? What is the probability this is not a bluff?"

No one answered, so President Callahan continued. "They just killed hundreds of people and blew up a U.S. landmark in the middle of the country. It could be a bluff, but at this point my gut is telling me they have something real, so I believe we have to assume the worst. This is the nightmare scenario we have worked so hard to avoid. And we know that if they have a nuke, they won't hesitate to use it on U.S. soil. The only questions are where and when. I want every man and woman you have on this starting two hours ago. Any objections?"

"Mr. President," said Tom Garrett of the FBI, "we have a number of high-profile cases under way right now, many of which include known terrorists ..."

President Callahan cut him off in mid-sentence. "Tom, I know we do, but this feels real. If they really have a nuke on U.S. soil, it will make 9/11 seem like a traffic stop violation. We need everyone on this. Brad, because of the NSA's intelligence gathering abilities, you have the lead. I am invoking the National Emergency Powers Act. Ben, document that now. Brad, you have full access to all records until we get through this emergency. Make it clear that I will publicly go after anyone who misuses this power with the same fervor that we are now using against the terrorists." President Callahan looked up at everyone, with as serious as a look as they had ever seen. "At this time, there are no more singular, independent agencies. Everyone in this room and every person that reports to your organizations now works for one agency, the United States of America, reporting directly to me. In his current role, Brad will be my singular point of contact for all information." President Callahan looked at Brad. "Brad, I want daily debriefs at 6:00 a.m., 12 noon, 6:00 p.m. and midnight. New breakthroughs will be shared as soon as you can validate the message. Nothing else will trump these meetings. Are we all clear?"

Everyone in the room nodded. President Callahan then looked at his Chairman of the Joint Chiefs of staff, Gen. McMullen. "Gen.

McMullen, how many troops can we return to the states to help beef up key city police stations, border patrols and port authorities, without jeopardizing our foreign interests, or creating new risks?"

"Mr. President, we have approximately 150,000 troops abroad. I will have a hard answer for you first thing in the morning, but I expect we could quickly and quietly relocate 20,000 to 30,000 troops back home on temporary leave within the next 30 days without creating undo visibility or risk."

"Thank you, general, you have my approval, but it has to happen in the next five days. Work with Brad to determine where best to locate them. Highest priority should be given to engineers and technicians that have nuke sensor experience. Relocating some of their nuke-sensing hardware to key U.S. locations will also be of utmost importance." The president was about to continue when Ben Tellinino looked up from his screen with a pained look in his eyes.

"Mr. President, you need to see this." Ben punched a few keys and looked up at the main screen. "CNN Breaking News" scanned across the monitor and the afternoon anchor started with "Breaking news from the *Washington Post* ..."

"Shit ..." murmured the president as he sat back in his chair and the CNN anchor continued.

"The *Washington Post* has just released that unknown sources in the White House have verified that this was indeed a terrorist attack and that worse yet, more attacks are expected in major U.S. cities starting as early as tomorrow ..."

"I want to know where this leak came from and I want to know before dinner. I want the SOB arrested today!" President Callahan yelled as he pounded the table with his fist. "Brad, get with CNN and the *Post* ASAP and get this thing limited to what has been released so far. We need to give the same direction to all of the new agencies – no releases without White House permission. Ben, get the writers going; I want to be on air with all major stations in no more than 60 minutes. We need to calm the American people before the panic level goes ballistic in every city in this country.

We need to be honest with people, but we also need to create some confidence. Let's get moving, people." And with that, the group dispersed except for President Callahan, Brad and Ben. They continued talking for another 15 minutes.

*****

A.D. 2029 (3312 C.A.E.); Jan. 9
Reagan I

The call from Houston had arrived early in the morning and it was exactly what Cmdr. Kline had expected. Nothing. They were on their own.

"Well, gents, it's up to us. No help is coming," he shared with his crew. "Let's review what we've come up with for countermeasures. Jimmy?"

"Okay, commander, we actually have quite a bit of material." Jimmy proceeded to run through a list of dead-weight items that would provide impact interference to the missile. He went on to explain how they would conduct a spacewalk to release the material and then use the retro rockets to slow the ship down and provide safe separation from the array of objects. "We'll tether all of the other countermeasures together at various lengths to ensure the objects don't float away into space, thereby providing a giant interference screen for us."

"That makes sense, Jimmy, but what about Maj. Martinez's concern for electronic or thermal tracking sensors?" queried Cmdr. Kline.

"We have that covered as well, and that's our capstone project." Jimmy said, grinning ear-to-ear. "We are going to use the Red Lander as a decoy directly in line with the oncoming missile. As the missile nears, we'll turn on electronic radio signals and the maneuvering thrusters. The side-mounted thrusters will provide a thermal signature that should be easy for the oncoming missile to detect and home in on."

"I like it, but are you sure we can control it remotely, Jimmy?"

"We think so. O'Dougherty helped me come up with some software that should allow us to do just that."

"Okay, but how about our safety relative to shrapnel that comes our way from an explosion directly in front of us? There is no atmosphere, so there is nothing to slow anything heading directly into our course, correct?" Maj. Martinez queried.

"Unfortunately John, you are correct. Depending on how big this explosion is, the shrapnel within our arc segment of the explosive sphere will impact the ship if it misses our countermeasure net. There's no avoiding the possibility." Jimmy looked over at Cmdr. Kline. "I'm afraid that this is the crapshoot part of this plan. I don't see any way to prevent damage from something incoming on our direct flight path. I think we have to assume that the hull will be breached somewhere, if not in multiple locations, so we will all need to don our spacesuits to ensure maximum safety. Once the explosion is over, assuming we are spared, we can then isolate undamaged sections of the ship that might be able to maintain an oxygen environment."

"Jimmy, I agree on all accounts." Cmdr. Kline jumped in. "But I also think we have one tough question that we need to answer yet, and I will support whatever decision this group comes to." He paused and looked from face to face. "Do we all stay in one section of the ship together, with the risk that an unlucky hit takes us all out, or do we spread ourselves out to reduce the risk that all are lost?"

Everyone looked at each other for a long minute and then Jimmy broke the silence.

"The way I see it is that we've all been family for a long time on this trip. If it's all the same with you guys, I'd rather wait this out together. If I'm going to die, I'd rather it be with people I call my friends, rather than die alone."

One by one, all acknowledged agreement.

"Okay, gents, we have a decision, and we have very limited time left before the missile is upon us, so let's get to work." Kline stood up and the five other men headed out to put their plan into action.

*****

A.D. 2029 (3312 C.A.E.); Jan. 10
Iran

"Make the call, Amir. Their time is running out," the unknown voice stated.

Amir picked up his laptop and called the main telephone number in the White House: 202-456-4533.

"The president, please," the voice requested.

"I'm sorry sir, but the president ..." and the White House receptionist was quickly cut off.

"Do not delay me, woman. The second bomb will detonate in two hours and 10 minutes unless you get me the president within five minutes. Your people know where he is; get him."

"Hold, please." The panicked operator immediately called the on-shift supervisor of the Secret Service, who in turn was able to get President Callahan on the phone within two minutes.

"This is the president," Callahan answered.

"You have seen what we are capable of doing to your country and your people, Mr. President. We have many more events ready to trigger and you cannot stop them without us. So, it is up to you, Mr. President; how many more Americans do you want to die for your delinquency? Our patience is thin. Publicly denounce Israel on national TV and begin withdrawing your troops from the Mideast, or more will die shortly."

NSA agents were feverishly trying to triangulate the call to get a location on the caller. Unfortunately, the call was made through Call2Friends.com online with an anonymous account relayed thru multiple internet paths. The days of tracing phone lines with ease had disappeared forever with the advent of online phone calls. It was no different than trying to trace the source of irritating spam emails. The caller could easily have been anywhere on the planet and there was simply no quick and easy way to tell, especially if the caller kept the call short and there were no background sounds to provide hints on the location; this caller was smart enough to avoid both.

"You know I can't do that and the United States of America will never bow to terrorist demands," President Callahan stated with as much bravado as he could muster. "Is this really how you want to represent your people? By killing innocent women and children who have done no wrong to you or your people?

"Mr. President, you have made your choice. Their blood is on your hands now." With that, the call ended.

President Callahan cussed a string of profanity never before heard during his administration.

"Ben, get everyone in the Situation Room in 30 minutes."

"Yes, Mr. President."

*****

Mazza Gallerie Mall, Washington, D.C.

It was 11:59 a.m. in the Neiman Marcus store at the upscale Mazza Gallerie Mall at 5300 Wisconsin Ave. NW, and the store was beginning to fill with shoppers. As the clock ticked to noon, two 20-kilogram C-4 charges detonated in a janitor's closet on the first level of the three-level Neiman Marcus store. Walls disintegrated as the blast consumed everything within a 50-foot radius. Structural supports for the floors above gave way, causing the upper floors to fall inwardly, directly above the explosion. The blast left a gaping hole and fire through all three levels. The weight of debris from the falling floors cascaded down onto the smaller stores on the concourse level.

Within minutes of the blast, the *Washington Post* received an anonymous call from a man with a Middle Eastern accent who took credit for the blast. The individual stated that there would be another blast somewhere else in the U.S. within the next 48 hours.

It wasn't until days later, when crews were able to clear away most of the debris, the bodies recovered and families of missing people contacted, that it was estimated that no fewer than 251 people had died in the blast.

CHAPTER 23

A.D. 2029 (3312 C.A.E.); Jan. 10
Hawaii

Diego and Harry sent a long update to Blake and were waiting on his response. It had been two weeks since they caught Harold Bessimer. They updated Blake on the investigation, and how little progress had been made, as well as the recent terror attacks. The team completed breakfast and gathered at the FBI office where they were sitting in a conference room by themselves. Pete Sullivan, FBI agent, had just left the conference room after letting them know that they had yet to uncover any new information.

"Bingo, Blake's response just popped up," Diego called Harry, "I'll pull it up on the monitor." The team all turned toward the 72-inch monitor at the front of the conference room.

> *"Blake here. Still batting zero on any new clues out here. 'Company' is getting close – relay that I demand you guys get full update. Sounds like you've been FUBAR'd, nothing from the FBI after two weeks? Sorry to hear. Must be frustrating. Acknowledge that you said the FBI scoured Harold Bessimer's place. They are the best, but can't help thinking they missed something. You guys will rust away without some activity. Recommend you get FBI permission to look at house and conduct your own sweep. You may see it from a different perspective. See if they have looked for Bessimer's fingerprints in Houston Control, too. Possible that 'system' may have been prebuilt into a module. Keep the updates coming. Good luck. Over."*

"Well, he's right on that," Diego commented, "we will go stir crazy for sure if we sit here on our asses for even one more day. Let's get Sullivan back here."

*****

Two hours later, the team, Pete Sullivan and two other agents were inside the Bessimer residence. It was a small, nondescript house located in a nondescript neighborhood on a cul-de-sac at the end of Hokulii Plaza, not far from the coffee shop. Li noticed that the location was perfect for anyone wanting a backyard escape.

Agent Sullivan walked them through the house and shared what they had looked for, found and not found.

"What computer assets did you find?" Harry asked.

"One laptop, two cell phones and one desktop PC. The lab boys have gone over them top to bottom and have found absolutely nothing," Pete replied, knowing what the group was going to ask.

Li jumped in next. "That doesn't make any sense at all, unless there are other computers located elsewhere. Did he have access to any storage facilities that you know of?"

"None that we've identified, but it is possible that he has an associate elsewhere and that additional computers are maintained there," Pete replied with a shrug.

The group split up and walked through the house, yard and carport. Nothing. They talked with some of the neighbors, who all had the same response about Harold: a quiet guy who never talked to anyone, but would provide a friendly wave and smile when he saw someone. No one knew where he worked or what he did. He minded his business and didn't bother them, so they did likewise. As far as they could tell, Harold never had visitors.

Just then, Harry stuck his head out the front door. "Can you guys come in here for a minute?"

Harry pointed to the laundry room and asked Sullivan what they found when they checked this room.

"Nothing," Sullivan replied. He now knew enough about Harry to say, "But I'm assuming you just did. What is it, Harry?"

"Measure the length of the inside of the laundry room please."

One of the agents picked up a measuring tape that had been left on the counter from a previous FBI visit and stretched it from the door entrance to the far wall.

"Seven feet, four inches."

"Okay, now please measure the length of the outer wall of this room."

The agent complied as requested, exited the room and laid the measuring tape down along the outside of the room. He sat back, puzzled.

"What is the measurement?" Harry asked.

"Nine feet, 10 inches ..." The agent looked shaken, but continued. "There's a 30-inch difference." Everyone in the room started murmuring.

Sullivan responded first. "Harry, it could be ducting or something that goes up the inside of the wall."

"I thought about that as well, but this house doesn't possess a heating or a cooling system, just windows and the Hawaiian air from outside. Note that the dryer vent exhausts through the roof, directly above the dryer. I believe there is a defined space behind that back wall of the laundry room. Even if we assume five-inch thick walls, that leaves 20 inches unaccounted for."

"Okay Harry. I don't disagree with you, but how is it accessed and what could you do with only 20 inches?"

"I agree that's a pretty tight space, but if someone is trying to hide something really important, they will go through great lengths to do so. Relative to access, I didn't find any access points on any of the walls, and the roof is flat, so there's no attic to drop down through. The only other option would be from underneath, suggesting there may be a trap door that leads to some type of tunnel."

Sean jumped in. "Diego, how about we put a hole through this wall right now?"

"Whoa, not so fast," Sullivan replied. "I agree we want to get inside of that wall, but this is still an active investigation site. We can't do that without approval."

"Then use that damn phone of yours and get it," Sean answered tersely.

"Hang on, everyone," Harry countered. "I don't want to damage what's on the other side. If there is an access from underground, then we should be able to find it. Let's comb the back yard, especially near that clump of palm trees. Pete, go ahead and make the call anyway, just so we don't lose any time."

The group headed for the back yard and split up, looking for anything they could find that might hide a crawl space entrance. Harry went directly to the clump of palm trees. Diego walked off the back end of the property, where the hill slanted downwards. It was a small yard, so it didn't take long. Thirty minutes later, the team reassembled near the back door.

"Well, that didn't work," Sean said.

"Harry, did anyone check the carport yet?"

"No Pete, but that's a great idea; let's go."

The group spent the next five minutes looking for a secret entrance, but found nothing. They had gotten excited when they found a 15-foot-long by 6-foot-wide rubber mat on the floor, and quickly rolled it up and out of the way, but there had been nothing but oil-laden Hawaiian dirt underneath it.

"Sullivan. Any word on that approval yet?" Diego asked.

"Not yet."

"Where are you going, Harry?" Patty asked as Harry walked back into the house.

"Come on, he's onto something. Harry never does anything without an end game in mind."

As the group followed Harry into the house, Harry asked them to check every light switch they could find to see if it opened a secret panel somewhere.

Ten minutes later, the team gave up. Nothing.

"Now what, Harry?" Patty was feeling sorry for their team's genius. Harry was looking at the ground. Then he looked up with a glint of expectation in his eyes.

"Agent Sullivan."

"Yes, Harry?"

"Where is Harold's car?"

"At the lab, why?"

"Call the lab and see if the car has a garage door opener in it."

"Harry, this house has a carport. There is no garage door," one of the other agents replied, looking at Harry as if he had finally lost it.

"Exactly," Sullivan replied for Harry. "The simplest things in life are so easily missed. I'm on it, Harry." With that, Sullivan contacted the lab and sure enough, there was a garage door opener in Harold's car.

"They'll be here in 20 minutes. I know we shouldn't get our hopes up, but I think you're on to something."

Twenty minutes seemed like an eternity, but a young lab tech showed up, slid into the driveway with his brakes locked, jumped out and ran to Agent Sullivan.

"Is this what you needed, sir?"

"It most assuredly is, but the honors belong to Harry." Agent Sullivan took the remote and handed it to Harry. "Your move, Harry."

Harry requested everyone move out to the street, just in case it was more than just a remote door opening. Harry pushed the button one time. Nothing happened. Harry frowned, then looked over at the tech's car and asked, "How many times do you have to hit your trunk button for it to open."

"Twice or one long push, why?"

Harry smiled, raised the remote again and pressed the button twice. Shortly thereafter the sound of breaking glass could be heard inside the house.

"What the ..." Sean uttered.

"Let's go see," Harry volunteered.

The group reentered the house and gathered in the kitchen, which coincidentally happened to adjoin the laundry room. The broken glass was from a sugar bowl that had been on the kitchen table and was now in pieces on the floor. The table and chairs had been pushed back.

"Well I'll be damned. Harry, you are a genius." Sullivan put his hand out to shake Harry's while still focusing his gaze on the now open room. Harry took the offered hand in his and just smiled, still looking at the laundry room wall. The remote had activated a panel that opened outward like a Californian garage door, exposing a wall of computers and telecommunications gear. Agent Sullivan pulled the table back further so that the door could swing fully open. The panel turned out to be the entire wall, including molding strips, which explained why it was so hard to detect.

"OMG Harry, it's the mother lode!!!" Patty shouted and hugged Harry.

Agent Sullivan was scanning the secret room. "This is expertly done. No way this guy acted alone. Very impressive work, as good as anything we can do. It also explains why 20 inches was adequate as it was only for storage, not actual use of the equipment. Everything is turned off, which also explains why we didn't sense any electrical activity, either. Harry, let me take this from here. I'll get the tech squad back in here. There has to be a treasure trove of information in this room."

Two hours later, the house was again surrounded with black, unmarked sedans and tech vans with no fewer than 20 agents pouring over the equipment and data.

Sullivan looked at Harry. "Thank you, Harry, I think this is the first significantly positive piece of information we've had. Do you think there is a connection between this and the recent bombings?"

Harry chewed on Pete's question for a few seconds before replying. "It's possible, and I guess your crew will find that out shortly, but I don't think so."

"How so?"

"This guy clearly did not want to be identified and has not been part of any messaging whatsoever relative to the Armstrong, as if he wants to stay out of the mainstream. On the other hand, the terrorist hits have been very public and they want everyone to be aware of their activities. Because of that, I'm afraid that we may have two independent activities. If they are related, I doubt our Harold has any idea of what is really going on in the bigger picture, but there is a very real possibility that he could still be an information conduit."

"Harry, I have to admit that your logic is pretty sound. I guess it's wishful thinking on my part and I'm guilty of wanting it to be the same source, but I can't argue with what you just stated." Pete looked over at the man he was getting to know better each day and added, "Harry, if you ever want a position in the FBI, just let me know." Pete smiled, slapped Harry's shoulder and headed for his car.

*****

On Board the Reagan I

The predicted time had come and the missile remained on course, heading directly toward the Reagan I and its crew. It had taken a herculean effort by all to get the equipment together, conduct the space walk, prepare to "launch" the equipment and then slow the ship down. Cmdr. Kline looked out the front of the Control Deck and although he couldn't see it, he knew the Red Lander and its array of countermeasures were now flying intercept for them. They had not informed Houston due to the concern that whoever might be listening would change their game plan and they wanted to make sure the Reagan I had maximum surprise on their side.

The crew gathered in the Control Room, together, as proposed by Jimmy and agreed to by all. The men were all in their space suits, visors open. The air was solemn among the group of astronauts that had now become close friends.

"Okay, Tom, how about we fire up the Red Lander and get this show on the road."

"Aye, aye, skipper. 3 ... 2 ... 1, rockets on." Tom paused and looked down at the hand-built control panel. "Shit, let's try that again ... 3 ... 2 ... 1 .... Damn it! Could anything work for us as planned? Jimmy, give me a hand; our homemade RC is not working."

The two men checked all the circuitry and power, while the rest of the crew watched.

"No pressure, guys, but we're down to less than an hour before impact. Is there anything we can do to help? Are there other options?" Cmdr. Kline kept his composure as he asked. There were no answers.

No one noticed Maj. John Martinez leave the Control Deck.

Seven precious minutes passed as Jimmy and Tom worked feverishly on the remote control unit – until an alarm sounded on the main control panel.

"Skiles, what is that?" Kline asked.

"OMG … Commander, it's the dock alarm. Someone has opened the dock."

"What?" Kline yelled. "Who is … wait, where the hell is Martinez?"

No sooner had that name been uttered, than Skiles responded by speaking into the mic on the panel.

"John. What are you doing? John, speak to me, buddy."

"We don't have time. I'm sorry guys, but we have to light that lander up. You guys came up with a great idea; it's my turn to do something."

"John, this is Cmdr. Kline, turn the rocket sled around and come back. We agreed it was all or none."

"Yes, we did, and it still is. We all know that the cargo on this ship has to make it back to Earth. But even more important is the human cargo on this ship."

The sled was accelerating and Maj. John Martinez was quickly disappearing in the direction of the Red Lander.

"Gentlemen, this is my choice. We didn't have time to draw straws. I've already left messages for my family when we first knew a missile was on the way. Please make sure that the recordings are delivered. I am proud to have been part of this crew and mission and wouldn't wish any other outcome. Get strapped in, gentlemen, it's going to be a bumpy ride. I will let you know when I'm on board." With that, the mic clicked off.

"I understand, John. I don't agree, but … thank you. You're a good man, John." Cmdr. Kline spoke into the mic and then clicked off.

Jimmy was close to tears. Cmdr. Kline knew he couldn't let emotion take over now; he had to get everyone to safety and strapped in pronto.

"Everyone, let's move into the Control Module. There's nothing more we can do here."

The group took one final look in the direction of Maj. John Martinez and turned to depart the Control Deck. Lt. Pat Skiles saluted in John's direction and then relayed that he would stay in the Control Deck to monitor John's progress before he rejoined them. The Command Module, where the rest of the group was heading, was a separate unit of the Reagan I intended for re-entry into Earth's atmosphere.

"Okay, Pat, but as soon as you know he's good, you hustle back here pronto; that's an order."

"Yes, sir, with urgency." Pat smiled as the other four left.

Twenty minutes later, the mic clicked and Pat could hear John's labored breathing.

"I'm in. Anyone there?"

"I'm here, John; it's Pat."

"Thanks, Pat. I'm at the controls." Another five minutes went by. "Radio is on. Rockets in 1 … 2 … 3, fire. Hit your retro rockets and get further back, Pat."

"I see you, John. Good to go. Slowdown is in process; distance between us is increasing quickly. Can you get back here now? The window is tight, but I think you can still make it."

"Sorry Pat, but there isn't enough fuel for a return trip with the growing gap between us, and there really isn't time. I need to get this thing as far out in front as possible to minimize the blast arc that can actually impact the Reagan I. Don't go mushy on me now, because I don't want that to be our last memory. It's been a great ride, Pat, and I'm good with going out with a bang if it truly makes a difference. Keep in mind that we really don't know it's a missile yet, so we may be getting all dramatic for nothing. Good luck, my friend, now get your ass into that Command Module, pronto!"

With John's last comment, the mic clicked off and Pat sat alone in the darkened Control Deck looking forward to where the barely visible rockets on the Red Lander with his friend John Martinez were. Pat wasn't going anywhere. Ten minutes later, a bright flash of light was seen far in front of the ship. Tears rolled down Pat's cheeks as he angered over this senseless loss of life. There was no doubt Maj. John Martinez was gone. This was supposed to be a trip of adventure, hope and discovery, but instead it had turned out to be a trip that included murder. It just wasn't right, Pat agonized.

Now it was a matter of waiting a couple of minutes to determine if any of the shrapnel would indeed head their way, risking the loss of more innocent lives or the integrity of the ship.

Pat started a counter on the control panel. The panel read 1:06 when a 3-foot-long segment of the Red Lander's starboard landing strut catapulted off the left front window of the Control Deck. It careened off the glass and left severe cracks, but maintained its integrity. Pat continued to watch in horror as he saw other parts of the debris field fly by the ship, some missing, some bouncing off the ship's structure, one taking off an antenna on the port side of the ship. He heard a barrage of pings and bangs as debris continued to hit the ship. Pat had intentionally left his communication gear off and he couldn't see the Command Module from where he was sitting, so he had no way of knowing if the Command Module was still intact or not. He was confident there was a great deal more of the ship's structure separating the debris field from the Command Module than there was with the Control Deck, so he hoped his friends were also surviving the storm. The control panel counter was at 1:37 as Pat wondered how much longer this could last. At 2:08, a long, 1-inch diameter mounting bolt, still attached to an 8-inch-long section of a landing strut, penetrated the right front section of the Control Deck, creating a hole the size of a basketball. Pat never saw it coming, but for a brief instant he detected the distinct noise of a major vacuum breach and saw the flying papers associated with a leak to vacuum conditions before the strut section ricocheted off his helmet, knocking him to the floor. Pat rolled to his knees. He had not closed his visor yet, but when he attempted to do so, he found it hopelessly shattered.

Within seconds, as the water within Pat's body rushed to turn into vapor under the growing vacuum conditions, his body swelled and began to compress against the suit. The pain was horrific, but he was unable to scream. His skin began to turn blue as the oxygen in his blood reversed its dissolved state. His body began to go through the bends, like a deep-sea diver who rises too quickly and risks nitrogen bubbles forming in his blood. As the conditions worsened, Pat suffered a debilitating stroke because of the formation of nitrogen bubbles in his brain. As the pressure continued to drop, Pat's blood literally began to boil. At 2:10 on the counter, Lt. Pat Skiles was dead.

*****

Cmdr. Kline tried numerous times to hail Lt. Skiles or Maj. Martinez on the radio, to no avail with either man. The remaining astronauts were strapped into their seats in the Command Module when the debris field had begun hitting the ship. It seemed like an eternity, although in reality it lasted fewer than 90 seconds. When it was finally over, the four men looked around at each other and checked the gauges on their suits. The Command Module was still intact, but there were numerous red lights on the Command Module's control panel. Cmdr. Kline gave the other three men the thumbs-up to release their seating straps.

"The panel shows that the Control Deck has been compromised. Leave your suits sealed. Bob, you stay here with Jimmy. If anything happens to us, you are in charge. Tom, you come with me."

Five minutes later, the two men had reached the entrance to the Control Deck. The door was sealed, meaning only one thing. The deck had indeed been compromised and the door closed and sealed automatically.

"Pat. Lt. Pat Skiles. Please answer." Dutch repeated the order 10 times before Tom put his hand on his shoulder.

"Dutch, it's not your fault. He's not going to answer."

"I'm the commander, Tom. I take full responsibility for everyone on this mission, and I've just lost two very good men." The men stood there for a full 30 seconds, immersed in their own thoughts and eulogies for the two men, until Dutch finally spoke.

"Tom, we're going to have to depressurize this hall before we can open the Control Deck door and assess what's on the other side. Bob, Jimmy, have you been following?"

"Yes, sir, we heard everything. Sorry, Dutch. What can we do now to help?" It was Bob, providing as calm and reassuring a voice as he could muster.

"Release pressure slowly in the hallway after I close the bulkhead behind us. We'll assess the damage and then determine next steps."

*****

Five hours later, Dutch and Tom had completed their initial assessment of the damage inflicted on the Reagan I. Pat was, indeed, deceased. Both men had expected it, but it was still a staggering blow when the ugly reality was validated. They wrapped Pat's distorted body in a sheet and sealed him in a body bag, suit and all, so that the other two men would not see the ghastly effects of his exposure to space. Cmdr. Kline had all he could do to maintain his own composure.

The Control Room had been breached by something that left a large, ragged hole; big enough to fit his helmet into. Tom used a special plate and sealing kit to close the hole and Dutch then ordered Bob to re-pressurize both the Control Deck and the hallway. At that point, the other two crewmembers joined them in the Control Room.

"Gentlemen, we have more to do to fully assess and understand our status, but at this point, both Maj. John Martinez and Lt. Pat Skiles have been killed in action, and I use that term intentionally. This was an act of war.

"With the room resealed, I believe we are safe to remove our suits. The good news is that the ship is intact. Unfortunately, I do have additional bad news. As best I can determine at this time, one fuel tank and one control rocket have been lost. The fuel may not be overly critical as we can maintain our current velocity without it and reserve everything else for retro activity when we reach Earth. My biggest concern is that the loss of a control rocket greatly reduces our ability to maintain course direction. We also know that we are now off by at least two degrees from our target flight path because of the various debris impacts. At our current distance from Earth, that means we could easily miss our target by 2,000 kilometers, assuming our trajectory error remains constant and doesn't worsen.

"Jimmy and Tom, this is your bag; I need you to start looking at ways we can utilize the remaining control rockets to get back on course. Bob, you and I need to alert NASA so they can start planning for recovery efforts from their end as we get closer to Earth. We may be a little further away, but we're not as bad off as the Apollo 13 crew was, gentlemen. They made it back alive, and so will we, so keep your chins up and let's get some answers."

*****

On Board the Jarisst I

"Thjars, I'm positive of it. It was definitely an attack." Juulys summarized what she had been tracking over the past two weeks and she was positive that the latest event had culminated with an attack on the C2 contact traveling back from the fourth to the third planet. The attack had come from the C4 contact traveling the opposite direction toward C2, starting from near the third planet.

"During the final day, the C2 contact appeared to separate into two sections, with the smaller section moving well out in front. The C4 vessel impacted this smaller section and both had now disappeared. All of the data I have suggests that the C4 vessel must have been a missile of some type and that the C2 contact must have used a part of their ship as a sacrificial target to protect the remainder of the ship. I've heard communications from C2, and it appears that they have sustained both damage to the ship and loss of life, but they are still somewhat operational. Thjars, what is going on here?" Juulys cried out.

"Juulys, your assessment sounds correct and I, too, am very disappointed with what we're seeing. But recall that we agreed earlier that they are hundreds of years behind us in societal development. This may be a very natural maturation process as the planet moves from multiple, independent countries to one, unified society."

"I know, Thjars, you're probably right, but … how do we know who we can trust?"

"Juulys, not to burden you, but I think that is your call. You have been listening to the communications more than anyone else has. You also have a woman's intuition. I am happy to bounce ideas back and forth, but I believe you and you alone will have the best assessment of who is the safest group to make contact with." Thjars looked at Juulys with both understanding and trust. She was an amazing lady.

"Juulys, if it helps, consider that *not* making contact is not a viable option. We are stuck here and there doesn't appear to be any hope of a Cjarian rescue, so we have to make a choice. Another way of saying it is, even a bad choice is better than no choice. However, just for the record, I am not concerned about you making a bad choice. I think what you are struggling with is the decision between the best option and perhaps a good, but lesser option. In that case, both are acceptable. Does that help?"

Juulys was quiet. Her gaze was locked on the floor for a full minute after Thjars finished talking. Then she looked up at Thjars.

"Thank you, Thjars. This is just so hard for me. Yet, what you just said does help. I think I was too focused on finding the perfect answer, rather than an acceptable answer. To be honest, I think I already know an acceptable answer."

Thjars smiled back at her.

"That's good to hear, Juulys, I assumed you did. So, just out of curiosity, what decision would you make if you had to make one right now?"

"It would be either the United Kingdom or the United States," she replied, looking Thjars directly in the eyes.

"Okay, of the two ships coming this way, does either one of them fit your criteria?"

"C3 is definitely out. Everything I have in my women's intuition, as you pointed out, feels sinister."

"And the C1 contact?"

"Their predominant language during communications has been English, which is the language of both the United Kingdom and the United States. The leadership of the flight appears to be from the United States, as best I can tell. However, they also have many other dialects and languages spoken from the ship, almost as if it's some kind of multi-national consortium."

"That well may be true, Juulys. If it is, does that not bode well for a positive contact?"

"Yes, Thjars, yes it does. Thank you, for what it's worth, that helped immensely."

"Okay, how about we test it?"

"How so, Thjars?" Juulys wasn't quite sure she knew where Thjars was going with this.

"How about you attempt a message with the C1 contact before they arrive. Something simple, yet something that makes them realize you know more than they think you know, as well as make them think twice about harming us. How about a start like this that you can translate into their English:

> *"Greetings. It appears that your craft, as well as the craft attempting to catch up with you, might be planning on meeting at our current location near your outermost planet. Please advise your intentions. We do not wish to initiate defensive activities, but will if deemed necessary."*

"Send it in a narrow band that will exhaust before the second ship can receive it."

*****

On Board the Armstrong I

"Holy shit …" exclaimed Cmdr. Jack Pavlik to the empty Comm Center. He immediately called Blake.

"Blake, I need you in the Comm Center, ASAP!"

Within two minutes, Blake was at his side. "What's so hot, Jack? Did we finally receive news from Houston about our bomb?"

"No, it's much bigger than that," Jack said slowly as he looked up over his shoulder at Blake and then directed Blake's attention to his monitor.

Blake read the message and stepped back. "Can you tell where this came from, Jack?"

"Absolutely. It's a weak, but highly concentrated beam from out there, in front of us. Definitely not from behind us."

Blake paused and then a huge smile lit up his face. "Jack, this is it. Not only do we have proof of intelligent life existing elsewhere, but they are alive!" Both men looked at each other with a loss for words, until Blake spoke again. "We need to verify that. We need to send a message back to see how they respond. Hopefully, that will validate that this isn't just an auto response warning."

"Okay Blake, this is your show. What would you like to say?" Jack sat back in his chair with a big smile and humorously posed his hands in the air over the keyboard like a maestro for a major symphony.

"Well, I sure as hell don't want to start an intergalactic war, especially as we already have enough crap going on." Blake chuckled. "But I've actually spent quite a bit of time thinking about this ever since we left Earth. Now I just have to figure out how to make it fit their opening message; I wasn't expecting that. How about this?

> *"Greetings. My name is Maj. Blake Thompson on board the spacecraft Armstrong I from the third planet that we call Earth. We came to see what or who you are. We come as friends and wish you no harm. Important. We do not believe the second ship is friendly and they may reach you first. To be fair, you should be wary of both ships until you can validate for yourself. That is the safest path for you. I likewise have a crew to keep safe. Can you verify that you are real and alive, and not an automatic ship response? If you feel safe telling us, I would like to know where you are from and what your intentions are."*

"Interesting, Blake, it's definitely not a Neil Armstrong speech, but I think it's perfect for this situation. Heck, Armstrong had it easy; he only needed to keep the media and our president happy." Jack laughed.

"Okay, send it and let's see what comes back."

*****

On Board the Jarisst I

"Thjars, they must have responded immediately."

"What do you make of it?"

"This *Blake* entity claims he is coming as a friend, but he says the second ship is not friendly. That could be to throw us off, but he looks sincere based on his comment to not trust either of them. He wants to know about us. What should I say?"

"Juulys, I am out of my league here. This is where you shine. I'll be happy to review and critique, but I'd like you to keep the lead."

"Okay, Thjars, let's give it a shot."

> *"Hello, Maj. Blake Thompson. My name is Juulys Lystnyng. You may call me Juulys. Our ship is called the Jarisst I. We come from a star system that is very far from here, from a planet we call Cjar. We mean no harm, but are very capable of protecting ourselves if needed. We are real. I was tracking four ships, your two ships and the two between the third and fourth planet, one of which is gone now. I must know why the two ships attacked each other and why we should trust anyone in this star system."*

"I couldn't have said it better, Juulys. Perfect, send it."

*****

On Board the Armstrong I

"There is no way that message is an auto-reply from a computer," Jack concluded. "Mr. Blake, we are unequivocally talking to alien beings for the first time in recorded history!"

"Yes, but what the hell just happened with the Reagan I? Someone is not keeping us up to date. I'll give them a quick response, but I need to know what happened before we can talk much further. We are also getting tantalizingly close to meeting our new friend, Anatoly Domashev, and that has to become our top priority going forward.

> *"Juulys, you may call me Blake. I am embarrassed to say that you know more about the other two ships than*

I do. That is disturbing news you share. I need to talk to my superiors on Earth. We also need to prepare for the meeting with the second ship that will occur in what we call 12 hours. Assuming we all survive the meeting of ships, we will have plenty of time to talk before we reach your ship. I look forward to talking to you further. I hope to build trust between our two ships. Good luck to you. Please contact us if you have any concerns that may impact our meeting."

*****

NSA Headquarters, Fort Meade, Md.

"Mr. President? This is NSA Director Brad Watters."

"Yes, Brad, this is President Callahan, and my staff is here as well in the Situation Room."

"We have the Saudis on line, sir. They have confirmed that there is a Saudi mole. He appears to be a top-level diplomat, one of only a handful of people in Saudi Arabia in the know about the Armstrong I."

"How did they identify him?" President Callahan asked.

"It was really Harry Lundrum, sir. One of Maj. Blake Thompson's team."

"Blake? The major on the Armstrong I?"

"Yes, the same. Long story made very short, sir, Mr. Lundrum, or Harry, found a secret room in the house of the Hawaiian Al Qaeda suspect, Harold Bessimer. All of us had missed it – the FBI, the NSA, the police, everyone – except Harry. We've had a field day with the data on the computer gear. The gear was well hidden, but it was woefully unprotected from a hacking perspective. We are sharing the data with our allies as we speak. This will be the single biggest harvest of Al Qaeda activities and personnel that we have uncovered in decades. The owner of the house appears to be an information conduit to many different groups."

"That is excellent news, thank you, Brad. What about the bomb on the Armstrong I and the terrorist attacks underway in the U.S. right now?"

"Mr. President, we are confirming the existence and location of the bomb on the Armstrong I as we speak. Unfortunately, we have not yet determined if it really is on the Armstrong I or not, and assuming it is, if it can be safely defused or overridden. It also appears that Lt. Col Ataullah El-Hashem is innocent. That may be tough for Blake to believe at this point, but the data is pretty clean. As for the terrorist attacks, we have seen no connection between this Al Qaeda cell and that activity yet. We do, however, assume with a high probability of accuracy that the missile that blew up part of the Reagan I is tied to the fanatic on the ship that is closing on the Armstrong I. This ship is clearly an independent attack and not tied to the ongoing terrorist activities. Sorry I don't have more, sir."

"Understood, Brad. I will let your people work out the bomb investigation with the crew of the Armstrong I; please let them know they are in my prayers."

"Yes, Mr. President, I will. Thank you."

"Brad, I cannot overstate the importance of uncovering the terrorist cell behind the attacks. They have invoked an unprecedented level of panic and fear across the entire country. You must have something else for me, yes?" The president formed his statement as a question, but it was clearly a directive.

"Mr. President, we still have nothing substantiated ..."

"Brad!" The president interrupted. "Give me something to go on. I don't give a damn what you have substantiated or not yet. I need to see some progress. Do you have a theory? Do you have some leads?"

"Sorry, sir, but the trail is cold to non-existent. The one lead we're working may be nothing at all."

"Sorry, Brad, I know you guys are working 24/7, but that is what the American people expect of us. We have to solve this. Now, tell me about this lead."

"To be fair, it's Mr. Lundrum, Maj. Thompson, and their team again."

"Go on." President Callahan sat forward in his chair.

"The group has been bouncing ideas back and forth over the past two days. Harry and Blake came up with the idea of identifying cities that have had unexplained shootings in the past week that do not appear to be gang-related. Harry found that both of the bombs that have detonated so far were coincidentally in cities where a recent killing had taken place that just didn't fit the typical murder profiles. No domestic violence, no gang fights, no robberies. But two individuals were shot at close range for no apparent reasons. One was shot on his bicycle and one for answering his door. Both were middle-income people who had no previous infractions with the law."

"I agree, that feels pretty thin, Brad. I assume you have more."

"Yes, Mr. President. The biggest variable in their analysis is that both individuals were deep in debt, and had recently received a large sum of money in their savings account. So far, the source of that income has been untraceable. If this theory is correct, then people were hand-picked because of their financial records, and their good standing with the public – someone that you would never look at twice from a security perspective."

"How could the terrorists know they had financial problems?"

"Great question, Mr. President. Blake and Harry challenged us to find that answer as well. Turns out that both men had accounts with J.P. Morgan. Recall that J.P. Morgan had one of the biggest cyber breaches ever back in 2014. A lot of financial information was compromised on millions of people. We are now scouring the records of every murder in every major U.S. city for names that match the J.P. Morgan database. If the theory holds, then the terrorists have been sitting on this data for years, waiting for the right opportunity to use it."

"But I'm sure many of these people have either defaulted, changed their passwords, or cleaned up their finances by now, correct? That was 15 years ago."

"Correct, Mr. President. Unfortunately for the two individuals identified so far, they were either still deep into the red, or recently deep into it, and neither had changed their passwords after the 2014 hack. We have identified eight more names that fit that description, and who have also been murdered within the past two weeks, sir. The cities where they were killed include Atlanta, Los Angeles, Boston, Minneapolis, St. Louis, Miami, Seattle and Dallas."

"This doesn't feel so thin to me, Brad. Matter of fact, it feels pretty damn solid. Too many very disparate variables line up to make this a coincidence."

"That's the same thing that Blake and Harry argued, too," Brad added.

"Am I correct in assuming that you have focused all resources on the primary government buildings and public venues in these cities?"

"Yes, Mr. President. We have created a prioritized top 50 list in each of those cities and are marshalling every resource we can to inspect the buildings. If we are correct, we should find something soon."

"Let me know as soon as you know anything, Brad. And if this theory pans out, I really would like to meet Blake, Harry, and their team. They sound like quite an impressive group. Thank you."

CHAPTER 24

Blake looked at the screen, having just read Harry's message, and even though he knew Harry couldn't hear him, he still spoke out loud.

"Harry, are you sure Ataullah is innocent? After all, you're telling me that if the data on Harold's computer is correct, the bomb is actually hidden in Ataullah's room, correct?" Blake was frustrated with the ever-growing distance from Earth; this form of communication was extremely frustrating, taking four hours to send and another four to receive a response.

"What's that, Blake?" Jack asked.

"Sorry, just voicing my thoughts from Harry's message. The data is pretty damning for the Al Qaeda terrorist group being behind this, but more importantly," Blake paused and looked up at Jack before continuing, "Harry claims that the data is equally supportive of Ataullah's innocence. Sadly, as Patty found out in Yemen, Ataullah's brother Ahmed is guilty. That will not be easy for Ataullah." Blake bowed his head and then continued. "My hatred for the radical terrorists made it way too easy for me to *want to believe* that Ataullah was guilty."

"It's okay, Blake; we all did. Pretty natural given the current state of affairs."

"Thanks, Jack, but I will need to level with the man at some point." Blake added, "What about Popov? Was Vladimir able to get anything else out of Domashev?"

"No, nothing at all. It appears that Domashev is a pretty cold customer, with a very singular focus."

"Okay, James, you and I will go see Ataullah right now and see if we can't locate the bomb. We are down to, what, eight hours before the Domashev is within striking distance? Time is getting very tight."

*****

"Ataullah." Blake knocked on his door while James stood nearby. "Ataullah, we need to talk. A major incident has come up."

The door opened and Ataullah greeted them in his native attire. "What is it, Blake? Hello, James."

"Does the name Harold Bessimer or Aikane mean anything to you?" Blake watched his face closely for any response that might suggest a connection. He needed to verify his innocence for himself. He saw no response of acknowledgement.

"No, not that I am aware of. I don't recognize the name at all. Why, should I?"

"How well do you know what your brother Ahmed has been up to of late?"

That got a response.

"Unfortunately, my brother is no longer my brother; I do not talk to him anymore. What has happened?"

Blake spent the next 30 minutes getting Ataullah caught up with the events from the last few weeks.

"Ataullah, I apologize for suspecting you and keeping you in the dark about it. To be honest, I carried over 20 years of distrust with me when I first met you, but for what it's worth, I honestly struggled believing it was you after we had that long talk during our first game of backgammon. You hit me as a pretty straight arrow."

"Ataullah, I can vouch for that. Blake wanted to believe in you," James added before Ataullah could respond.

"I believe you, Blake, and I also understand why. I would have done the same myself," he responded respectfully.

Blake thanked him, shook hands and then continued. "Not to rush things along, Ataullah, but there are two more things you need to know, and quickly. First, it appears that not only is your brother Ahmed involved, he is guilty of many sins against our country, including what I am about to tell you. NASA and the NSA are convinced that there is a bomb onboard this spacecraft that will be detonated when we reach the ship near Pluto. And we are convinced your brother is involved."

Ataullah's face turned white, and then red with rage. "My own brother. We have known for years that he was running with a crowd we did not approve of, but this? This is unforgivable. I am so sorry, Blake."

"It's not your fault, Ataullah."

"But, yes it is. It is my family and henceforth my ownership. Where is this bomb?"

"That's another twist of fate, Ataullah. I doubt your brother, or anyone else in their group knew who would have which room when the bomb was planted many months ago, then built into a subassembly that was shipped off to be later assembled into the Armstrong I during final assembly. But we believe it is in your room, sleeping quarters #5."

Ataullah did not hesitate a second. "Then let us find it now." He stepped aside and invited the two men into his room.

James was carrying a bag of tools as he walked in and patted Ataullah on the back. "We will find it, Ataullah. Then the next question will be to determine if it is booby-trapped or not." James didn't add that they had already searched his room while Blake and Ataullah were on their spacewalk. It didn't seem like that would add any value at this point, and this time they knew where to look.

Two hours later, they had found the bomb and removed it. It had been located in a panel structure behind a grooming mirror, hard-mounted to the wall. Fortunately, no booby-traps were found.

"Blake, I'm not a bomb expert, but if I had to guess, this looks like about two or three kilograms of C4, big enough to blow a hole through the wall and rupture the fuel tank only a couple feet behind it," James volunteered.

"I agree with you, James. This would have resulted in a chain reaction that would have consumed our ship and anything near us if we had parked close enough to the alien ship," Blake added. "Unfortunately, the bomb is encased in some type of hermetically sealed plastic, so I don't see how we can remove the firing wire without risking detonating the unit ourselves." Blake then looked over at James, "That also explains why we couldn't detect it with Fido-Mutt – Ataullah, I'll explain that later."

"The information in Harold's computer outlined an electronics schematic that the techies believe could be triggered two ways; first by signal and second by when the velocity of the ship reaches zero. We believe the latter was based on an assumption that the Armstrong I would only be at rest once it had reached the alien ship and parked alongside of it. We also believe that this approach ensured the bomb could still be successful even if the terrorist ring were uncovered and taken out. Actually quite ingenious."

"Yes it is, Blake," Ataullah replied, "but clearly beyond anything my brother could do. He was not the sharpest tool in the shed, as you Americans like to say." He smiled, but it was clearly forced.

"So what do we do with this thing; take it on a spacewalk?" James added sarcastically.

"Actually James, that's a great idea," Blake responded. "Carry it up to the Control Deck and we'll get a message to Harry. I have an idea we had been discussing for days, but our time window is getting very tight and we'll have to change our plans based on the idea James just gave me. The Domashev is less than a day from being within reasonable range of firing on us."

Ataullah and Blake left for the Control Deck, carrying the bomb, as James, who was still standing in the same spot, spoke to their departing backs, "Okay, Blake, you say I gave you the idea, but I don't have a clue what it was… are you going to leave me hanging here?"

*****

Blake sent off a quick message to Harry.

> *"Harry, Blake here. I need you to do a little math for me."*

Blake explained to Harry in detail what they had found and what he was thinking of doing, and then waited for the intolerable delay for a response. He would eat, exercise, work on his project and take a nap before Harry's response would arrive … which it did in slightly fewer than nine hours.

> *"Count me in, and by the way, I like it. There's some pretty complicated gravitational components to make sure we get this right, but I think it will work, Blake. Give me an hour to do my calcs while you complete your assembly. I've already started, so you should receive it in another 60 minutes."*

An hour later, Blake looked up from the computer and said, "Thank you, Harry" to an empty room.

Four billion kilometers away, at the precise time Harry knew Blake would be reading his second message, Harry looked at the clock and spoke out loud, "You're welcome, Blake." Harry lived for this kind of stuff. Complicated algorithms, calculus, and physics all rolled into one neat little homework problem. It just didn't get any better than this. Harry smiled and started typing away on his laptop on a new problem.

*****

Blake and James had not yet returned to the Control Deck. Jack and the rest of the crew were growing more nervous by the minute. The Domashev could now be seen in their rear, without the aid of magnification. If it were carrying missiles, it was only a matter of time before they would launch, if that was indeed the intention.

The Comm Center beeped.

"Blake, we can see the Domashev. It's getting close. How much more time?"

"Almost there."

A collision alarm sounded throughout the ship.

"Blake! It's a missile from the Domashev!"

"Bastards!" Jack hollered. "We knew they'd try. Let it get closer before you turn the Asteroids debris gun on. On full auto, you'll exhaust ammunition in 32 seconds, so we need to make sure it's in range and too close to maneuver."

"I wish we could have come up with an anti-missile solution to keep the explosion farther away from the ship, but I guess this is as good as it will get. Jack, let it get as close as we dare. Hang on folks; it's about to get interesting," Blake relayed to the crew.

"Your definition of *interesting* leaves a little to be desired, major," Vladimir smirked at Blake.

"Counting the missile they shot at the Reagan I, then they might have one more missile, but here's hoping they only had two to begin with," Blake added.

"Five minutes, then bring the sled controller down to the docking door."

"What?"

"Trust me; you're gonna love this. See you in five."

Five minutes later, the rest of the crew, except Jack and James, showed up at the docking bay door. Everyone had previously suited up. James was already there and appeared ready for an exterior ship mission, while Jack remained in the Control Deck, ready to activate Asteroids.

"You gotta be kidding me ..." Rakesh Deshpande spoke first. "I think I see what you're planning. That's pure gold, Blake."

"Well it looks good, but let's see if it actually works as planned. Hand me the controller."

Blake synched up the sled and controller so that he could steer it remotely. The bomb was mounted directly over the sled's fuel tank.

"Okay, James is suited up and waiting, and seeing as it was James himself that suggested a spacewalk, whether or not he realized it," Blake chuckled, "that means he volunteered, too. James is going to take this modified unit for a short space walk. Everyone close your visors. From this point on, there is risk of secondary damage."

"Brace yourselves; Asteroids has lock-in at the desired distance. Firing, 3 ... 2 ... 1, now!" Jack relayed over the speakers. The entire ship shook and the sound resonated throughout the ship for exactly 20 seconds and then the ship went eerily quiet. Blake made sure that Jack had programmed the gun to stop at 20 seconds to ensure they had a second option – even if it were only 12 seconds' worth.

"Jack?" Blake was the first to speak.

"Blake, I'm looking ... I'm pretty sure I saw a small explosion, perhaps from the fuel tanks ... it was *really* close to our ship ... Moving the camera ... zooming in ... there's something .... yes! I see two distinct sections, and both are rotating freely in opposite directions … both sections will miss the ship! I repeat, no missile, no debris threat. Damn, that was close!"

The crew broke into cheers.

"Just the way we planned it, Jack; it had to be close. Send out the emergency distress signal, flare some fuel and start sputtering the rear maneuvering engines to make it look like they are damaged."

"Okay, James, now it's your turn. First, we need to get all of that junk, and our little gift, outside, and fast! Close the door and vent it to space. Let's move, people. Clear the area. This has to be fast."

"I'm not sure I understand … please explain, Blake," Rakesh asked, but James jumped in to answer for Blake.

"It's an old World War II submarine trick, Rakesh." He nodded at Blake and then continued, "We simulate a direct hit and dump a lot of material out to make the hunter think they've damaged the ship, but we'll also have our little surprise for them well hidden within the debris field so that they don't expect anything. The fuel flare and emergency distress message will get their attention, and the sputtering engines will hide what we are doing, as well as further convince them that the ship is damaged. Anything else, Blake?"

"Perfect, Sir James. Hopefully, this will entice Domashev into letting his guard down – and then we wait. James, time to get outside."

James was already in the dock with his helmet closed and gave Blake the thumbs up.

"Are you crazy? Why are we sending James out? It's suicide!" Jie screamed into his mic.

"It's okay, Jie, trust me. James is going out on a spacewalk to create the illusion that he is inspecting the ship for damage, but he will really be guiding our package within the debris field we created, waiting for the perfect moment to reverse engine thrust on the sled. If Harry's calculations are correct, the sled, and its explosive package, will achieve zero relative velocity just as the

Domashev goes by the debris field, and James will still have time to get back inside before it detonates."

Twenty minutes later, James was back inside the dock, laboring from the exertion.

"Tell Jack to send the next message."

"Got it!" Jack echoed.

> *"Houston, this is the Armstrong I. We've taken significant missile damage from the attack. Maj. Snyder inspected the main engine nozzle ... the damage is unrepairable. The Domashev is closing. The Asteroids gun is exhausted. We expect they will attempt to board us. Maj. Thompson has armed the crew. Preparing now."*

"Ten minutes to go. We cut this one pretty tight, gentlemen. Everyone strap in. Vladimir, please get Mr. Domashev on the line." Blake smiled, looking noticeably more relaxed for the first time in days.

"Anatoly, Vladimir here. May I again ask your intentions?"

"Vladimir, Vladimir. Does it really matter anymore? You may have eliminated our missile, but we saw the explosion and you are trailing debris, so we have damaged part of your ship in the process, as I am sure your spacewalk just verified. We also picked up your distress signal and the fact that your guns are exhausted. Am I correct?" Domashev paused for effect and then continued. "You need not answer, Vladimir; I will finish your ship's engines and let you float into eternity. You will all die alone."

Blake reached over and put his hand out for Vladimir's headset. "Cocky bastard, isn't he?" Blake smiled at Vladimir.

Vladimir removed the headset and set it gently in Blake's hand with a reassuring smile and nod. Blake then nodded to James, who had the controls for the sled.

"Mr. Domashev, Maj. Blake Thompson here."

"That is Gen. Domashev to you. Where is my friend, Vladimir?"

"General? I don't think so. In my country, a person must earn the title of general. You, sir, have done nothing to earn such a title. Indeed, you have also killed two of my fellow astronauts with your missile launch against the Reagan I. I am not sure why you felt the need to kill innocent astronauts, but that surely does not warrant a promotion in my book. As for your friend, I don't think I see your name anywhere on Vladimir's Facebook page. Sorry to rain on your parade, as we Americans like to say." Blake took a long, slow breath, and then continued.

"Now, for the final time, Anatoly, I am asking you to disclose your intentions. Do you really intend to board our ship?"

A short pause was followed by a low, almost guttural chuckle.

"You pompous American. You think you can talk your bravado around the world and do whatever you want. Ever since your President Reagan shouted, 'Mr. Gorbachev, take down that wall,' and that weak son-of-a-bitch did. That alone was enough justification to shoot down the Reagan I."

"Ahh, you assume too much, Mr. Domashev. It turns out that you were outwitted by Reagan again; this time though, it was the ship named in his honor. Yes, they did lose two great men, greater than you'll ever be, but one of those men, a Maj. John Martinez, flew the Red Lander out front as a target to take the blast and save the Reagan and its occupants – sacrificing his own life to protect his crewmembers. That, Mr. Domashev, is what a true leader and hero does. Take a lesson."

"If you speak the truth, then they have been spared, but only temporarily. I will return to finish the job before they can ever reach Earth. I will own space. But first, I will destroy your putrid ship. Then I will recover the technology in the alien ship. And there is nothing you can do to stop me."

"We are fully prepared to battle the Domashev's crew to the death when you attempt to board us." Blake lied, wanting to delay him just a little more.

"Board? Why would I board your inferior ship? Within moments, we will be close enough to fire our guns from your now unprotected rear. We will save the boarding activities for the alien ship."

"What?" Blake mocked his response in fear and surprise, and then intentionally questioned Maj. Snyder out loud so that Domashev could hear him. "Maj. Snyder, are you ready yet?"

"You are delirious, Mr. Thompson; why should I care if you are ready or not? That would be injudicious and stupid. I never had any intention to make this a fair fight."

Jack quietly announced over the suit mic system that the sled had achieved zero relative velocity ... but there was no explosion.

"It didn't work!" Klaus stammered. "What do we do now?"

"Blake, use the controller and detonate the bomb!" Rakesh joined in.

"I can't," Blake added quietly.

"We will miss our chance; he will be on us any second!" Klaus was panicking – uncharacteristic for the German.

Blake smiled and gestured to the group to stay calm. He quietly held up 10 fingers and then closed one hand and held up five more. Fifteen seconds to go.

"I wasn't talking about my time. I was talking about yours, Mr. Domashev. If Mr. Harry Lundrum is correct, which by the way he always is, you are down to less than 10 seconds as of right ... now."

"What are you talking about ... Harry who?" It was the first sound of doubt in Anatoly's voice.

"Five, four, three ... I'm sorry, Mr. Domashev, but I believe this conversation is over. Goodbye." With that, Blake nodded to James. He was rewarded by a thumbs-up and replied loud enough for all to hear, "We are now at true zero."

A bright light suddenly lit up in space behind the Armstrong I. Seconds later, an even bigger light show erupted as the Domashev's fuel tanks exploded.

Blake released a heavy sigh, looked at the ceiling of the Control Deck and said: "Thank you, Harry. Jack send the follow up message to Houston that we are okay, and that the Domashev has been destroyed."

"I don't get it." Rakesh was perplexed. "The vehicle reached zero well before it was next to the Domashev and it didn't explode, even though the relative velocity achieved zero … what happened?"

"Harry happened. With all of his detailed calculations, a simple detonation time delay was the only guess he needed to make. He was convinced that the software would require a fixed delay at zero velocity prior to detonating to reduce the risk of prematurely detonating on a false signal."

"But how did he come to a conclusion of 15 seconds? Five or 25 would have missed the Domashev, how could he possibly have guessed that 15 was perfect?" Klaus interjected.

"All I know is that he said he assumed a standard 99.9 percent signal accuracy, thereby leading to a 0.1 percent error probability. Over a four-hour and 12-minute signal distance to Earth, that created a 15-second maximum delay error, so Harry added 15 seconds."

"But what if it had been minus 15 seconds?" Klaus pounced on Harry's analysis, trying to point out an error. "The error analysis would have to include both a plus 15-second value, and a minus-15 seconds. He can't ignore the minus-15 option!"

"Correct. I thought the same thing and asked him. He responded that if the ships were truly parked alongside each other, it would be for extended time, therefore the designer of the bomb would have assumed that any longer value would still result in a successful explosion and that the designer only had to protect against premature firing – i.e. the short value. So Harry added 15 seconds and called it a wrap. Why did he base his calculation on the time delay between Earth and Pluto? I have no idea, but it worked, and I've learned over the years to enjoy a win – regardless of if I can fully take credit for it or not. I suggest you all do likewise."

Weeks later, after NASA analysts had spent countless hours simulating the event, addressing the various speeds of the two vehicles in question, as well as the sled-turned-IED, the rotational aspects of the solar system and the gravitational pull of Pluto, they were finally able to approximate the analysis Harry had done on his computer in just 65 minutes. Harry had nailed it, directly amidships.

The fact that the Al Qaeda bomb had actually saved them was an irony all would thoroughly enjoy for a long time.

"Is there any chance of survivors?" Jie spoke for the group.

"I doubt it, as I don't see any ship sections that could be big enough to represent an intact module. The flames extinguished as soon as the fuel sources were gone and I have a pretty clear view. I think we can safely conclude 10 KIAs, but to be honest, I really don't care if there were any survivors," Jack replied.

"Gentlemen, we are not out of the woods yet." Blake jumped in. "The debris field from the explosion can still impact us just like it did to the Reagan I. Strap in."

Everyone had already suited up earlier by Blake's order. Now they understood why. Blake made a mental note that space fights were better handled over large distances. Without an atmosphere to slow debris down, a close kill could easily become an unintentional double kill.

The next 20 minutes would decide their fate. As the time of danger came and passed, a number of small pings and bangs were heard, but nothing as serious as what the Reagan I had encountered. The Reagan I had been much closer to the exploding Red Lander than the Domashev had been to the Armstrong I. In addition, the blast occurred alongside the ship, forcing most of the debris to fly harmlessly and perpendicularly to the flight path the two ships were maintaining.

It was only after everyone had unsuited that Klaus Schneider, the German astronomer, had noticed that a large section of the light sail had been damaged by debris that must have flown through it. There was a large hole that had caused a full quarter of the sail to fold in upon itself. The overhanging tangle of fabric and struts was disrupting the ability of the sail to work effectively. Worse yet, it was throwing them off course because of the asymmetry of the functioning sections.

"Jack, this is a mess." Blake summarized. "We're going to have to cut away a good section of that sail. We might be able to rebuild some of it, but we definitely need to clear away the debris blocking the rest of the sail. We are going to lose some efficiency, but right now it's more important that we regain the proper flight path. I'll talk with NASA, but we need to get a team out on that sail ASAP; I'll join you as soon as I can get a message to Houston. Until then, I recommend we work in shifts of two, for two hours each. Jie and Klaus, you take the first shift. Ataullah and I will take the second, James and Vladimir will take the third. I will go out again on the fourth with Rakesh. Jack, you stay at the ship's control."

*****

The crew worked feverishly through their shifts to fix the sail. In the end, they were able to recover about 65 percent of the sail's efficiency, far less than what Blake had hoped for. How that would impact their safe return to Earth was now being analyzed by every expert in NASA, less Harry, who was still helping the feds with the terrorist bombs back on Earth. As much as Blake knew they needed Harry's help now, he also knew that there were greater risks back home and that their journey, as important as it was, included signing up to the inherent risks that came with it.

*****

On Board the Jarisst I

"Thjars, as best I can tell, it appears that C3 has been destroyed, and C1, although possibly damaged, is still heading toward us. From the communication between the ships, I believe that the crew on C1, which they call the Armstrong I, are honorable people. I don't think they realized I could hear everything that was being said, as they made no attempt to hide their communications."

"Perhaps that was intentional on the part of the one you call Blake so that we could listen in and make up our own minds. He was the one that recommended we be careful with both ships, correct?"

"Yes, but I'd like you to listen to the tapes I recorded just to make sure you agree. Blake did seem genuine and open. The other ship, the one Blake referred to as the Domashev, clearly had ill intent. The Domashev's commander also claimed ownership for the attack between the third and fourth planets, as well as voicing their intent to destroy the Armstrong I, and then board our ship. It actually feels like the Armstrong I's crew may have saved both themselves and our ship."

"See, Juulys, your intuition was correct again," Thjars reminded her.

CHAPTER 25

A.D. 2029 (3312 C.A.E.); Jan. 11
Staples Center, Los Angeles

It was midway through the third quarter of the L.A. Clippers/
N.Y. Knicks basketball game. The Clippers were destroying the
Knicks 87-62, even though the Knicks' rookie sensation, Jamal
Towers, was singlehandedly keeping the Knicks in the game
with 32 of their 62 total points. The time-out buzzer sounded and
was immediately followed by an explosion that rocked the entire
Staples Center.

Players were thrown to the floor; smoke and fire filled the air.
Sections 317, 318, 319, PR13, PR14 and PR15 were immediately
consumed by the explosion. The center, when full, seated 19,067
fans, and although this was a top-billed game, the fear associated
with the recent terrorist threats had dropped game attendance to
9,543. The NBA and players' union had both stated firmly that
they would not allow terrorism to impact the game. Unfortunately,
147 people were killed instantly by the explosion and subsequent
fire, and at least another 500 were injured, many critically. It was
expected that the death count would only increase.

Five minutes later, a Middle Eastern voice called the Beast II
980 AM radio station to claim credit for the explosion, repeating
the threats from previous attacks. The Beast 980 had been the
longtime voice of the Clippers, but was shut down in 2016. New
management bought the rights to the station and led its rebirth
in 2021 as the Beast II 980. Unfortunately, the sports announcer
immediately played the recording over the radio and it was
quickly replayed on every major news desk and social media

app in the country. The news was out, and mass anger and panic quickly escalated across the country.

President Callahan was on the air within 15 minutes, once again trying to calm an exceedingly nervous nation, but the time for confidence building was already past. It was time to share reality and focus on saving lives, so President Callahan ordered a shutdown of all professional sports and music events. More details were promised to follow, but it was now clear that additional attacks were expected at major cities and event locations over the next week. People were advised to stay home when possible, and to report all suspicious activities; Americans were now at war, on their own soil, with an unknown foe moving invisibly among them.

*****

A.D. 2029 (3312 C.A.E.); Jan. 12
On Board the Armstrong I

It was not going to be a good day. Earlier in the morning, Blake had received word that the Reagan I was floundering. They had been unable to counteract the loss of the critical port thrust rocket destroyed during the missile attack that blew up the Red Lander. The ship was now slowly spiraling, and falling further off the planned target path to Earth. NASA was still attempting to develop a solution, but relayed its concern to Blake that there was a growing expectation that the ship and crew would be lost.

The list of significant, unplanned issues that Blake was trying to keep up with seemed to be growing by the day. At this point, Blake had all he could do simply to react to each new emergency; there wasn't any amount of planning that could have prepared for this. In addition to what he was dealing with, Harry had also messaged Blake with the latest update on the terror attacks – that picture was not very reassuring, either. Harry provided Blake with a number of recommendations he wanted to give President Callahan. Blake spent two hours going through the detailed data summaries and analysis that Harry provided and sent his approval back.

"Harry, great work. Concur with analysis. Recommend share with NSA. Request President Callahan convene Situation Room TODAY. Need massive troop support to search & recon. Recommend no TV coverage. Recommend evacuation of those areas. Minimize opportunity for terrorists to prematurely detonate bombs while search personnel are on site. Do NOT repeat 9/11. Please confirm. Keep me posted."

Blake sat back in his chair, stunned. There was no way to quantify the full threat, but at this point, Harry remained convinced that, at a minimum, the seven other U.S. cities they had identified earlier were still at risk. They had unfortunately been correct on Los Angeles, but not in time to avoid almost 700 casualties. The only good news Harry communicated was that the number of large targets within those seven cities was a significantly smaller, and somewhat more manageable subset. Harry and Blake had agreed on a Top 10 list within each remaining city, including Atlanta, Boston, Minneapolis, St. Louis, Miami, Seattle and Dallas.

With everything that had occurred over the past two days, the onboard bomb, the attack of the Domashev, the precarious condition of the Reagan I, the terrorist attacks on Earth and the standard ship duties, Blake had not forgotten about the alien ship they called the Jarisst I, but he literally hadn't managed any time to dedicate to it. He decided to attempt a quick communication, especially as they were only one week away from reaching their ship.

"Juulys and the Jarisst I. Greetings from the Armstrong I. Hope all is good with you. We've had a couple of rough days here and also at home, but we expect that we will still reach you in seven days. Would like to meet. Do you concur? If yes, what do you recommend? Also, thank you for learning our language. Blake."

Blake stood up to go work out; he was a day overdue. But before he could reach the door, the panel beeped the arrival of a new message. Blake turned and walked back, expecting to see a response from Harry, but it was Juulys.

"Blake. Hello. Yes, we have seen some of the activity and the destruction of the other ship. We were also able to hear your communications with the other ship during the attack. Thjars, our commanding officer, believes that was intentional. Is that correct?"

"That was fast, and totally unexpected." Blake told the empty room, and then sat down again.

"Thjars is correct. I thought it fair for you to hear everything to make your own opinion on the intentions of the two ships."

Ten minutes passed, but Blake remained at the console. He decided to check further.

"Are you still there?"

Only 30 seconds passed this time.

"Yes."

Blake was confused. He wondered why were they hesitating, and decided to ask.

"Something still seems to be a problem. Please share."

Blake sat back and looked at his watch. If they didn't feel like talking, then he was fine with getting some exercise. He was both mentally and physically exhausted after the past two days.

"You are correct. We believe that the other ship did have ill intentions, but we are still very hesitant about your ship. Everywhere we look, we see aggression. How can we trust that you come in peace?"

Whoa. Nothing like getting to the heart of the matter, Blake thought.

"Sorry. I understand why you're concerned. We need to figure this out before we get too close. I am not looking to get blown up because you are nervous."

Twenty seconds passed. At least now they were truly talking.

"Likewise, neither are we. We saw how you fooled the other ship. You must understand that as you get closer, we will become more alert for some form of trickery."

Blake realized that he would be saying the same thing if their roles were reversed. He wasn't sure how to resolve it right now, but at least they had a couple of days to work it out.

"I can tell you that we mean well, but I understand your position. I would say the same. I am also assuming that you must be having ship problems; otherwise, you would have left by now. Perhaps we can help. Regardless, let us both go back and think about ways we can increase our mutual confidence levels in order to work out a meeting. Can we get back together tomorrow morning?"

"Yes."

"Okay, thank you. We will talk tomorrow."

This time, Blake did get up and walk away, but not to go exercise right away; instead, he went to see Cmdr. Jack Pavlik and briefed him on the conversation.

"Jack, can you update NASA while I exercise? Hopefully, they've calmed down from when they first heard about the ship having live crew. We could actually use some help on this one."

*****

A.D. 2029 (3312 C.A.E.); Jan. 13
NSA Headquarters

The progress had been better than anyone could have hoped for. The Pentagon, NSA, CIA, FBI, military, local fire departments and police departments had all worked together around the clock on the targets identified by Harry. Thousands of dedicated personnel across the country had been consolidated at the 70 sites they had identified. Overnight, the effort had exponentially grown to become the single largest search and recon effort in U.S. history. The dedication of thousands of highly trained officers, engineers and soldiers, and the speed of the on-site execution had paid off; Harry's search had been validated in six of the seven locations. In each case, the bomb had been in a large, public center, typically in a well-selected area that would maximize damage, carnage and death.

After initial failure in Seattle, Harry had gone on a hunch and widened his search area beyond the city and was rewarded when they found the bomb on his tenth priority, the Victoria-to-Vancouver ferry named Spirit of British Columbia. The ship, built in 1993, could hold more than 400 cars and associated passengers. The bomb had been placed in a storage room six feet below the water line and near the engine compartment. The ship would have definitely been lost, and given the cold January waters, it was doubtful there would have been many survivors by the time rescue boats could have arrived.

Boston's bomb had been located in a storage room deep inside the Thomas P. "Tip" O'Neill, Jr. Tunnel, a highway tunnel under the Boston downtown, built during Boston's famous Big Dig project. Minneapolis's bomb was actually in Bloomington, at the Mall of America. It had been well hidden in a storage room on the ground floor near the three-story-tall Christmas tree display. The St. Louis bomb had been found in the Cathedral Basilica of Saint Louis.

The Super Dome had been the #1 priority on the Dallas list and was quickly found in a locked bathroom closet in the lower level of the Super Dome. The Miami location, on the other hand, had been relatively hard to find. The team assigned to Miami had exhausted its top 10 list and moved on until it reached #15, the J.W. Marriott Marquis Hotel. Once again, the bomb was located in a janitor's closet on the ground floor. That bomb appeared strong enough that the FBI feared it would have leveled the building.

Only Atlanta remained unsolved. There were currently 400 personnel still combing through the #7 priority on the list, CNN headquarters at the corner of Marietta Street and Centennial Olympic Park Drive in downtown Atlanta. They were five hours into their search when one of CNN's own news helicopters flew overhead with cameras running. George McNally, head of the CNN building search, screamed into his phone for the police copters to force him down, but it was too late. The copter was broadcasting live, and the news was out.

"Evacuate the building, immediately!" McNally yelled into his phone, set on the emergency band mode to contact all personnel in the building simultaneously.

Firefighters, police officers, Army troops and FBI agents began spilling out of the building as fast as they could, creating commotion at every exit. Two minutes later, McNally's worst fears were realized, which also simultaneously validated that Blake's prediction was correct; the terrorists had been watching the major news feeds looking for any viable attempts to locate their bombs. Once they knew that one of their targets was possibly compromised, they auto-detonated the bomb inside the CNN building. The blast was immense. There were still at least 150 safety and security personnel in the building when the massive explosion hit, totally destroying the CNN World Headquarters Studio 7 and killing or injuring a large percentage of the remaining security personnel trying to escape the building. The U.S. had not suffered the loss of that many dedicated service and security personnel since the World Trade Center attack on Sept. 11, 2001.

The most pressing question for the U.S. authorities now became determining how many more bombs might be out there. U.S. authorities had no way of knowing if there were only 10 bombs originally planted, or if more existed; only the terrorists knew that. Brad Watters quickly redeployed his 9½ remaining search and recon armies to the next 10 cities on the list. However, now that the terrorists knew the U.S. government was on to them, and searching for the remaining bombs, it was expected that the terrorists would watch the sites more closely and detonate any remaining bombs as soon as search teams arrived – making the new searches even more dangerous. And beyond that danger, the terrorists still had the grand finale they had been threatening.

Once again, President Callahan took to the air in an attempt to console a scared and mourning nation. The latest losses added to a toll that only continued to mount, despite the most intensive efforts the country could mount. He chose not to share the good news about the other six cities, where bombs had been found and deactivated, as he did not want to expose that information to the terrorists yet.

*****

A.D. 2029 (3312 C.A.E.); Jan. 15
On Board the Armstrong I

Blake had Vladimir and Jack at his side as he began typing on the screen; James was flying the Armstrong I. They were now within four days of reaching the Jarisst I and began to slow their approach so as not to overshoot the ship's position.

> *"Juulys. Good morning. Any ideas on how we can make this work without making your ship's gunner trigger-happy, as we would call it on Earth?"*

> *"Blake. Hello. I think I know what you mean by trigger-happy and I do not want a war to start. I hope that goes for your crew as well."*

Juulys' response had been almost instantaneous.

"I swear, these people, or beings, whatever they are, must not sleep," Blake said before responding to Juulys.

> *"Juulys, do you ever sleep? You are always there to answer. You have not left yet, so I must still assume that you are either not capable of flight, or you are sincerely considering my offer. Have you or your crew come up with any ideas on how we can make this meeting occur safely for both sides?"*

The response came quickly.

"Our drives are operational and we will move shortly to prove that, but we have not yet come to terms regarding how to meet with you. Please do not close to less than 1,500 of your kilometers."

Vladimir was looking over Blake's left shoulder.

"If I was a betting man, which I am, that suggests that their weaponry range is slightly longer than 1,500 kilometers and that their ship is incapable of sustained flight operations."

"I'll take that bet, Vladimir," Maj. James Snyder called from the other side of the Control Deck. "How about a bottle of your best vodka against a bottle of Johnnie Walker Black Label?"

"You're on, Major," Vladimir replied with a smile.

"I think we can figure this out; give me a minute," Blake replied.

> *"Juulys, you may be in better shape than we are. We are having trouble steering with the damaged light sail and I do not think we are going to be able to steer to get alongside you. I am not asking for assistance, but could you please move your ship 500 kilometers toward the planet we call Pluto?"*
>
> *"Yes, but I am not sure how that will help; isn't that farther from your preferred line of approach to us?"*
>
> *"You are correct. To be honest, I would rather we risk passing by you, and make sure we don't hit your ship."*
>
> *"Okay, we will do so shortly."*

Juulys turned to Thjars and requested that he move the ship accordingly.

Thjars turned to Cryells and formalized the request to officially move the ship. Cryells, in turn, began pushing buttons.

"Cryells?"

"Nothing is happening, Thjars … I don't understand it … the drives are on …?" Cryells looked up in confusion.

Thjars was looking down over Cryells' shoulder. "You are correct, Cryells; we are obviously missing something."

"The drive sequence has two initiation steps; is it possible only the first has been approved by the C-Pod?" Qulys asked.

"Please explain, Qulys."

"The first step is to literally activate the drives, which it appears has been accomplished. The second step is to actually engage the drives. That is what Cryells is now attempting to do, correct?"

"I believe you are correct, Qulys. We may still have a problem. … Juulys?"

"Yes, by now they will know we have an issue as well. I should notify Maj. Thompson."

"Are we sure we want to do that?" Thjars asked.

"I am not totally comfortable with telling them either, but they will lose trust if we are not honest with them."

"Okay, go ahead, Juulys. Qulys, just in case, you verified that weapon systems are active, correct?"

"Yes, but based on what just happened with the drives, I would prefer to test it on something first."

"Fair point. Juulys, please explain to the other ship what has happened, and then explain how we are going to launch a time delay missile that will explode harmlessly in space, just to ensure our weapons truly do work. I would also give them a little of our background on how we found ourselves here. I think you are right. It's time to be more open with what I hope will be our new friends. I pray to Glysst we have not made a bad decision."

"Okay, I will."

Juulys began typing a long message to the Armstrong I. Ten minutes later, Blake looked up in total surprise.

"What?" It was James, and he could clearly tell that Blake had received something he didn't expect to receive.

"It's a long story, but they may be in deeper trouble than we are. They truly thought their drives were working, but they aren't. They also don't know if their weapons are on line. It appears that they are lost and came out of a very long suspended sleep state and more than half of their crew is dead. Like I said, the story is significantly longer than that, but they first want to test their weapon systems to see if those are functional before we get any closer. They wanted to warn us so that we didn't take it as an attack."

"That makes sense, especially given their situation. It's also a sign of good faith to warn us, knowing that if their weapons don't work, they've left themselves at our mercy."

"Good point, James."

"So," Vladimir was the next to talk, "we have two damaged ships with each ship trying to figure out if the other is friendly or not. And if that is not enough, we are not sure if either ship can get back to Earth."

"That about sums it up, Vladimir; at least we know what we're dealing with. Hopefully, we have finally run out of new surprises."

"Okay. Juulys, we are ready; please target something well off to the side, but on a line perpendicular to the midpoint between our two ships."

"Prepping now, Blake."

"Okay, we are also ready; it will be to the right of your ship and should detonate at least 500 kilometers from either of our ships. It is a general purpose explosive used for position identification and does not have any radioactive or fragmentation risks."

"Thank you for clarifying, Juulys; we were concerned about that."

"Missile has launched; you should see a small, quickly extinguished bright light in just a few more seconds .... there ... see it? Thank Glysst, at least our weapons work."

"That was a pretty small explosion," Jie stated with both relief and disappointment in his voice.

"That's because the only explosion or flame that you can see in space is one that is fed by an ignition or burn source, like air. In the absence of air or fuel, the flash you saw is limited only to the chemical substance the bomb burns, and that is exhausted pretty quickly," Blake explained, and then continued with Juulys.

"Juulys, I am sure that was good news for you, but I have to admit, your excitement of having your weapons on line was a little unnerving on this end. We are assuming that was purely from the standpoint of being able to protect yourselves, rather than launch an offensive on us. Is that a fair assessment?"

There was a slight pause and then Juulys responded.

"Yes, my apologies Blake, but it is purely defensive from our perspective."

"But still no drives, correct?"

"Yes, that is correct, Blake. The more we discuss it amongst ourselves, we are convinced that the drives are activated, but they are still waiting for a signal from us that allows us to engage them. We think it's a safety mechanism to ensure that a ship couldn't be stolen by our enemies, yet select weapons were enabled to allow a ship to at least attempt to protect itself."

"Okay, that makes sense, but how is it you have everything else turned on? I would think the ship's

captain would have access rights to all aspects of the ship, yes?"

Thjars gave Juulys a quick glance that clearly said *no*, so Juulys didn't explain any further about their long lost captain.

"You are correct, Blake: we are at a loss and not sure what is wrong yet. We have our engineers working on it."

The two ships broke their radio connection.

"Hmmm. Seems like everyone is having trouble," Vladimir stated aloud. The group sat in silence for what seemed like a very long moment until Vladimir spoke.

"Blake, speaking of trouble, what is the latest with the terrorists? Has your government caught any of the bombers yet?"

"No, Vladimir, they have not. At least not that I have been told. In some way, I wish I was there to help out."

"I'm quite confident you would go through hell's water and back again if you could, leaving a trail of dead terrorists in your wake."

"Yes, I would." Blake grumbled with a steeled look. "Yes, I would. Wait a minute, Vladimir."

"What is it, my good friend?"

"I've been so focused on our own issues that I forgot about the rest of my team."

"But you have been working with Harry, yes?"

"Yes, but Diego and Sean are likely looking for some way to help, just like I would. The NSA must have some data on the various terrorist cells that are in the U.S. I'll recommend that they tie Diego and Sean into their efforts and let them deal directly with any leads. Those two and a team of SEALs will be lethal. They just need to be let loose."

With that, Blake started typing a message to the White House. Running an op that targeted terrorists was nothing new for Diego and Sean, but running one in the U.S. ... now that would be different. Blake knew just who to contact to make sure Diego and Sean were given a green light quickly. President Callahan. And he knew just what he wanted them to do ... and that was exactly what he would be doing right now if he were there.

CHAPTER 26

A.D. 2029 (3312 C.A.E.); Jan. 16
White House, Washington, D.C.

President Callahan had called the Situation Room to order at 6 a.m.; there was a lot to cover. Various parties reported in on the declining status of the Reagan I; the continually evolving status of the Armstrong I; the latest knowledge of an alien ship called; the fact that the ship was damaged and did, indeed, carry live and potentially friendly aliens; the latest casualty totals from the four terrorist bombings; the status of additional bomb searches; the latest data recoveries from the computer gear that had been in Harold Bessimer's house; other critical world events; and finally, the latest threat from the terrorists. It was a daunting list of topics, even for these hardy veterans.

"Ben, please pull up the message we received earlier this morning." President Callahan slowly scanned the faces of his trusted advisors to see their responses as they read the message on the screen.

"Mr. President, we have tried to get you to see the futility of your ways, but you continue to resist. You have refused to denounce Israel. You have not withdrawn your troops from the Middle East. You have not apologized for the targeting and killing of innocent Muslims with your fighter aircraft. It is now time to take our message of jihad directly to the U.S. people. The following message will be released to the internet and to your major news networks at 9:00 a.m. EST if you do not meet our demands.

"American people. The time has come for you to pay the price for your government's continued murders of so many innocent Muslims, as well as for your continued sins for ignoring Allah's direction to follow Sharia law. We have already detonated bombs in four of your major cities. You have witnessed the results, but you still do not conform. Our resolve remains firm. We have additional bombs and fighters prepared to deliver more death and destruction to your country, but we also have worse. We have succeeded in eluding your security nets and have placed a nuclear bomb within your territorial borders, where it can inflict the most harm. If your government does not denounce Israel, pull your troops home and then terminate all air traffic around the world, including both military and commercial activity by midnight seven days from tomorrow on Jan. 24, we will detonate the nuclear bomb. Seven days, like the seven heretical teachings in your Bible; that is more than enough time to meet our demands. If not, we will kill millions, and forever change the course of your country, but the blood will be on your hands.

We cannot be stopped; Allah Akbar."

The room was silent. Everyone looked at President Callahan.

"How could they have gotten a nuclear bomb into our country and why are they waiting so long?" he finally asked the room full of advisors and staff.

Brad Watters was the first to respond.

"Mr. President, we don't know for sure, but I expect they are biding their time in order to maximize the terror effect and further degrade our government's ability to maintain control. They want a mass panic. Relative to the 'how,' our ocean ports, airports and natural borders with Canada and Mexico are heavily monitored and we are confident that the sniffer systems we have would have caught anything greater than 100 grams of plutonium-239 or uranium-235. We have also triple-checked our nuclear stockpiles and are confident nothing is missing. We don't know how this could have happened, sir."

"What if they had amounts that were fewer than two kilograms?"

"That is possible, sir, but we don't believe they could have secretly set up labs capable of assembling the bomb within the States. Our experts believe that they would have to import the bomb's explosive unit fully assembled and have at least four kilograms of Plutonium-239 or Uranium-235 in it."

"What is so special about the four kilogram level, Brad?" the president asked, "Short version please."

Gen. Landon McMullen volunteered to speak for Brad.

"Mr. President, the 'Fat Man' atomic bomb that destroyed Nagasaki in 1945 used 6.2 kilograms of plutonium and produced an explosive yield of 21 to 23 kilotons. Although some argue that as little as one kilogram of plutonium can suffice to make a bomb, the Department of Energy estimates that a minimum of four kilograms of Plutonium-239 is required to make a small nuclear weapon. Below that level, there is insufficient critical mass to sustain the explosion."

"Are you sure we can't do it?"

"Sir, we do have a Top Secret program where U.S. scientists were able to successfully develop a one kilogram plutonium bomb, but its reliability is still in question, and the technology to successfully build that sophistication into a bomb is simply not in the grasp of the rest of the world."

President Callahan contemplated his response options before carefully asking, "So, you are telling me that the U.S. *can* do it with one kilogram; is that correct?"

"Yes, sir, but for someone else to do it … that would mean that our nuclear system has been infiltrated and compromised. I don't believe that is possible."

"Ladies and gentlemen, we have a terrorist who claims to have a nuclear bomb in our country, yet all we can say is how that isn't possible. We are looking at this wrong. We need to stop saying it can't be done and figure out how it could have been done." The president's expression was fierce. "Meet back here in two hours; I want answers. All dismissed, except Ben Tellinino, Gen. Landon McMullen and Brad Watters." He waited for the room to clear.

"Ben, get the writers in here; I need to go on live television within 30 seconds of that news release. Get the networks ready. Brad, Landon, get with whoever you need to in order to prepare to ground all commercial U.S. flight operations and stop all offensive military operations. Continue recon and CAP operations."

"Sir, we are giving in to the terrorist demands?" Brad's face was ashen.

"No, Brad, but I am trying to buy some time, which we desperately need. We will make it public so that everyone knows. We will need to establish martial law and freeze any travel in the country; our citizens will need to know why."

"What about the growing protests we're seeing in every city? People are demanding that we give in to the terrorists. Do we shut down the protests?"

"No. I'm concerned that will only result in taking critical security resources away from our investigation and search activities – that is exactly what the terrorists want. Crowd control should be kept at a minimum unless violence erupts. In that case, we will shut it down fast and hard with the military. That will be part of my speech. We simply do not have the time to waste on idealistic idiots who have no clue how the world truly works. That may sound cold, gentlemen, but desperate times call for desperate measures."

"President Callahan ..."

"Yes, Ben?" he said more calmly as he looked over at his National Security Council Secretary, Ben Tellinino.

"We just received another message, but this one is directly from the Armstrong I. It's Maj. Thompson."

"Maj. Thompson … what does he want? Our hands are pretty full right now with our own nightmares."

"Mr. President, he is offering his help."

"What?" President Callahan stammered out. "What could he possibly help us with right now?"

"He's recommending that the NSA pull two of his team members in: Diego Velasquez and Sean O'Rourke. He wants you to direct the NSA to make a short list of likely terrorist cells that could be connected to the bombings, and then let Diego and Sean pick a crack team of SEALs and start taking them out."

"Good God, Ben, on American soil? What if the NSA is wrong?"

"Sir, with all due respect, you said it yourself … desperate times call for desperate measures."

The president paused, his head down for a few seconds before responding.

"I'm sorry, Ben, you are correct; I can't believe I even hesitated, but … on American soil … this will change everything." President Callahan paused before continuing. "Make it happen, Ben; it's time to team our elite killers with our stealthy bloodhounds and start turning the tables.

"Gen. McMullen, please make sure this team gets whatever they need."

"Absolutely, sir, and for what it's worth, I think it's way past time to start kicking some ass, sir."

"Brad, what can you pull together from the NSA?"

"A lot, sir, and for that matter, we already have some information of interest."

"Why hasn't that been shared yet, Brad?"

"The problem is that none of it has been validated yet. We have pictures and we have fingerprints, but we haven't tied them together yet. None of the terrorists appear to be in the system for doing anything suspicious. It's like they are invisible. More than likely, they're not homegrown and probably came in across the border, not through customs."

"The borders? How does this happen?"

"Sir, the U.S.-Mexico border covers approximately 2,000 miles and the U.S.-Canadian border is almost another 4,000 miles by itself, much of which is pure wilderness. It is truly impossible to block it all. On top of that, it would be relatively easy for a small ship to land on the northern shores of Maine or Washington, and avoid all detection. The borders are simply too expansive to cover every inch of, or to be able to catch every individual or small group of people."

"I know you're right, Brad; it's just frustrating. So how are we supposed to find them then?" President Callahan asked quietly, getting more agitated.

"We need something to break in our favor, sir. We need the suspect fingerprints or faces to show up somewhere and trigger an alert. We have the best facial recognition algorithms in the world, but they don't help if the individuals don't show up somewhere. The NSA has been integrating and interrogating video databases from around the country, especially at formal points of entry, as well as at major public venues, but the truth is, most of the video surveillance systems in this country are independent systems purchased by homes and businesses. Fortunately, most of these systems are internet-based, and given that, we can usually find a way to infiltrate their data systems. However, at the end of the day, the best chance and fastest path we have is with the integration of major security companies, but that crosses the line between government and business agreements. We'll need White House direction to do that."

"Approved, make it ASAP, Brad; no paper trail or Congressional review is required: this now falls under the War Act. Everyone will know the depth of this crisis to national security soon enough, if they don't already. Make sure the CEOs of each of the companies understand the criticality of the situation and that they need to act yesterday. If there is any hesitation, get me on the phone. Make it happen, Brad."

"I will, sir."

*****

New York City, N.Y.

Diego, Sean and six SEALs were on foot and had just converged on a building up the street from The Mosque of Islamic Brotherhood at 55 Saint Nicholas Ave., just three blocks north of Central Park in Upper Manhattan. This was the team's first assignment against known terrorist cells within the U.S., initiated by the discussions between Blake and President Callahan. A second team of six SEALs was stationed in three military Humvees at the intersection of Saint Nicholas Avenue and West 115th Street as backup. Although the mosque was not suspected of any terrorist activity, a rental on the fourth floor of the seven-story brick building at the corner of Saint Nicholas Avenue and West 113 Street was. The rental was above the Gourmet Deli, and housed known terrorists who had been on an FBI watch list. The FBI had staked out the group for six months, waiting for them to tip their hand to a hoped-for larger connection, but that effort was now trumped based on the events at hand.

It was just past midnight and the SEAL team was slowly walking up the back stairs, having disabled the alarm system and picked the lock on the back door. One SEAL remained at the back door as a guard against any surprise intruders. The other seven men, including Diego and Sean, were heading up to the terrorist rental, with guns in hand, rotating left to right and up and down to cover all angles of potential danger. At the fourth floor, Diego hand-signaled for two SEALs to form on the left side of the door that led to the suspected terrorist cell, and two to the right. One SEAL on the right side of the door quietly placed a det-cord-laced wooden lath across the door, while two SEALs guarded the hallway approach, one on each side of the door. Diego, Sean and the remaining SEAL were poised to storm the door immediately following the detonation. Once the det cord was in place, Sean held up one hand with five fingers, and silently counted down to zero fingers.

The explosion shook the entire building, filling the hallway with dust as it blew a designed four-foot-tall by two-foot-wide hole in the door, thereby avoiding any reinforced hinges or locks. Diego dove through the door first, followed immediately by three SEALs and Sean, all with night vision goggles now in place. The others remained in the hall as backup, as well as to monitor any hallway traffic that might come their way from other rooms.

Three men had been sitting at a table with what looked to be small bomb-making equipment, cell phones and circuit cards. They were now in various stunned positions on the floor from the force of the explosive door breach. Dust and door splinters were everywhere, and each of the men was bleeding from the flying wooden splinters. Based on the newly minted wartime rules provided by the White House, this was ample evidence to commence military action. Diego and the SEALs opened fire, killing the three men with two shots each before either could react. Two SEALs spun off of Diego's left to probe the room on the left side, while Sean and the other SEAL headed to the room on the right. Diego searched the rest of what looked like a living room and headed to the kitchen. Gunfire erupted in all three rooms, the majority of which came from the SEAL team. Sean and the SEAL on his side killed four men in the bedroom to the right, while the two-man SEAL team to the left shot and killed two more in the left bedroom. Sean found one more terrorist hiding in the kitchen, unarmed, and quickly knocked him out with his rifle butt and tied him up. In less than 30 seconds, the 10 terrorists had only managed one burst from an AK-47 that went harmlessly into the bed as he fell dying, and nine were dead.

Diego called in the backup SEAL team with the Humvees to help set up a guarded perimeter around the building. The FBI quickly followed suit with no less than 12 agents in three black SUVs. Dozens of New York City police cars converged on the site to complete the entourage. Computers were harvested and the unconscious terrorist was whisked away for interrogation by the FBI. Scared neighbors were consoled by the police. Twenty minutes later, the 14-member team departed in the three Humvees, allowing the FBI and police to clean up while they prepared for their next assignment.

*****

A.D. 2029 (3312 C.A.E.); Jan. 17
On Board the Armstrong I

The Armstrong I was within two days of reaching the Jarisst I. The building excitement levels associated with the anticipation of the upcoming meet had now replaced that of the anxiety of the previous unknown for everyone on the Armstrong I. The long trip, filled with many periods of high stress, was now coming to a climax beyond what any of the crew had hoped for when they left Earth slightly over two months ago. It was hard to believe this was really happening. No one wanted to remind himself that at the end of all the excitement, they had another two-month-long trip back to Earth. That wasn't exactly something Blake and the crew was looking forward to.

Relative to events back home, the White House had finally approved classified news updates for the entire crew of the Armstrong I. Everyone was devastated to hear about the nuclear threat facing America – regardless of their country of origin. The world powers might have their differences, but on the topic of terrorism and nuclear threats, there was no difference of opinion.

During the past two days, Blake had continued to work details with Juulys to reduce any risks associated with their first meeting. They were beginning to feel much more confident about the upcoming encounter, even setting up a draft agenda of topics to discuss. Most important was verification that all were safe, followed by an introduction of the two races, a review of the different cultural and planetary histories, some linguistics education, and of course,

Harry would disown Blake if he didn't ask about *some* of their technology capabilities in the first meet.

Rakesh was working feverishly to complete a software adaptation of a copy of Babylon Pro Package translation software for their portable digital camera system. They had expected to video the interior of the ship when they first left Earth, but regardless of expectations, no one had really expected they would interface with actual living beings from another planet. Rakesh was attempting to put a system together that would record everything the crew from Cjar spoke aloud and then attempt to create an understanding of what they were saying. He wondered what the Cjarians had done to pick up the English language so quickly.

Blake still wished Patty were with him. She would pick up on their linguistic speech patterns way quicker than any of them. On the positive side, at least he knew that he could send whatever Rakesh recorded back to Patty on a daily basis to get her opinion the following day.

Klaus Schneider was assembling star charts for Blake to use to assess where the Jarisst I may have originated. Maj. Vladimir Popov was not yet needed, but it was Blake's hope that the crew of the Jarisst I would at some point allow them to look at the engine systems. When they did, Vladimir and his chemical engineering background was Blake's top consideration.

Ataullah and Jie's core importance was as backup pilots for Pavlik and Snyder, but that need had also been deemed more important if there were any possibility of flying the alien ship back. As exciting as the finding of live aliens had been, it unfortunately greatly reduced the importance of the two men on this flight. A major disappointment for both men, yet they still had a front seat to one of the biggest moments in human history. Cmdr. Jack Pavlik and Maj. James Snyder would keep their primary area of focus dedicated to flying and controlling the Armstrong I.

Blake would be the primary contact with the crew of the Jarisst I. He hadn't given any thought to the formal aspect of the responsibility until he heard Vladimir refer to him as Ambassador Thompson, obviously in humor, but the more the two men joked about it, the more they all realized that Vladimir was correct; they were indeed *all* ambassadors from Earth. If this had been a movie, then the president would be making a speech for their new guests with all kinds of pomp and circumstance. The reality was that the president had way more critical tasks to deal with, but even if he hadn't, the distances were too large to allow for a true conversation anyway. So it was left to Blake and his crew to be his ambassadors for both the U.S., and the world.

The Armstrong I had now slowed to below 100,000 kilometers per hour and was continuing to decelerate as they prepared for the final approach to the Jarisst I.

> *"I think I have an idea, Juulys. Are you willing to entertain a proposal?"*

> *"We will consider it, but no promises. What are you thinking?"*

"Yes, Blake, what are you thinking?" Cmdr. Pavlik queried. "Keep in mind that I have the dual responsibility of getting you to their ship, as well as protecting this ship and its crew."

"All good points, Jack. Here's what I'm thinking." Blake outlined his plan to Vladimir and Jack.

"Blake, I agree that would reduce their concern, but it's highly dangerous. You could easily be killed, Blake," Jack volunteered as Vladimir nodded agreement.

"I agree, it does have risks, but this is one of those rare happenstances where one has to take that leap of faith and go for broke," Blake responded resolutely. "And I am 100 percent A-okay with it." Both men nodded agreement.

> *"Juulys. Here's an idea that I believe will protect both ships once we arrive. Do you have the ability to send someone on your ship out to meet me halfway between the ships, once we've parked two kilometers from you?"*

Two long minutes came and passed.

"Yes, Blake, continue."

"Once parked, I will use a second rocket sled we have on board. Yes, it is similar to the one we used on the Domashev you saw a few days ago. I will maintain maximum speeds at less than 10 kilometers per hour. That will take me a little over what we call 10 minutes to transit to the midpoint of one kilometer, including time to slow down to a stop. If at any time I exceed that speed, or I don't stop at the rendezvous point, you are free to fire if that is your desire. Once there, I will put on a reserve air tank that has four hours of air, release myself from the sled, allow the sled to return to our ship via an anchored towline, and await your pickup. I will be at your mercy at that point. If you are willing, you can pick me up and take me to your ship, where we can meet and talk, but I would need to be returned to my ship before the four hours are up."

This time, 10 minutes passed.

"Juulys?"

"We are still discussing, Blake."

The three men talked very little, sitting, staring at the screen and waiting for the anticipated response. Then it came.

"Your plan sounds very dangerous, Blake. If you trust us to get you, then we will trust you to meet us. We will prepare the dock for your environment, so that you may conserve air while you are in our ship. We will communicate with you through an airlock to ensure we do not exchange what could be deadly microbes to either of our races. We believe your air is approximately 78-80% nitrogen and 20-22% oxygen. Please verify. Based on the light emitted from your star, and the distance of your planet from your star, we will prepare lighting levels to what you call 320 watts per square meter. Please verify. Juulys."

"Holy cow …" was all that Blake could say at first. "They have done their homework! They know so much about us, yet …"

"We know nothing about them." Vladimir completed Blake's sentence for him. "Are you sure you are ready for this, comrade?"

"Thank you for the promotion to comrade, my good friend," Blake responded sincerely. "To be totally honest with you, I can't wait to get started."

"Yes, Juulys, all verified. Thank you."

CHAPTER 27

A.D. 2029 (3312 C.A.E.); Jan. 18
NSA Headquarters

Blake had exchanged ideas with Harry about the nuclear bomb's location late the day before, but the growing distance between Earth and Pluto now required hours for transmission, each way, so it was nearly impossible to maintain a legitimate conversation; it was almost analogous to mailing letters back and forth in the snail mail days.

Blake theorized that the terrorists might have made a mistake and unintentionally tipped their playing hand by using the word "territorial" borders. Blake directed Harry to request Brad Watters to look at the message again, but consider that the term "territorial borders" might actually refer to "maritime territorial" borders, rather than the more typically assumed "continental" borders. That would be one way to explain why the feds hadn't identified anything yet – it was highly possible the feds had been looking in the wrong places.

Brad had just finished listening to Harry's spiel on the phone, summarizing Blake's thoughts on the territorial borders.

"Harry, I won't say that we haven't looked at our coastal waters, but I can definitely say it hasn't been our focus. We were definitely landlocked in our theory generation process."

"No problem, Director Watters, that's why I guess it's always good to have fresh eyes in a brainstorming session. You guys know things that we will never know, but you may also assume things that we see as totally new. Pretty natural. What now?" Harry asked.

"Hang on, Harry, let me get Adm. Zach Taylor, the commandant of the Coast Guard, and Gen. Landon McMullen on line first; that way, we can all have one discussion."

Thirty minutes later, the group had been re-energized and laid out plans to assess the coastal waters on both the East and West coasts, as well as the first 140 km of international waters beyond the coastal waters. Coastal, or territorial, waters were defined by the 1982 United Nations Convention on the Law of the Sea. They represent a belt of waters extending, at the most, 12 nautical miles (22.2 kilometers; 13.8 miles) from the mean low-water mark of a state or country.

From the perspective of a nuclear explosion, a boat would have to be more than 162 kilometers, or approximately 100 miles, from shore to ensure little-to-no impact from a nuclear explosion; so coastal waters were well within the death and damage zone of a nuclear explosion. Harry also pointed out that they might want to include the Great Lakes area as well because of the connection to the Atlantic Ocean via the Saint Lawrence Seaway. Brad quickly concurred.

"Tell Blake nice work for us, Harry. This may be the breakthrough we have been waiting for. Talk to you when we know more, Harry." With that, he hung up and headed to see President Callahan with his latest update.

*****

Dam Neck Annex at NSA Oceana
Virginia Beach, Va.

Diego and Sean had been called back from their New York mission before they could join the other SEALs in the next planned attack in Queens. All they were told was that their priority had been changed by the White House and they were then whisked away to the West 30th Street Helipad on the east bank of the Hudson River, not far from the Jacob K. Javits Convention Center. As soon as they arrived at the helipad, the rotor blades of a waiting V-22

Osprey began turning and three U.S. Marines motioned Sean and Diego to board; they were airborne 30 seconds later.

Three hours later, the two men were standing in the middle of an op room at the Dam Neck Annex at NSA Oceana, but with a different crew of SEALs, this time with 14 hardened members of the world-renowned SEAL Team Six. It was only then that Diego and Sean understood the magnitude of what the U.S. was undertaking; it wasn't just New York City, it was across the country. The thought of these highly trained and lethal soldiers being turned loose across major American cities was something no one ever expected to see. Diego was confident that within just a few short days, the number of thought-to-be-hidden terrorists who would meet their maker was going to be very sizable. Many terrorists, who thought they were operating in the secret, were in for a nasty surprise. Uncle Sam's secret monitoring systems kept track of more than the public was aware of – specifically for pre-emptive strikes and for times like this. Diego was also confident that civil rights lawyers would have a field day once they found out, but right now, the country was operating under martial law, and as long as that was the case, "cleansing" was the word of the day.

They had just completed an NSA debrief that was the source of their mission change. The debrief identified a match between a video of a shooting in Chicago, and a video of a person that had purchased gas at a BP Gas Station near Dayton, Ohio. The video hit might have been lucky, but it was also part of an extensive plan by the NSA to integrate video systems across the country and run them through the NSA facial recognition systems – all in the hope of finding something that might shed light on the current terrorist threat.

The Chicago video was grainy, but it showed a clear picture of a man's face as he leaned out of a car window and shot a man who had been identified as Jim Morrati. NSA had used its highly classified enhancement algorithms to enhance the picture to the point that it felt like you were holding an actual photograph of the individual. The technician said it was better than most – a very high-quality photo. Then the video match showed up from Dayton.

The Dayton video had been taken at a BP gas station located at 129 E. National Road in Vandalia, just north of Dayton. The individual of interest had not entered the store, but was shown pumping gas into a car. The car's license plates had been traced within seconds to the Avis car rental at 33 E. First St. in Dayton, Ohio. The car turned out to be a blue Nissan Pathfinder, but according to the woman who answered the phone, the Avis video and data systems that would identify the renter were not available to the public. She further stated that someone would have to come to the office with police or proper government identification to access their information. The NSA operative thanked her, hung up and went to work. It took him less than 20 minutes to hack into their system and be rewarded with a name and the crystal clear photograph matching both the shooter and the gas station customer. It was a match.

This was what the team had been waiting for: a break. Now it was time to pack up and get to Ohio. The team would land at Wright Patterson Air Force Base and use that location and its assets as their home base. The team would then break up and scour the grocery stores and gas stations around the Vandalia area, waiting for the next lucky hit. Terrorists were no different than anyone else; they still needed food to eat and gasoline to fuel their movements.

The NSA increased their integration and interrogation levels of video sources across the surrounding Dayton area. The location of the Chicago killer had now become one of the top non-nuke-related priorities in the country. The NSA, CIA and FBI all brought in additional surveillance teams to electronically infiltrate every business and home security system they could legally, or semi-legally engage in the area. The data was being integrated into the massive data-crunching, self-learning AI systems the NSA maintained to track high-value suspects.

The greater Dayton area, an area of more than 6,000 square miles, had just become ground zero for the U.S. counterattack. The area extended south to Centerville, north to Piqua, east to Springfield and west past Lewisburg. A large area for a small team to cover, but they now had multiple teams that were searching for a very specific car and face. Available space-borne surveillance systems that weren't being used to search for the offshore nuclear threat were also pulled in to assist. As the 2008 movie thriller, "Eagle Eye," depicted, these satellites had the ability to read license plate data from Earth orbit, and could easily spot a blue Nissan Pathfinder driving or parked in the open – as long as there wasn't a continuous cloud cover. If all of the data were correct, then at least one terrorist had located himself at a major crossroad in the U.S.: the intersection of U.S. interstates 70 and 75.

*****

Eight hours into the search, code named "Go for Broke," and after multiple flights by multiple planes up and down the East and West coasts, a specially modified high-altitude, semi-stealthy, Boeing WC-135 Constant Phoenix, tail number 61-2667, having just refilled in flight, flew over a private yacht due east of Atlantic City when a light went off on the main sensor panel. As there were no commercial flights in the air, they were flying black with lights out to reduce any chance of detection.

"Sir, we have a hit: Plutonium."

"Mark location."

"39.3773° N, 74.4511° W"

"Orders are to get that information to NSA Director Brad Watters ASAP, eyes only, no one else. Clear?"

"Yes. Transmitting now."

"Roger. We'll keep flying in case that is a false alarm. The NSA will utilize high-intensity, narrow-beam satellite X-ray sensors to look into those holds and validate our findings."

*****

"Director Watters. Eyes-only transmission."

"Thank you, lieutenant."

Forty-five minutes later, Director Watters picked up the secure line and called President Callahan.

"Mr. President, the satellite has validated the Constant Phoenix's sensor pickup off Atlantic City. We have a target. Satellite imagery shows it to be flying a Union Jack flag under the name of Manchester United."

"Have we contacted the Brits?"

"Yes, sir, they have no record of the yacht. It feels like this could be a rogue ship, sir."

"Where is our closest nuclear attack sub, Brad?"

"The Virginia Class, USS Virginia is two hours out, Mr. President."

"Order them to close in. Call the Situation Room together."

*****

Thirty minutes later, the Situation Room was fully staffed. Director Watters briefed the room and turned the meeting over to President Callahan.

"Gentlemen, let's talk options and risks. Gen. McMullen, what do you think?"

"Mr. President, from a risk perspective, there are two primary issues. First, is the actual nuclear explosion and the immediate aftermath that will result in deaths and damage to our communications infrastructure due to electromagnetic pulse, or EMP. Second, is the longer-term aftermath associated with radiation fallout. Death and destruction will be severe, numbering in the tens of thousands expected casualties, especially if the yacht attempts to go upstream. For example, like on the Delaware River, all the way to Philadelphia, or through the Great Lakes, to Chicago."

"Gen. McMullen, that is a frightening, but an excellent observation." President Callahan exclaimed. "I need immediate knowledge of any attempt this yacht makes to move toward the shore. Continue, general."

"Thank you, sir. Continuing on, although we are concerned about radiation fallout, it may not be as critical as one might think because the prevailing winds on the East Coast should take the cloud farther out to sea, but as we just discussed, this is assuming that the detonation is out to sea. EMP on the other hand is very concerning. A high altitude burst would impact every city on the East Coast. Obviously, the fact that the bomb is on a boat at sea level will greatly diminish EMP risks, but it would still put many major U.S. cities at risk, including Washington D.C., Baltimore, Philadelphia, New York and all of the smaller cities and towns in between. The EMP from the blast would be expected to shut down more than 80 percent of all electrical power and computing capabilities in those areas. The cold weather would only aggravate the condition as homes and businesses lose power. After years of preparation and investment, key government and hospital sites are better prepared, but we still expect at least a 40- to 50-percent loss of those facilities as well."

Gen. McMullen paused to survey the stunned expressions of those in the room. President Callahan nodded to continue.

"From an options perspective, if we want to recover the bomb, we could attempt to board with Navy SEALs, from either the air or sea, but speaking honestly, I think that has too much risk. The probability that the terrorists could still detonate the bomb, by themselves or remotely, before we could kill everyone on board is too high. The USS Virginia could easily take the yacht out with torpedoes, or we could send in F-18s at night at supersonic speed to take them out before they could hear or see the planes coming. Cruise missiles could be another option, but I think we need to consider that any airborne attack might carry a higher risk of detection depending on what level of radar sophistication they have on board. I doubt they have the ability to detect our submarines, but the sound of a tracking torpedo might be something they could identify early enough to still react and detonate the bomb. Ship-to-ship attacks are not recommended as they could easily be detected. We need to keep in mind that those on board the yacht have likely already signed up for a one-way ticket; they know they will die a martyr's death no matter what happens, so they are fully incentivized to detonate the nuke at the earliest concern that something has gone wrong.

"One last thing, Mr. President."

"Yes, general?"

"Unless we know there is really only one nuke, destroying this nuke could alert them to immediately detonate any other nukes they have."

The room went silent. Everyone had been considering a single nuke scenario. President Callahan was the first to speak.

"General, you're right on all points – again, a frightening, but excellent summary. We will reserve the sub attack as a last-ditch alternative until we can convince ourselves that we have ruled out the existence of any other devices. Or until we fear they are truly ready to go. Have the Virginia hold at attack depth and distance, at full battle stations, ready to launch as soon as they receive word – and make sure they understand that word comes directly from me, the president – no one else. If that yacht moves even one hundred meters closer to the shore, I want to know about it within 30 seconds."

"Yes, sir."

"One other thing, what about the passengers on the yacht? Do we have any information that would suggest they are all part of the attack, or is there a chance we are risking innocent people if we destroy their yacht?"

"Sir, there is no way to guarantee that everyone on board is part of the attack or not, but we feel it's a pretty safe bet that a pleasure yacht, even a big one at that, could not possibly do what they are doing without everyone being part of the mission. The sad fact is that we have to make some hard decisions and, in the small chance there are innocents on board, we will still need to move forward. The collateral damage that will be incurred by not taking out this ship is far greater than the loss of a few innocents, no matter how distasteful it seems," the general concluded.

"Acknowledged, Landon, but I don't have to like it. I just wish I knew in advance," the president replied.

Harry had been included in the latest Situation Room meetings via a secure phone from his remote location at NASA in Houston. He had been very impressed with the meeting. It was good to see the government functioning as a single, cohesive unit.

President Callahan looked over at Harry's projected image on one of the side monitors.

"Harry, we sure could use some of your genius right now. Thoughts?"

"Thank you, sir. I need to chew on it some more, but I think you have it correct. We need to buy as much time as it takes to convince ourselves this is the only nuke involved, even if that means giving some ground to the terrorist's demands. I'd also like to update Maj. Thompson and get his thoughts again. Is that acceptable?"

"Heck yes, he was the one who got us looking over the water in the first place. And who the hell is he going to tell anyway, sitting five billion kilometers away from Earth? Thanks Harry, but make it quick."

"On it, sir."

*****

Harry attacked his keyboard to get a message out to Blake quickly, knowing full well that his haste would quickly turn into queue time while the message traversed space to get to Blake, be read, analyzed and responded to, and then returned.

"Blake. Highly confidential – you only. Callahan approved discussion. You nailed it. Yacht is off East Coast, near Atlantic City. Could attempt to destroy boat, but terrorists would be certain we attacked. If other nukes exist, they could detonate those or pre-detonate existing bomb if any threat is detected. Game over. Commercial flights shut down. Buying time. Looking for ideas. Six days left. Harry."

CHAPTER 28

After significant effort, Jack and James had been able to slow the Armstrong I down and actually steer it back on course with the Jarisst I. And after multiple readjustments in position, the Armstrong I had finally arrived and stopped at the agreed to distance of two kilometers. The long anticipated day had finally arrived.

Earlier that morning, Blake, Rakesh and Juulys had established radio contact between the ships and were able to tie Blake's suit microphone directly into the communication channel with the Jarisst I. Blake would be able to talk his way to the Jarisst I, meter by meter if that was necessary, so that all could maintain status awareness, but most importantly so that Juulys and the Jarisst I could tell him to stop at any given time if he somehow accidentally crossed a concern line with them. Blake still recalled the first time he heard Juulys' voice … it was not what someone would call "non-human," but it was definitely different than what he had ever heard. It had an almost melodic, warm theme to it. He was definitely looking forward to talking further with the travelers from Cjar.

He and Rakesh had also been able to follow up on a strong recommendation Patty had provided a couple of days earlier. Patty has stressed the need for both crews to see pictures, preferably video, of each other prior to the meet. In that manner, they would both know who it was they were expecting to meet, but more importantly, if there were extreme differences in physique that might be hard to accept on either side, Patty had said that it was very important to get that out of the way before the meet and allow adequate time for all parties to prepare.

As it turned out, to the relief and surprise of all parties involved, the two races were not as drastically different as they had expected. The Cjarians were on average slightly taller, thinner, almost fragile-looking humanoids. Their faces were as equally expressive as humans'. They had five fingers on each of two hands and all appeared to have hair in similar locations. It had been a momentous moment that was quickly dwarfed by the realization that there was so much commonality, one could not argue against the thought that there might actually be a common tie.

Blake and James were making final adjustments to the sled. He had been thinking about Harry's latest message all morning and wondered what he would be returning to, a long two months from now. The President definitely had his hands full. Blake hadn't come up with any ideas yet, but he knew he had to put that aside to focus on his trip to the Jarisst I.

"Jack, Juulys … I think I'm ready to go. Please verify status on both of your ends."

Jack was first to answer. "Roger."

There was a short pause and Juulys' voice came through with an undertone of uncertainty … "Roger? Who is Roger? We were preparing for just Blake …? … Please verify."

Blake chuckled and Jack laughed heartily. "You haven't even left the ship yet, Blake, and I've already screwed things up! Sorry, Juulys, but we have a long history of using the word 'Roger' to acknowledge that we understood something or that we are ready to go. Only Blake is traveling to visit you. Let me try this again. Blake, all systems ready on this end. Commence when ready. Is that better?"

Now Blake was laughing and he was pretty sure that he heard multiple sounds of what could be translated as laughter coming from the Jarisst I as well, until Juulys' voice overrode them and she said, "Roger. The Jarisst I is also ready."

Blake smiled and added, "Very good, Juulys, the first point goes to you and the Jarisst I. See you shortly. I will keep communicating along the way."

Blake stepped into the air dock with the waiting sled and signaled Jack to evacuate the dock and open the exterior doors. Two minutes later, the dock's doors began to open. Blak untethered the sled, disconnected his lifeline and pushed the sled and himself out from the ship. He knew roughly where the Jarisst I was, but at this distance he couldn't see it. As he floated away from the ship into the blackness of space, his heart rate increased from his standing 60 beats per minute to over 95 beats per minute, quite unusual for him.

"Blake, are you okay?" Jack asked. "Your heart rate just jumped up higher than I've seen before."

"Yes, I'm okay, thanks." Blake labored into his mic. "It really doesn't hit until you're out here. It's an extraordinary view as you move away from the ship. But there is one thing that could help."

"What's that?" Jack answered.

"I know I have the coordinates of the Jarisst I programmed into the sled's controls, but it would definitely help once I get close enough to be able to see the ship."

Five seconds later, Blake was rewarded with the sighting of a beautiful blue, strobing aura coming from where the Jarisst I was supposed to be.

"Juulys, was that you? That is impressive."

"Yes, Blake, hopefully that helps."

"Absolutely, always better than flying blind. Thank you," Blake responded.

The crew watched as Blake's heart rate slowed slightly, dropping to about 85 beats per minute.

Vladimir, like the rest of the crew, was in the Control Room watching and listening to everything unfold. He reached down to the panel and hit the mic's mute button, and then held up a wait sign for Jack with his hands. Vladimir was smiling. "Interesting."

"What is?" Jack replied.

"It appears that we actually found something that can throw our Maj. Thompson off a little. It just took a free, untethered spacewalk, five billion kilometers from Earth, into total nothingness, on the way to meet an alien life form for the first time in history to finally show a crack in his armor, even though he won't admit it. I'm so disappointed with him."

Everyone in the room laughed, and Jack clicked the mute setting back off.

"Looking good, Blake. We all know what kind of movie line buff you are, so contrary to that old movie line, please DO go into the light." Jack chuckled.

"Touché, Jack. 'Poltergeist,' early 1980s, correct?"

"Bingo."

Juulys entered the conversation as well. "Just when I think I know what you are talking about, you lose me again. Sounds like I may have missed something that was funny?" she asked.

"Yes, but it will take a long time to understand where that came from. Sorry, we will try to keep our banter to levels that both ships can follow. I surely don't want to use a joke that isn't received as a joke," Blake responded seriously.

"I'm at 100 meters," Blake announced a few seconds later. "Ready to initiate sled rockets. Rendezvous point estimated in slightly over 10 minutes."

"Roger," Jack stated mechanically, now fully in operational mode.

"Roger," echoed Juulys.

The 10 minutes passed like seconds. The views were stunning. The entire sky was filled with an unending supply of stars and clusters in every direction. Blake also discovered that in the immenseness of space, with nothing nearby, it was very hard to gauge one's relative speed, especially as it was no longer easy to see the Armstrong I. Without the sled's console, it was hard to tell that he was even actually moving.

"Beginning retro rockets to slow down. 3 … 2 … 1, engaged. Slowing down. I should be at rest shortly."

"Blake. Juulys here. Recommend one change. We have already launched our sled as agreed to as well. Look for a green flashing strobe shortly."

"Got it. I see it. Thank you."

"It should be there in less than what you call 10 minutes. It is unmanned. We will guide you back to our ship. Use the safety line to ensure you don't get separated from the sled."

"Roger."

*****

Fifteen minutes later, Blake was nearing the Jarisst I. It was an amazing moment to actually experience close up, and in person: an alien ship. It was different than anything Earth had ever constructed. It was huge, at least three times as long as the Armstrong I by Blake's estimate. It was also beautiful. The sleek lines of the ship revealed a hint of the importance of design aesthetics to their race.

"Blake. You will need to remove your suit before entering our ship."

"What?" Jack almost yelled into his mic before Blake could answer.

"I expect Juulys is learning to joke with us, Jack. Would that be correct, Juulys?"

"Yes, how did I do?"

"Quite well. Even better now that I know you caught Jack off balance." Blake laughed. "What *really* happens now?"

"The sled will bring you alongside our air dock. The door will open and a mechanical arm will extend out of the bay, grab the sled by the forward docking joint, and guide you into the air dock. You will not have to do anything. Are you ready?"

"I've been ready for this all my life. Yes."

Everything occurred as Juulys described. Fifteen minutes later, with the sled locked into place, the air dock closed and Blake could hear the unmistakable sounds of the vacuum being replaced with air. He looked around at the unmistakably alien controls and designs.

"Jack, can you still hear me?"

"Loud and clear. Congratulations, Blake. A true first for humanity. I'm envious, my good friend."

"Thanks, Jack, is the video working, too?"

"Crystal clear. I have no idea what I am looking at, but it sure looks impressive."

Juulys spoke up. "Blake, we just completed our moment of trust, allowing you into the ship. Now it is your turn. First, open your visor. We have established your air environment."

With a hissing sound, Blake released the visor, hesitated for a brief instant and then took a long breath of air. He continued breathing for 60 seconds. Everything seemed fine. The air smelled and tasted somewhat metallic, very similar to air in the Armstrong I before they added air freshener to it.

"Now you may remove your outer space suit, Blake. Just so you know, we have scanned you and the suit as we discussed. We have not detected anything that could be considered a weapon, other than the unit you have reassured us is a system for taking video and recording our discussions."

"That is correct, Juulys; I come totally without protection."

Blake did as requested. He also unclipped the video camera system from his helmet and suit, and attached the mic to his ear.

He gave a thumbs-up to the darkened window in front of him, in a position Jack could see as well from the video camera.

"Still following, Jack?"

"Roger that."

"Blake, what was the meaning of that gesture?" Juulys asked.

"Sorry, Juulys. We have many customs in our world. This gesture is somewhat like the word 'roger' we laughed about a few hours ago. With the thumb pointing upwards, it means all is good. If the thumb were to point downwards, that would mean all is *not* good. I am sure things like this will happen many more times. Please continue asking when I do something unexpected."

"Thank you, Blake, we understand."

With that, the 3-foot-tall by 1-foot-wide window began to lighten until it became a panel of clear glass. As Blake watched, an individual with beautiful eyes and long flowing reddish-gold hair gracefully moved in front of the glass, raised her hand with a small smile and gave a distinct thumbs-up. Blake knew immediately that it was Juulys from the video and pictures they had exchanged. He needed to thank Patty; that had been an excellent recommendation.

Juulys was wearing a sleek, light-gray garment that conformed tightly to her body. The suit extended to her wrists and her feet from what Blake could quickly surmise without gazing too long at her figure.

"Greetings from Planet Earth. I am honored to be here, and we all wish to thank you for allowing this meeting," Blake said while holding his hands out flat and extended away from his body in a sign of openness.

"Blake, thank you for honoring our trust requests. Greetings from Planet Cjar. We are also honored to be here."

"Juulys, how is it that you are walking, and not floating?"

"It is something we call simulated gravity. This suit I have on is specially designed to interact with sensors throughout the ship to create various magnetic attraction forces on different points of the body that somewhat simulate how gravity would impact the body. Obviously, we could not design a suit for you without knowing much more about your anatomy, but one of our engineers, Cryells Elysst, set up a number of these sensors with individual straps that you may attach to your body, if so desired, to test it out. It will not be as effective as our suits because we have hundreds of these sensors throughout our suits; your straps will be predominantly on your hands, elbows, shoulders, waist, knees and feet." Juulys nodded to her left as a younger man stepped into view, smiled and gave a thumbs-up signal.

"Absolutely, please direct me and please thank him."

With that, Cryells spent the next 10 minutes, with help from Juulys' English expertise, directing Blake where to place each sensor, as he simultaneously held onto the ship to avoid rolling in the weightlessness. When he had completed attaching all of the straps, as directed, Cryells gave Blake a thumbs-up signal, and was awarded with a returned gesture and a chuckle from Blake. Cryells held up a remote control unit so that Blake could easily see it, and then pushed a button to activate the system.

"Oh, my God …" were the first words out of Blake's mouth, followed by a string of revelations as his feet slowly moved toward the floor. "This is amazing. Jack, are you following?"

"Yes! How much do we have to pay to get one of those for each of us? That is incredible. What does it feel like?"

"It's just a slow, gradual pull that feels different at each location the sensor is mounted. I'm sure it will take some practice to get used to, but it's way better than floating all the time."

Juulys and Cryells were both smiling, imagining what it must be like to stand and walk normally for the first time in over two months.

"Blake, who is this God I've heard you mention a couple of times over the past few days; is that in some way related to Roger?"

Blake smiled. "No, Juulys, it is actually in reference to a greater being that we believe created us and the universe."

There was a long pause as Juulys looked at her crewmembers before responding. There was the appearance of a tear in her eyes.

"Blake, we will need to explore this further another time. We, too, have a similar belief. In our world, we refer to our creator as Glysst."

"Yes, we will, Juulys, and I look forward to that discussion. I believe I heard you mention that phrase a couple of days ago as well. Ataullah, did you catch that?"

"Yes, I did Blake, and if you leave me out of that discussion, I will never talk to you again." They both laughed.

Juulys went on to introduce Thjars and the rest of the crew. Blake had been very interested in the one she had called Qulys; he had the look of a military man you could rely on. Blake looked forward to meeting him another time when they could really communicate. The conversation began flowing freely between the three of them. There were many times they had to stop to recalibrate what was intended, but the conversations were understood better than Blake had ever expected, thanks mostly to Juulys' amazing expertise with the English language.

Juulys provided highlights of Cjar and Cjarian culture. Blake responded in kind about Earth and human history. Juulys then went on to describe how they believed they had arrived in this solar system and gave a little background on the war with the hated Klaxx. That was a concern that Blake had not prepared for. Humankind had only previously been threatened in science fiction movies; this was real and Blake had no idea how close or far away the Klaxx system was, nor did the Cjarians.

They gave Blake a few lessons in the language of Cjar and provided him with some written material to take with him. Finally, Blake asked the question he had promised Harry.

"Thjars, is it possible that you can teach us about your propulsion systems?"

Juulys jumped in for Thjars. "Blake, we assumed you were going to ask that. In all fairness, we believe it is too early to share advanced technology with your race. We believe you are sincere, but unfortunately, we have seen a great deal of aggression from your planet that concerns us."

"That is totally fair, Juulys, but I needed to ask. So, where do we go from here?"

"Great question, Blake."

Before Juulys or Thjars could answer, Blake was interrupted by a call from the Armstrong I.

"Blake, come in." It was Jack. "We have an issue; can you talk offline?"

"I can, but I would just as soon not have any secrets in front of our Cjarian friends at this point."

"Okay, understood."

"We took multiple hits on the ship about 15 minutes ago. I was not going to bother you, but James was outside using the down time in an attempt to work on the damaged sail, trying to make repairs, and we haven't heard from him ..."

"Hits? What kind of hits, Jack? Is James okay?"

"It must be remnants from a comet tail or some other kind of debris in space. It shredded the remainder of the sail. We can see him and have hailed him, but he hasn't responded yet; he does not appear to be moving. I have Jie and Ataullah suiting up for a recovery mission."

"Jack, what direction did the material come from?" Blake asked.

"No, Blake, it was not from the Jarisst. It came perpendicular to the line between our two ships."

"I will return as quickly as I can, but that will still take some time," Blake responded before turning to address the Cjarians.

"Sorry, Juulys, but I absolutely need to go. We have a serious problem on our ship; it has been hit by something else and we appear to have an injured crewmember. I need your help to get back to my ship."

Juulys and Thjars were talking to each other in their native tongue. It was clear whatever they were discussing was serious. They talked to their two engineers, who quickly reviewed a number of items on what looked like a computer screen, but it was hidden from Blake's view.

"Blake, everyone was focused on watching and listening to you, so we didn't see it. However, one of our crew just rewound and reviewed our video files of your ship, which we were recording while you were here, just in case anyone else made an attempt to come over. My apologies, but I trust you will understand. We can clearly see the impacts from what looked like a small cloud of rock and ice debris, and the resultant damage does look severe. Unfortunately, it also appears that your crewmember was hit. Suit up; we will begin moving the sled toward your ship as soon as you're ready. Once there, we can join you on the recovery mission. Our sergeant-at-arms, Qulys Plyenysst, will assist if you desire; he is among the best we have and is highly experienced."

"Thank you, Juulys; I accept your offer."

Qulys joined Blake in the air dock, already wearing a very tech-savvy spacesuit. The two men greeted each other with nods and Blake began to suit up.

When both men were ready, Thjars dropped the pressure in the dock and then opened the outer door once it had equalized with the vacuum. The two men then hooked onto the sled and prepared to head back towards the Armstrong I. Qulys also hooked a large bag onto the sled and quickly noticed Blake's questioning look. He opened the bag. He spoke into his mic and Juulys quickly notified Blake that it was a bag of tools that might be useful to recover their crewmate and possibly help fix any of the structure.

"Good luck, Blake. Qulys, please be careful."

Blake gave the ship a thumbs-up and reaffirmed his hook up to the sled. The sled began to accelerate rapidly and in fewer than 20 minutes, they were at the Armstrong I's side.

Blake looked up and could clearly see Ataullah and Jie climbing the sail. Ataullah was in front of Jie by seven meters, Blake estimated, when the main sail structure snapped and folded inward, ejecting Ataullah into space with no lifeline.

As Blake stood helplessly by, he watched Ataullah fly by and then gasped as the folding structure collapsed on Jie, clearly piercing his midsection and exiting the back of his suit. Blake was stunned.

"Damn it! I need to get up there. Jack … are you seeing this?"

"Yes, Blake. I'm on my way."

"No, Jack, stay. You must remain at the ship's control if we have a chance of recovering Ataullah. Track him and don't lose him."

Qulys and Juulys were talking in their native tongue again.

"Blake, this is Juulys. Qulys will drop you off and take the sled to get your crewmember. Don't worry; Qulys will get him. You deal with your crewmember on the sail. I will communicate between you and Qulys."

"Okay, thank you, Juulys. Over and out." This was time for action, not talk.

With a push, he ejected himself from the sled and headed toward Jie. He quickly covered the 100 meters of distance and grabbed onto the structure.

"Jesus, Blake, what if you had missed?" Jack snapped.

"I didn't," was all Blake could say with labored breath. He started working his way up to Jie. He didn't bother looking back, as he knew Qulys was already on the way to find Ataullah. Five minutes later, he called Jack.

"Jack?"

"I'm here, Blake. How is Jie?"

"Jie is dead. I'm moving up to James," Blake said through very heavy and labored breaths. Three minutes later, he reached James.

"Blake. Talk to me," Jack urged Blake.

"I'm sorry, Jack; we lost James, too." The weight of the news reduced both ships to total silence. Jack finally broke the silence.

"Roger that, Blake; I will notify Houston," Jack spoke with a heavy voice.

"Juulys?"

"I, we are so sorry, Blake. We didn't see it coming."

"Understood, but we are not in the clear yet. What is the status of Ataullah?"

"Qulys caught up with him. He appears to be injured, but alive. They are heading back to your ship as we speak."

"Thank you, Juulys. I will contact you later, after we have recovered the bodies and are back on board the ship."

"Understood. Please be careful; we have both lost too many friends."

"Blake? Jack here. You are down to two hours and 42 minutes of air. Do we need to switch positions?"

"No. Give me the rest of my air for first shift. If I can't complete it, then we can switch."

"Roger that. Be careful, Blake. Juulys is correct; I don't want to lose any more of this team."

Two hours later, Blake had recovered James' body and then returned to the Jarisst I. All were now safely inside their respective ships, with the exception of Major Jie Gao. Jie was still impaled on the sail's structure and they would have to cut him free in a separate recovery effort.

"Juulys?"

"Yes, Blake, we are here. We are sorry for your loss."

"Thank you Juulys, and thank you for your assistance today. Please let Qulys know how much we appreciated him putting himself at risk to save Ataullah. He has a broken arm, but will recover fine. We will forever be grateful to Qulys and your crew."

"I will, Blake. Thank you. I am guessing that we may be better prepared to recover the body of your other crewmember. May we assist?"

"If you can and are willing, I would again be grateful for your assistance. Thank you."

"Okay, let us know when and we will suit up and send out Zalmyt Wylmysst and Platsys Flysst, two of our ship's technicians, along with Qulys on the sled."

"I need Jack to remain on the ship as our primary pilot. I have another crewmember, Klaus, who can assist me." Blake responded. "Can we meet in one hour?"

"Yes, Blake."

Six hours later, after the Cjarians had used cutting torches to slice through the structure, Blake pulled Jie's body into the air dock. He relayed his thanks to Zalmyt, Platsys and Qulys via messages to Juulys. Blake was impressed with all three Cjarians, but it was clear that Qulys came from a cut well above the average; Blake expected Qulys would be as good as any SEAL he had trained and fought with.

The Cjarians headed back to their ship, while the crew of the Armstrong I, down two men, began the chore of dealing with their losses. It was going to be a long night for the surviving members of the Armstrong I. Jack had already messaged Houston about the disaster, but it would be many hours before the ship would receive Houston's response.

"Juulys, we have a new problem."

"Yes, Blake, what is it."

"I don't believe our sail will get us back to Earth."

A long silence ensued.

"Blake, we were afraid of that. We now have two ships that cannot make it to safety," Juulys responded with a heavy heart.

"Let's get some sleep and regroup in the morning. I have a friend back home who may be able to help; his name is Harry. I will send some information to him tonight and see if he can come up with anything. We will talk tomorrow."

CHAPTER 29

A.D. 2029 (3312 C.A.E.); Jan. 19
On Board the Reagan I

The days had been long and sobering on the Reagan I since the attack.

"Houston."

Four minutes passed.

"Yes, Cmdr. Kline?"

"We are a dead stick; we cannot course direct. The ship is below 50 percent operational status and only 40 percent of the ship can maintain livable conditions. We have exhausted all attempts to fix the ship. We have 12 months of provisions. I believe we are out of options at this end. What is the chance that NASA will be able to launch a recovery vehicle within the next nine months?"

Another four minutes passed.

"Commander, we are looking into it. NASA cannot, but we believe the Russians can. We are working on it and will provide updates to you. I wish I had more, Dutch, but it's all I have right now."

Cmdr. Kline severed the link and looked out into space. How could such a promising journey with such great dreams have come to such ruin? What the hell was he supposed to tell his crew?

"Damn it!" he spoke aloud to the empty Control Deck. "I cannot allow this crew to lose faith. As far as they need to know there is a pending launch in three months and it's up to us to ensure we are ready to be retrieved."

With that, Cmdr. Kline went to see his remaining crew.

*****

A.D. 2029 (3312 C.A.E.); Jan. 19
The White House

President Callahan had just been briefed in the Oval Office about the Armstrong disaster and the fact that the ship might not be able to return to Earth.

"This year has already seen so much disaster, yet we are only 19 days into it. Two spaceships possibly lost. Multiple terrorist attacks across our country. And the threat of a nuclear attack." He looked up at Ben Tellinino, who was standing in front of his desk.

"Remind me, Ben, why did I run for this office?"

"Because you truly care and because you are still the best man for the job," Ben replied sincerely.

President Callahan contemplated Ben's response for a few seconds before replying quietly, but resolutely.

"Thanks, Ben, I hope you're right, but it sure as hell isn't feeling that way right now. Let's get over to the Situation Room and see what the latest update on the nuke hunt is."

The two men walked from the Oval Office on the first floor down to the Situation Room. Ten minutes later, the room was fully staffed and ready. The standard noon update had been delayed 90 minutes due to the news on the Armstrong I and the loss of two respected astronauts, as well as the fact that President Callahan demanded that he and he alone be the one to inform both the family of Maj. James Snyder and the government of China.

"Let's get started. Brad, what do you have?" President Callahan launched into the meeting.

"Mr. President, we are highly confident that there is only one nuke. Confidence levels are above 80 percent."

"That's still not good enough, everyone," the president responded. "We owe the American people more than that. What does it take to get that above 95 percent?"

"More time, Mr. President. There's a lot of territory to cover and very few assets that can detect nuclear material at the levels required for this search," Gen. McMullen volunteered.

"I know, Landon, but we're running out of time."

President Callahan paused and then looked at NSA Director Watters. "Brad, what was the latest deadline from the terrorists – five days from today?"

"Yes, sir. If we do not denounce Israel, ground all commercial and military flights and demonstrate a sizable withdrawal of American troops from the Middle East by Jan. 24, they claim they will detonate the nuclear bomb."

"Are the Israelis on board with the message we drafted last night?"

"Yes, sir, they are, as are other world leaders, but it truly takes a hit to our relationships with countries around the world because, for decades, America has stated and backed with actions that we would never cave to terrorists' demands."

"General, what about troop movements?"

"We can start any time you command. I know that you are aware of this, sir, but it will create a huge destabilizing effect around the world, one that the terrorists are likely planning to capitalize on."

"I understand," President Callahan replied. "Perhaps I'm just trying to buy some time before the inevitable occurs, but I don't see any other options. Harry, are you on?"

"Yes, Mr. President."

"Anything from your end?"

"Sorry, sir, nothing back from Blake, either. I expect his plate is pretty full right now."

"Understood."

President Callahan sat quietly, scanning the faces in the room.

"Okay, gentlemen, the time has come. The final decision will be mine, but I want your opinions. Option A is the Virginia sinks the yacht at 6 a.m. on the 24th, hoping that another option develops before then. Option B is we release the Israeli denouncement to world media and begin withdrawing troops and grounding flights. Ben, start the roll call."

"Sir?" It was Harry.

"Yes, Harry."

"I know this is one of the toughest decisions that someone sitting in your office has ever had to make, but there have been others. Just to name a few, the Civil War, Hiroshima and the Cuban Missile Crisis were likely pretty big. I am confident that your selection of options is truly in what you believe to be the best interests of the country. I am also confident that I know what Blake would say if he was on the phone."

"And what is that, Harry?"

"Many times while we were on an op, Blake would repeat something he heard in SEAL training. 'You don't have to like it; you just have to do it.' And then for all his Marine Corps friends that he deeply respected, he would end with 'Semper fi' and we would implement the plan. Mr. President, we never had all the data we wanted in the field and yet we were still expected to meet the objective. Blake is the best I've ever seen at taking what he had and making that hard decision to do the best he could – all based on the intel he had at that moment in time. Never quitting and never looking back. Just like previous presidents did with the Civil War, Hiroshima and Cuba, and many other very tough decisions. They made the hard decision to stand strong and proud, and deal with the consequences.

"Sir, there is not a doubt in my mind that Blake would advise you to take option A and advise against taking option B. Otherwise, terrorists around the world will know they can do it again. The message has to be that America stands strong at whatever cost it takes. And while Blake was at it, he would continue to work on creating a better option C, but until that time, he would remain committed to option A."

President Callahan surveyed his staff; many sat up straighter in their chairs during Harry's speech. Gen. McMullen was nodding. The room was quiet for a full 60 seconds.

"Are there any nays to option A?" President Callahan asked the room.

Total silence.

"Ben, cancel the roll call. Harry, thank you. Gen. McMullen, you will show the world an absolutely devastating destruction of that yacht. The attack is a go at 6 a.m., Jan. 24.

"God bless this country, and pray that a better option C presents itself soon."

*****

Vandalia, Ohio

Diego was driving toward a barn located in a cornfield northwest of the Dayton airport. Although the NSA contact had referred to the location as Vandalia, it was actually the southwestern part of the township of Tipp City. The NSA satellites had identified the suspect Pathfinder as it drove north on Dog Leg Road earlier. It just now passed the intersection with Old Springfield Road. The Pathfinder turned right onto a tractor trail in the center of the cornfield that led to the barn, and then drove directly into the barn.

Diego had been camped out in Vandalia waiting for any updates, so it was a quick five-minute drive to get to the NSA-identified location. On the way, he called Sean and requested that he leave his watch zone in Piqua to join him. He also recommended that the SEALs remain at their assigned zones until they knew more;

that way, if the barn turned out to be a false lead, the others would still be equally spread out across the Dayton area to facilitate a quick response if a second hit was received from the NSA.

While Diego waited for Sean, he drove calmly past the cornfield to eye the barn. Like the rest of the team, he had been given an older model car to drive that would better blend in with the surroundings. This was not the time to be driving government-issued black SUVs. Sean's car was a beat up, dark gray, nondescript 2018 Ford Explorer that secretly held plenty of horsepower in case he needed it. The barn looked relatively new, as if it had been built within the last five years. He wondered if they had been planning the attack that long, or if they simply bought property for sale that conveniently had a barn located on it. Not that it mattered, he was simply curious. Diego was more concerned with the number of visible cameras he could see on the barn. The cameras were definitely an early warning system.

As it was mid-January, the cornfield contained only post-harvest stalk nubs with a slight covering of snow. Diego wished it was late July, as he could have used the corn to hide an approach to the barn, but unfortunately, it was the dead of winter and there was no cover whatsoever. As any special ops guy knew, you had to make do with what you had. There was no other way. Sean noted a small creek and hedgerow at the back, eastern side of the lot. Google Maps quickly identified it as Mill Creek, something that might come in useful as it was less than 1,000 feet from the back of the barn.

Diego drove back to Vandalia via a different path to ensure that no one inside would take notice of a repeat drive-by and stopped at the local Wendy's to grab a sandwich and wait for Sean. He also called NSA to send an electronics eavesdropping team with their youngest-looking agent from Wright-Patterson Air Force Base (WPAFB) to meet up with them, as well as a linguist that could at least identify Middle East dialects. Diego wished Patty was with him, but she was assisting Harry's other efforts at the moment. Hopefully, WPAFB had someone with at least half of Patty's capabilities available. Relative to the youthful-looking agent, Diego had an idea he wanted to try out.

A.D. 2029 (3312 C.A.E.); Jan. 20
On Board the Armstrong I

It had been a long night for the remaining crew on the Armstrong I. After two months of relatively incident-free travel prior to the Domashev attack, the loss of two of their crew had been totally unexpected, especially because it happened after the safe arrival at their mission objective. Blake had looked forward to Diego, Jack and James getting together when they returned to Earth – a meet that would never occur now.

Blake knew that everyone needed to go through their own grieving process on their own timelines, but he also knew it had to be quick in order to keep the mission on schedule, as well as to reduce the risk that any of them would inadvertently join the list to be mourned for because of a momentary lapse of attention. Having always appreciated the importance of routine, Blake rose at 5 a.m., exercised, cleaned up, ate breakfast and was now heading to the Control Deck to check on messages from Earth. There was one, from Harry. The message summarized the plan agreed to by President Callahan to take out the yacht at 6 a.m. on the 24th. The biggest concern was the possible existence of other nukes and how the terrorists might react once the U.S. took out the yacht. Still, Blake agreed with the decision. Hit them hard and send a message, then deal with what comes. Blake wished he could help more, but he had pressing problems of his own to handle. It was time to contact the Jarisst I.

"Juulys. Blake here. Can we talk?" Blake hit the send button.

"Yes, by radio, please."

Blake moved over to the radio panel and put on a headset.

"Blake here. Can you hear me?"

"Yes, Blake."

"We are looking for ideas. The sail is definitely inoperable and beyond our ability to repair."

"Blake, there are 11 of us on board the Jarisst I. We lost the majority of our crew due to an event that we still don't understand, and I haven't told you this yet, but we also lost our captain during that event, as well as the first officer. That is why we can't activate the drives. Relative to your ship, I don't believe we have the materials or the ability to fix your sail in a reasonable timeframe, if at all."

"I'm sorry to hear that, Juulys. I can only imagine how tough this has been for you and your crew. As for our ship, I assumed that might be the case," Blake added emotionlessly. "Juulys, I hate to put this on you, but I see only one option where we all survive. That option being that we have to get your ship drives activated."

"Blake, we have tried everything we know and can't figure it out. I don't mean to insult you, but how could you possibly fix what we don't know how to fix?"

"I have something that you don't have."

"What is that, Blake?"

"My team back on Earth, specifically Harry, as well as an entire world of technical experts at my fingertips that can be applied to this problem, if and only if you allow us to better understand your technology. I understand the predicament, but as I mentioned, I don't see any other options."

"That is a logical proposal, but it could also have impact and significance way beyond what any of us could predict, Blake. Let me talk it through with Thjars and I'll get back to you. If there was any way that you could get the C-Pod back to us, that might offer the best opportunity we have, but based on what you shared about your other ship, we don't even know if they still have it, let alone be able to get it to us."

"That is actually a great question, Juulys. I'll check and see what the status is and we can talk more tomorrow."

*****

Blake had a million thoughts running through his head, all competing for his attention, but foremost was to make a quick connection with Harry.

> *"Harry. Blake here. Need you to find out if the device on the Reagan I is still with us. It is called a C-Pod. If they still have it, you and I will need to find a way to communicate between you, the Reagan I and the Armstrong I, and more quickly than what we do now."*

Blake hit the send button and turned in for the night, confident that Harry would have an update for him first thing in the morning.

*****

A.D. 2029 (3312 C.A.E.); Jan. 21
White House Situation Room

"Report in. What new developments do we have?" Ben Tellinino asked the president's cabinet members.

Chairman of the Joint Chiefs of Staff, Army Gen. Landon McMullen, was the first to speak. "We have covered additional ocean and the Great Lakes since yesterday, as well as revisited a couple of key suspect areas and have not identified any other nuclear material, outside of our own ships and one Russian boomer parked off Maine. I can now increase our confidence to 87 percent that there are no other nukes the terrorists might be hiding."

"Thank you general. It's not 95 percent, but it's a whole lot better. Anything else, anyone?" Callahan scanned the room.

The room was silent.

"General, keep raising that number. Harry? Anything from you or Blake?"

"Relative to the terrorists, no. Relative to our predicament in space, it's too early to know, but Blake did message me last night with some new information. It appears Blake has an idea where our new friends might be able to help – and that they also need our help."

The room broke into pandemonium. President Callahan spoke for everyone, "Our new friends? That's an interesting opener, Harry. Please go on."

Harry quickly filled in the details from the past 12 hours.

"Do we know the status of the device, or C-Pod as we now know it to be?" Harry queried the group.

"To be honest, with all of the events of the past few days and the losses on both ships, I don't believe anyone has asked. I'll follow up for you after this meeting, Harry," Brad Watters replied.

"While we are on the topic, Harry, how about our men on the Reagan I? Any chance of recovery of those brave people?" President Callahan had already moved on to the next agenda item.

"Yes, I think we have the beginnings of a plan. We'll need the Russians to help and we need to do a little work on the Reagan I, but there's a better than fair chance we can be successful – not great, but better than what the Apollo 13 crew had. We still have plenty of time to work the details out, so I think we can spare your time on this issue."

"Okay, thanks Harry. As you hinted, my top issue remains the terrorists. I have the draft message to deliver to America, but I still need to make some refinements. Brad, you work with Harry to make sure he gets everything he needs for the Reagan I and the Armstrong I, but in no way does it get in the way of terrorist activities. Understood?"

"Yes, sir."

With that, President Callahan and most of his cabinet left the room, leaving Brad to talk with Harry.

"Harry, stay on the line. It may take two to three minutes, but I can tie the Reagan I into this call."

"Will do."

Five minutes went by and Cmdr. Dutch Kline answered.

"Kline here, what's up, Houston?"

"Dutch, this is Brad Watters, in President Callahan's Situation Room."

A few minutes passed. "Oh … Okay, what can I do for you, sir?"

"First off, our thoughts and prayers for you and your crew, especially for the families of your lost friends."

Four more minutes were exhausted.

"Thank you, sir, that means a lot. I will pass that on."

This time, the four minutes seemed appropriate, based on the acknowledgement of their losses.

"I almost hate to ask, but it's an emergency. Do you still have the device?"

Four more excruciating minutes went by.

"That's a rather odd question based on our current situation, but yes, we do. Why, may I ask?"

Another four minutes.

"Dutch, I'd like to introduce you to someone named Harry Lundrum. Harry, Dutch. Dutch, Harry. And Dutch, you'd better sit down; this is going to come as a major surprise to you, and not the way in which we planned to break the news to you. Harry, could you provide Dutch with a high-level update on what else is going on in the world, and our solar system?"

"Sure, my pleasure."

With that, Harry launched into a 15-minute-long, uninterrupted update of what had transpired with the Armstrong I, acknowledging what a disappointing surprise that would be to Dutch. He also updated Dutch on the Cjarian ship, the Domashev and the current status of both ships now out at Pluto. He ended his discussion by explaining what the device on the Reagan I was, now known as a C-Pod. Blake and the Cjarians wanted to know if Dutch still had the C-Pod on board, as well as if it remained operational, or if it had been damaged during the attack. He then waited the standard four minutes for a response.

"That's truly incredulous, Harry." Dutch paused, something clearly brewing in his head, "Brad, why were we not told?"

Four more minutes expired.

"To be honest, Dutch, we were concerned over the emotional impact it might have on you and your crew when you found out, and the risk that would create over a very long flight. Right or wrong, a lot of high-level folks were involved. For what it's worth, I'm sorry. I wish this could have been different."

A short pause ensued and then Harry added, "I need you to send me pictures of anything you have that might provide insight into the C-Pod's command and control functions."

Another agonizing four minutes went by. With everything else going on, Harry couldn't believe that someone hadn't extracted Brad from the call yet for some other reason.

"Well, it's spilled milk now, but still smells like spoiled milk, Brad." Dutch paused, and then moved back into operational mode, "What can we do to help, Harry? Would something like a keyboard help? Assuming yes, I will have Jimmy jump on it; he must have taken a thousand pictures of it already. I should be able to have something for you in your inbox in say … 30 minutes. That quick enough?"

"Yes, exactly, as well as some overall unit photos. I'll forward them to Blake and he'll share it with our new friends to see if they can help. Thirty minutes is perfect. Thanks, commander. By the way, I understand your current predicament. Don't give up hope. I'm working with Jimmy to see if we can rig something that will allow you to get back on the right trajectory and establish a better chance of creating an intercept window when you approach Earth. It has to do with releasing a large quantity of shipboard air through a vent created in a very specific location in the side of the ship. I think it has a good chance of succeeding. But this approach also requires that you stop the rotational movement of the ship first; Jimmy is working that angle with me now."

Four minutes went by, seemingly quicker this time.

"Oh, you're *that* Harry. Jimmy has talked quite a bit about you. Anything you can do to give us some hope would be greatly appreciated. As you can imagine, it's a pretty tough going out here right now."

"Understood, commander. I'll be back in touch."

With that, Brad disconnected the call and Harry began sending an update to Blake.

*****

On Board the Armstrong I

Jack was already up when Blake entered the Control Deck.

"Morning, Jack. How're you holding up?"

"Okay, considering the recent events. Heck, it's not like I could sleep even if I wanted to right now. I thought my days of losing friends due to battle engagements were long over. It's been a long time since feeling a loss like this."

"I know. One never gets over it. They were both good men, but I understand the extra tie that you and James had. Sorry we couldn't do more, Jack."

"Thanks, Blake. By the way, you have a message from Harry. Just came in a little less than an hour ago. I didn't read it."

Blake sat down and scrolled to the latest message from Harry.

"Whoa! Pictures! Check this out, Jack. This is their C-Pod. We have to get this to Thjars and Juulys. Have you had any contact with them today?"

"Not yet, let me see if I can raise them." A minute went by.

"Blake?"

"No, this is Cmdr. Jack Pavlik. Hold on, Blake is here; he has something for you."

"Hello, Juulys. Blake here. I'm opening up the video feed. Let me know when you can see the pictures."

"Yes! That is definitely our C-Pod! Does your other ship still have it?"

"Yes, and they state that it still appears operational. There is no way we can get it to you, but check this out. They were able to open it and expose what looks like a keyboard."

"I'm surprised they were able to get into it. Did they cut it open?"

"No, my understanding is that a couple of smart young engineers figured out how to open it with acoustic signals."

"Perhaps we have underestimated some of you. That is impressive you were able to figure out that it needed an acoustic signal, let alone figure out which signal."

"Like I said, there were a couple of our brighter young engineers involved, but to be fair, I believe a little luck played a key role as well."

"Either way, it's good to know that it's still operational."

"The battery or energy-retaining systems are clearly beyond anything we currently have on Earth, or anything that we have even dreamed of," Blake said, with clear admiration in his voice. "I hope you will be able to share some of this with us one day."

"Yes, that would be good if we can ever figure out how to make that day occur safely, Blake."

"So, what can we do with this device now that we know what we have?"

"I'm not sure, Blake. It requires a password to provide authority to release and engage the drives. The captain's brother, Jarns, couldn't even figure it out."

"Well, that may be one thing we Earthlings are good at: hacking code."

"Hacking? What does that mean?"

"It's a way of getting into software systems that the software creator or user does not want to occur. Perhaps it would be better to compare it to cheating your way into something."

"Okay, I think I follow … you do this?"

"No, not me or anyone else on this ship, but I know some people who can. One of my team back home is named Li, and I actually call him 'Hack' for his ability to hack into systems, but he has some others he can work with as well."

"Are there any keys on that keyboard that you would consider dangerous, like for example, a self-destruct button?"

"Glysst no, Blake!"

"Well that's good to hear. How about the code word we are looking for, any hints?"

"None whatsoever, Blake. Jarns tried everything he could think of and came up empty-handed."

"Okay, let me see if Harry has any ideas and I'll get back to you. One last question. How would they know if they succeeded or not?"

"They won't, but we will know as soon as the drives are activated."

"Okay, but no thoughts of leaving us stranded out here alone when you decide to head for home, correct?" Blake asked innocently, but seriously.

"I understand the intent of your question Blake. No, you have my honor that we will not leave you. You will know as soon as we know, but I am not expecting a breakthrough."

"Roger that."

Blake disconnected the call and then looked over at Jack.

"Who would have thought that one of our greatest, but least respectable talents, computer hacking, could be our primary ray of hope right now?"

Jack laughed, "Quite fitting for the lowly human race. Who do you have in mind?"

"Harry, Li and Patty of course, but remember that kid that first spotted the device on Mars with the Mars Rover? I think his name was Robert Stern, he's the kid that was a college intern at Lyndon B. Johnson Space Center."

"Yes, I recall the person, although I have to admit his name never registered."

"He has some pretty natural hacker skills. Those four coupled with Jimmy on the Reagan I ... now that fivesome could be an interesting and formidable team to take it on. Let me get this off to Harry."

*****

"Interesting."

"What is, Harry?" Patty looked over at Harry, who was deeply focused on his laptop.

"Blake wants us to hack the aliens."

"He wants *what*?"

The rest of Blake's remaining team also took notice. Sean and Diego were on the phone listening from their post in Ohio.

"Sorry, Patty, that wasn't meant to sound so criminal. Blake needs to send a code that is in the device on the Reagan I to talk to the alien ship that is out by Pluto so that they can fix their ship as well as help Blake and his crew, well his space crew to be more specific. The code can override the password from the ship's commander, who died centuries ago."

"Oh, is that all?" Sean asked sarcastically. "Where do you get this stuff from, Harry? We couldn't make this crap up if we had a year to think about it!"

They all laughed, except Harry.

"It's all fact, Sean, and pretty straightforward. Just an unusual circumstance from our perspective."

"You tell him, Harry." Patty put her arm around Harry and stuck her tongue out at the phone for Sean's benefit. "Is there anything we can help you with?"

"I'll need you and Li to help, and I also need to get a hold of that Robert Stern kid down at NASA, but I have to ask permission first."

"Okay, that's even dumber than your last commentary. Let me see if I got this straight. The world is in danger. Blake is in danger. We need an alien ship to help out. Everything depends on some 20-year-old college kid. And you want to ask permission to get his help?"

"Yes, Sean, I believe that is a fair summary."

"I think I'm losing it. Who are you going to ask, President Callahan?"

"Yes."

"I need a beer." With that, Sean dropped off the phone call, mumbling about the crazy state of insanity that seemed to be contagious these days and how much he missed the days when they were given an assignment and simply took care of it.

"He'll get over it, Harry. Go get the kid."

"I'm on the president's call in 35 minutes. I'll ask."

CHAPTER 30

A.D. 2029 (3312 C.A.E.); Jan. 21
The White House Situation Room

"Harry." President Callahan had begun to think of him as a permanent fixture of his cabinet. "What's the latest on the Armstrong I?"

"I need to add Robert Stern to our Armstrong I support list."

"Who?"

"Robert Stern, the college kid who first found the device on Mars."

"Okay, I trust you know who this kid is, and what he might be able to do, but Harry, do you really want to bring a college kid into one of the most tightly held secrets in the world?"

"Yes, sir, I do. I'll assume responsibility for him and make sure he understands. Sir, the lives of many people now stranded in space depend on us resolving some software-related issues, and this kid is good."

"Okay, Harry, I'm just the president of the United States, who am I to question it? You have my approval."

"Thank you, sir."

"Brad, you may want to have someone in a black suit emphasize what we can do to him if he doesn't cooperate, just to re-enforce Harry's message."

"Absolutely, sir," Brad replied with a rare smile during the past few days of activity.

*****

Vandalia, Ohio

"Diego, waz da plan?" Sean spoke while he reached for his burger. He just grabbed a meal at Wendy's, and the two of them were sitting in Diego's car.

"The NSA has one of those 30-year-old, looks like a high-school-musical kind of guy ..."

"What in 'ell air ye talking aboot Diego, 'ave ye lost it, too?"

"Give me a minute, ya Irish bloke. I asked for an agent that still looks like a kid. I'm going to have him deliver a Domino's pizza to the barn and see what he can find out."

"Okay, now I follow; I like it. When will he be here?"

"Shortly. We need to wait for dinner time, but not too late, maybe 5:00 to make sure there is a little light in the sky. It gets dark pretty early this time of year in this neck of the woods."

"What's his name?"

"Joe Welch."

"Welch? Like grape jelly Welch?"

"Good Lord, Sean, how the hell does that gourd of yours work? Yes, like Welch's grape jelly."

"Sorry, but I was hungry. All the way down I-75, all I could think of was a peanut butter and jelly sandwich, and then you mentioned Welch. Makes sense to me."

"Whatever. Anyway, I want Joe to deliver the pizza with a bright Domino's sign on top of his car; you know, the magnetic ones. He can walk up like some dumb high school kid and knock on the door. They will obviously tell him they didn't order any, but hopefully, he can learn something, like how many guys are there?"

"Okay, sounds like a plan, Diego. What do we do?

"We'll be just down the road at the intersection with Old Springfield Road, in case anything goes wrong."

Fifteen minutes later, "Joe" showed up with an unexpected partner and parked next to Diego's Ford. He was perfect. Diego and Sean eyed Joe over from head to toe. Floppy, untied shoes. Baggy pants hanging just a little too low, T-shirt under his coat and a mop of hair from some local hairdresser poster.

"OMG, he's perfect, Diego. Looks like a friggin' brain-dead, pot-smokin' high school idiot."

"I'll take that as a compliment and an affirmation that this is what was ordered," Joe replied smoothly as he stuck his hand out. "And this is Sarah, an Arabic translator."

"Spot on Joe, and one of the few times I'll agree with this Irish lackey. You're perfect." Then he looked at Joe's partner. She was not what he expected for an Arabic translator; rather, she looked like a regular, blue-eyed, blonde-haired American girl.

"Sarah what?"

"Sorry, gents, all you get is 'Sarah' on this one." Joe inserted himself, "We keep her pretty well under wraps these days."

The quartet spent the next 90 minutes laying out plans and discussing options. The kid looked young, but it was clear to Diego that he had been around and could be depended on in a crunch. As it turned out, Joe had spent most of the past six years working the drug wars in the Dayton area, so this was familiar turf for him. They'd made progress against the opioids and heroin nightmares that had ruled the state since the mid-2010s, but the truth was, it was still a major crossroad that remained a battleground for illegal drug shipments. Sarah was quiet, only speaking when a direct question was asked, and even then, it was "no" or "yes" in most cases.

It was closing in on 4:30 and the two cars drove down the road just a little farther west from Wendy's and stopped to see the manager at the Domino's in Vandalia. Sarah stayed in the car while Joe flashed a badge and said that he needed to buy a pepperoni pizza and borrow one car sign, and he would be back in an hour. The manager seemed to know better and didn't even ask a question as he nervously eyed Diego and Sean. Even under cover, the two looked more than a little menacing.

Fifteen minutes later, with the sunlight waning, Joe jumped into his beat-up 2013 Chevrolet Spark and headed to the target. Sean and Diego followed behind by about a half-mile, with Sarah in their backseat. She said nothing, but focused intently on her headset to listen for whatever comments Joe was relaying and more importantly, any conversations he might have with the barn's occupants.

A few minutes later, Joe pulled into the driveway and headed directly to the barn, while Sarah listened via his hidden mic. Sarah seemed to read Diego's and Sean's minds, pushed a couple of buttons and the sounds from Joe's mic quietly flowed into their car while she stayed insulated and focused on her headset with a recording device on her lap.

To further sell the pizza delivery masquerade, Joe left the door to his car open to allow the deep bass emanating from his car radio to flood the surroundings.

Joe exited his Spark and looked around with that stereotypical teenage "what the f---" look, shrugged and walked up to the side door entrance and knocked.

Immediately, a voice responded.

"We didn't order any pizza, go away."

Back in the car, Sarah nodded and said, "Yemen."

"Look, man, don't make me go back empty-handed; my boss will fire me. I got one pepperoni pizza for 11510 Dog Leg Road."

The door opened a crack. It was dark inside, but the man pointed to his left and said, "I think you want the house just south of us in that wooded parcel."

Joe looked to his right and said "Oh, thanks, man." He turned around, headed back to his car and jumped back in, seemingly without a care in the world. He then backed out and drove down to where the man said the address was. Fifteen minutes later, all four were back at the Wendy's parking lot.

"Well, what did you see, Joe?"

"It was pretty dark, but with that quick opening of the door, I know two things."

"What's that?" Diego almost begged.

"There are lots of computers in that place and definitely more than one person living there."

"Bingo. Great job, Joe." Diego spoke, for the first time getting excited. "Let's get everyone back to Wright-Patt Air Force Base and lay out some plans. Sounds like NSA wants to watch the place for a few days."

"Why not hit it hard and fast right now?" Sean asked.

"We don't know if this is a singular safe house or if there are others. NSA wants to know more before we take it out. They will also set up some listening equipment to see what else they can learn. I expect we will be on hold for a few days," Diego replied.

"Cripes, do we really have that much time?"

"Good question, Sean. I'd rather hit 'em hard and fast, too, but we don't have all the data, so I guess we'll have to rely on the folks in Washington that do."

"Sucks, but I understand."

"Oorah."

"Whoa, what about the pizza? That sounded good … where is it? What did the people in the house say?" Sean threw multiple questions at Joe all at once.

"Well, I had to make it look good in case they were watching, right? So, I drove there, knocked on the door and no one answered, but their mangy German shepherd looked pretty cold, hungry and friendly, and definitely lonely in his outdoor pen …"

"You gave it to the dog?!!"

"Hell, yes, man. I like dogs, okay?"

The three men laughed and Sarah simply smiled as they started their cars and headed to Wright-Patt.

*****

"Robert?"

"Yes … who is this?"

"Harry Lundrum. I'm working with Jimmy Decker and President Callahan."

There was a long silence before Robert spoke again.

"Prove it."

"Which Dr. Seuss character would you like me to quote for you?"

"That's pretty good, but to be honest, all of my friends know I use his characters for nicknames."

"Okay, do I need to detail how Jimmy called you and you asked for forgiveness for borrowing a certain oscilloscope, or should I ask your professor about it?" Harry said, chuckling.

"You're blackmailing me? Jimmy said he would protect me if I got in trouble."

"No, I'm just trying to get you to the finish line quickly. By the way, Jimmy says hi, but more importantly, he and others need your help now. Can I count on you?"

"Okay, if Jimmy is involved, yes. What do you need?"

"Look out your window. There should be two black SUVs outside with a bunch of black suits in them. I expect one is holding a door open for you right now. His name is Lynch."

"Holy shit, where are you taking me?" Robert panicked.

"Calm down, Robert. They are taking you to a classified room at the Houston Space Center. I'll meet you there with a lady named Patty and a man named Li. We'll hook you up with Jimmy and a man named Blake who is on a separate space mission. All of this will remain top secret, classified."

"Really? That's way cool! But, I can't … I have testing this week that I can't miss; can we do it next week?"

"Robert, lives are at stake, including Jimmy's. You let me know who the professors are and we'll take care of it. I need you to get your laptop and get in the car with Mr. Lynch. He will also explain the secrecy expectations to you for this assignment. Who are the professors?"

Robert was speechless for 20 seconds.

"Robert?"

"Holy cow, is this really happening? What do I tell my family?"

"Tell them your Mars project has gotten a special request from the White House and that you will be staying at the Houston Space Center for the next couple of weeks. You will be able to talk to them, but you won't be able to share any details with them."

"Okay. That should work. Let me get my stuff; I'll be outside in two minutes. How do I know this Mr. Lynch is real?"

"If you really need to, call the White House phone that is listed for the public. Ask for Brad Watters …"

"The NSA director?"

"Yes. I'm surprised you know who that is, but you are correct. Ask him if he ordered Mr. Lynch to pick you up. I need to go now, Robert; see you in Houston. Don't forget to tell him your professors' names."

Robert hung up and looked at his cell phone in utter disbelief.

"Okay, Mr. Harry, let's see if this is real." Robert Googled the White House reception line and called it.

"White House, who may I connect you with?"

"Umm, Mr. Brad Watters."

"May I ask who is calling?"

"Yes ma'am, Robert Stern." He tried to sound as formal as he could.

"Oh, Mr. Watters has been waiting for you. I'll connect you right away."

Robert nearly jumped out of his chair.

"NSA Director Watters here. Hello Robert … Robert?"

"Yes, sorry, sir, just thought this might be a prank. You know, I am in college after all."

"Yes, you are, but this is not a prank. This comes straight from President Callahan. Are you in and ready to help your friends, and your country?"

"Absolutely! Yes, one thousand times!" Robert stammered into the phone.

"Thank you, Robert. Please get into the car with Mr. Lynch. He will answer additional questions for you, but first I need to talk to your professors for you; is that correct?"

"Ummm, yes. Thank you, sir. Their names are—"

"Let me see, I think I already have them right here in front of me … Prof. Espinoza for English. Prof. Lu for physics, Prof. Lewis for advanced algorithms and Adjunct Prof. Hardy for software development. Is that correct?"

"Dang! … How did you … Never mind. Yes, you have them correct. Thank you, sir. Will I be in trouble?"

"No, quite the opposite. We will give each of them the full government show, in person. We will also visit the dean and the school president. I will guarantee their support; you can trust me on that one. Thank you, and welcome to the team. As you can imagine, I have many other tasks at hand that require my attention right now. I hope you are as good as Harry says you are." With that, the NSA director hung up, leaving a stunned, but excited 20-year-old college student rushing to throw things into his backpack.

Robert would have paid anything to see the faces of his professors. He imagined a number of black-suited guys walking up to them in class, flipping open their badges and having a quick conversation with them. He loved it. He wished he had asked Director Watters to make sure they gave Prof. Espinoza a little extra grief. After all, that guy was a royal, arrogant, pain in the ass – a real Yertle. He needed to be put in his place.

*****

On Board the Armstrong I

"Juulys, are you there?"

"I'm here, Blake. Anything new?"

"Yes. I have some photographs for you to look at. Do you need anyone else to see these?"

"That is good news. Yes, I'll call you back in five minutes. I need to get Cryells, Allympht and Jarns first."

Five minutes seemed like an eternity. The console buzzed, acknowledging an incoming call.

"Juulys?"

"Yes, and I have Cryells, Allympht, Jarns and Thjars with me."

"Good. Can you see my screen through the video transfer?"

"Clearly. Let's see what you have."

Blake began pulling up the photographs he received from Jimmy, via Harry.

"Stop. Go back one. Yes, that one. That is the operational interface for the unit. That is how our technicians manually program it if they are lacking a wireless hookup."

"That is what Jimmy referred to as a keyboard in our world."

"Understood, then keyboard it is. Cryells, your turn." Juulys turned and faced Cryells. "I'll translate for you as you speak." Cryells began speaking, and Juulys translated for him.

"There are two ways to activate the drives. The normal path is for the ship's captain to enter his password. The backup path is for another Cjarian vehicle to send a code that enables and then activates the drive. In this manner, all Cjarian ships are protected."

"But what if that code got into the wrong hands? Wouldn't that be catastrophic to all your ships?"

"Yes, Blake, it would. That is why every ship has its own code system and it changes with time. It is one of the most highly protected codes in our world, and all ships are synchronized with it. It requires the first ship to initiate the request and then a second ship, any ship, must respond with the appropriate code response. If the code matches the planned sequence, then the drives are re-engaged. It's a pretty complex system, but it also occurs within the ship's computer system, so from our perspective, it's almost invisible and automatic."

"So, if you sent out a signal already, and that was adequate to initiate the C-Pod's response, why hasn't it answered yet?"

"That's the question we don't understand, either. Allympht thinks it may be due to damaged circuitry on the C-Pod that is associated with wireless communication. But as long as the operational interface … ahh, I mean *keyboard* is functional, then a person should be able to enable it from that end – if they can figure out the access code to the C-Pod."

"Wait, why would it be easier to crack the code on the C-Pod rather than your ship? Seems like if one is possible, then both would be, yes?"

"Good question. The biggest difference is one that we forgot about for many weeks. Not only does our ship require the captain's password, but it also requires an eye scan from either the captain or the first officer to ensure proper access, both of whom are long dead. Unfortunately, there is no way to simulate Capt. Blissiart's eye, nor is his … are his remains able to do so." Cryells looked down, away from the camera for a second and then continued. "The C-Pod, being unmanned, does not require an eye scan, only the password."

"I understand. Juulys, please pass on my respects to Cryells and the rest of your crew. From what you have shared, I think I would have really enjoyed meeting your captain."

"Yes, I think you would have; you both seem to have been made from the same mold," Juulys said with a smile.

"I hope you are correct, Juulys." Blake smiled back. "So, what are we to do now?"

"You suggested that you might have people who are good at cracking codes. Allympht is as well, but we need someone on site to actually push the keys. There are 36 keys, so there are many different combinations of characters that could be used, but we can rule out the top row of six keys as they are not used for codes. That leaves us with 30 keys."

"Okay, I understand. Let me get this off to Harry and he will work with Patty and the rest of the team to see what they can do. Unfortunately, it will take hours to get the response to them, as well as an equal or longer time for them to respond."

Qulys smiled. "We thought about that, Blake, and we may be able to reduce that time significantly."

"Really? How?"

"We can launch an additional C-Pod that can transmit a message while it flies by your other ship to avoid unnecessary delays due to deceleration. The C-Pod can then swing through a wide arc, returning by the ship to pick up messages and return to us in less than two total hours from when it left. We can program it to be there in approximately 45 minutes."

"Forty-five minutes? But that can't be done …. that would be …"

"Yes Blake, faster than light. The irony is that our C-Pods can be sent at faster than the speed of light, but our ship can't travel that fast until it has re-engaged its Q-PAMS drive."

"Mind blowing … absolutely mind blowing. Harry will go nuts when he hears this." Blake looked over at Jack, who held his hands up in the air and shrugged in an expression of "don't look at me; this is way over my head."

"How quickly can you have a message ready, Blake?"

"Sorry, I'm still struggling to absorb this. I honestly never anticipated faster-than-light travel … In our world, that is considered impossible and just a fantasy for people to write books about."

"It was in our world once upon a time long ago as well, if that helps."

"No, but thank you just the same; I just need to process it. I'll have the message ready in five minutes … no, make that 10 minutes just to be safe. I'll transmit as soon as it's ready. How long will it take the C-Pod to get ready?"

"It's ready to go now. Qulys thought it would be a good move to get it ready ahead of time based on what you had relayed to us yesterday."

"Please tell Qulys that I am definitely looking forward to working with him. I like the way he thinks." Blake smiled and gave the now mutually accepted thumbs-up sign to Juulys. "How long will Harry have to respond to the initial message?"

"The C-Pod will have to make a very long arc to get back to them at that speed, even considering high gravity turning radii. I would assume it will be approximately 30 minutes."

"Okay, as hard as it is to believe that, 30 minutes it is. We just have to hope they are ready and listening." Blake paused and then asked, "Juulys, wait a minute, why are we trying to crack the code on a C-Pod that is billions of kilometers away when we have one right here? Why can't we work on the C-Pod that you have ready to launch?"

"Yes, that does seem like a reasonable option, Blake, but unfortunately for us, the designers of these ships were very concerned about a stolen ship and what the Klaxx might be able to do with the information if the codes were compromised. For that reason, C-Pods were designed to only allow the capability to be enabled in two scenarios. The first is when their launch was associated with an emergency, like the Jarisst I must have had so long ago when it first came to rest in your star system. The second is when the C-Pod is programmed by the ship actually launching it. The later approach requires full ship access, which we clearly do not have. The end result is that we have no way to override that design feature and therefore no way to even begin attempting to crack the code, as the system that requires the code cannot be enabled."

"You have very complicated restrictions for your ships, and those restrictions are unfortunately working against us, but it is what it is, so we can only work the options that are presented to us, even if that option is billions of kilometers away. I hope you and Thjars have a backup plan in the works, Juulys, because the chance of this working, feels pretty small right now."

Blake immediately started typing.

> *"Harry, Patty, Li, Robert, Jimmy. Hold on to your seats. You should have just received a highly unexpected message from me. Jimmy, you may also have detected*

something different near your ship. It will return in 30 minutes to pick up your response. I'll explain later.

Jimmy, ignore the top six keys. The other 30 require a code that you'll have to decipher. Once the correct code is entered, the device, which is called a C-Pod, will send a message to the C-Pod's owner, which is the ship near the Armstrong I.

Harry will explain more.

Unfortunately, it will take us five hours to receive the C-Pod message once you crack the code, but you won't know it, so you'll have to keep trying until you hear otherwise from me.

Good luck. I believe this is our only remaining hope for both your ship, and both ships that are out by Pluto. Blake out.

"Juulys, it's done and I just hit transmit to your ship. It's in your hands now."

"Thank you, Blake. The C-Pod will launch in two of your minutes. If you are able to, the acceleration may be worth watching."

*****

A.D. 2029 (3312 C.A.E.); Jan. 22
St. Louis, Mo.

Another bomb had struck. This time it was a suicide bomber inside the emergency room of the Barnes-Jewish Hospital in St. Louis, Mo. Thirteen people were killed instantly, including two physicians, three nurses and eight patients. Another 59 were injured, many critically. The Barnes-Jewish emergency room was now useless and a makeshift field hospital was immediately set up in the main entrance of the hospital. All normal services were now shut down to focus on the victims of the latest bombing.

Although the bomber was actually unrelated to the current terrorist cell, and acted totally independently of them, he did so in support of the Muslim common cause he believed in. The terrorists were quick to take responsibility for it, knowing that the American people would easily believe it and further elevate panic levels. Their message went out to all major media outlets.

> *"Your time of acceptance continues to shrink, America. Your evil and corrupt Government needs to be overtaken and removed. If you will not do it, we will do it for you. The Mother of All Bombs, to use your own nicknames that you used on our people in Afghanistan, will be detonated in two days, on the 24th of January."*

The president received the latest word in the office and looked up at his NSA director.

"Good God, Brad, these people are truly insane – but unfortunately, also extremely smart and well prepared. This will drive the panic and protests to an even higher level. Make sure Gen. McMullen gets the message. We need to let our citizens know we are here to protect them, but if they insist on violence, they will be met by violence, quickly and harshly. Martial law is in effect and will be enforced. The people need to understand that we do not have time to investigate the difference between a terrorist and a protestor. Right now, protestors and terrorists are all the same; they are against the government of the United States and its people. Get me on TV in 10 minutes."

"Yes, sir. It will not be a well-received message by many, but I agree it needs to be sent and enforced."

*****

Three hours later
White House, Oval Office

"Breaking news just in. Twenty-two people have been killed in downtown San Francisco, and another 75 injured after the Army opened fire on rioters. The dead include two U.S. Army soldiers. A mass protest of more

than 500 people disobeyed President Callahan's call for martial law and rioted at police headquarters on 1251 Third Street in San Francisco. This is the third major clash this week involving protestors and sympathizers, each one more violent than its predecessor. As the Army moved in, one rioter opened fire, killing two soldiers and injuring five others. Soldiers immediately returned fire on the crowd, killing 20 and injuring at least 68 more before the crowd dispersed.

President Callahan has expressed deep concern over the loss of life, but has restated his policy of martial law, now including the use of deadly force as a deterrent to future rioters.

We urge everyone to stay in your homes and remain safe.

More updates will be provided as we get them. This is Charles McBrady reporting for ABC News, directly from downtown San Francisco."

President Callahan was in the Oval Office with Brad Watters and could only shake his head in despair as he listened to the broadcast.

"This is quickly getting out of control and uglier by the hour, exactly what the terrorists want. They are building pandemonium to a climax, and then when they detonate that damn nuke it will end any form of control we have remaining. We are already seeing localized gas shortages, grocery store closures and bank runs; I can only imagine what it will be like in two more days. Supply systems will fall apart, banks will run out of cash, grocery stores will be emptied. The risk of localized anarchy will be greater than at any time since the Civil War.

"Brad, this may well become the single most critical day in the history of the United States, minimizing even the days of the birth of this great nation. The nation will survive, but there will be great loss of life and wealth. The nation will never be the same again and the terrorists will have won a major victory. I pray that we can pick up the pieces and rebuild when it's finally over."

"I can't disagree, Mr. President, but we also need to start thinking about where to go before the bomb goes off, sir. All of the experts have identified Washington, D.C., or New York as their likeliest target. We need to get you out and to a safe bunker location."

"We've had this discussion already, Brad; I'm not leaving. I have to stand strong. What would the people of this nation think if I went into hiding while they remained at risk, unable to protect their families because of the martial law that I activated? No, I can't do it. I'll take my risks just like every other citizen is doing right now. They have to see us as remaining strong, Brad, no differently than a general standing with his soldiers at the front battle lines. Our country has a rich history of people who have stood for honor and courage during the worst crises of their times. No, I cannot run and hide, and I won't run and hide. There will be no more discussion on the topic Brad; it's a done deal."

*****

On Board the Reagan I

"What the hell was that?" Tom O'Dougherty looked over at Cmdr. Dutch Kline.

"What was what, Tom?"

"The stars to our portside just blurred for a second, then there was a flash of light and shortly after that, the message transit lights went on."

"You're tired, Tom; it's just your eyes playing tricks on you and telling you to get some sleep."

"No, Dutch, I'm sure it wasn't. I was just staring out at the Big Dipper and all of a sudden, the stars blurred, then there was a quick flash of light, and a second later everything looked normal. And then the message transit light went off."

"Well, what does it say?"

"Let me see …" Tom looked puzzled as he attempted to read the message.

"Well, what does it say, Tom?"

"I'm … I'm not sure. It's garbled, almost like it was … backwards …?" Tom spoke slowly. "Hang on for a minute, Dutch; let me see if I can save and flip the message to come out backwards."

"Backwards? That would be a pretty weak attempt to encrypt a message, wouldn't it?"

"I have a feeling that it wasn't meant to be encrypted, at least I don't understand why it would be … it looks like it is simply backwards."

A couple of minutes passed and suddenly Tom sat back in his chair. His face was aghast and his mouth wide open.

"Tom? You okay? You better not be having a stroke on me … Are you okay?" Dutch was now concerned that something had befallen another of his shrinking crew.

"Dutch, you gotta read this. It's from Blake. And my eyes are not playing tricks on me; it was backwards." He looked over at Dutch, his eyes pleading for him to come over to his terminal.

"What the …? That's not possible. It can't be …." Dutch was totally confused.

"Regardless of if it's true or not, it says we have 30 minutes to prep a response." Tom leaned over to the intercom system.

"Jimmy, get to the Control Deck immediately. I repeat, immediately."

Ninety-five seconds later, Jimmy arrived in the Control Deck, laboring from his full-out sprint.

"What the hell is up now, Tom?"

"Read this." Tom moved back from his terminal to allow Jimmy to read.

"Holy shit, Tom, is this for real?"

"As best as I can tell, yes. We now have 26 minutes to craft a reply until the C-Pod comes back around; start thinking, Jimmy. And this time I'm definitely watching those stars again."

Six minutes into his effort, Tom relayed that Harry had also gotten the message, two minutes after them, and then another two minutes to message the Reagan I.

"Harry said to finish your response first and call only after you have transmitted," Tom relayed.

Twenty-three minutes after he had arrived on the deck, Jimmy was done and hit transmit. Three minutes later, with all three men watching the constellation known officially as Ursa Major, but better known as the Big Dipper, they all saw the blur, as well as the subsequent flash of light.

"Holy shit is right, Tom; I saw it this time, too," Dutch said with open amazement.

"So did I, Tom," Jimmy quietly echoed while still gazing out the window. "Faster than the speed of light. God, I wish we had some of that action right now, but that might explain why the message came in backwards. They sent an analogue message while the vehicle was moving faster than the speed of light, so the end of the message got here first, and the beginning got here last."

"Say what, Jimmy?" Tom asked, dumbfounded.

"Okay, enough stargazing, gentlemen – technical explanations can come later. Jimmy, you need to call Harry, pronto," Dutch commanded.

Six minutes later, Harry was on the phone with Jimmy. The two men had come to agreement on where to place the hole in the ship. To maximize the ability to turn the ship, they needed to vent the air as near the rearward end of the ship as possible. The front end would have been preferred, but there was simply too much damage from the missile attack. They agreed to wait until later in the week to attempt the vent, but Harry wanted to make sure they did it soon enough to enable maximum change in position relative to their pass-by of Earth. Once agreement was reached, Harry spent most of the precious few minutes they had updating Jimmy on the C-Pod, the Armstrong I, the Jarisst I, and outlining a plan on how to crack a password on the C-Pod.

"Damn," Jimmy uttered.

"What does Harry need you to do?"

"There is a crap-ton going on that we don't know about – I mean a real crap-ton. But I'll update you all on that later. First, Harry wants me to get set up to put passwords into the device's keyboard – I mean the C-Pod."

"That sounds pretty simple; don't you just type it?"

"Not in this case."

"Okay, I'll bite; why not?"

"It's about permutations and combinations, Tom."

"There you go again; what the heck does that mean, Jimmy?"

"It's a calculation that tells you how many trials you would have to make to cover all options. For example, we have 30 characters. If the sequence has six characters, and the characters can be repeated and don't have to be in any special order, then there are ..." Jimmy typed feverishly on his LB, "over 1.623 million options. You and I can't react that quickly and our fingers would be worn out before we were even 10 percent through all the options. Furthermore, at 5 seconds per entry, which is really fast, that would still require over 90 days, working continuously 24/7 to enter every possible combination. We need to get that down significantly. If, for example, we were fortunate enough to have a three-character string without repeats, then there would only be approximately 24,000 options – that would still require 33 hours of continuous typing."

"Wow! That sounds like a nightmare. So, how are you going to do it?"

"Remember that FANUC R-2000iC robot I argued long and hard for?"

"Maybe …"

"Well, I expected to need it to do a lot of repair work with, so that's how I got it approved for the mission, but it will actually be a better fit for this. It's teachable, extremely reliable and fast, and if we keep the range of motion only above the keyboard, it will be even quicker. I just need to make a special robot fingertip so as not to damage the keys that we'll be touching millions of times. I also have an idea or two that will allow me to increase the typing sequences even more. Patty, Robert, Li and Harry are working the software right now and should have it ready to download by tomorrow morning; then we start typing."

"And how will we know when we're done?"

"When it turns on their ship's drives and they send us a return message. Even if they do it with the faster-than-light C-Pod again, it would still require hours before we know we had success."

"So, what did you ask Blake?" Dutch asked Jimmy.

"I really didn't have much to ask until after we start trying to break the code. I acknowledged getting the message and recommended that they resend the C-Pod tomorrow morning after I've had enough time to play around with it. I also let him know that I would be talking with Harry and his team. The only other questions I had was first to ask if there was an expected character string length for their codes, or if that was a variable, too. I also asked them how I can reduce the chance that one of our random strings doesn't shut the device down, or strings that cause other undesirable effects – they should know those as standard operating procedures. We'll program those out of our planned sequences."

"It took you 23 minutes to write that?" Tom asked exasperatedly.

"No, that was quick. Then I asked a ton of questions about their technology; wouldn't you?"

"You're a damn geek, Jimmy, but we love you just the same. Now get your ass down there and get to work!"

All three men laughed, and Jimmy left with Tom to go see their now favorite C-Pod.

Dutch suddenly realized that this was the first time they had laughed since the missile attack. He was still angry and hurt over the loss of John and Pat, but he knew that he needed to continue to keep the remaining crew focused on getting home – and this was helping.

*****

Houston Space Center

Patty, Harry, Li and Robert Stern were all huddled together in one small room. Patty was researching classified cryptanalyses algorithms used by the FBI and NSA, Harry was pencil-whipping something out on a stack of papers, and Robert and Li were typing away to set up the overall password-cracking software structure they would send to Jimmy. Their number one concern was to make sure it interfaced with the FANUC robot's software.

Robert was using Python software to write his codes because it was easy and fast to use; it also had tons of free libraries of useful pre-made software routines that you could download without having to re-create them.

Robert was modifying a subroutine that would receive Blake's list of keyboard sequences that they were not to use. He wanted to make sure he could integrate their independent responses as quickly and seamlessly as possible, so he set it up to receive Microsoft Excel files, as that was the software Blake was most comfortable using. His next programming task would be to find and modify a subroutine that would parse the Excel data through the Python application. Many experts argued that C/C++ was a better software package, as it was typically voted the number one software for robotic programming, but Robert was more familiar with Python and Python was definitely easier and quicker to use, so the tiebreaker went to speed. That would save him a lot of time – time that he drastically needed right now.

*****

It was late evening when it finally hit Harry.

"Patty, wake up."

Harry was shaking Patty. Both Patty and Robert had finally succumbed to the need for sleep and had asked Harry to wake them up in three hours. Harry was running fine on his fourth bottle of Mountain Dew. Li was still typing a way like a machine, trying to complete the overall interrogation structure.

"Wow, three hours already?"

"No, Patty, sorry, it's only been 45 minutes, but I just realized we're working on the wrong problem."

That woke Patty and Robert up quickly, and Li stopped typing. "How so, Harry?"

"I was reading through Jimmy's messages to make sure we didn't miss anything. Remember he asked us to double-check his calculations for the number of iterations we would have to type? Well, I had put it aside to concentrate on what I thought were more important issues. Long story short, I finally got to it 20 minutes ago. Jimmy's numbers are correct."

"That's good news, isn't it?" Robert asked sleepily.

"Yes, and no. It's good that he was correct, but it's also bad that he's correct."

"What … ?"

"The numbers are huge, easily over a million combinations. It could take Jimmy months to type everything in, even with the robot Jimmy is working with. We simply don't have that type of time available. Cmdr. Kline and the Reagan I may have that kind of time because their ship planned on a year-long trip. Blake and the Armstrong I were planning on a much shorter trip and could easily exhaust life support options before this is completed."

"What do we do now?" Patty asked.

"We need to get this down to less than 24 hours. There are two primary tasks we need to do. First, we get Jimmy on the line; we need to drop the robot. Remember how he had installed jumpers on all the keys? Well, I think we can use that to bypass the electro-mechanical key interface. We can use software to run electrical pulses way quicker and reduce cycle time by more than 50 percent easily, perhaps even as much as 75 percent. Robert can still use most of his software he created so far, but he'll need to interface it directly with the keyboard jumpers now, rather than the robot."

"That makes sense, Harry. What else?" Robert asked.

"Remember that routine you found, Patty, the one that used statistics on the probability of use for each number and letter and cheated the string selection based on the various probability distributions it set up for each character?"

"Yes, but we said it wouldn't apply here because the statistics were based on English," Patty replied.

"Correct, Patty, but if we can get the Cjarians to create a probability distribution for us, even if it's their best guess, then that could eliminate thousands of lower probability combinations on the first pass through. If we get lucky and hit it the first time through, we could achieve success in hours."

"Harry, that's an enormous observation. We need to send that to Blake ASAP, but it will take 10 hours to get there and back to us again, and that's before we even begin to start programming it."

Harry was smiling.

"Harry, I really don't see how you can find humor in that. There has to be a better way."

"There is." Harry kept smiling.

"Well what is it, Harry!"

"Remember that book 'The Hitchhiker's Guide to the Galaxy' by Douglas Adams?"

"Good grief, Harry, I don't know if I ever read it, but I think I recall hearing the name and laughing about it."

"Well, we are going to hitchhike there." Harry smiled broadly; he was obviously feeling good about whatever he had found – a true rarity for Harry's self-assessments.

"Okay, Harry, hit us with it because I'm just seeing blanks right now."

"The C-Pod from Blake and company is due to pass by the Reagan I in about 16 minutes on its second homeward-bound trip to the Cjarian ship. I've already drafted the message; all I have to do is hit send to Jimmy and he bounces it to the C-Pod. Blake will have the message in less than 45 minutes from now. Knowing Blake, he'll force a quick, low-fidelity analysis of the characters and have that C-Pod refueled and back past the Reagan I in another 60 minutes max. Total time elapsed less than 100 minutes. We'll be pumping codes within 30 minutes of that if Sir Robert here has his code ready. Anyone want to bet that we have an answer by lunch time tomorrow?"

"Good Lord, Harry, as much as I think I know you, you continue to absolutely amaze me. Let's get Jimmy on the horn now. Okay, why did the smile go away, Harry?"

"Don't get me wrong, Patty; it was one of those times where I actually felt good about my own work, but the truth is I should have thought about this when we first started talking. Net-net, one bad move and one good move, so I'm really at break even."

"Harry, break even in your world is still better than 99.9 percent of the rest of the world." Patty bent over and kissed Harry on the forehead. "Thank you, Harry; now call Jimmy."

One hundred and 19 seconds later, to the second, Cmdr. Kline answered.

"Reagan I here. Cmdr. Kline speaking."

Another two minutes passed before Harry could say, "Jimmy needs to read my email immediately. Over. Thank you."

CHAPTER 31

A.D. 2029 (3312 C.A.E.); Jan. 23
On Board the Reagan I

Jimmy read Harry's message after Cmdr. Kline woke him up. He, too, had succumbed to the need for sleep and was literally lying half over his FANUC robot, asleep.

"OMG, that is out of this world! Move out of the way, commander." Jimmy was nearly yelling at Cmdr. Kline as he half-pushed him to get to his computer console. He copied the message from Harry and pasted it into a new message to send to the C-Pod, hit transmit and then sat back in his chair, exhaling a significant volume of air in a sigh of relief and completion.

"Okay, can you get me up to speed now, Jimmy?"

"Oh, yeah, sorry, commander, I was pretty focused on getting that message out and had very little time to connect. Sorry about that shove."

"I'll let it go this time, but next time?" Dutch lifted his eyebrows and crossed his arms over his chest. Both men laughed. Jimmy explained Harry's revelation and the new game plan.

"Actually, that sounds pretty damn impressive; it should work."

"I agree, commander. I'm bummed that I won't be using the robot that I argued we needed so badly, but this puts us into action way quicker than what we had planned earlier."

*****

On Board the Armstrong I

"Harry has come through again."

"What's that, Blake?" Vladimir looked over at Jack and Blake. The three were in the Control Room.

"Let me get Juulys on the line first; then I can explain it to all four of you at the same time." Blake hit the speaker button so the others could hear and then transmitted to the Jarisst I.

"Juulys here."

"Juulys. Blake, Jack and Vladimir here. Harry just gave us a hot action to do. How quickly can Qulys refuel the C-Pod and send it back?"

"It really doesn't need refueling, so it's just a matter of reprogramming ... In an emergency, 30 minutes, otherwise, maybe one to two hours."

"Okay, tell him it's an emergency. And here is what I need you and the rest of your crew to do."

Blake spent the next five minutes explaining the probability problem with the various keyboard characters. No one had a clue of what the true answer was, so Blake simplified it and asked them to put each character in one of five different buckets: bucket one for the least expected use, bucket three for average expectations and bucket five for the most commonly used characters. Buckets two and four were to be used for anything that seemed like it might be in between the others. They completed the simplified task in five minutes and Blake quickly typed out the response.

"Jimmy: See attached picture of the keyboard – same as you sent earlier. As I can't pronounce the letters and you wouldn't know what I was saying anyway, let's use position. There are five rows of six characters each; we'll start on the bottom row and work our way from left to right, and then go upwards and repeat the process. Below are the probability buckets: 1 = low, 3

= average, 5 = high. 2 and 4 are for tiebreakers that were in between.

Row 5 (top):	*2, 3, 4, 2, 5, 1*
Row 4:	*3, 1, 1, 5, 5, 1*
Row 3 (middle):	*2, 4, 5, 1, 4, 2*
Row 2:	*2, 3, 2, 4, 5, 2*
Row 1 (bottom):	*1, 3, 3, 2, 5, 1*

Good luck – Blake out."

The message was loaded just in time for Qulys to start the launch protocol. Three minutes later, the C-Pod was on its third trip to the inner solar system.

*****

On Board the Reagan I

It had been 97 minutes since the C-Pod transmission Jimmy made. He was truly clock-watching now.

"Ding." The receive button lit up on the console.

Jimmy opened the message, read it quickly to ensure it was what they were waiting for and then hit forward to Harry at the Houston Space Center. He then went back to his C-Pod, as he was now referring to it, and started double-checking the jumper wires. Everything looked good.

Thirty-four minutes later, Jimmy received the code back on the Reagan I, loaded the algorithms and hit start. He also fired up a response for the second C-Pod to take back to Blake on its return trip.

> *"Good to go, Blake. Computer is loading and running sequences. Let us know when we get a hit. Thank you. Harry says hi. Jimmy out."*

He then sent a message to Harry.

"Harry, we are running live. Great work. Keep your fingers crossed. Jimmy out."

The computer was whirling away, and without the robot. Now it was just a matter of time. Jimmy knew that even if he did hit the right combo early, it would be hours before he knew anything had worked, so it seemed like a good time to get some sleep.

*****

Harry received the message at exactly 101 minutes from the start of their exercise.

"Not bad, Harry, but you're off by a whole 1 percent. We'd miss the Earth by over 50 billion kilometers if you were doing the return calculations."

"Thanks for the vote of confidence, Patty. I think that's a wrap, lady and gents; now, we wait."

*****

On Board the Armstrong I

Ten hours had passed since Blake received Jimmy's startup response, making it a little less than 11 hours since Jimmy had started. He had no way of knowing how long it would really take, but he was hoping that the probability matrix he had sent to Jimmy, coupled with Patty's algorithm, would have gotten a hit on the first pass with the highest probabilities. If it did, then they would have achieved success within the first six hours; add another five hours and he would have received a message by now.

"Well, it was a good shot, Jack. Damn it, I'd really hoped we'd get a quick win this time."

"It sure seems like we're due, Blake, but it is what it is. How long until the second run of options with the wider probabilities complete?"

"I'm not sure, but I'm guessing that will be longer, perhaps 15 hours, plus the five-hour transit time. That would be late tomorrow."

"That could be after the terrorist deadline, wouldn't it?"

"Yes, I think it would be," Blake replied. "I can only imagine how tough this must be on President Callahan and everyone else involved back home. The good news is that the last I heard, the NSA was claiming that the search activities had raised the confidence level to slightly greater than 95 percent that there's only one nuke. As long as those subs can approach undetected and hit quick, there's still a good chance we can stop the nuclear detonation."

*****

Two more hours passed. Blake decided to go exercise and work off some steam. He was 15 minutes into his workout when the intercom sounded.

"Blake to the Control Deck. All crew to the deck." Jack sounded like he was in a military drill.

Blake grabbed a towel and headed to the Control Deck. Shortly thereafter, all were gathered.

"Blake, we were waiting for you," added Ataullah.

"Do we have good news from Jimmy?"

"No, Blake, unfortunately not. This isn't about Jimmy. It's the terrorists."

"Now what?"

"Brad Watters, the NSA director, messaged me. One of our nuclear attack subs moved in closer in preparation for tomorrow's attack. We have no idea how they gained this technology, but the enemy must have had passive sonar sensors in the water that picked up the submarine as it approached. These subs are super quiet, so I expect some mechanical malfunction must have occurred. Regardless, the terrorist immediately called the White House and informed President Callahan that they were ready to detonate now. President Callahan had no other choice than to agree to their demands to publicly sever our ties with Israel in order to barter some additional time to begin withdrawing all troops, but it is clear that action is now under way. I don't know what else to say, Blake; it sounds like Callahan didn't have many options left."

"Why won't they attempt a nighttime HALO with SEALs? They could jump with infrared goggles and take these guys out while they're still in the air. I'd take that shot if I was there without a second thought."

"They discussed that exact option, Blake, but they were concerned that the terrorists are now on high alert. It was deemed too high of a risk that the HALO would be detected and the terrorists would detonate the bomb."

"Why don't the terrorists just detonate the bomb now and get it over with, especially now that they know we're on to them? It just doesn't make sense," Jack stated, his frustration building.

"They can, at any time, assuming all of this is true, but the terrorists don't want to give up on any of their goals and demands until they absolutely have to. Remember that they want us to denounce Israel, which we just did, but they also want us to pull back our forces from around the world – that goal hasn't been achieved yet. If they detonate now, they might lose the latter objective. If I was them, I would keep my finger on the button and wait as long as I could to maximize the chance of meeting all of my goals," Blake replied. "They really are in the driver's seat at the moment, but I still like the idea of a nighttime HALO op. Nighttime goggles would highlight everyone on the boat and our snipers could take them out while still descending on their chutes, above and below the decks."

Just then the incoming call alert popped up on Jack's screen.

"Jack, come here. It's the Jarisst I."

Everyone followed Blake over to Jack's pilot seat.

"Blake here."

"Blake, it's Juulys. Have you looked outside lately?"

"What? No, we were just reviewing an update from back home. Things are not good."

"What happened?"

Blake quickly reviewed the latest status, as well as what had occurred over the past two days.

"I'm sorry, Blake. That doesn't sound very good. Perhaps we can help."

"I don't know how, Juulys, but I appreciate the offer."

"I don't think you heard me just a minute ago. Blake, please go look out your portside window, now." The last word was stated as more of an order than a request.

Everyone in unison turned as Blake looked out the window. The Jarisst I was now within 200 meters of the Armstrong I.

"Oh my God ... Juulys, the drives are on? When?"

"About 10 minutes ago. We headed right over."

"This changes everything, Juulys. Is your offer to help still open?"

"We've all talked it over, Blake, and our answer is yes. It was, how-do-you-say-it, unanimous. We also believe you can still help us as well as only our sub-light speed drives are operational. The Q-PAMS drives that allow us to travel at greater than the speed of light need refueling. We are hopeful that Earth has the resources we need to refuel and then hopefully we can attempt to reconnect with our home planet."

"Sounds like a win-win, Juulys. Please thank all of your crew for us. Jack, send a message to Harry and Jimmy."

"Okay, what would you like me to say?"

"On second thought, hold that thought. I've got something I want to think through first. Juulys, can you hook up and tow the Armstrong I?"

"Yes, that is an option, but Thjars has another proposal."

"What is it?"

"Cjarian ships are all outfitted with magnetic beam tugs that allow us to move units around in space. Your ship obviously does not have the coupler design built into it, but Cryells has estimated that your ship has adequate metal content, so it should still work. If it does, we could actually magnetically tow you back to Earth's orbit."

"How long do you estimate the trip would take?"

"We estimate slightly under 12 hours; most of that time would be during acceleration and deceleration in order to ease acceleration forces on your crew as you don't possess the protective systems we have on board the Jarisst I. It might be longer if the acceleration forces are too high. We have other units that we call G-Cells that we could use if we transferred your crew to our ship, but we have no idea how they would impact your physiology, so we recommend not using that approach."

Blake was stunned. He couldn't utter a word for what seemed like 30 seconds.

"Blake? Are you still there?"

"Twelve hours?" he stammered back. "Juulys, it took us two months to get here," he added, still stunned.

"We understand, Blake. We would be traveling at a maximum of 0.9 times the speed of light once acceleration has been completed. The actual flight will only take six to seven hours. Even under those conditions, there are precautions we will have to take to protect your crew. We would like to attempt a tow to see if this option is available. May we try?"

"Yes." Blake began to regain his composure. "Give me 10 minutes to gather the crew and strap in."

Fifteen minutes later, with all six crewmembers strapped into their seats, Blake gave Juulys the go-ahead. The crew felt a very slight bump and then little thereafter.

"Juulys?" Blake asked, wondering what happened.

"All is working fine. Cryells is excited that his assessment was correct. We can easily couple with your ship and move – which is what we are doing right now. We can pull you and place you anywhere you want to go."

Blake's gaze bolted upwards from the control panel.

"Say that last part again, Juulys ..." Blake was thinking of something else.

"We can place the Armstrong I wherever you want it to be delivered to. That part?" she asked, wondering where Blake was going.

"That's it!" Blake shot out.

Jack looked at him as if he had lost his sanity. "Blake, you want to let the rest of us in on this?"

"Harry's message about the one nuke they found. They're pretty sure there is only one, but the terrorists are alert for any manmade responses that will cause them to instantly trigger the bomb."

"Keep going, I'm still not there yet ..."

"We can use the Armstrong I as a simulated meteor hit."

The room was silent.

Jack was still puzzled. "Why go through all that trouble when we can just light the yacht up with torpedoes or cruise missiles?"

"It's the message we deliver with it that will keep them from pushing the button. The terrorists are all self-proclaimed religious fanatics fighting in the name of Allah, or so they claim. I agree that their true intent can easily be debated. But, regardless of that point, this is an opportunity to deliver a counter-message to terrorist groups around the world. We put President Callahan on national and world news, every media path we can access. Have him request an hour of prayer across the world at 11:00 a.m. EST tomorrow. Shortly after that, we have ABC News, or some other major news network, broadcast that they have detected a meteor on line to impact the Earth. The latest estimates show Washington, D.C., to be in the crosshairs, but the entire East Coast will be impacted. The terrorists will claim that it is an act of God, that Allah has heard them. They will raise rifles around the world that their claims of the great Satan have been proven correct. Think about it; they won't be able to resist the urge. It will be totally intoxicating to their leaders. And once they commit to that claim, there is no backing away from it. We will use their own lies and claims against them.

"At the end of that hour, a streaking meteor, what we know to be the Armstrong I, falls across the sky toward the East Coast as predicted. They will see the fireball and believe it to be the hand of Allah coming to strike President Callahan dead. But it doesn't hit Washington, D.C.; instead, it takes out the yacht. At the speed it will be traveling, they'll never have time to react. I agree that it's complex, risky and a little hokey all at the same time, but if the media then lights up the airwaves with news of a meteor impact, and that by an act of God, it missed the U.S. and fell into the Atlantic Ocean, instead taking out the terrorists, how could the terrorists then claim additional continued attacks in the name of Allah, knowing that the meteor, a.k.a. Allah himself, just took out their nuke and saved the United States and President Callahan?"

"We would need to inform our major allies around the world of what we are doing because they will have satellite surveillance that might leak the true identity of the meteor, but notification would only be shared within their highest government levels. The U.S. would indeed look like it was saved by the hand of God. The question to consider is: could this approach possibly destabilize the terrorist cell activity around the world more than what our entire military could do? I think it could only help. Ataullah, think back to that conversation we had weeks ago over the backgammon game; this might be the solution we both thought didn't exist. Our military could definitely eliminate the bomb and the terrorists on the boat, but there is no scenario where the military could reduce the resolve of the terrorists to attack again. Rather, it would only galvanize them to try again. The meteor option might create enough doubt to rethink their plans in the U.S., as well as many other areas of the world. At a minimum, it might make their recruitment propaganda a little bit harder to sell, knowing that they're actuality fighting *against* the hand of God, which they claim to be their justification for jihad in the first place."

"It's an interesting idea, Blake," Jack interjected, "but it feels like a pretty tough target to hit and I'm not sure I'm comfortable with what could be viewed as a fake prayer setup. I would think that would be an issue for you as well, yes?" Jack asked seriously.

"Yes, it is tough to do, but have we not done this on every space vehicle that we have ever recovered? We aimed it at a target zone. The only difference is that the re-entry vehicles were built to survive re-entry and not burn up. The Armstrong I was not built to re-enter the atmosphere, and it has plenty of mass and fuel to burn long and bright. It's also big enough that re-entry should not totally consume it. This is doable. The debris field will be huge and should easily cover any minor errors in impact location that might occur. We will also keep the USS Virginia attack sub in attack mode to ensure destruction – in as stealthy a mode as the Navy can muster. Near the time of impact, everyone, including the terrorists will be looking upwards. They won't be paying any attention to underwater reconnaissance efforts. No one will know that the yacht was destroyed by torpedoes if a meteor impact has been validated. As to your other question, Jack, relative to prayer or religious fidelity, is it not legitimate to pray for the protection of the U.S. and for our attack to be successful?"

"I like the idea, and your prayer clarification helped as well, but from an attack perspective, I like it even more with the USS Virginia joining the attack – but their timing has to be perfect. If the torpedo explosions are too early or too late, the watching world may pick up on the disconnected explosions. And let's also make sure they're far enough out of the probable impact area that we don't take a submarine out as well. Uncle Sam may not look too favorably on that outcome," Jack added and then continued. "What about having the Jarisst I blow it out of the water? I'm sure they have something powerful enough, and adequately non-earthy they could use?"

"Jack, I really don't want the relationship between Earth and Cjar to start with an attack. Towing to our selected drop point is one thing, directly attacking is another."

"Fair point, Blake."

"I'll have Harry and NASA run an estimate to see what they think before we get to Earth. If it looks bad, we can stay with the USS Virginia option. Juulys, when can we get started?"

"We already did, Blake. At a very high level, from what you have shared with us, it appears that your physiology is not terribly different than ours. To protect you during flight, we will need you and your crew to get into your chairs and tilt them back into horizontal mode, feet forward, to minimize the impact of the acceleration rates. We are using our G-suits and specially designed chairs to do likewise."

"Okay, Juulys, give me 10 minutes to send off a message to my team on Earth and we'll be good to go, but I do have one more request."

"What's that?"

"Can we stop by the Reagan I first? We will transfer to their ship, so that you can deliver the Armstrong I to the terrorists and then return to tow the damaged Reagan I back to our Space Dock, where everyone can be rescued. At that point, it will be up to you to stay or leave, but I will feel better that you aren't stuck with our crew or have concerns relative to your safety with us on board your ship."

"That is very admirable of you, Blake, and I commend you for that offer. Thank you, sincerely. We have not decided what we will do yet, or when we will do anymore beyond delivering you and the two ships as we just discussed. That might mean that your Harry will be very disappointed to see us depart without an opportunity for him to learn more."

"Yes, you are correct, but it will be my call, and I believe this to be the best call for all involved. I need five more minutes, Juulys. I need to send one last message to Harry before we depart."

A minute later, Blake was back.

"Time to roll; we're ready, Juulys."

CHAPTER 32

A.D. 2029 (3312 C.A.E.); Jan. 23
Tipp City, Ohio

It had been a couple of days and no one had entered or left the barn. Diego assumed that the occupants must be holed up for the final days of the looming attack in order to minimize their risk of being uncovered. What plans they had ready to deploy in an effort to further destabilize the U.S after the explosion were unknown at this time, but Diego was confident it was part of their grander plan. Their current location was perfect for it. The major crossing of I-70 and I-75 was further enhanced by the fact it was far from the planned destruction on the East Coast and nowhere near a major city, as the U.S. might suspect.

"What have the sound boys come up with so far?" Diego asked.

"They have some pretty sophisticated jamming software inside the barn, which is adequate to say they are bad guys. Hard to tell if they're drug lords or our bomb team, but the fact that our Chicago video hit man came here is enough to answer the mail in my book," replied Mark Moore, the local NSA agent.

"Amen. So, when do we hit? Any word yet?" Diego replied.

"Soon. I've been told to give you and your SEAL team the green light tonight."

"What's the play?"

"The SEALs already had it laid out. You, Sean and I will take the front of the building. One team of SEALs will come through Mill Creek up to the back of the barn and the second team of

SEALs will parachute onto the roof to blow a hole in it and drop in simultaneously. We'll kill the power to the entire neighborhood one hour before the hit."

"Why one hour before, why not simultaneously?"

"We want to take them by surprise. When the power goes off, we expect they'll grab guns immediately and be prepared for an attack. This way, when nothing happens, they will hopefully let their guard down. When they go outside to check it out, they'll see that power is out as far as they can see and will assume it's a widespread power outage that has nothing to do with them. We'll even send out a radio news alert to back it up."

"Okay, then what?"

"They have a lot of computer power in there that they will want to keep on line, and it might all be at risk as it's getting colder; it's already 22 degrees outside and dropping fast. We expect they must have a generator in the small shed behind the barn. Once they decide all is safe, they'll send someone out to fire up the generator. During the time between power out and generator startup, our sound boys will be free to listen in on their discussions. That will give us a head count as well as inside information."

"Damn, I like it," Diego responded.

"How about we drive up in a utility truck, like we're here to help?" Sean chimed in with an evil grin.

"Actually, that's not a bad idea as it provides some decent cover as well," Mark responded. "I'll get that arranged. I expect at least one occupant will likely come out to greet us, the more the merrier."

"And he or they won't be standing long," Diego stated coldly.

*****

Houston Space Center

Harry had just completed reading Blake's message. He had to read it three times to make sure he had it right.

> *"Harry. Tell President Callahan we will be there by noon tomorrow. See attached plan for my proposal details. Hoping I will have a chance to introduce you to my new friends. Blake."*

Harry continued staring at the monitor … "Tomorrow? At noon? That's today … six hours from now?" he said aloud to an empty room. "Blake, what in God's name did you figure out?" A big smile crossed his face as he realized that they must have successfully cracked the code and re-engaged the drives. Harry locked the screen, pushed back the chair and decided it was time to relay a message. A message from over 5 billion kilometers away, to President Callahan himself. It was going to be an interesting day. That, Harry was confident, was a fact. After that, he would get to figuring out the re-entry data Blake requested.

*****

Aboard the Reagan I

"Cmdr. Kline?"

"Yes, Kline here."

"This is Blake on the Armstrong I. Our ship is beyond repair and we will need to ditch."

"I'm sorry to hear that, Blake; how long will the crew be able to survive in the rescue module?"

"I don't think that will matter much, commander, so let us pass on that discussion for now. What shape is your vessel in?"

"Ours isn't much better, Blake, but we're moving, and with Harry's help, we are getting ready to attempt a major vent that should push us back in proper trajectory to reach Earth."

"That's good news, but I'm recommending you hold on that action, Dutch."

"Hold? What? What the hell are you talking about?"

"Requesting permission to scuttle the Armstrong I and come aboard. Are you in position to take on survivors?"

"Maj. Thompson … are you okay? I don't find this humorous at all."

"Commander, the truth is, I've brought help with me. Jimmy was successful; you can tell him to turn off the code breaker. We are moving alongside you now. It's going to take a bit to explain this, but let me give you the nutshell version first. After that, we'll need to transfer over to your ship until our new friends can return later today and tow us all home."

*****

The Barn

It was 1 a.m. local time. As predicted, the occupants of the barn had turned on the generator in the shed behind the barn about 30 minutes after power went out. During that 30-minute window, the NSA sound boys had been able to validate at least 11 different voices. They were also able to cleanly tie them to the terrorist cell based on the comments they had made. This was, indeed, their safe house, or one of their safe houses, for the operations they had initiated around the country. NSA's best guess was that they had travelled singularly or in pairs to establish their drop points, stayed there until the drop was completed, killed their unwitting delivery personnel and then returned to this barn to detonate the bombs remotely when directed, and then wait for the final attack.

The first SEAL team was in position in the creek behind the barn. The second SEAL team had just left WPAFB in a modified MC-130E/H Combat Talon II. The quartet of Diego, Sean, Mark and one other SEAL sharpshooter named Richie, were in a Dayton Power and Light truck parked at the now familiar intersection of

Dog Leg and Old Springfield Roads. All three groups were armed to the teeth, and outfitted with night vision goggles. Mark would approach the barn in a Dayton Power and Light uniform, without any visible military gear. A dangerous position to be in, but he knew that the other three would be alongside the truck and had his back. They would leave the headlights on and aimed at the barn to help mask their positions in the darkness behind the truck.

All three teams heard the call sign simultaneously, once the plane was in position. "Restore power is a go."

The SEAL team on the MC-130E/H parachuted out into the cold, dark sky. Mark engaged the truck's drive and started up Dog Leg Road. The SEAL team in Mill Creek crawled forward and took position on the ground at the edge of the hedgerow. The group carried multiple grenade launchers to punch holes in the back of the barn for rapid-entry points and to take out the generator. The airborne team was similarly outfitted to punch entry holes into the roof that they could shoot through and then rappel down through. Although computer recovery was a secondary objective, the primary and foremost objective was the quick elimination of all the terrorists. To ensure safety between the various teams during the chaos while they would all be converging on the same target, each member was outfitted with green infrared identifiers located on each helmet, backpack and shoes. Without night detection goggles, the signals were invisible. But with night goggles on, the various IR arrays created a kaleidoscope of bright green signatures throughout the attack zone. Anyone without such an array was by definition a target. Mark's Dayton Power and Light helmet had been similarly modified to ensure his safety.

Sean pulled the truck into the driveway and drove up to within 50 feet of the front door. Leaving the engine running and the lights on, Sean stayed in the driver's seat with the window down while Mark slowly stepped out of the passenger door, blowing on his hands and pulling his coat collar tighter around his neck as he walked into the well-lit area illuminated from the truck's headlights. He knew they would be watching and he wanted to ratchet down their concerns as best he could. He approached the door while Diego quietly climbed down the back of the truck to cover Mark from the side. Richie stayed on top, prone, with his M24E2 Enhanced Sniper rifle aimed directly at the door. Sean was prepared to barrel through the side of the barn with the big utility truck as soon as shooting erupted, further adding to the chaos of the moment.

Without looking up, they all knew the airborne SEAL team was within seconds of landing on the barn. At that moment, the door opened and a flashlight blinded Mark.

"Who are you?" the man called from the door, concern heavy in his voice.

"I'm from Dayton Power and Light," Mark stated calmly while pointing back to the truck that was masked by the bright headlights. "We're trying to find out what happened. What time did your power go out?"

The man walked farther out to see the truck. It was indeed a utility truck and he began to relax a little. Then something caught his eye.

"You said Dayton Power and Light. This is Tipp City and we are serviced by Tipp City Electric. Why are you here?" he added in an agitated voice.

Mark continued to act calmly, but Richie tightened the grip on his M24E2. "The power outage covers a very large area and all of the major utility companies have been called out to help, especially as cold as it is."

Suddenly, multiple explosions took place on top of the barn and then a flurry of explosions erupted behind the barn. Richie dropped the man with one clean shot through the head. Mark entered through the barn's door while Sean drove the massive utility truck through the main tractor entrance doors, with Diego right behind him. Diego immediately dropped the first two men who appeared in the dust and debris of the smashed barn door. Both were holding shotguns, but neither moved quick enough to fire a single shot. The first went down with a bullet in his forehead and the second took three consecutive shots to his chest, all of which could be covered by a three-by-five card.

It was a shooting gallery, except that all of the shots came from the attackers. The occupants, actually numbering 15, never had a chance. The chaos created by the multiple explosions on the roof and the rear door, coupled with the near simultaneous disintegration of the tractor doors, caught the terrorists by surprise. From that point on, the ground troops coupled to provide a massive cover barrage of gunfire while the SEAL team on the roof methodically eliminated anyone still standing. The battle was an array of dancing green infrared identifiers intermixed with the red beams of the SEAL's laser locaters. It was over in fewer than 90 seconds. None of the attacking forces were even injured, and 15 terrorists lay dead in the gunsmoke-filled ruins.

After placing one phone call, scores of police vehicles converged on the scene to ensure all was cordoned off. Within 10 minutes, power was magically restored to the area.

Mark called the success into NSA headquarters so that the news could be relayed to President Callahan as quickly as possible. At that specific moment, there was no way they could guarantee that there weren't other safe houses in the country, but they knew this one was out of commission for sure. The NSA team set up jamming devices around the barn to reduce the chance that a remote terrorist could detonate the barn, and the computer collection process began in earnest. The jamming would surely mess up local TV service for a while, but if that was the only price the neighbors had to pay for freedom, so be it.

A number of computers had taken direct hits to the monitors and cases, but overall, it looked like a major trove of information would be realized from the raid that would, at the least, help determine if there were, or were not, other safe houses in the U.S.

Diego looked over at his longtime friend, put his arm around his shoulder and smiled.

"For a while there, Sean, it was beginning to feel like no one needed us anymore, but it sure feels good to bury a few more bad guys again, doesn't it, buddy?"

"It sure does, Diego; it sure does. How about we get word to Harry and Blake?"

"Amen, brother, let's go." They both traded their thanks with the SEAL teams and Mark, and then headed out. It was a safe assumption that the NSA, with the help of the two SEAL teams, had this site fully under Uncle Sam's control.

*****

A.D. 2029 (3312 C.A.E.); Jan. 24
The White House

The Oval Office was full of staff, reporters and cameras. Only a handful of people around the world truly knew what was about to happen, and all had taken an oath of secrecy that would last their lifetimes. It was also notable that the major media companies were not among that select few. However, most of them had been given special seating invitations to the president's speech and were now squeezed into the relatively small Oval Office.

President Callahan carried the ball perfectly, just as Blake had scripted. As it turned out, the biggest concern President Callahan had was that he not incite mass pandemonium and cause people to try to escape Washington, D.C. He was able to defuse the expectation that Washington, D.C., was in the target crosshairs by addressing the entire East Coast as the highest risk areas. Everyone was told to stay indoors and underground in basements, where they were available. It was emphasized that taking your risks in your own house greatly increased the odds of survival as compared to being caught in the open or in an attempt to drive away.

The world waited together as one, as it had not since the Apollo 13 days, praying as President Callahan requested, waiting to know the outcome. At precisely noon EST, as predicted, the sky lit up as the biggest fireball seen in decades descended toward the East Coast.

Harry had been successful in recommending the exact point of atmospheric entry. He had also made the recommendation to advise the Jarisst I to release the Armstrong I at a high rate of speed to ensure it looked like the meteor it was claimed to be. There would be no slow entry for this spaceship-turned-meteor. Meteors were known to enter the atmosphere at speeds as great as 70 kilometers per second, or 250,000 kilometers per hour, so Harry had the Jarisst I release the Armstrong I into Earth's atmosphere at a staggering 280,000 kilometers per hour; a previously unimaginable speed from Earthly perspectives, but a walk in the park for the Jarisst I.

The terrorists on board the Manchester United were being monitored from space by a military satellite and the president could clearly see the terrorists celebrating and firing their rifles into the air as the fireball became visible to the naked eye. It helped that every news station in the free world was carrying the video that the terrorists could follow as well. Five minutes later, the satellite video was drowned out by the spectacular fireball that plunged directly into the Atlantic Ocean, impacting within 50 meters of the Manchester United. At precisely the same time, a salvo of no fewer than 12 Mark 48 torpedoes found their target on the Manchester United. The resultant explosions only made the appearance of the fireball's impact look more realistic.

The satellite-based cameras left the impact scene and returned to show a relieved, calm and thankful president. President Callahan had maintained this demeanor in front of the cameras throughout the entire ordeal, and he continued, projecting confidence, empathy and hope. He told both the American people and the world that God had, indeed, spoken. America had survived again to continue to lead the free world, and the terrorist threat had been extinguished by none other than God's own hand. He thanked the world for their prayers and asked all in the U.S. to help stabilize the chaos of the past few weeks.

As all great presidents had done for generations before President Callahan, rather than trample on the enemy, he offered his hand in strength, but also in peace and friendship to the Muslim world, with the single request that they jointly work to eliminate the radical arm of extremism that had for so long plagued and devalued their faith. He completed his broadcast by stating,

"God bless America and God bless our friends around the globe. And may we be further blessed to enter a new era of peace around the world."

*****

EPILOGUE

Thirty minutes after the Jarisst I had delivered the Armstrong I to the terrorists onboard the Manchester United, they were again back alongside the Reagan I. Due to the extensive damage the ship received to its hull, Dutch was not confident about its ability to withstand high acceleration or deceleration rates. Blake had recommended they take a slower path home than the Armstrong I had taken. It would lengthen the return trip to Earth from fewer than two hours, to a full day, but as Jimmy pointed out, would still get them home months ahead of schedule!

One day later, on Jan. 25, 2029, the Reagan I was brought alongside the U.S. space dock. Only then could Dutch's crew see the full extent of the damage to the Reagan I. How the ship had maintained life support for the remaining four astronauts was a miracle in itself. Jimmy, forever the entertainer of the group, had recommended that they re-commission the ship as the USS Demolition Derby.

As both the Reagan I and the Armstrong I had returned home months earlier than expected, the number of personnel currently on the space dock was greatly reduced from the levels that existed just two months earlier when the Armstrong I had departed Earth's orbit. Those remaining were able to witness their return, accompanied and assisted by an alien spacecraft. All aboard had been briefed prior to the arrival of the two ships and educated on the fact that everything they saw or heard was now classified as "top-secret sensitive compartmentalized information," and were all sworn to secrecy.

Unfortunately, and sadly, the loss of four astronauts somewhat overshadowed the successful return of the two ships, as well as the proof of alien existence. Blake and Dutch had led the transfer procession of the two men from each of their ships as their remains were transferred from the Reagan I to the Space Dock. It had been a solemn moment, with all available personnel present to pay their respect, as the remains of the dead crewmembers were transferred to storage, one at a time. Dutch and Blake each provided last rites and a brief summary of who the men were, what they stood for, and the fact that once the activities of the past month became public, the men would be held in honor by the entire world.

President Callahan had called Blake while they were still being towed back to the Space Dock to thank him and congratulate all involved. He promised to come see them when they were safely back on terra firma. He shared that just before the Armstrong I was taking out the terrorists onboard the Manchester United, some of Blake's old SEAL Team Six friends had paid Gen. Shirazi a long overdue visit. Needless to say, the general would never be bothering anyone again. Although Blake would have preferred putting a bullet between the man's eyes himself, President Callahan had requested that he be taken alive so that they could extract whatever information they could. He added that once it was determined that Gen. Shirazi had no further use, he would be returned to Saudi Arabia for subsequent execution per Saudi law.

The long reach of righteousness did not stop there. The world had had enough of terrorism. Governments around the globe began to systematically shut down or attack known terrorist camps wherever they were suspected. Most world leaders clearly knew it could have been their country, and still could be next time – if a next time was allowed to occur. But there were still loose ends to tie up. Fortunately, the Saudi government had been able to identify Gen. Shirazi's contact within their own hierarchy: none other than the Saudi's own minister of the interior. He had been the principal organizer behind the planting of the bomb on the Armstrong I, the acquisition of the nuclear weapons, the financer of the jihad, and he alone had selected the actual targets within the United States – all set in motion once he found out about Ataullah's selection to the ultra-secret flight to the alien ship. Saudi's Prime Minister had allowed President Callahan and staff to watch by satellite feed as the traitor and perpetrator was arrested and subsequently executed. It did not stop there. As information was gathered, extracted and analyzed, arrests were made across many countries with ties to the cowardly and traitorous attacks, including Ataullah's own brother, Ahmed. Ataullah knew his brother would also be executed, but he had already dealt with that emotion when he had previously disowned him for his illegal activities and terrorist connections.

The only remaining terrorist link remained with Russia and the high-level mole who aided Domashev. Shortly after President Callahan's call, Vladimir received a call from the Prime Minister of Russia, Anton Titov. Domashev did, indeed, have a mole high in the Politburo; it had been the Minister of Foreign Affairs. Similar to the Saudis, the minister had been in the inner circle that knew about the selection of Vladimir to the ultra-secret mission, and he had secretly contacted Domashev to alert him of the plan. Domashev had known he had to beat the Armstrong I to the ship and quickly changed plans to ready for a launch. Subsequent investigations would prove that the Russian minister had clearly planned to topple the Russian government with the assistance of Gen. Domashev.

Titov then notified Vladimir that the role of the Minister of Foreign Affairs was open, as its predecessor was now deceased, and asked Vladimir if he was interested in the position. Titov had been surprised to hear Vladimir reply that he was most honored, but wanted time to contemplate his next move in life. Relative to the now cut-off base on the moon, Titov added that the remaining men on the lunar base were on their own until Russia decided it was time to return to the moon. They were clearly going nowhere.

Blake managed to set up a short video call with himself, President Callahan and both Juulys and Thjars while the latter two remained on their ship. It was a moment in history that none of the attendees would ever forget, but one that would remain a well-guarded secret for an indeterminate amount of time. President Callahan thanked the Cjarians for all they had done to help and promised to have the necessary fuel components delivered to them within the next two weeks. He asked if there was anything else he could do for them – water, food, and even assistance to identify where Cjar might be located – but the Cjarians said thank you, but no thank you; they were good for now. President Callahan asked what was next for them and if they planned on departing any time soon. Juulys replied that they truly wanted to find Cjar to see what the status of their home world was, but they also wanted to wait for a while before making any immediate decisions. They wanted to determine if it was still even safe to travel outside of this planetary system, as they had no idea how far the Klaxx had spread since departing the war. Juulys warned President Callahan that Earth needed to set up passive monitoring satellites at various points within its solar system to provide early notification of any impending visit from friendly, or unfriendly races from other planets, and that they should make this a top priority. Juulys added that they might stay nearby and tour the solar system for a couple of weeks while they tried to assess the constellations to better determine where they were in relation to Cjar. The president again offered that if desired, he had access to some excellent scientists and facilities that could assist their efforts. Juulys thanked him again and said they might just take him up on his offer, but not quite yet.

The two races agreed to electronically exchange language dossiers so that each could learn the other's ways of speaking. Blake had laughed and stated that he thought that was a one-way assignment based on how well Juulys already spoke English. They all joined the laughter when he added that Patty would be in heaven for a month or more with the newfound treasure, and he was confident the two ladies would be able to carry on a full conversation in Cjarian if and when they ever returned and met.

Before they signed off, Blake added his wishes and thanks one last time, then paused and added, "Juulys, I really hope you do stick around, or come back again. You never met Harry, but I can assure you that until he gets the chance to talk technical with you and your crew, he will be a royal pain in my butt, upset 24/7 over the fact that after everything he's done, we're all guilty of keeping him and his insatiable appetite to learn, locked outside in the cold."

Everyone laughed.

"Blake, I grant you approval to tell Harry that he will get his wish one day … perhaps sooner than you might think." Juulys gave Blake a thumbs-up sign, at which Blake smiled and immediately duplicated. With that, both parties signed off.

*****

Three days had passed and the crews from both ships, as well as Blake's earthbound team, were now all together back at the Johnston Atoll, enjoying its beautiful scenery and serenity. Earlier that day, Blake and Dutch had been requested to assemble everyone in the auditorium at 11:00 in the morning. The group assembled as requested and as the group sat and waited, the rear doors of the auditorium opened and to their surprise, in walked President Callahan. He spent two hours with the group, sharing personal stories, thanking them for their service to their countries and the world, as well as listening to each recount his or her experiences from the two journeys and the earthbound search as well.

Harry mentioned that there were only two gaps remaining, to which the president had asked, "And what would those be, Harry?"

"First off, we just lost an opportunity to accelerate our technology by centuries. The Cjarians are gone and we have nothing," he voiced with mocked despair.

"Blake? Would you enlighten my good friend Harry, please?" Blake shared what the Cjarians had stated prior to the end of their last transmission, including Juulys' thumbs-up sign. Harry grinned from ear to ear.

"What else do you have, Harry?"

Harry went on to question how they would explain that the two crews were back home, one without a ship, and that both crews were months ahead of schedule.

President Callahan looked slightly perplexed, but recovered quickly. He acknowledged that he would have to work on that solution, but as a minimum the group might be granted a fully paid vacation on this beautiful atoll for another couple of months until the timing was more appropriate to have them *publicly* arrive. That seemed to be received well by everyone in the room. Vladimir raised a glass of water and stated that it should be Russian vodka, but just the same: "За здоровье! Or in your language, 'Cheers to your health,' Mr. President."

Blake smiled as he and the crews joined Vladimir's toast to the president and each other.

When it was time to depart, the president shook the hands of each man and woman in the room, once again providing them with his personal gratitude, and that of the countries from where they came. President Callahan made sure to provide a very personal tie to what each man or woman had specifically contributed in his final words to them. As he was able to thank them each in their native tongues, it was clear that someone had done quite a job preparing the president for this meeting, but it was also quite evident how much the president truly cared and the sincerity of his words. He repeated his request to Harry relative to the president's science advisor offer, to which Jimmy had quickly and humorously answered that he was open for it if and when Harry turned it down.

Blake found the president to be a good man, and a great leader, one he would easily follow anywhere.

Last, but not least, the president stood in front of an over-awed Robert Stern, the college intern. He thanked him for his outstanding service, reminded him of his oath and welcomed him to the big leagues. He shook Robert's hand and turned to leave, but suddenly stopped. He stated that he had almost forgotten one thing. President Callahan reached into his inner suit jacket pocket and pulled out an envelope, handing it directly to Robert.

He repeated his thank you and departed. Robert had yet to utter a single word; he was literally speechless.

"Well, aren't you going to open it?" Harry asked.

"What is it?"

"Open it and see."

Robert opened the envelope and read the contents.

"How did he know?"

"Know what?" Blake replied. "Are you going to share it with us?"

Robert read the letter aloud. It was a copy of a personal letter from the president of the United States to the chancellor of the University of Houston. It was a request that Robert be given full credit for any classes he missed while in the classified service of President Callahan himself. He went on to exonerate Robert's use of the oscilloscope he had borrowed to support the effort and said that the White House would fully reimburse the university if needed. In addition, President Callahan's office would be contacting them shortly to ensure that every expense Robert had for the remainder of his college program would be covered fully by the United States government.

Awestruck, Robert could only mutter, "How could he have known?"

"We all knew how worried you were about that oscilloscope, so when the president asked me if there was anything he could do for me after I had attended my last Situation Room meeting, I thought a get-out-of-jail-free card for our favorite intern, straight from the president of the United States, seemed like an appropriate request. The fully paid scholarship was his idea. Robert, we all know that without your discovery that night when you discovered The Big Brag, none of this would have been possible. Furthermore, if you think about it, Robert, many of the people in this room would not have made it back to Earth if it wasn't for you."

Robert reflected on the last comment for a bit, his eyes wide as he surveyed the group, most of whom were smiling back at him.

"Wow ... I hadn't looked at it quite like that ... umm, thank you, Harry."

"You're most welcome Robert. We all thank *you*."

"What else did the president say?" Robert stammered.

"All he wanted was a picture of your face at the moment when you read his letter, which I took and texted to him already – and I'm sure he's enjoying it even more than we are."

The entire room broke into laughter.

<>

MAIN CHARACTERS

Adam G. Rimlinger: Cornell University professor in archaeological theory

Admiral Stjssjen ("Sties-sin"): Cjarian, leads the combined Cjarian fleet on board the Stojesst IV

Admiral Zach Taylor: Commandant of the Coast Guard

Ahmed: Ataullah's brother

Allympht Allsysst ("All-leem-fit Alls-ist"): Cjarian engineer on Jarisst I

Anatoly Domashev: Ex-Russian General from the moon

Andrew Callahan: U.S. President

Anton Titov: Russian Prime Minister

Ben Tellinino: National Security Council (NSC) Secretary

Brad Martinez: NSA Director

Captain Fyslyl ("Fiss-ll"): Cjarian captain of the Stojesst IV

Captain Zyles Blissiart ("Ziles Bliss-e-art"): Cjarian captain of the Jarisst I, creator of the Q-PAMS

Captain Zyles Blissiart ("Ziles Bliss-e-art"): Cjarian captain of the Jarisst I, creator of the Q-PAMS

Cindy Thompson: Blake's sister

Colonel Armeen Khorasani: Works for General Shirazi, U.S. spy

Colonel Ataullah El-Hashem: Saudi Arabian Air Force, Armstrong I

Colonel Bill Stevens: Pentagon

Commander Cel Rylsst ("Sell Rye-l-ist"): Cjarian commander of the Stojesst IV

Commander Doug "Hammer" Jones: USS Avenger Flight Commander

Commander Dutch Kline: Commander of the Reagan I

Commander Jack Pavlik: USAF Commander of the Armstrong I

Corporal Diego Velasquez: Member of Blake's SEAL team, 27 years old, USMC

Cryells Elysst ("Cry-lls E-lee-ist"): Cjarian engineer on Jarisst I

General Keith McGraw: head of the Top Secret Space Corps

General Landon McMullen: Army, Chairman of the Joint Chiefs of Staff

General Shirazi: Iranian general who plans the nuclear missile attack

George Stratton: Robert Stern's manager at NASA Houston, professsor

Glysst: The common Cjarian reference for the religious deity of Cjar (God)

Harold Bessimer: Middle Eastern spy in Hawaii

Jarns Blissiart ("Yarns Bliss-e-art"): Cjarian, Captain Blissiart's younger brother, military scientist, on Jarisst I

Jenysys Thalysst ("Jen-e-sis Thal-ist"): Cjarian medical officer on Jarisst I

Jim Morrati: Chicago man who unwittingly delivered the bomb to the Museum

Jimmy Decker: Engineer on Reagan I

Joe Dodd: Director of the Armstrong I design and build teams

Joe Welch: Young-looking NSA agent

John Tatum: JT. Young engineer who helps program the Mars Rover after NASA takes over

Jose Velasquez: Diego's younger brother

Juulys Lystnyng ("Jewels List-ning"): Cjarian linguist on Jarisst I

Kay: The agent in the Pentagon who offered Blake the mission position

Knarls Rjissist" ("Gnarls Rye-jist"): Cjarian Private First Class, reports to Qulys, 35

Leo Tjassist (Leo "T-ah-sist"): Invented Leo-1253 and Leo 5321 for the Q-PAMS fuel

Lieutenant Mentyss Pfssiast (Men-tiss phys-c-ast): Cjarian Lieutenant on the Jarisst I

Lieutenant Pat Skiles: mission specialist on Reagan I

Lieutenant Sean O'Rourke: Member of Blake's SEAL team, 33, Irish, Blake's primary pilot

Lieutenant Thjars Chjssiast ("Thars Chiss-e-ast"): Cjarian in charge of Jarisst after it awakens

Lieytenant Tom O'Dougherty: mission specialist on Reagan I

Major Blake Thompson: 41, leader of SEAL team, leader of Armstrong I team, from NYC and Cobleskill, father killed in 9-11

Major Bob Chase: Co-Pilot Reagan I

Major James Snyder: USMC, co-pilot of Armstrong I

Major Jie Gao: Armstrong I, China, missions specialist

Major John Martinez: on the Reagan I

Major Pat Sullivan: F-18 pilot that flew Blake from India to Germany

Major Vladmir Popov: Russian, Armstrong I crew

Mark Moore: Dayton local NSA agent.

Mike Phalen: NSA operative

Nylsst Volysstmyn (Ni-list Vole-ist-min"): Cjarian technical specialist on Jarisst I

Oliver Wyatt: British MI6 organization, 31, Chemical Engineering

Patty Myers: Member of Blake's SEAL team, 31, linguist, cryptanalyst

Pete Sullivan: FBI Agent

Platsys Flysst ("Plate-sis Fyl-ist"): Cjarian technical specialist on Jarisst I

Qulys Plyenysst ("Que-Lis Ply-en-ist"): Cjarian sergeant-at-arms on the Jarisst 1, 125

Richie: SEAL sharpshooter

Robert Stern: Third year Aerospace Engineering student at the University of Houston, 21

Sarah: Unnamed NSA translator for the Middle East

Sir William Davies: Original UK member for the Armstrong I, withdrawn due to renal cancer

Specialist Harry Lundrum: Member of Blake's SEAL team, "Einstein"

Specialist Klaus Schneider: Armstrong I, astronomer from Germany

Specialist Li Zheng: Member of Blake's SEAL team, 26, Chinese-American computer expert, hacker

Specialist Rakesh Deshpande: Armstrong I computer specialist from India

Steni Qyissys ("Sten-E Q-ih-sys"): Created the Qyissys Rule

Tom Garrett: FBI Director

Zalmyt Wylmysst ("Zawl-m it Will-mist"): Cjarian technical specialist on Jarisst I

BLUNT FORCE MAGIC by LAWRENCE DAVIS

http://wbp.bz/bfma

Read A Sample Next

CHAPTER 1

The Deliverers' Deliverance

For a month and a half straight I'd been staring stupidly at this door.

Correction: for a month and a half straight I'd been staring at the green insignia carved *beside* the door with the same blank, dumbstruck face my father use to hate so much when I was a kid. Once a week I dropped a package from a fancy meal kit company on the welcome mat and just gawked. The symbol resonated with the life I used to live. It was an emblem of some kind, but who could say?

Most people imagined that when a ragtag group led by a hero was combing through tomes and scrolls, they usually happened upon whatever they were looking to find. In reality, that could take a *long* time. People and civilization were older than our concept of time, older than written language. Finding context for an archaic hieroglyph was tough work, I know; I used to be part of a merry band thumbing through those endless stacks of books. The search was maddening; you had to force-feed yourself so much information that you ended up brain-dumping half the lore you'd learned almost immediately after assimilating it once you were confident it wasn't what you were looking for.

Anyway.

For a month and a half straight I dropped the package down, stared, reflected, and usually just shrugged before leaving. It didn't just bother me because I couldn't place it; there was something about the insignia that didn't *fit*. Not my business anymore, though. I was an aging vagabond working a dead-end job because the benefits package was respectable and I could usually get through my entire day with only a few exchanged niceties as shallow as my faked smile.

Today wasn't any different, aside from the fact that I closed down the bar the night before and was suffering the consequences. At least it shouldn't have been. Package deposited, I gave myself the usual span of time to scrutinize the symbol. This time, I entertained the notion that it may have had some kind of localized Pagan origin. This area had an extensive and rich history, and, as I wasn't really an expert in it, maybe that was why it was such a mystery to me. I was about to return to my asinine, uneventful life, when I felt *it*.

When you've consorted with evil—and I'm not talking about a rambunctious frat boy or some hyper-aggressive meathead who's heavy-handed with a girlfriend, but actual evil: you feel it coming. It has a distinctive, suffocating presence. We all experience it differently, but the effect and impression are universal.

So, there I was, half a decade removed from a life I'd left behind, when everything went to absolute shit. Whatever the governing power behind timing was must have hated me. Once a week for a month and a half I'd spent no more than a minute on this doorstep. The disparity between the time spent there compared to the time spent everywhere else had to be astronomical, and yet there I was.

The hairs on my arms had just about fully risen when the door I was staring at exploded open. I was fast, but not supernaturally so. I'd spent more time in the thick of violence than I cared to admit or recall, and that alone saved me from getting a face-full of splintering wood. I spun out of the way just in time to see the guy who'd just wrecked his own door with a Spartan kick follow that up by leveling an old school, pump-action shotgun at the very quaint fence I'd just walked past to get here. There was a life-threatening fear in his old eyes, his hands shook as he aimed the barrel of the gun past me and toward the gate in his front yard. I turned to see what could possibly have driven so seemingly sane a man out of his mind.

That's when I saw it. That was when everything started to come together.

***

This isn't a world of make-believe, yet we still seek what we know to be impossible—from the wild extravagance seen in filmmaking to the outlandish lore built into any science-fiction series. It has a way of speaking to us, an escape from a reality that's grown stale or unforgiving. All of us have daydreamed about it, growing pensive while we wonder what it would be like to be surrounded by such wonder.

It's not everything you think it is. Walking in a winter wonderland is a cold, scathing trek.

Routine has a way of bastardizing normalcy which makes it seem so unremarkable that we strive for something completely outside of our understanding: fantasy.

The problem with fantasy is that we've largely relegated it to the *happily ever after* genre. It doesn't work that way, in real life. We're afraid of the dark because a cultivated sixth sense is warning us away from it. Our instincts were honed over countless centuries, a direct line to our subconscious protecting us from something. Man built fire not only for warmth, but to ward off the shadow that was eager to swallow us whole; it's why the Bible begins with the creation of light to divorce us from the darkness, that separation is foundational to our species. Over time we've lost that fear, the limelight of our neon paradise making us immune to it. You should know that there is an ugliness just beyond our understanding that if we invite it, if we consider it too long, if we happen upon it, will strike. It might flirt with us, all coy and suggestive, but like every arrogant predator, that's just it toying with a meal before devouring it whole.

I know, I'd been eaten alive. And here I was, in the middle of it again. They say the path to hell is paved with good intentions, and they couldn't be more right.

***

The shotgun thundered, the sound reverberated through my eardrum and it felt like half my head went numb. It snapped me back to the present. If you've never had the distinct pleasure of standing beside a powerful weapon when it's gone off, it wasn't everything Hollywood had made it out to be. It was deafeningly loud and incredibly angry.

The guy who'd just come out like a suburban Rambo had a mix of madness and betrayal in his stare; before he could fire again I slapped a hand beneath the barrel and directed it toward the porch roof. "Stop," I hissed with as much calmness as I could muster. "Get. Inside. Now." I was trying to stay calm even as adrenaline tore through me quick as a lightning strike.

The thing he had shot at was an abomination. Humanoid in shape, but warped by something insidious. Its fingers were spindled and long; halfway down each was a bloody opening where its claws started. Its knees were snapped backward like a bird and its legs ended with six-toed feet, gnarled and lethally clawed as well. Claws so sharp they cut back into its own body, leaving its hands and feet filthy with dried black blood. Literally rending the very flesh they sprouted from.

All of that didn't compare to its face. Night-black eyes glittered in sunken slits, the suffocating void in them a direct reflection of their indifference to dealing out so much death. An exaggerated mouth was not quite canine but in that cast, as if its maker couldn't decide what kind of monster this would be. The beast's teeth were several rows deep like the jaw of a shark, elongated, razor-sharp, and capable of biting clean through a person. Its arms were so long they nearly dragged those clawed fingers on the ground, which made it easier to sink down to all four limbs and prepare to pounce.

I had only ever read about this abomination, only seen estimations of its likeness inked on parchment, but it all came flooding back. It was an ancient enemy of mankind, a conjured creature with more names than I cared to cite. In most circles they called them Stalkers, as they were used to hunt down someone who was notoriously hard to find and even harder to capture or kill. Here's the breakdown: first, in order to bring one of those things to this reality, you had to be powerful—powerful enough to alter the future of mankind. The second part was that they were a perfect predator: fearless, nearly indestructible, and singular in their focus to obtain their prey. They tipped the scale somewhere between three and four hundred pounds, moved too fast to register with human eyesight, and they topped off at just beneath seven feet. We were desperately outmatched and wasting ammo was going to get us all killed.

I wasn't easing my grip on the gun, and the old man's shocked look turned into full-fledged panic. I'd had very little time to understand what was happening and less to react, and because this was just a banner day when the man started trying to hurriedly explain what was happening he was speaking in Spanish.

Perfect.

It wasn't all his fault. My complexion led a lot of people believe I was of Hispanic descent. I was short and stocky, five-seven if we're being honest, five-nine if it's a dating website. A fan of a good workout but also guilty of frequenting dive bars and burger joints so it wasn't like I was going to win any shirtless competitions. I had the everyday-guy thing going for me, though if the girl is desperate enough I think I passed as handsome in the right light. The confusion was caused by my jet-black hair and standard issue brown eyes that seemed to come stock to my tan skin and with that people assumed I was a card-carrying member of the Spanish-speaking community. I wasn't.

So, while he was yelling in Spanish, I had a major-league bad ass dropping to all fours—the telltale sign it was about to burst across the whole lawn and start ripping me to shreds—and five years of rust to contend with. You know, another Tuesday afternoon.

***

In the life before this one I was a budding Artificer. Now, the internet dictionary will tell you that's a skilled inventor or craftsmen. Beneath that there will be a description from Dungeons and Dragons. Don't believe me? Check it out, I'll wait. The idea was that I would become something between the two. The truth was that my mentor was an Artificer and I was a promising student who'd had all the right stuff to be one myself but couldn't quite put it together. That's how it is in this life. Hell, life in general—a quarterback with every tool and physical advantage who just can't step up in the big game, a wizard from the most esteemed family line unable to bring together the simplest spell. The optimist in me kept at it for as long as I could until the work I started to produce was actually becoming less helpful and more a liability, so eventually the pragmatist in me won out. Still, I had an ace or two up the old sleeve and a treasure trove of trinkets handed down to me when the old man, my mentor, was killed with the rest of our merry band of do-gooders.

It's like I said though, this life isn't an ideal escape into joyous adventure. This life also just had a way of finding you.

Even with the tragedy, hardship, and let-down that came with having to play second fiddle to the people I loved and respected most, I was never much of a quitter. If I was going to punch my ticket for that big ride in the sky, I would rather do it in the thick of a fight. Going gently into the night just wasn't my style.

***

A mix of adrenaline, youth, and momentum helped me wrest the shotgun clean out of what I assumed was the homeowner's grasp as I used my other hand to shove him back through the dangling door he'd just kicked almost clean off the hinges. I was trying to control the cadence of my breath and stifle the rise of fear, even with the incessant cries going on behind me. I could distinctly make out the old man and another voice. I had some modicum of success with gulping down the desire to run for my life. This creature was full of enough self-preservation to be wary when faced with someone who won't turn and run the second they laid eyes on it.

I imagined that this was what a gunslinger felt like when faced with an even bigger and badder opponent while being without a revolver to draw. This game was going to be based on a bluff, which was hard enough when my attention was undivided. Right now I was worried about whoever was yelling in the house, what this thing was doing here, and this nagging feeling about the pagan symbol next to the door. I fed the monster a smirk, playing my utter lack of hand with this all-in gambit for what it was worth.

That is when I heard it. *Maria.* That was the name the old man called the female voice inside. Apparently, the name got the mud-stuck wheels in my hungover head going because the symbol I had been wrestling with trying to figure suddenly leapt out at me. *The Morrigan.* The Irish goddess of witches and about everything else. That was what bothered me. The symbol guarding the door was wrong, which was a pretty common thing when trying to decipher an ancient text that was based off another, even older text and translated into a foreign language that hadn't even been invented yet. The stalemate on the lawn was ending fast, the beast was either growing too restless to give a damn about the fact I hadn't backed down or it simply had seen through my guise of worthy guardian. It gave a stilted sniff that drew in the still air between us for a taste. The action somehow came off as a kind of snide cackle to me.

There it was: the calm. The calm right before the storm.

Those powerful, twisted haunches flexed and both it and I exploded into motion. It crossed twenty feet with one incredible leap, bounding right for me. Me? I slapped the broken door as hard as I could, the familiar sensation of pain lanced through my hand and down my forearm. One of the fractured shards of wood cut into my hand producing an ugly cut that bled freely, but I didn't slow. Slowing down would get me killed. I turned to the symbol that I had stared at for a minute a week for six weeks and finally solved at least one mystery before an untimely death.

Dipping my free hand fingers into my cupped one where the blood from my laceration was pooling, I drew one last line above the circular singlet decoration just outside the door frame, crossing a lone line that rose from above the oval that the symbol was held inside of. That last bit was the missing piece to complete the circle of power. It didn't require blood or anything so dramatic, but I was out a pen (packages are signed for with a digital pen now) and it wasn't as if I had a lot of time to work with. Plus, with the language barrier between me and the owner of the house, it wasn't as if I could convey what I needed quickly enough. Still, blood has power in it too. Magic is a funny thing, anyway. Belief in something can empower it.

The Stalker was so close that I swear I could feel that *thing* breathing down my neck. It hit the invisible barrier like the force of nature it was, shaking the entire foundation of the house and sending a literal *whoosh* of air washing over me. I could smell its acrid breath and taste the sheer foulness of it. I was half in the door and half on the small porch when a very human urge came over me. Despite knowing better, I turned back around to get a real good look at this old, ancient evil. For a long time we took measure of one another. They say it's dangerous to stare into the abyss because it will eventually notice you. There was a cold intelligence in these wild eyes and I knew it had marked me, from the way it was glaring to the deep draw of breath that was thick with my scent. In a heartbeat I'd made mortal enemies with the most powerful thing I'd ever had the distinct displeasure of crossing.

And it wasn't even three o'clock yet.

http://wbp.bz/bfma

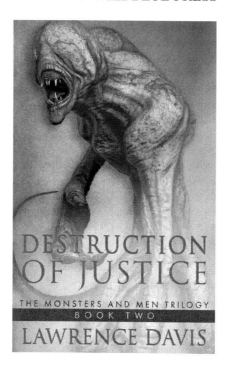
Janzen Robinson is no longer a man torn between two worlds, having decided to come off the bench and dive head first into Cleveland's magical underworld. With his new partner and perpetually exhausted friend Grove, he's just starting to get a handle on all the supernatural happenings when disaster shows up at their doorstep and doesn't even have the decency to knock.

Gale stands accused of disrupting the Balance, and Janzen finds himself abruptly tasked with finding out who's behind the accusation. It's a charge as serious as it is vague, at least to Janzen, but that doesn't stop the two governing bodies of the In-Between from showing up in his hometown and unleashing a Blind Judge to exact justice.

The House of Unet and the Tribe of Masarou don't share Janzen's sense of humor, nor do they have anything in the way of patience or lenience when it comes to dealing with infractions of their laws. Janzen's already impossible job only gets harder when he finds the fingerprints of old enemies all over this case.

Now, with a wanted fugitive hiding in their makeshift headquarters and the entire magic community painting a target on his back, Janzen and Grove must step outside their normal alliances for help while attempting to stay ahead of the brutal enforcers hot on their trail in their attempt to get to the bottom of who it was that framed Gale...

...if she was framed at all.

http://wbp.bz/doja

Made in the USA
Middletown, DE
01 April 2021

36749774R00285